IT'S SIMP

Matt watched closely a[...] drifted through a cloud of [...] touched, with his pointer, p[...] in the far side of the star cloud. "These are the enemy's fortified star systems."

Matt nodded in agreement.

The general put down his pointer. "In brief," he said, "ordinary military movements can't win the war. Diplomatic measures can't end it, because the enemy won't make peace. We can't settle down to fight it out here forever, because the enemy's larger civilization gives him a cumulative advantage in productivity and manpower.

"A while back," said the general, "we discovered a means for the very rapid transmission of matter from point to point. We should be able to compound this advantage into a first-rate catastrophe for the enemy. The device will throw a ship as a radio throws the human voice. But it's no good unless there's a *receiver already set up where you want to go*."

Matt nodded, in dawning recognition of what was to come.

The general touched the pointer to a little white dot close to the green cable. "When we have a station set up here, we can send a fleet through, rip that supply line wide open, seize the star systems nearby, set up more stations around them, and cut the enemy off from his base. With superior mobility, we should be able to throw him into a fog of uncertainties at the very moment when he has to hit hard and fast."

The general paused, and got control of his enthusiasm.

"However," he said, "before we can do that, *someone* has to go in and set up the station."

He looked at Matt.

Matt looked at the little white dot behind enemy lines.

"That," said the general, with enthusiasm, "is *your* job."

—from "Foghead"

Baen Books

By Christopher Anvil

THE TROUBLE
WITH ALIENS

by
Christopher Anvil
Edited by
Eric Flint

BAEN

THE TROUBLE WITH ALIENS

Copyright © 2006 by Christopher Anvil. Preface copyright © 2006 by Eric Flint.

A Baen Books Original

Baen Publishing Enterprises
P.O. Box 1403
Riverdale, NY 10471
www.baen.com

ISBN 10: 1-4165-5601-X
ISBN 13: 978-1-4165-5601-5

Cover art by Bob Eggleton

First Baen paperback printing, November 2008

Distributed by Simon & Schuster
1230 Avenue of the Americas
New York, NY 10020

Library of Congress Cataloging-in-Publication Data:
2006012262

Printed in the United States of America

10 9 8 7 6 5 4 3 2 1

TABLE OF CONTENTS

Acknowledgments

"The Prisoner" was first published in *Astounding Science Fiction* in February, 1956.

"Seller's Market" was first published in *Astounding Science Fiction* in December, 1958.

"Top Rung" was first published in *Astounding Science Fiction* in July, 1958.

"Symbols" was first published in *Analog* in September, 1966.

An earlier version of "Foghead" was first published in *Astounding Science Fiction* in September, 1958.

"The Ghost Fleet" was first published in *Analog* in February, 1961.

An earlier version of "Cargo For Colony 6" was first published in *Astounding Science Fiction* in August, 1958.

An earlier version of "Achilles's Heel" was first published in *Astounding Science Fiction* in February, 1958.

This is the first publication "Of Enemies and Allies."

"The Kindly Invasion" was first published in *Worlds of Tomorrow* in March, 1966.

"Mission of Ignorance" was first published in *Analog* in October, 1968.

"Brains Isn't Everything" was first published in *Analog* in June, 1976.

"The Captive Djinn" was first published in *Analog* in May, 1965.

"The Uninvited Guest" was first published in *Analog* in March, 1967.

"Sabotage" was first published in *The Magazine of Fantasy and Science Fiction* in December, 1966.

"Mind Partner" was first published in *Galaxy* in August, 1960.

"A Question of Identity" was first published in *Analog* in July, 1995.

"Advance Agent" was first published in *Galaxy* in February, 1957.

PREFACE

by Eric Flint

One of the constant themes in Christopher Anvil's writings is the interaction between humans and aliens. That issue stands at the center of the Pandora's Planet stories, with which we began this major reissue of Anvil's works, and it is an important if not predominant theme in the Federation of Humanity stories. (Those have now been reissued in their entirety in the second and third volumes of this reissue, *Interstellar Patrol* and *Interstellar Patrol II: The Federation of Humanity*.)

All the above stories take place in one of Anvil's two major settings, which, taken together, comprise about one-half of his entire corpus of work. But the theme can be found in many of his other writings as well, and the next two volumes of the reissue will revolve around it.

This volume, *The Trouble With Aliens*, looks at the problem primarily from the standpoint of humans. The volume is anchored by a related group of stories that Anvil wrote for his third important shared setting, which he calls "The War With the Outs."

Anvil never finished that cycle of stories, however, until now. For this volume, he rewrote three existing stories to make them fit into the setting. ("Foghead," "Cargo For Colony 6," and "Achilles's Heel.") And he wrote a new story for this anthology—"Of Enemies and Allies"—which finally completes the story cycle. This volume is its first publication.

1

The fifth and next volume of Baen Books' reissue of Anvil's writings is titled *The Trouble With Humans*. That forthcoming volume will deal with the same issue, but this time primarily from the standpoint of aliens. Among the stories included will be some of Anvil's most popular works, including "The Gentle Earth," and "Behind The Sandrat Hoax."

THE WAR WITH
THE OUTS

THE PRISONER

ROUTINE   04-12-2308-1623 TCT
STAFF
COMGEN IV TO OPCHIEF GS CAPITOL
REQUEST PERMISSION ADVANCE DEFENSE
LINE TO SYSTEM CODE R3J RPT R3J

☆ ☆ ☆ ☆ ☆ ☆

ROUTINE   04-13-2308-0715TCT
STAFF
OPCHIEF GS CAPITOL TO COMGEN IV
PERMISSION ADVANCE DEFENSE LINE TO SYSTEM
CODE R3J RPT R3J REFUSED RPT REFUSED

☆ ☆ ☆ ☆ ☆ ☆

URGENT   04-14-2308-150TCT
PERSONAL
COMGEN IV TO OPCHIEF GS CAPITOL
STINKO IT IS VITALLY NECESSARY THAT I TAKE OVER
R3J RPT R3J BEFORE THE OUTS GET HERE STP YOU

KNOW THE SIZE OF MY FLEET STP LOVE TO TANYA
AND KIDS MART MARTIN M GLICK COMGEN IV

☆ ☆ ☆ ☆ ☆ ☆ ☆

ROUTINE   04-15-2308-0730 TCT
PERSONAL
OPCHIEF GS CAPITAL TO COMGEN IV
SORRY MART I CANT LET YOU DO IT STP R3J RPT
R3J IS TOUGH NUT TO CRACK AND NOT ENOUGH
TIME TO CRACK IT STP ONLY QUADRITE IN
SYSTEM IS ON FIFTH PLANET STP TWO PREVIOUS
ATTEMPTS TO TAKE FIFTH PLANET ABORTED STP
SYSTEM AS A WHOLE IS NO GOOD WITHOUT
QUADRITE AND WE COULD NOT SUPPLY YOU
FROM HERE YOU KNOW THAT STP CANNOT HAVE
YOUR FORCES IN STATE OF DISORDER WITH
MINOR CONFLICT GOING ON WHEN OUTS
ARRIVE STP I KNOW YOUR POSITION BUT R3J RPT
R3J IS NO SOLUTION STP CAN ONLY HOPE THEY
WILL ATTACK ELSEWHERE STP JACKIE IS FINE
STP YOUNG MART HAS GROWN STP GOOD LUCK
STP STINKO J J RYSTENKO OPCHIEF GS

☆ ☆ ☆ ☆ ☆ ☆ ☆

VITAL   04-16-2308-1632 TCT
STAFF
COMGEN IV TO ALL STATIONS
U EXPLOSION D308L564V013
U EXPLOSION D308L562V013
U EXPLOSION D308L560V013

U EXPLOSION D308L562V015
U EXPLOSION D308L562V011
EXPLOSIONS SIMULTANEOUS TIME OF OBSERVATION
04-16-2308-1624TCT
VITAL TRANSMIT TRIPLE AT TEN-MINUTE INTERVALS

☆ ☆ ☆ ☆ ☆ ☆

URGENT   04-16-2308-1640TCT
PERSONAL
COMGEN IV TO OPCHIEF GS CAPITOL
STINKO THEY ARE NOT GOING SOMEWHERE
ELSE THEY ARE COMING HERE STP IF THEY GET
BY ME THERE IS NOTHING FROM HERE TO CAP
BUT THE GR AND THAT WILL NEVER HOLD
THEM STP THEIR TIMING PERFECT STP MAXIMUM
CONFUSION STP IF THEY CAME ANY SOONER
THEY COULD HAVE VOTED IN THE ELECTION
STP IN CIRCUMSTANCES DESPERATELY NECESSARY
TO TAKE R3J RPT R3J STP SEND PERMISSION
BEFORE WE WASTE MORE TIME STP MART MARTIN
M GLICK COMGEN IV

☆ ☆ ☆ ☆ ☆ ☆

(Reply requested today.)

Office of the Secretary for Defense
Dear General Rystenko:

As a member of the new President's cabinet, responsible
for the overall direction of the defense effort, I am

determined to acquire, as soon as possible, some appreciation of the overall strategic picture.

So long as I do not understand the meaning of certain technical terms, this will be impossible. These terms are regarded as secret, and no civilian has any sure idea of their meaning until he is thrust into an office where his ignorance may be fatal. Looking at the dispatch copies which come to my office, I find the following terms I would like defined: a) quadrite; b) GR; c) CAP; d) U explosion; e) Henkel sphere; f) SB; g) abort.

I also want a brief summary, on no more than two sheets of paper, of the overall defense strategy, a similar summary of known enemy capabilities; and a brief point-by-point comparison of our important weapons, considering not only quality but amounts, and present and projected rates of production.

You need not handle this yourself; but if you do not, I want you to check the papers before they come to me. You will be held personally responsible for their accuracy.

Sincerely,
James Cordovan
Secretary for Defense

☆ ☆ ☆ ☆ ☆ ☆.

4-17-2308

Office of the Chief of Operation
Dear Mr. Secretary:

Quadrite is a crystalline substance used as fuel in the non-radioactive, or N-drive. A small safe quantity of radioactive material starts the reaction, which may be stopped by removal of this material. The mass radioactive, or R-drive, is useless against the present enemy because he possesses a means of exploding it before our ships come into ordinary firing range. Thus we use quadrite on warships.

GR means General Reserve. CAP means Capitol. A U-explosion is a large explosion of uranium or other radioactive material by the enemy's device, or, occasionally by us. Henkel sphere is a large self-contained unit carrying impulse torpedoes and magnetic-inductive direction finders. SB means solar beam; a concentration of the rays of a sun for offensive or defensive purposes. "Abort," as we use it, merely means "fail."

The overall defense strategy is simple. Our forces are located around the surface of a flattened spheroidal defensive border. At the outer edge is a triple layer of warning devices, the U markers, which explode on approach of the enemy. Next comes several layers of Henkel spheres, stretching from one sun system to the next. Each sun system is equipped with solar beams, so far as possible, so that these sun systems constitute strong points in the defense perimeter, or, if they are cut off, may function for some time as isolated fortresses in the enemy's rear. Behind this outer line of defense lie the fleets, which help service the Henkel spheres, fight to repair small breaches in the defensive perimeter, and in the event of large breaches, fall back in an orderly manner and assist in forming the next defensive line.

As for the known enemy capabilities, and the comparison of their important weapons with ours, the first item to consider is their manner of attack. They come in huge masses of ships, moving at a tremendous velocity, and often making two nearly simultaneous attacks at far separated parts of our defense lines. A series of U-explosions signals their penetration through successive lines of our U-markers, and then they hurtle through the lines of Henkel spheres. The spheres automatically discharge their impulse torpedoes on precalculated courses, and at the same time, our fleet on the spot sows a series of new layers of spheres along the estimated course of the enemy attack. There is no such thing as a general engagement between the two fleets, because ours is always too weak at the point of attack. It is guarding a vast area which the enemy can, if he chooses, attack at any chosen point with his full force.

Usually, however, just as the situation becomes desperate, and we feel compelled to rush the general reserve to the spot, a second and even stronger attack strikes us at some widely separated point from the first. At this stage, all resemblance to plan and order ceases, and we are forced to resort to expediency. Fleets are rushed from all around the perimeter to the estimated position of the future enemy penetration. Solar beams are concentrated in a webwork across the line of enemy attack. It is impossible to generalize beyond this point. We do what we can. Usually we are forced to commit the fleet to battle at a heavy loss, which weakens us for the next attack. The enemy cuts a swath through the whole system, burns out a number of vitally important planetary centers en route, and erupts outward through some place which has already been stripped for defense elsewhere. After the enemy has gone, we draw together the bits and pieces, reapportion the weakened forces, and wait for the next blow.

We know very little of enemy weapons, save that they are similar to ours and used in overwhelming concentrations. As for the enemy personnel, only one individual has been captured following a fluke individual dogfight in which Colonel A. C. Nielson was killed and the enemy ship ruined. This enemy individual showed a) human form, very compact and muscular, with peculiar eyes; b) fantastic recuperative power, with healing of very severe wounds, such as killed Colonel Nielson, taking place spontaneously and practically visibly; c) fanatic hostility, shown as soon as the individual recovered consciousness; and which was followed apparently by the use of some poison, as the enemy's body then at once decomposed, too fast to permit further examination on the spot.

As for our present rate of production, it is suitable to replace approximately forty per cent of the losses suffered during enemy attack. This refers to warship production. Production of the cheaper Henkel spheres would be quite respectable if it weren't for the fact that it takes ships to put the spheres in position. Projected production of ships was cut further in the last budget.

As for recruitment of personnel, it is barely adequate to man the continually decreasing strength we are able to maintain. Training facilities are inadequate, but the need for men is so drastic we have no time for adequate training. The quality of recruits is poor, since the population does not believe the situation serious, and thus has little respect for the services.

I hope this answers your questions satisfactorily. I shall be glad to help you in any way I can.

Respectfully,
J. J. Rystenko
Chief of Operations

☆ ☆ ☆ ☆ ☆ ☆

4-17-2308

Office of the Secretary for Defense
Bart:

I am enclosing an answer from General Rystenko, the
Chief of Operations, to some questions of mine. I hope
you will read it now and let me know what you think.
Unless Rystenko is exaggerating for some reason, this is
worse than we ever imagined.

Jim Cordovan

☆ ☆ ☆ ☆ ☆ ☆

4-17-2308

Office of the President
Jim:

This is horrible. Let me know immediately if you find
out anything more about this.

Bart

☆ ☆ ☆ ☆ ☆ ☆

(Immediate action)   4-17-2308

Office of the President
General Rystenko:

Report to my office immediately unless you are occupied
with matters of vital importance.

Barton Baruch

☆ ☆ ☆ ☆ ☆ ☆

4-17-2308

Office of the President
Jim:

Rystenko is all right. But our predecessors have gutted the defense establishment to balance the budget. Cabinet meeting tonight at 8:30.

Bart

☆ ☆ ☆ ☆ ☆ ☆

URGENT   04-16-2308-2210TCT
PERSONAL
COMGEN IV TO OPCHIEF GS CAPITOL
STINKO MY POSITION HOPELESS HERE IN PRESENT CIRCUMSTANCES STP ONLY JUSTIFICATION FOR INACTION WAS TO AVOID INVOLVEMENT IN MINOR WAR AND THUS INABILITY TO REINFORCE IF ATTACK CAME ELSEWHERE STP ATTACK IS COMING HERE STP IF I STAY WHERE I AM I AM LIKE A MOUSE IN AN UNBLOCKED HOLE WITH THE WEASEL COMING ON THE RUN STP I CANT HOLD THEM HERE STP THIS TIME THEY WILL GO ALL THE WAY TO CAP STP STINKO I HOPE YOUR PERMISSION IS ON WAY AS I AM GOING TO TAKE R3J RPT R3J OR DIE TRYING STP LOVE TO TANYA AND THE KIDS STP GOOD LUCK IF THEY GET THROUGH STINKO STP MART MARTIN M GLICK CONGEN IV

☆ ☆ ☆ ☆ ☆ ☆

ROUTINE   04-17-2308-1100TCT
STAFF
OPCHIEF GS CAPITOL TO COMGEN IV
IN ABSENCE OF GENERAL RYSTENKO MY DUTY
TO INFORM LIEUTENANT GENERAL GLICK NO
PERMISSION TO ADVANCE TO R3J RPT R3J
WAS SENT OR CONTEMPLATED STP IN EVENT
YOU ADVANCE CONTRARY TO REITERATED
COMMANDS TO CONTRARY MY DUTY TO
INFORM YOU YOU ARE HEREBY RELIEVED OF
COMMAND AND HEREBY ORDERED TO TURN
OVER COMMAND TO DEPUTY COMGEN IV AS
PRESCRIBED RGC 6-143J SECTION 14 STP Q L
GORLEY COLONEL FOR GENERAL J J RYSTENKO
OPCHIEF GS

☆ ☆ ☆ ☆ ☆ ☆

ROUTINE   04-18-2308-1625TCT
STAFF
COMGEN IV TO OPCHIEF GS CAPITOL
ALL RECEIVING APPARATUS OUT OF ORDER STP
POSSIBLY BY ENEMY ACTION STP ADVANCE
ELEMENTS OF FLEET IV APPROACHING SYSTEM
CODE R3J RPT R3J

☆ ☆ ☆ ☆ ☆ ☆

VITAL   04-18-2308-1640TCT
STAFF
COMGEN IV TO ALL STATIONS

U EXPLOSION D288L564V103
U EXPLOSION D288L562V103
U EXPLOSION D288L560V103
U EXPLOSION D288L562V105
U EXPLOSION D288L562V099
EXPLOSIONS SIMULTANEOUS TIME OF OBSER-
VATION 04-18-2308-1635TCT
VITAL TRANSMIT TRIPLE AT TEN-MINUTE
INTERVALS

☆ ☆ ☆ ☆ ☆ ☆

(Reply requested immediately)

4-18-2308

Office of the Secretary for Defense
General Rystenko:

As you know, OPCHIEF dispatches move through my
office as a routine so I will know what your office is doing.
Now I want to know why this General Glick is being kept
on a short leash. I have gone over a set of star charts, and
if I can make anything out of them this System R3J is a
vital link in your defense system. Who is this Q. L. Gorley,
colonel, who sent the order removing General Glick? Why
did *he* send the order? Are you dodging the responsibility
for it? Unless you are occupied in vital matters I want
the answers to these questions by tube within fifteen
minutes.

J. Cordovan
Secretary for Defense

☆ ☆ ☆ ☆ ☆ ☆

4-18-2308

Office of the Chief of Operations
Dear Mr. Secretary:

I had no knowledge of Gorley's action till you called it
to my attention. I am reinstating Glick immediately.

Rystenko

☆ ☆ ☆ ☆ ☆ ☆

VITAL   04-18-2308-1125TCT
STAFF
OPCHIEF GS CAPITOL TO COMGEN IV
BY ORDER GENERAL J J RYSTENKO OPCHIEF GS
EFFECTIVE IMMEDIATELY LIEUTENANT-GENERAL
MARTIN M GLICK IS RPT IS IN FULL COMMAND
SECTOR IV STP BY ORDER GENERAL J J RYSTENKO
OPCHIEF GS FULL DISCRETION RPT FULL
DISCRETION GRANTED RPT GRANTED LIEU-
TENANT-GENERAL MARTIN M GLICK COMGEN
IV INCLUDING RPT INCLUDING ANY ACTIONS
REGARDING SYSTEM CODE R3J RPT R3J TIME
OF ORIGINAL ORDER 02-18-2308-1125TCT
VITAL TRANSMIT TRIPLE AT THIRTY-MINUTE
INTERVALS

☆ ☆ ☆ ☆ ☆ ☆

URGENT   02-18-2308-1128TCT
PERSONAL
OPCHIEF GS CAPITOL TO COMGEN IV
MY GOD MART I AM SORRY STP YOUR REASONING

REGARDING R3J RPT R3J IS PERFECTLY CORRECT
STP GORLEY ACTED WITHOUT MY KNOWLEDGE
STP WE ARE IN MIDST OF CHANGE OF ADMIN-
ISTRATION HERE STP SOME CONFUSION STP
YOU HAVE FULL AUTHORITY STP DO WHAT YOU
WANT STP BEST OF LUCK AND GOD BE WITH
YOU STP STINKO J J RYSTENKO OPCHIEF GS

☆ ☆ ☆ ☆ ☆ ☆

4-18-2308

Office of the Chief of Operations
Dear Mr. Secretary:

I have sent orders reinstating General Glick and giving
him full authority to take System R3J. Two previous
attempts to take the only planet in the system that possesses quadrite have failed, with no survivors returning;
but it is worth trying.

Rystenko

☆ ☆ ☆ ☆ ☆ ☆

(Reply requested immediately)

4-18-2308

Office of the Secretary for Defense
General Rystenko:

That is fine. What about my questions concerning
Colonel Gorley?

J. Cordovan

☆ ☆ ☆ ☆ ☆ ☆

4-18-2308

Office of the Chief of Operations
Dear Mr. Secretary:

Colonel Gorley was sent here by the former President.
He acted in an advisory and liaison capacity between this
office and that of the former President. I know his action
in this instance has proved to be unfortunate, but he was
entirely justified by regulations covering the situation. I was
with the President at the moment, and immediate action
was necessary to maintain the balance of the situation.

Respectfully,
J. J. Rystenko
Chief of Operations

☆ ☆ ☆ ☆ ☆ ☆

(Reply requested immediately)

4-18-2308

Office of the Secretary for Defense
General Rystenko:

Do you mean that Gorley advised the former President
on matters of defense?

J. Cordovan

☆ ☆ ☆ ☆ ☆ ☆

4-18-2308

Office of the Chief of Operations
Mr. Secretary:

That is what I mean. Yes.

J.J. Rystenko
Chief of Operations

☆ ☆ ☆ ☆ ☆ ☆

4-18-2308

Office of the Secretary for Defense
Bart:

  I am enclosing some correspondence between myself
and Rystenko, regarding a Colonel Q. L. Gorley who has
just taken a step I regard as well calculated to throw our
defense arrangements off balance at the decisive moment.
I am enclosing the dispatch referred to. You will note that
Rystenko takes a progressively stiffer tone in protecting
Gorley. Personally, I think if Gorley was defense advisor to
the previous Administration, he must be no good.

Jim

☆ ☆ ☆ ☆ ☆ ☆

(Reply requested today)

4-18-2308

Office of the Secretary for Defense
Comptroller of the Records:.

  I would like a digest of all pertinent data in the service
record of Colonel Q. L. Gorley, now attached to the office
of the Chief of Operations.

James Cordovan
Secretary for Defense

☆ ☆ ☆ ☆ ☆ ☆

4-18-2308

Office of the President
Jim:

I have been in office three days and it feels like three years, all thanks to the miserable defense picture. If you think Gorley is no good, select some distant and unimportant asteroid and put him in charge of it. Don't bother me with this trivia.

Bart

P. S. The time on this dispatch from Gorley to Glick is 1100. Rystenko was not with me then.

☆ ☆ ☆ ☆ ☆ ☆

4-19-2308

Comptroller of the Records
Dear Mr. Secretary:

I have been able to ascertain that there is a Colonel Q. L. Gorley attached to the Chief of Operations office, but the Master Recorder merely remains blank when I try to obtain his service record. No Colonel Q. L. Gorley is listed in the Officers' Registry. There is a Q. S. Gorley, Captain, now serving with the Tenth Fleet, and a Brigadier General Mason Gorley, Ret'd. Upon code-checking the rolls of the National Space Academy at Bristol Bay, I find no mention of any Q. L. Gorley within the last hundred years.

It is possible to bar access to the service record of any

individual if the President or Secretary for Defense approves the action. But this is not the case here. There simply is no record. Do you wish me to cross-check the coded Administration records of the past few years to see if any mention is made of this man in these records?

> Respectfully,
> Ogden Mannenberg
> Comptroller of the Records

☆ ☆ ☆ ☆ ☆ ☆

(Reply requested today)

4-19-2308

Office of the Secretary for Defense
Comptroller of the Records:

Yes, by all means cross-check the administrative records back to the time Gorley was first mentioned.

> James Cordovan
> Secretary for Defense

☆ ☆ ☆ ☆ ☆ ☆

(Immediate Action)

4-19-2308

Office of the Secretary for Defense
Birdie:

Get down to the Chief of Operations' office and play the part of the Undersecretary getting acquainted with the team. Find out all you can about a Colonel Q. L.

Gorley, who is now attached to the Opchief's office.
Gorley appears to have no service record and I am a little
curious about him.

Jim

☆ ☆ ☆ ☆ ☆ ☆

ROUTINE   04-19-2308-2300 TCT
STAFF
COMGEN IV TO OPCHIEF GS
CAPITOL FLEET IV NOW BASED ON SECOND
RPT SECOND PLANET OF SYSTEM CODE R3J RPT
R3J STP SB BEING PLACED NOW STP ADVANCE
HENKEL SPHERE-PERIMETER BEING HEAVILY
REINFORCED STP BULK OF FLEET IV NOW
MOVING TO OCCUPY FIFTH RPT FIFTH PLANET
OF SYSTEM CODE R3J RPT R3J

☆ ☆ ☆ ☆ ☆ ☆

ROUTINE   04-19-2308-2314TCT
PERSONAL
COMGEN IV TO OPCHIEF GS CAPITOL
STINKO I HAVE OCCUPIED THE SECOND PLANET
OF R3J RPT R3J AND FIND POPULACE AND GOV-
ERNMENT FRIENDLY AND EAGER TO HELP STP
THEY HAD CIVILIZATION BASED ON FISSION FIVE
HUNDRED YEARS AGO BUT THE OUTS WENT
THROUGH HERE AND KNOCKED THEM INTO A
QUOTE PILE OF DUNG END QUOTE STP THEY
HAD SPACE TRAVEL BUT KEPT AWAY FROM FIFTH
PLANET AS HAD NO NEED FOR QUADRITE

WHICH IS ONLY ATTRACTION STP ALL THEY CAN TELL ME IS THAT ONE OF THEIR RELIGIOUS LEADERS PREDICTED MY ARRIVAL AND SAID OF THE FIFTH PLANET QUOTE HE WHO WILL FEED ON IT SHALL LIVE OF IT STP END QUOTE SOUNDS GOOD STP AM ON ROUTE NOW STP MART MARTIN M GLICK COMGEN IV

☆ ☆ ☆ ☆ ☆ ☆

4-19-2308

Office of the Undersecretary for Defense
Jim:

I have covered the situation for you down at the Opchief's office, and I am sure you must be mistaken about Colonel Gorley. He seems straightforward and solid, and explained the defense setup to me in such a way that for the first time it made sense to me. I can think of no one we might pick who would make a better advisor to the President on military matters. As for Colonel Gorley having no service record, the idea is fantastic. Several of the officers present spoke familiarly to Gorley of events which happened while he and they were at Bristol Bay together in their Academy days. It could hardly be a case of mistaken identity. Colonel Gorley is a very striking man, very compact and muscular—a very powerful, magnetic, dynamic type. He has peculiarly keen intelligent eyes, and an incisive, clear positive manner of speaking. Personally, I think that instead of investigating Gorley, we should raise him to high rank and get a little decision into the war effort.

Birdie

P. S. The only thing resembling criticism I have heard of Gorley was a joking reference that he has a ferocious appetite and has to diet constantly to keep his weight down. Surely you won't hold this against him.

☆ ☆ ☆ ☆ ☆ ☆

ROUTINE   04-20-2308-0756TCT
STAFF
COMGEN IV TO OPCHIEF GS CAPITOL
ADVANCE ELEMENTS FLEET IV HAVE LANDED
ON PLANET FIVE RPT FIVE OF SYSTEM CODE
R3J RPT R3J NO OPPOSITION STP ONLY INHABI-
TANTS APPEAR TO BE GRAZING ANIMALS OF
INTERMEDIATE SIZE

☆ ☆ ☆ ☆ ☆ ☆

4-20-2308

Comptroller of the Records
Dear Mr. Secretary:

I list below in chronological order the portions of past Administrative records apparently referring to Colonel Q. L. Gorley:

★ ★ ★ ★ ★

4-25-2304 . . . Thank you so much for sending me Colonel Gorley. The defense position is more clear to me

President to Opchief.

★ ★ ★ ★ ★

5-4-2304 . . . I approve the new plan of dynamic

containment. I was a bit uncertain as to the effect this would have should the enemy renew offensive action, but Colonel Gorley has assured me it will be possible to concentrate reserves quickly. On this basis, I approve the plan. Certainly it seems much less risky.

President to Opchief

★ ★ ★ ★ ★

2-23-2305 . . . I do not understand your difficulties in repelling the latest enemy attack. What exactly has happened here? Why were you not able to concentrate your reserves quickly enough to prevent the enemy from traversing the whole length and breadth of the system and leaving a trail of ruin behind him such as we have not seen in twenty years of warfare? Who ordered these cuts in production? What do you mean you cannot replace the losses? I have no memory of these Executive Orders you speak of, or of any Colonel Gorley. Send this man to me immediately, or better yet, come yourself.

President to Opchief

★ ★ ★ ★ ★

2-24-2305 . . . Colonel Gorley has explained the matter to me satisfactorily. Of course it is unfortunate that these things happen.

President to Opchief

★ ★ ★ ★ ★

6-1-2305 . . . Colonel Gorley will explain to you the recommended new cuts in the defense budget. The improved foreign situation makes these cuts possible.

Opchief to President

★ ★ ★ ★ ★

4-2-2306 . . . Rystenko, these losses are horrible. Why has

this thing happened twice? The purpose of censorship is not to hold the people in ignorance and hide the festering wounds from view. The point of censorship is to keep information from the enemy and to prevent over-violent public reaction to unimportant temporary reversals. But these disasters are not unimportant! They are terrible defeats! I find your reaction grossly inadequate. Who is this Gorley you are sending to me, as if this would correct the situation?

President to Opchief

★ ★ ★ ★ ★

4-4-2306 . . . Colonel Gorley has explained the matter to me satisfactorily. I see now clearly it was bound to happen in this phase of our defensive effort.

President to Opchief

★ ★ ★ ★ ★

6-2-2306 . . . I approve the new defense budget, as explained to me by Colonel Gorley. I am, of course, pleased though surprised that you can now give us more defensive power at lower cost. Please check this and be sure that the situation has stabilized to this extent.

President to Opchief

★ ★ ★ ★ ★

6-6-2306 . . . That Colonel Gorley be attached to my office until these complex arrangements are completed . . .

President to Opchief

★ ★ ★ ★ ★

6-7-2306 . . . We will miss Gorley, but are sure he will prove as helpful to you as to us.

Opchief to President

★ ★ ★ ★ ★

9-15-2306 . . . The food must be much better here than in your mess. Poor Gorley has to go on another diet.

President to Opchief

★ ★ ★ ★ ★

10-23-2306 . . . I am very sorry to have to bother you with these petty trivialities, Mr. President, but they may prove vital. I can't send men to Cyros with such inadequate equipment as this budget allows for. This one trivial substitution of separate interliners and thin semi-detached boots may cost a delay of up to ten minutes when the men go into action. This equipment has already proved itself worthless. I will gladly consider Colonel Gorley's suggestions, but this matter was disposed of years ago. I have also discovered several other aspects of our present arrangements which make me extremely uneasy . . .

Opchief to President

★ ★ ★ ★ ★

10-25-2306 . . . I have talked with Colonel Gorley and can see that these plans are perfectly suited to the situation. Perhaps he could remain with our office for some time till these other matters are ironed out.

Opchief to President

★ ★ ★ ★ ★

4-15-2307 . . . Poor Gorley is on a diet again.

Opchief to President

★ ★ ★ ★ ★

4-16-2307 . . . Who? Gorley? Am I acquainted with the man?

President to Opchief

★ ★ ★ ★ ★

4-29-2307 . . . Terribly shaken by this hideous disaster. Why has this happened to us when our arrangements were supposed to be invulnerable? The enemy has torn your battle line like tissue paper. Why are we so weak everywhere? Your talk of "elastic counter-defensive" makes no sense to me whatever. If these fleets were held concentrated at one central point instead of strewn all over the universe, we could return the blow. What do you mean by offering to send "Colonel Gorley" to me? If any personal explaining is to be done, you will come yourself, not send a stooge. Make out immediately a list of all requirements needed to correct this hideous situation.

President to Opchief

★ ★ ★ ★ ★

Note: These are all the direct references made to Colonel Q. L. Gorley in the Administration records. Would you like me to cross-check the Departmental records?

Respectfully,
Ogden Mannenberg
Comptroller of the Records

☆ ☆ ☆ ☆ ☆ ☆

4-20-2308

Office of the Secretary for Defense
Comptroller of the Records:

Thank you. These references are amply sufficient for the present.

James Cordovan
Secretary for Defense

☆ ☆ ☆ ☆ ☆ ☆

4-20-2308

Office of the President
Jim:

I have now absorbed the substance of the report
Rystenko sent you concerning our defenses, and which
you forwarded to me. I have slept on it, and thought of it
when I was not otherwise occupied. It seems to me: 1)
This policy of locating the main bulk of our fleet in a thin
shell around the periphery offers us about as much
defense as an eggshell does to an egg. 2) Since in the present
arrangement the fleet does not engage, it is worth no
more than so many civilian ships. 3) Therefore, let us draw
all the fleet to the center (with the possible exception of
Glick's IVth, which is actively occupied), and replace it
around the periphery with civilian ships and crews to service
the layers of Henkel spheres. Enough men could be left
behind to train these crews, but no more.

My final observation is that everything I have said so far
is fairly obvious, therefore why hasn't Rystenko carried it
out on his own? He impressed me very favorably in our
interview, but further consideration leads me to think he
may be one of these men who expend their sense on the
package instead of the contents. I am going to talk to him
again, and would like your view of the subject.

Bart

☆ ☆ ☆ ☆ ☆ ☆

4-20-2308

Office of the President
General Rystenko:

I want to see you within the next hour regarding the overall strategy of the war effort, and regarding the present recruitment and material replacement situation, and regarding the present arrangements for advancement of high officers.

Barton Baruch

☆ ☆ ☆ ☆ ☆ ☆

4-20-2308

Office of the Chief of Operations
Dear Mr. President:

I shall be at your office at 3:00 p.m. if this is agreeable to you. As it happens, my aide, Colonel Q. L. Gorley, left my office a short while ago to bring you some important data sheets. I am sure you will find him most helpful also on these other matters if you choose to consult him.

Respectfully,
J. J. Rystenko
Chief of Operations

☆ ☆ ☆ ☆ ☆ ☆

4-20-2308

Office of the President
Jim:

I have just had a very illuminating talk with General Rystenko's aide, Colonel Gorley, and he has very clearly explained the logic of the present defense setup to me. I am sending him along to brief you. He is a most capable man, and I am sure you will profit by contact with him.

Bart

☆ ☆ ☆ ☆ ☆ ☆

VITAL   04-20-2308-1654TCT
STAFF
COMGEN IV TO ALL STATIONS
U EXPLOSION D280L564V193
U EXPLOSION D280L562V193
U EXPLOSION D280L560V193
U EXPLOSION D280L562V195
U EXPLOSION D280L562V191
EXPLOSIONS SIMULTANEOUS TIME OF OBSER-
VATION 04-20-2308-1646TCT
VITAL TRANSMIT TRIPLE AT TEN-MINUTE
INTERVALS

☆ ☆ ☆ ☆ ☆ ☆

4-20-2308

Office of the Undersecretary for Defense
Jim:

Colonel Gorley is out here cooling his heels in the anteroom. He is here at the President's personal order, and yet
when the receptionist tries to let him in, your door is
locked. Have you turned childish?

Birdie

☆ ☆ ☆ ☆ ☆ ☆

4-20-2308

Office of the Secretary for Defense
Birdie:

Who is Gorley? Is he the one who made the fuss
removing a general yesterday or the day before? If he has
anything from the President, he can leave it outside. If he

wants to see me, he can make an appointment for tomorrow. I am working my way through a pile of business as high as your head, and I do not want to be disturbed till I am finished. Say, while he is out there, pump him discreetly about Rystenko. See if you can find out whether the Opchief used Gorley for a cat's paw in trying to get rid of that general . . . what's his name? . . . Glick.

Jim

☆ ☆ ☆ ☆ ☆ ☆

4-20-2308

Office of the Secretary for Defense
Chief Dispatcher:
Send the following:

VITAL   04-20-2308-1621TCT
PERSONAL
DEFSEC CAPITOL TO COMGEN GR CAPITOL
REPLY IMMEDIATELY YOUR OPINION WILL
PRESENT DEFENSES REPEL ENEMY ATTACK OF
MAGNITUDE SIMILAR TO THAT EXPERIENCED
LAST THREE YEARS STP REPLY IMMEDIATELY
CATEGORY VITAL TO DEFSEC CAPITOL
THROUGH CHIEF DISPATCHER STP THIS
INQUIRY AND REPLY CONFIDENTIAL STP JAMES
CORDOVAN DEFSEC CAPITOL

☆ ☆ ☆ ☆ ☆ ☆

(reply requested immediately)

4-20-2308

Office of the Secretary for Defense

Comptroller of the Records:

Find out for me what happened to the body of the enemy captured after a dogfight in which Colonel A. C. Nielson was killed.

James Cordovan
Secretary for Defense

☆ ☆ ☆ ☆ ☆ ☆

VITAL   04-20-2308-1642TCT
PERSONAL
COMGEN GR CAP TO DEFSEC CAP THRU CHIEF
DISPATCHER CONFIDENTIAL
MY OPINION PRESENT DEFENSES WILL COLLAPSE
IF ENEMY ATTACKS WITH SAME STRENGTH AS
FORMERLY STP OR WITH ANYTHING LIKE SAME
STRENGTH AS FORMERLY STP VERNON L
HAUSER COMGEN GR CAPITOL

☆ ☆ ☆ ☆ ☆ ☆

4-20-2308

Comptroller of the Records
Dear Mr. Secretary:

The body of the captured enemy was brought here under refrigeration, to be examined by physicians and chemists. It arrived at night and was placed, still in its box, in a small room off the autopsy room. The intern on duty ordered the lid of the box pried up, examined the remains, and noted that the object within appeared to be in a state of advanced decomposition, with, however, very little odor. The room was refrigerated, and next day the surgeons entered to carry out a preliminary examination, and upon raising the lid found nothing within but a quantity of water, some of which had seeped out through the sides of the box.

The above summary is condensed from voluminous reports on the occurrence, and equally voluminous reports attempt to explain the matter, but the substance of these latter reports is that the authorities do not know what happened.

>   Respectfully,
>   Ogden Mannenberg
>   Comptroller of the Records

☆ ☆ ☆ ☆ ☆ ☆

(Reply requested immediately)

                                              4-20-2308

Office of the Secretary for Defense
Comptroller of the Records:

Send me a summary of the physical characteristics of the captured enemy during life.

>   James Cordovan
>   Secretary for Defense

☆ ☆ ☆ ☆ ☆ ☆

                                              4-20-2308

Office of the Undersecretary for Defense
Jim:

Colonel Gorley was ordered by the President to see

you now, today. Why try to put him off till tomorrow? You can get back to your work after he has a few minutes to deliver his message.

Birdie

☆ ☆ ☆ ☆ ☆ ☆

4-20-2308

Office of the Secretary for Defense
Birdie:

I am snowed under. Tomorrow.

Jim

☆ ☆ ☆ ☆ ☆ ☆

4-20-2308

Comptroller of the Records
Dear Mr. Secretary:

The captured enemy is described as having during life the following physical characteristics: a) human form; b) extremely compact and muscular physique; c) peculiarly keen sharp eyes; d) very great recuperative power.

Respectfully,
Ogden Mannenberg
Comptroller of the Records

☆ ☆ ☆ ☆ ☆ ☆

4-20-2308

Office of the Secretary for Defense
Chief Dispatcher:
Send the following:

VITAL   04-20-2308-1708TCT

PERSONAL
DEFSEC CAP TO COMGEN GR CAP CONFIDENTIAL
REPLY IMMEDIATELY THROUGH CHIEF DIS-
PATCHER YOUR OPINION ON OUTCOME OF
COMING ENEMY ATTACK IF ALL OUR FORCES
NOW CONCENTRATED AT CENTRAL POINT
LEAVING SMALL TRAINING CADRES AND CIVIL-
IANS TO MAINTAIN HENKEL SPHERE DEFENSES
STP REPLY CONFIDENTIAL CATEGORY VITAL
STP JAMES CORDOVAN DEFSEC CAPITOL

☆ ☆ ☆ ☆ ☆ ☆

VITAL   04-20-2308-1714TCT
PERSONAL
COMGEN GR CAP TO DEFSEC CAP THRU CHIEF
DISPATCHER CONFIDENTIAL
MY OPINION OUR CHANCES GOOD STP THIS IS
FIRST SENSIBLE PLAN TO COME OUT OF CAP
IN FOUR YEARS STP BUT YOU WILL NEVER
GET IT BY RYSTENKO OR HIS CREATURE
GORLEY STP SEE GORLEY DOES NOT GET TO
PRESIDENT STP GORLEY IS GLEVER MAN
WITH THE BUTTER KNIFE OR WHATEVER HE
USES STP MR SECRETARY ONLY CHANCE YOUR
PLAN GETTING ACROSS IS TO SEE PRESIDENT
REMOVE RYSTENKO APPOINT ANYONE WITH
ALL HIS FACULTIES STP ANY SANE MAN CAN
SEE PLAN NOW IN USE IS SUICIDE STP VERNON L
HAUSER COMGEN GR CAP

☆ ☆ ☆ ☆ ☆ ☆

4-20-2308

Office of the Undersecretary for Defense
Jim:

Colonel Gorley was *ordered* to see you by the *President* and he was *ordered* to do it *today*. The colonel is a very powerful and determined man when his duty is at stake, Jim, and I think it would be wise not to get in his or the President's way. I say this as a friend, Jim. Gorley is *going* to *see* you *today*.

Birdie

☆ ☆ ☆ ☆ ☆ ☆

4-20-2308

Office of the Secretary for Defense
Birdie:

Why didn't you tell me Gorley was here at the direct order of the President to see me *today*? He can see me when I am through, probably about an hour-and-a-half from now, or, as he would put it, about 1854 hours. Birdie, would you repeat what you said about Colonel Gorley's appearance? I think he reminds me of someone I knew as a kid.

Jim

☆ ☆ ☆ ☆ ☆ ☆

04-20-2308

Office of the Secretary for Defense
Chief Dispatcher:
Send the following:

VITAL   04-20-2308-1722TCT

PERSONAL
DEFSEC CAP TO COMGEN GR CAP CONFIDENTIAL
REPLY IMMEDIATELY THROUGH CHIEF DIS-
PATCHER STP SITUATION HERE HIGHLY
PRECARIOUS STP GORLEY HAS ALREADY GOTTEN
TO PRESIDENT AND USED WHATEVER HE USES
STP PRESIDENT NOW CONVERTED STP GORLEY
AWAITING ME IN MY OUTER OFFICE STP EAGER
TO USE WHATEVER HE USES STP MY THOUGHT
THAT ONLY SOLUTION IS THROW AWAY PRESENT
SITUATION AND START ALL OVER STP INCIDEN-
TALLY WHY CAN I NOT PERSONALLY ORDER
REGROUPING OF FORCES STP IS THERE ANOTHER
CAPITOL AS I HAVE HEARD RUMORED ALL SET
UP WITH SKELETON CREWS AND READY TO
TAKE OVER IF ANYTHING HAPPENS TO PRE-
SENT ONE STP WILL YOU CONSENT TO ACT AS
OPCHIEF IF SO DIRECTED BY ME STP I PROPOSE
GIVE YOU DIRECT ORDER TO PERFORM VERY
HAZARDOUS THANKLESS MISSION OF VITAL
IMPORTANCE STP WILL YOU OBEY IMMEDIATELY
AND WITHOUT QUESTION STP REPLY IMMEDI-
ATELY THROUGH CHIEF DISPATCHER STP
REPLY CONFIDENTIAL CATEGORY VITAL STP
JAMES CORDOVAN DEFSEC CAPITOL

☆ ☆ ☆ ☆ ☆ ☆

VITAL   04-20-2308-1730TCT
PERSONAL
COMGEN GR CAP TO DEFSEC CAP THRU CHIEF
DISPATCHER CONFIDENTIAL

HOW DOES GORLEY DO IT STP YES YOU CAN
ORDER FORCES DIRECT BUT WHAT GOOD IF
PRESIDENT COUNTERMANDS STP YES AUXILIARY
CAP EXISTS READY TO TAKE OVER STP BUT IF
WE LOSE THE PRESENT CAP THRU ENEMY
ACTION IT WILL BE BECAUSE OF GREAT WEAK-
NESS AND THERE WILL BE LITTLE FOR AUX
CAP TO DO BUT SIGN SURRENDER STP YES I
WILL BE OPCHIEF IF YOU SO ORDER STP I WILL
FOLLOW ORDERS REGARDLESS HAZARD OR
THANKLESSNESS STP I WILL ACT IMMEDIATELY
WITHOUT QUESTION STP BUT I CAN FOLLOW
YOUR ORDERS ONLY IF NOT COUNTERMANDED
BY HIGHER AUTHORITY THAT IS THE PRESIDENT
STP VERNON L. HAUSER COMGEN GR CAP

☆ ☆ ☆ ☆ ☆ ☆

4-20-2308

Office of the Undersecretary for Defense
Jim:

Come off it, fellow. You can't expect a man like Colonel
Gorley to wait around in your outer office when he is on a
mission direct from the President. As for Colonel Gorley's
appearance, as I said before, the colonel is a splendid figure of a man, very compact and muscular, with peculiarly
keen sharp eyes. Eyes indicative, I might add, of great
force of character, and you are standing in this man's way
and the President's. Colonel Gorley says he thinks it is
"unlikely" you knew him as a child. He came from a place
where as a child he didn't ever have enough to eat, which

explains his periodic little indulgences in food. He is angry with you, Jim, and he is close to the President. I don't think he will wait much longer, Jim, when it is his duty to see you. Wake up, Jim.

Birdie

☆ ☆ ☆ ☆ ☆ ☆

4-20-2308

Office of the Secretary for Defense
Chief Dispatcher:
Send the following:

VITAL   04-20-2308-1734TCT
PERSONAL
DEFSEC CAP TO COMGENS ALL SECTORS
EFFECTIVE IMMEDIATELY GENERAL J J RYSTENKO
IS REMOVED RPT REMOVED FROM POST AS
OPCHIEF GS STP EFFECTIVE IMMEDIATELY
LIEUTENANT-GENERAL VERNON L HAUSER
COMGEN GR IS APPOINTED RPT APPOINTED
OPCHIEF GS STP I HAVE FULL AND COMPLETE
CONFIDENCE IN GENERAL HAUSER STP ANY
DELAY IN CARRYING OUT GENERAL HAUSER'S
ORDERS IN THE UNUSUAL CIRCUMSTANCES
ABOUT TO OCCUR WILL BE A DIRECT THREAT
TO THE SECURITY OF THE RACE STP IN THESE
TIMES STEADINESS AND INSTANT OBEDIENCE
TO ORDERS ARE THE VITAL QUALITIES STP GOD
BE WITH YOU AND HOLD YOU STEADY AGAINST
THE FOE STP JAMES CORDOVAN DEFSEC CAPITOL

☆ ☆ ☆ ☆ ☆ ☆

VITAL   04-20-2308-1735TCT
STAFF
DEFSEC CAPITOL TO ALL STATIONS
FOR YOUR INFORMATION EXPERIENCE WITH
ENEMY CAPTIVE HERE SUGGESTS OUTS POSSESS
GREAT HYPNOTIC POWERS AT CLOSE RANGE
STP ADVISABLE TAKE NO PRISONERS

☆ ☆ ☆ ☆ ☆ ☆

VITAL   04-20-2308-1736TCT
PERSONAL
DEFSEC CAPITOL TO COMGEN GR CAPITOL
DIRECT ORDER YOU DESTROY RPT DESTROY
CAPITOL RPT CAPITOL AT EARLIEST POSSIBLE
MOMENT CONSISTENT WITH SAFETY OF
FORCES UNDER YOUR COMMAND STP THEN
CONCENTRATE MAIN FORCES AS YOU THINK
ADVISABLE STP JAMES CORDOVAN DEFSEC
CAP

☆ ☆ ☆ ☆ ☆ ☆

4-20-2308

Office of the Undersecretary of Defense
Jim:

You have gone a little too far in defying Colonel Gorley
and the President, and Colonel Gorley has decided to wait
no longer in performing his duty. He is coming in to see
you now, Jim, door or no door.

Birdie

☆ ☆ ☆ ☆ ☆ ☆

4-20-2308

Office of the Secretary for Defense
Birdie:

Tell Colonel Gorley I have a service revolver in my hand and am only too eager to test Gorley's fantastic recuperative powers against this and one other weapon. Go after him and tell him this.

Jim

☆ ☆ ☆ ☆ ☆ ☆

ROUTINE   04-20-2308-1700TCT
STAFF
COMGEN IV TO OPCHIEF GS CAPITOL
OCCUPATION OF PLANET FIVE RPT FIVE
COMPLETE STP NO RPT NO OPPOSITION STP NO
RPT NO INDICATION OF PREVIOUS ATTEMPTS
TO TAKE PLANET STP HUGE RESERVES OF
QUADRITE STP MINING NOW UNDERWAY

☆ ☆ ☆ ☆ ☆ ☆

4-20-2308

Office of the Undersecretary for Defense
Jim:

What do you mean? What is going on here? May I go home, Jim? I feel strange.

Birdie

☆ ☆ ☆ ☆ ☆ ☆

4-20-2308

Office of the Secretary for Defense
Birdie:

    Thank you for sending Colonel Gorley in to me. He has explained our defense setup to me most clearly.

Jim

☆ ☆ ☆ ☆ ☆ ☆

VITAL   04-20-2308-1750TCT
STAFF
COMGEN GR CAP TO ALL STATIONS
U EXPLOSION CAPITOL
U EXPLOSION CAPITOL
U EXPLOSION CAPITOL
U EXPLOSION CAPITOL
U EXPLOSION CAPITOL
EXPLOSIONS RAPID SUCCESSIVE NOT BY ENEMY ACTION
TIME OF OBSERVATION 04-20-2308-1746TCT
VITAL TRANSMIT TRIPLE AT TEN-MINUTE INTERVALS

SELLER'S MARKET

Captain Nathaniel Corder, of Cryos Expedition, lay in the deep cold snow under the tracksled. He shone his light on the rapidly spinning drive-shaft, then shone the light carefully back along the shaft to the universal joint. He saw that it was spinning, too.

From the darkness beside the sled, Corder heard the Sergeant's low voice. "Sir, I found some heavy wire. If the universal's broken, maybe we can fix it."

Corder blew out a cloud of frozen breath. "It's not the universal. It's another broken axle."

There was a moment of silence, then Corder said, "Divide the men up, and put them in the other sled."

"Sir, the tracksleds are overloaded already."

"That may be, but we can't leave anyone here."

There was the sound of a tailgate dropping, and Corder heard a muffled order. From the bed of the tracksled over Corder's head came a slow dragging scuffle of feet. Corder began to worm his way out from under the sled.

Now that the problem of the tracksled was no longer on

his mind, Corder became conscious of his own sensations. His hands and feet were numb. His face felt deadened and chilled. The bridge of his nose ached with the cold, and he had a dull pain over the eyes. His heavy overcoat bound him without giving a feeling of warmth. When he wanted to move, he found that it took a concentrated effort to make his body perform.

Corder rolled carefully free of the sled, and got to his feet. All around him was darkness, with here and there the dim glow of a moving flashlight. The only sounds around him were the low mutter of tracksled engines, and the rustle of steadily falling snow.

One of the flashlights wavered toward him, and the Sergeant's voice said, "I got them all in, sir. But I hope we don't hit any more of those burrows."

"How badly are the men crowded?"

"Three deep."

Corder and the Sergeant waded through the snow in silence. Corder was trying to think what to do if yet another tracksled broke an axle.

The Sergeant caught his arm. "Watch it, sir. There's a burrow about here."

Corder waded cautiously forward. His boot hit a hard slippery surface and slid ahead. Corder took an awkward hasty step to recover his balance. The Sergeant stumbled and lunged forward. Corder caught him. They stepped around the dark hood of a tracksled, and Corder shone his flashlight on the door. The Sergeant pulled it open, set one foot carefully on the step, reached up, grabbed the doorframe with both hands, and clumsily heaved himself in. Corder wondered if the Sergeant's feet were as cold as his own, which felt like loosely hinged blocks of wood. He reached up, hauled himself in, and shut the door.

The Sergeant leaned forward over a faintly-humming box mounted between himself and the driver. A bluish glow from the box lit his face like a mask. "Swing a little north," he growled.

"O.K.," said the driver.

The engine speeded up, there was a smell like hot rubber and the tracksled began to creep forward. Corder pushed back the sleeve of his coat to glance at his watch. The glowing dial told him that it was already 0550. The attack was to start at 0630, and the tracksleds were proving so defective that Corder wondered if they'd make it.

The Sergeant cupped his hands to blow on them. Corder worked off his mittens, undid a coat button with numb fingers, and slid his hands inside his coat under his arms. The tracksled crept through the darkness, and the snow pattered as it blew against the windshield. Corder's mind drifted back to the first day of the expedition, when he'd listened as the Colonel described the situation on Cryos.

★ ★ ★

The officers were gathered in the ship's maproom, and the Colonel, straight and spare, was standing before them.

"The background of the situation," said the Colonel, "is that we have our fleets spread thin all over the universe. We're strong nowhere, so the Outs can hit us anywhere. In their last fanatical attack, they stabbed through the region we're now approaching. During the advance, they dropped a small landing-party on Cryos, an unimportant planet of an out-of-the-way sun. A scout ship of ours was caught in the path of this Out penetration and saw the landing.

"The Outs could easily have destroyed this scout ship, but they let it get away. Since then, they have made three showy attempts to supply this little force on Cryos, and all three have been turned back without a genuine struggle."

The Colonel frowned. "Cryos, to the best of our knowledge, has no value either to the Outs or to us. Its ore deposits aren't exceptional, and it is located away from any sizable communications route. The axis of Cryos is sharply tilted, and its climate runs to violent extremes. The highest known form of life on the planet is a hardy burrowing omnivore. This creature looks like a huge caterpillar, has an oversize appetite, and kept our first exploratory team in a constant state of emergency by burrowing into the stocks of supplies. Gravity and atmosphere on Cryos are bearable, but these are the only known points in the planet's favor.

"So," said the Colonel, "the Outs dropped a landing party on this place, and, ever since, they've been advertising it to us." The Colonel glanced narrow-eyed at a Manila folder lying on a table nearby. He took hold of the folder, and held it up. It was stamped in big block letters, "Top Secret."

"This," said the Colonel, "is the General Staff's answer to the problem. As you may have noticed, gentlemen, in the past three years there have been some peculiar changes in the manner of thinking of the General Staff. To begin with, they dispersed our strength on the frontiers. The Outs have punched through twice, and show every sign that they are getting ready for a new and bigger attack. When we try to warn of this, we find that we might as well try to talk through a dogged-down spacedoor. We aren't heard. The worst part of it is, if we send someone back to hammer things out with them, he vanishes into the Capitol, and comes out after a few days convinced everything is fine. I came back myself about fifteen months ago and tried to sell some kind of gibberish called 'elastic counterdefensive.' Whoever goes back to the Capitol comes out with the idea. After a few days, the sense of certainty evaporates, and it's possible to see that it's all doubletalk. It won't work. But the General Staff keeps handing down stuff on the same level, and now we come to the plan for Cryos.

"Anyone," said the Colonel, "ought to be able to see the possibility that the Outs are laying a trap. But the plan specifically prepared by the General Staff makes no mention of the possibility of a trap. It says instead, that we have taken no prisoners, and therefore this collection of Outs offers a splendid opportunity for study. We are supposed to go down and *capture* this Out expedition. We're supposed to bring them back alive and in good shape. Let me read just one paragraph:

"'The objective of Operation Coldfeet is the capture, alive and well, of all enemy troops on the planet Cryos. To this end, the initial landing will be made at Point Q, precisely forty miles southwest of the enemy base on Able Hill. The expeditionary force will form three separate columns of attack, advance under cover of darkness and total silence along diverging routes of march, turn at predesignated points and converge upon Able Hill in a three-pronged pincer movement. This advance will be so timed that the three columns strike the hill simultaneously from the south, west, and east. The troops will immediately deploy, and halt ready to advance up the hill. The Expedition Commander will then contact the enemy and demand his immediate surrender.'"

The Colonel put the manila folder on the table nearby and pushed it away. The room was dead quiet. The Colonel said, "Anyone who can land a ship precisely forty miles southwest of a given point on the winter hemisphere of a strange planet, and throw troops out into the night in three different directions at three different rates of march through deep snow, assemble them again simultaneously at a place forty miles away, where they have never been before, and do it without benefit of any signal the enemy might pick up—anyone who can do this has *earned* the right to go out and try to make his enemies give up without firing a shot. But," said the Colonel, "with all due respect to the people who framed this order, I think *we* had better go at it a little differently."

* * *

Corder felt a heavy jounce and a crash. He was sitting in the tracksled. The tracksled hesitated a moment, then crept forward.

"Amen," said the Sergeant.

"Keep praying," said the driver. "There's generally a bunch of burrows together."

The tracksled tilted again, climbed, and came down with a smash. There was a moment's pause, then the sled crawled sluggishly ahead.

Corder leaned forward and scraped a layer of frost from the windshield. Outside the night was fading to a dark gray, and Corder seemed to see a darker bulk far ahead and slightly to his left. He visualized the map the Colonel had shown them, with its long narrow hill in the center. The Outs had been sighted on the hill, and the Colonel had decided to land to the east, then advance toward the long east face of the hill in parallel columns of tracksleds. Each column of sleds would help the other if they were attacked en route. If not, the plan was to hit the hill to the north of its center, split the Outs into two parts, and crush each in turn.

Only, Corder thought, if that dark bulk to the left was the hill, he was too far to the north.

"Sergeant," he said.

"Sir?"

"Take a look out there."

The Sergeant leaned forward. The tracksled crawled up and crashed down. The Sergeant steadied himself, turned his head away, then looked back. "Sir," he said, "it looks like the hill to the southwest there. But it's too dark to be sure." He looked ahead, then squinted off toward the north. Then he turned and looked back to the southwest. "I don't know. It could just be heavy clouds in that direction."

Corder leaned forward and peered into the gloom. If he looked straight ahead, it seemed noticeably darker to the left. If he looked to the left, he could see nothing there at all.

Now, Corder thought, if that *is* the hill, I am off the course and will get carried right straight out of the battle entirely; and then only part of our force will hit the Outs, and we will lose. Or, on the other hand, if that *isn't* the hill, and I do swing southwest, we will probably hit the center column going west, and cause such a mess—including the possibility that they will mistake us for Outs and open fire—that again we will lose the battle.

The Sergeant leaned forward tensely and wiped off the windshield.

"Damned if I can tell," he said.

To Corder, the dark blot seemed to be gradually falling to the side as they moved ahead.

"Swing southwest," said Corder. "And if you see anything that looks like a tracksled swing west again."

"Yes, sir."

They peered ahead into the grayness and the tracksled now began a rolling motion, rising up at the right in front, then pitching forward so the left rear was up. Corder glanced at his watch. He had less than twenty minutes to get into position.

They rode for a while in silence, trying to see ahead. The sky was growing lighter, but they still couldn't be sure.

To the south, a bright white glare lit the sky. A series of orange flashes puffed out like long fingers and faded away. Then they could see the hill, tall and white, and much closer than it had seemed.

Corder felt his muscles tense. For a moment, he didn't breathe.

Then the hill was swinging close, looming high above them.

★ ★ ★

In the gray light of dawn, Corder could see nothing on the hill save a smooth slope of snow.

The tracksled tilted as it began to crawl up the first slope of the hill.

"Sir," said the driver, "do you want to go up here, or farther south?"

Corder was thinking that if they went up the hill here, they would be north of the place where they should have been, but if they went south, the whole column would trail along the base of the hill, offering an excellent target, and they might still be out of action when they were needed most. But, if they could get up the hill here, while the Outs' attention was distracted by the attack to the south—

"Go up here," said Corder.

The tracksled tilted more steeply, and churned its way soggily up the slope. As the sled climbed, the slope steepened and the engine labored.

Something ticked lightly on the roof of the cab.

The engine was racing, and the tracksled was moving more and more slowly. There was a stench of burning rubber.

"Sir," said the driver, "I think this is about as far as we're going to go."

Outside, it was growing steadily lighter, and had stopped snowing.

The windshield in front of the driver starred but didn't break.

Corder reached down to a shelf under the dash, and took out a small hand comset. Then he studied the hillside. In the growing light he could see nothing but a rising sweep of smooth snow. There were no irregularities save an occasional ripple in the snow, running straight up the side of the hill and fading out of sight.

Something bounced off the hood and starred the upper edge of the windshield directly in front of Corder. The tracksled crept to a dead stop.

Corder opened the door and jumped out. His feet landed on crusted snow that broke with a crunch. He took a step, and the crusted snow at first supported his weight, then gave way, so that his foot came down with a jolt, hit another layer or crust about eight inches lower, broke through that, and jammed into a third layer that caught his heel. The crust was hard, so that when he came to take another step he had to pull his foot straight up to get it free. Corder walked in this spine-and-joint-jarring way about half the distance from the cab door to the rear of the tracksled. Then he stopped, the comset raised to his mouth to give the order, and saw in his mind just what would happen if his men started up the hill through this stuff.

The air overhead and to one side was now growing thick with things that went *Whick! Whick! Whick!* as they passed. Corder looked around for some kind of cover, and saw, thrust up here and there through the crust, what looked like the naked top branch of a tree. The stems thrust up a yard or two at an angle, and were too thin to hide a cat.

It was very plain to Corder that if he gave the order he was supposed to at this point, his men would be shot to pieces or pinned down in isolated snowholes in no time at all. The Outs would have a little brisk early-morning target practice, and that would be the end of it.

Something whacked the front of the tracksled beside him, thumped on the roof at the rear, and fell in the snow at his feet. Corder picked up a little metal cylinder with small fins set on it at an angle. The point of the dart looked like the bent end of a pin, and was covered by a thick coating that had partly cracked off.

Corder glanced at the fabric covering over the rear of

the tracksleds, and knew his men couldn't stay there, either. He brought the comset close to his mouth, studied for an instant the sled's ground clearance, then said slowly and clearly, "Get your men out and under the tracksleds. Let the first few men open fire from behind the tracks. Have the rest dig out under the sleds. As soon as you can, dig connecting trenches between the tracksleds."

Corder repeated his orders carefully, heard tailgates dropping along the line of tracksleds, and made his way bone-jarringly to the rear of his own tracksled, where the first men to hit the crust filled the air with outraged disbelief, then dove under the sled.

The air was now filled with whizzing darts, and an occasional something that made a droning buzz. From under the sleds came the first sharp reports as Corder's men began to return the fire. So far, it was possible to stay here. But already one of Corder's lieutenants had reported two men hit by darts and unable to move. Moreover the Outs could be expected to bring up heavier weapons as quickly as possible, and they might, Corder thought, have tunnels already dug for the purpose of doing it unseen. Corder crawled under the tracksled and studied the hillside in the growing light. He frowned at the low ripples in the snow, running up toward the top of the hill, then realized that they were probably burrows under the snow.

Corder traced the ripples up the hill, where they vanished completely. Probably, he thought, because the burrows ran deeper there under the snow. He looked down the hill, and saw the ripples fan out onto the snowfield. The tracks of the sleds showed where they had crossed them.

Corder traced the nearest of the ripples back, and saw that it passed under the third tracksled in the line.

The men from Corder's sled were digging steadily and silently. Corder glanced back at the hill and scowled thoughtfully at what looked like a vapor rising from the snow far up the hill. Then, when his sled was connected with the one behind it, he ducked through the slit trench, to the third tracksled back. The men here, in order to move freely beneath the sled, were chopping through the side of the burrow that ran under it. With the snow dug away, the burrow looked like a giant pipe about three feet thick.

From up the hill, a shout went up. Corder turned to look out through the sled's tracks. A heavy gray fog was rolling slowly down the hillside. Corder turned back to the burrow and saw that the men had chopped a large hole into it. He shone his light inside. The burrow stretched off in both directions farther than the light would reach. The whole inside wall was rippled like corrugated iron, and roughened as if it had been stippled by thousands of stiff tiny wires.

Corder crawled in, and ordered his men to follow in single file.

* * *

Corder crawled forward as rapidly as he could, and the men hurried after him. The burrow sloped more steeply, and the corrugations deepened. After a time the muscles of his whole body began to ache. He was repeatedly thrown off balance by his long overcoat. He was breathing hard, and his lungs hurt, as much from the constriction of his heavy clothing as from the effort. On the other hand, he was warm, for the first time since he had set foot on the planet. He thought of the possibility that a grinning Out was sitting at the other end of the burrow with a box of grenades, waiting till they got good and close before rolling the first one in. Corder told himself that he had only had so many choices since he had started out, and he had tried to pick the best ones he could.

Instead of making him feel better, the thought of the fewness of the choices made him feel frustrated and resentful. He yanked forward the heavy skirts of the overcoat and thrust them through the coat's belt. He crawled ahead fast and steadily, matching his motions to the harsh indrawing of his breath.

Behind him trailed the clatter, heavy breathing, and dogged cursing of his men, laden down with their equipment, and driven by the same frustration that drove him.

It was a long way to the top. Corder had to call a halt three times, and each halt was accompanied by a bumping and a piling-up that shortened tempers to the point where fights threatened to break out along the whole length of the line. At the third stop, Corder had to calm a soldier, somewhere in the blackness behind him, who had gotten banged in the face with a rifle butt twice and now furiously announced that he would kill everyone present if it happened again.

Each stretch of the burrow was worse than the one before, as the slope steepened and accidents and bad temper piled up. By the time the burrow had begun to level out, a new source of trouble became evident. The burrow roof was beginning to get lower. Corder hit his head twice, and from the dull burst of cursing behind him, he knew he wasn't the only one. The burrow tilted slightly downward, flattened out more and more, and the corrugations grew shallower, longer, but more sharply ridged, so that they bit into his knees, which were already sore and tender, while the roof forced him down so that he had to use his knees regardless.

Corder passed the word back to come ahead more slowly. Then he crawled forward as fast as he could to find out where the burrow led. As he crawled, the cross section of the tunnel progressively changed from a flattened circle, to an oval, to a flattened oval, to a kind of wide horizontal slit that forced him to lie perfectly flat and pull himself ahead by his fingernails. By this time, the burrow was wide enough for three men, and the concave corrugations in its floor were long and shallow, and edged almost like knives. The burrow slanted sharply downward, then sharply upward. Corder breathed a silent prayer, slid down, squeezed himself through, felt ahead, and his fingers closed around a lip of ice. He pulled himself up and came out in a dark place with a flat floor.

Corder released the safety on his service automatic, and came cautiously to his feet. He turned on his flashlight. The beam lit a pile of big, odd-looking tins, then shone on a wall of grainy snow. Corder swung the beam around, and it lit the six walls of a room about fifteen feet across. He shone the light up. The ceiling of the room slanted up from each wall to a round hole about two feet across and ten feet up from the floor. The hole extended up a little over a yard, and ended in what looked like a trapdoor. Hanging down the side of the hole, was the top end of a rope ladder. About two-and-a-half feet down from the trapdoor, the ladder ended, its ropes frayed as if they'd been cut off with a dull knife.

Corder studied the frayed rope, then shone his light on the pile of tins. The tins were about sixteen inches high, flat on both ends, and six-sided in cross section. Each one Corder picked up was roughly torn open along an edge.

Corder's men were now pulling themselves up out of the burrow. Corder had them move the tins to see if there was any other way out of the room. Behind the piles of empty cans, the men found the entrances of four more burrows. Some of the burrow entrances were deeply scratched, as if the big cans had been pulled down into them.

Corder turned around to see more of his men climbing into the room. In time, there would be about two hundred of them in here, jammed together like bullets in the clip of a gun. Corder stared up in exasperation at the trapdoor. Then he stepped to the mouth of the burrow and said, "Just one more man."

He had the men form a human pyramid under the hole. Then he climbed cautiously up, steadied himself with the rope ladder, and tried to raise the trapdoor. The trapdoor wouldn't move. Corder hit the edge sharply with a rifle butt. Then he raised it cautiously and looked out to see the backs of half-a-dozen fur-clad beings, each carrying a long slender gun. Trudging past them was a group of about fifty Earthmen, their faces blank and unseeing, their hands clasped above their heads. Corder peered cautiously around and in the other three directions saw only snow. He let the trapdoor back in place, bent down, and briefly explained the situation. "Don't move till I do," he warned, then he inched the trapdoor up.

★ ★ ★

He saw one of the Outs from the side, as the fur-clad

figure bent to prod a finger into the side of a passing Earthman. The Out's face was like that of a man, but gray, and thin to the point of emaciation. His movements were very slow. Corder's sights swung into line on his head and he squeezed the trigger a little harder. The rifle jumped and the Out jerked and staggered forward.

Corder aimed deliberately at a second Out, and fired. The Out fell. For a moment, the other four stood frozen and still, then their long slender guns started to swing up as they turned. Corder fired deliberately a third time, then he heaved himself up out of the hole, sprinted hard to his left, and dove.

Whick! A dart flew over his head. *Whick!* One ticked his helmet as it passed.

Corder landed awkwardly faced in the snow, and had no time to change his position. He switched hands on the rifle, fired it left-handed and missed. He corrected his aim, took first pressure, then he couldn't move.

A solid rank of fur-clad Outs watched him over leveled guns. Their faces were pink and glowing with health and well-being. Their eyes were large and bright, peculiarly keen and sharp, and Corder felt a wave of unfitness that he should have attacked these superior beings. He felt ashamed to be human and eager to do whatever these master men might—

Crack!

The line of Outs was gone, and a thin fur-clad figure tumbled forward. From the corner of his eye, Corder could see a bulky shape heave itself up from the trapdoor, sprint to the right, and dive.

A long slender gun spun to cover him. Corder took aim.

Corder's gun swung erratically, a tiredness and weakness making his hands too feeble to hold it, too weak after the long struggle, and the insufficient food, the lack of water, and now he was so tired. No one could blame him if—

Crack!

One fur-clad figure was still standing, his long slender gun aiming toward the trapdoor where Corder could see in a swift glance that a man looked out with his eyes focused on the far distance, and his face trancelike and blank, and Corder's sights settled into line on the slender fur-clad figure, and as he squeezed the trigger his rifle bucked and his ears rang with the concussion.

The fur-clad figure bent at the knees, tipped and fell to one hand, looking at Corder with his brilliant eyes.

And Corder stumbled to his feet, half-sobbing, and ran forward to catch him, to give first aid, to—

Crack!

The figure jerked and slammed down on the snow.

★ ★ ★

Corder stood stock-still, his lungs sucking in breaths of the bitter-cold air. He was looking around, the whole scene vividly clear as he saw the still-trudging procession of Earthmen, their hands clasped over their heads, and the six huddled figures on the snow. More of his own men were climbing out of the trapdoor now, and Corder turned to tell them to spread out and— He jerked around suddenly.

Out of the corner of his eye he had seen the first of the Outs start to roll slowly over. For an instant, Corder seemed to see two things at once. The Out was slowly coming to a sitting position, and the Out was lying flat on his face.

He couldn't have sat up, Corder realized, so it must be a trick of the sun on snow, there was nothing to worry about, nothing at all— But—

Corder sucked in a sharp breath, and jerked his rifle up. He fired and fired again.

The image lying in the snow was gone, and Corder saw the Out halfway to his feet, the long slender gun in his hand. The Out sat down backwards, and the gun flew out of his hand to lie on the snow.

Crack! Crack! The men were firing again at the Outs.

Corder strode to the Out he had just shot, and rolled him over on his face. In the back of the skull was a mark like a little mouth. Even as Corder watched this mark slowly smoothed out and grew fainter. Corder raised his gun and rolled the Out over. The clothing over the Out's chest had a neat round hole in it. There was no blood.

The Out's eyes slowly opened. They were peculiarly bright and keen eyes. Corder saw the Out's chest move to take in a deep breath. Corder brought the raised butt of his gun down hard. The bright eyes shut, then opened, and Corder knew he could never kill, never even harm, these beings who were of a superior race, far wiser, far stronger—

The Out's thin hand groped, and his eyes flickered for an instant. Corder brought the gun butt down hard, and rolled the Out over on his face. Corder looked up and saw a tense group of his men firing down into a patch of empty snow, while a spare fur-clad figure nearby slowly came to its knees, its brilliant eyes intent on the men. Corder brought his gun butt down again on the back of the head where the scar of the shot was almost gone.

Then he lay down by the Out, and taking the Out's gun, studied it a moment and rested it across the Out's back as he aimed. He squeezed the stud.

Whick! The gun jerked just a little in his hand.

He squeezed the stud again.

Whick! Whick!

The other Out fell over on his face, and Corder fired a dart from the weapon into the Out near him, who was starting again to move. After that, the Out lay still.

* * *

It took from the morning far into the afternoon before the Out position was completely under control. By then, Corder, the Colonel, and every man present in the whole expedition knew why the Outs had put this base temptingly far forward inside the human star system.

Before finally leaving Cryos, the Out position on Able Hill was thoroughly explored. There were dugouts in the snow that seemed to be barracks, headquarters dugouts, and dugouts that apparently served as recreation rooms. There were a large number of supply dugouts, and all of these had been burrowed into on a grand scale.

Corder, the Colonel, and a number of other officers and men, found themselves staring bemused at a huge pile of red-painted structural beams in the center of the Out camp. Each of these beams had holes about an inch across spaced along it at regular intervals. The beams were free of snow; several brooms were stuck in the snow at each end of the pile; and to one side was a stack of red hexagonal kegs, or drums, drifted over with snow.

"Granted," said the Colonel, "that they wanted to let us see plainly where they were, I can understand why they kept that pile of beams clear of snow. But I fail to see why they didn't make something useful out of it."

"Sir," said Corder, "we haven't found many tools here that they could have used. There are picks, shovels, and so on, but nothing in the way of mechanical tools."

A Major standing nearby spoke up. "Thank God. If they'd gotten their food supply up out of reach of the burrowers, we'd all be Out recruits by now."

The Colonel frowned at the stack of hexagonal kegs. "Sergeant, take a few men and break open one of those six-sided drums."

The Sergeant called to several men and waded through the snow toward the pile of kegs.

Corder shifted his grip on one of the Outs' long guns and looked around warily.

The Colonel smiled. "Uneasy, Captain?"

"Sir, I can't get rid of the feeling that there might be one we haven't caught."

The Major laughed boomingly. "God forbid."

The Colonel said in a quiet voice, "There is one we haven't caught."

Corder glanced sharply around. "Where?"

"In the Capitol."

"*Sir?*"

"When I was sent back to the Capitol," said the Colonel, still in his quiet voice, "I had the same sensation I had here when the Outs took us over. I'd forgotten it, but the memory came back when it happened a second time. The sensation when I was convinced of the 'dynamic counterdefensive' was exactly the same as the sensation here; but it was much stronger than what happened here."

"Good God," burst out the Major, "then they've got a spy through to the top. *That's* why our orders are all cockeyed!"

The Colonel didn't turn his head. Dryly, he said, "It seems to be a possibility."

"Then," said the Major after a pause, "we've lost the war."

Corder opened his mouth angrily, then clamped it shut. The Colonel turned his head to look at the Major.

"We might just as well," the Major was saying heatedly, "throw in the—" His eyes strayed to meet the Colonel's gaze. The Major's voice cut off, and for an instant his lips moved with no sound coming out.

The Colonel, looking at the Major, spoke in a flat toneless voice. "You're a good man in combat, but you'd better learn to control what thoughts make use of your tongue."

"Sorry, sir."

The Colonel looked away, and said broodingly, "Things are so connected together that it's impossible to tell what leverage any single event will have. But if we do our best, at least we have nothing to reproach ourselves for afterward." He turned to the Major, and said in a voice edged with anger, "Always remember, our own wounds and troubles are painfully close to us. The agonies of the enemy are too far away to appreciate. Just do your job and don't complain except when it will do some good."

"No, sir," said the Major miserably.

The Sergeant let out a shout. Corder turned to see that the Sergeant was holding up in one hand a wrench, and in the other a bolt with washers and a nut threaded on it. Corder squinted at the bolt and washers, glanced at the holes in the red beams.

The Colonel said, "Captain, do you see what I seem to see? Come on."

They waded through the snow.

The men were breaking open more of the six-sided drums.

"Sir," said the Sergeant, "they all seem to be the same size."

Corder took one of the bolts, and passed it—washers, nut and all—easily through the holes in the stacked beams. "Too small," he said. "But how did they ever make a mistake like that?"

"That wonderful convincing ability of theirs," said the Colonel. "If it's like any other ability, they have it in varying degrees. What happens, I wonder, if a lazy, high-convincing Out competes for a position with a conscientious, skilled, but not-so-convincing Out? And if there's mismanagement, how does it get rooted out, when the bungler can convince everyone in his mind that he's right?"

They stared at the pile of beams, and the Major blurted, "Well, I'll be da—" then cut himself off and bit his lip.

The Colonel glanced at the Major and smiled faintly. "It would be a little premature to give up, wouldn't it?"

"Yes, sir."

"Why?"

"They have their troubles, sir."

The Colonel nodded, and the Major looked like a boy who has gotten off the cracking ice onto hard ground, and resolves to stay there.

Corder looked at the piles of beams and stacks of bolts and shook his head.

Late that afternoon they took their captive Outs and blasted off.

TOP RUNG

James L. Kevv, newly-appointed ambassador to Knackruth, stood up as the Secretary of State opened the door of his inner office. Kevv said, "Good morning, sir."

The Secretary of State eyed Kevv critically. "Come in," he growled. He studied Kevv's trouser creases, glanced at Kevv's shoes, squinted dubiously at Kevv's tie, grunted, and shut the door. He walked over to his desk and growled, "Sit down."

Kevv frowned and slowly sat down. The secretary scowled at him like a rocket engineer looking over an engine of doubtful design. "Hm-m-m," he said finally. "What do you know about Knackruth?"

Kevv took a deep breath and related, "Knackruth's the fourth planet of the sun Ostrago III. Principal export, quadrite. Form of government, heterogeneous independent states. The leading state is Gurt."

"You realize that for all intents and purposes, you will actually be ambassador to Gurt?"

"Yes," said Kevv. "I realize that."

"And what kind of government does Gurt have?"

"It's called an 'elective monarchy.' Actually, it amounts to a dictatorship."

The secretary seemed to relax slightly. "Know the language?"

"Of course."

"What do you think of it?"

"Well, it can be pretty straightforward and direct."

The secretary took out a thick black cigar. He studied Kevv with what looked like the first microscopic beginnings of approval. "For instance?"

"Well," said Kevv, "if a man wants to compliment a girl, using the Gurt language, he has a hard time being subtle. About the most roundabout thing he can say is, she 'heats his blood.'"

The secretary nodded and settled back in his chair. "What's the climate like?"

"It's mostly extreme—a sodden spring and fall; a hot, dusty summer; in the winter, blizzards and severe cold."

"Hm-m-m." The secretary opened a drawer, and pulled out a long wooden match with a big pink head. "Now," he said, "You've never actually been in Gurt?"

"No. But I've read a good deal in the native tongue. I think I have a working picture of the country."

"That's a help," said the secretary. "But I'll be brutally frank with you. Earth needs quadrite. Gurt has quadrite. It's important that you get along with the Gurt dictator, and I can tell you right now that is no easy job. Up till now, we've used military men for ambassadors, and limited their stay to one year. One year was about all they could stand."

Kevv blinked. "Why?"

The secretary touched the edge of his desk, and the lights in the room faded. His voice came to Kevv out of the blackness.

"Our last ambassador presented his papers with sight-and-sound recorders sewn into his suitcoat, so I can explain it to you very clearly. Turn your chair so you're facing toward the wall to your right."

Kevv turned. At his side there was a scraping snap, and the secretary's face and hands appeared cupped about yellow murky flames. The flames waved in the air and went out. The reek of burnt wood and hot fish oil filled the room.

"That," said the secretary. "was a Gurt match." A red glow the size of a man's thumbnail brightened and darkened. An odor like over-heated rubber began to seep across the room. "This," said the secretary, puffing, "is a Gurt cigar. The dictator is very fond of them. He smokes them constantly." The secretary coughed. *Whew*. Well—" Kevv choked on an overpowering stench like burning rubber, flue gas, and sulfur fumes. "There," said the secretary's voice, "now we have the right background." He sucked in a whistling breath. "Now just imagine you're going in to present your credentials on Gurt. Watch that wall opposite."

Kevv sucked in a breath of smoke. His eyes watered, and a sharp pain shot across his forehead. "O.K." he said.

* * *

A room seemed to light up around him, with a low ceiling, and unshielded lights set at six-foot intervals along the wall. The room was bare, and Kevv sat on a chair in a thick layer of smoke that hung about three feet above the floor, its bottom edge as clearly defined as a cloudbank. Opposite Kevv was a heavy door with a peephole. To the left of the door, a snout like that of a machine gun was thrust out a slit in the wall, and aimed at Kevv. In front of the door, like a mat, lay a polished metal plate, with a black rubber cord plugged into a socket at the base of the wall nearby. The doorknob was of polished metal the exact color of the plate. To the right of the door, something long, bright and thin, flicked out and back like a snake's tongue. Kevv watched, and saw it was a highly-polished blade, that flashed out sometimes toward the space before the door, and sometimes over the black cord.

The door opened. A man wearing a gray-and-blue uniform with silver insignia glanced at Kevv, looked around at the gun and the long sharp knife. He said dryly, "Vrin, ven tu dupit nal spung, spoopt, slitzt ater ossonplopt."

After an instant's hesitation, Kevv caught his meaning: "Come in, if you can do it without getting shot, fried, slit open, or squashed."

The officer stepped back, and a massive block of concrete dropped about a foot-and-a-half from the ceiling near the doorway. The block hung on a taut cable, turning slowly.

Kevv's viewpoint shifted rapidly. Walls and door swung sidewise and rushed forward. The polished plate flashed past below. The floor came up. Behind him there was a heavy shock and echoing blasts. His viewpoint shifted again, and he was standing in a room filled with smoke, and lined along the wall with maps. The Gurt officer in gray-and-blue helped brush him off.

"Nice jump," said the officer. He straightened up. "No

doubt you will want to strike light with our ruler. But right now he has his teeth in General Potakel. Look there."

Kevv glanced around and saw, through the smoke, a powerfully-built man of above average height, a black, smoking cigar jutting out of the corner of his mouth, his hand gripping a fistful of a pale officer's gray-and-blue uniform jacket. Words were flying thick and fast, and both men's faces were twisted with violent emotions.

"Damn it!" shouted the general. "I tell you, we've got to retreat!"

"Not an inch!" roared the ruler. "We're going to attack!"

"Attack? Thundering damnation! What with? I tell you, I've got a fourth of my men up to their ears in that sink-hole! The Znyth line's a fortress from one end to the other. With twenty-five per cent of my men half-drowned in Bogmurk, I couldn't lead a decent attack on an army of starving cows!"

"All right, you've made your point. Now stop using your mouth for a minute and use your head. We aren't fighting cows, we're fighting Znyth! How many times in the past couple of hundred years have they chopped us into pieces? You want that to go on forever?"

"No. But now we've got them out of the country—"

"And who planned that?"

"You did. I concede that. I give you full credit. But this is risky, dangerous. If the Znyth attack us while we're mired in the swamp—"

"Didn't you tell me the Znyth line was a fortress from end to end? Didn't they just get collected from their worst licking in two hundred years? Do you think their minds and emotions are fit for an attack? I tell you, they're grown into the earth in their fortress line! They'll fight in it. But they won't come out of it. Not yet. Wait till they mend their wounds and brood on their defeat and then it will be another matter. The idea is smash them now and *end* this hell!"

"Yes, fine, but the swamp in impassible, and their line is too strong. Unless, my ruler, we take twenty divisions from Santok's front—"

"What a bright idea *that* is. Take those twenty divisions and the Ghisrans will have us ground up and stuffed in sausage skins before we know what hit us. Your mind is working like a loadbeast with its head down and all four heels dug into the ground. You can't see the answer unless you *listen* to me."

"My ruler, I have listened. But I tell you—"

"Listen again. Don't just stand there waiting for me to finish so you can pound your argument into my head. Put your mind on what I say and listen hard. There are only so many things we *can* do. If we attack the Znyth defenses head on, we fight on their ground, with everything planned and laid out to their advantage; and they'll fight to the death on the spot, while some of our men will hesitate because they see how strong the Znyth position is."

"I see that."

"Good. And right now we can't switch men from other places. There's too much danger. To do that now would be like pulling stones out of a thin dike in one place to build it higher in another. Furthermore there is no use hoping we can raise new troops fast enough to change matters, because the Znyth, too, get reinforcements. All that leads to is more men on both sides. And, of course, we can try to make peace with them. Since they look forward to chopping us into little pieces as soon as possible, you can see what that would be like."

The general shook his head. "Yes, my ruler, I see. Still—"

"Hold on a minute. Listen to me. The west end of their fortified line rests on Bogmurk. They think the big swamp is impassable, so it isn't defended—"

"Yes, yes. But—"

"All right. Here's the key to the whole problem. Build the causeway through Bogmurk. Mass our main strength on the left flank. Pour the troops over the causeway and stab like a knife into the rear of their line. And right then, a hard attack from in front. A sledgehammer blow on the hinge at the same instant the bolts are sheared from in back—"

"Yes, yes, but this swamp drains the men that ought to attack!"

"What do you expect? Do you want to stroll through on a purple carpet? If we lose one out of the four in that swamp, the three remaining are still worth ten!"

"My ruler, you don't know. You haven't seen—Mud, fog, drizzle, quicksand, snakes, clouds of stinging bugs, half-an-acre out of a hundred dry enough to camp on—"

"If it were easy, the Znyth would do it themselves."

"The men are worn out, discouraged—"

"Did you come here just to tell me that? Get it across to them what they're doing. Tell them what it means. Give them honest reasons and they'll give you honest work. Do you think they'll be worn out when the Znyth scatter in front of them like leaves in the wind? Every step through that swamp is a step closer to that. Show them that, and think what it will mean to *you*. Now, get out of here. Put your mind on it. You keep coming back here to yell complaints in my ear and you'll end up with your head in a basket."

Kevv had the vague impression of someone stepping forward. Then it all faded out, and he was sitting in the dark.

A light switched on. The Secretary of State looked at Kevv with a rueful smile. "I wanted to give you some idea of what you're getting into. My understanding is, that was a comparatively calm day on Gurt. Now you're fore-warned, I think you can appreciate them better. Study them carefully." He shoved forward a thick stack of papers and microfilm, and reached out to shake Kevv's hand.

* * *

Kevv boarded the big, spindle-shaped spacer the next day. He immersed himself in the documents, and one word beat at him from nearly every page: quadrite. Earth needs quadrite. Quadrite is rare. Gurt has quadrite. Gurt has kept her agreements faithfully, and Gurt must be protected to safeguard the quadrite.

Kevv scowled, scanned the microfilm and studied the reports. Quadrite, he knew, was used to stabilize the drive tuning of Earth's interstellar fleet. He began to see the importance of Gurt in helping to supply quadrite, and he began to see his own job in helping to defend this supply. The only question was: How? Vigorous digging through the reports unearthed the fact that the total investment in Gurt seemed to consist of one ambassador, one communications technician, a general practitioner and a lung specialist.

Kevv spent the rest of the trip absorbing information and exasperatedly trying to understand the situation. But a piece of the puzzle eluded him. His first act in landing on Gurt was to see Colonel Martins, the retiring ambassador.

Martins turned out to be a weary-looking elderly man with a ramrod back and a twitching left eye. He also had a look of contentment. He greeted Kevv cheerfully, and after a few words lay down on a cot.

"Excuse me," he said, "I'm a little tired. It helps to get off my feet." His face settled into an expression of contented achievement.

Kevv, noting the expression, said, "I don't mean to sound trite, but is this assignment here a . . . er . . . a rewarding experience?"

Martins grinned. "Not exactly. But leaving here certainly is rewarding."

"Oh."

"No, I don't mean that exactly, either. Some experiences are rewarding after you're out of them. For instance, shooting the Belt at six g's in a scout spacer after an unsuspecting dope runner in a converted Class-B cruiser."

"That sounds nice," said Kevv, without enthusiasm.

"This has it beat," said Martins.

"What do I do?"

"First go see the Doc, get your nose plugs fitted. Try not to take a breath with your mouth open when you're around the ruler. And don't let your plug charges get run down or the effect is just as bad. If you have to smoke a ceremonial cigar yourself, don't inhale any more than you have to. Ah . . . oh, and you might as well get your audience over today, one way or the other. Pray first. When your time comes, wait till the sword takes a stab toward the door, then go through the doorway *fast*. Take a flying leap over that plate, and don't brush the doorknob."

"What," said Kevv exasperatedly, "is the point of that thing, anyway?"

"The theory is, if you have any treachery in mind, you'll hesitate. That's all it takes. But if you get through, you're O.K. You only have to do it once."

"Assuming I live through it, exactly what is my function here?"

"You come back afterward, and I'll give you a few pointers."

"No," said Kevv, "maybe you'd better tell me now."

"You can take it in better after you have an audience with the ruler. Just act natural and you'll be O.K. It's hard to explain."

"Can't you at least give me an idea?"

"Well—" Martins hesitated. "O.K. What does an absolute ruler have that his followers don't have?"

"Position. Final authority."

"And what do the followers have that the ruler doesn't have?"

Kevv frowned. "Well—" He tried to analyze the problem, but it evaded his grip like smoke. "I don't know."

"Figure it out," said Martins. "Now, unless you want to get fumigated at the audience, you'd better get your plugs. It's bad enough with them, believe me."

Kevv located the Doc, who went to work on him with

pincers, hoses, and thimblelike objects of varying sizes. The Doc had a gift for one-sided conversation, and a grip that held Kevv struggling but helpless with his head bent over the back of a chair. In the end, Kevv wavered off to the audience with his own built-in air purifier.

★ ★ ★

"Vrin," said the officer in gray-and-blue, "ven tu dupit nal spung, spoopt, slitzt ater ossonplopt."

Kevv prayerfully watched the blade lick out past the door, took a flying leap, heard a heavy crash and a hammering blast behind him, and stumbled to his feet. He expected to hear roars of rage, oaths and orders, but the smoky room was almost oppressively quiet. Somewhere, a voice said, "Yes, my ruler."

At Kevv's elbow, the officer remarked, "We've conquered Znyth. Think of it."

Kevv frowned, and saw the ruler wandering amongst groups of officers gathered around maps and tables. The ruler's face was an unhealthy gray, and he was being followed around by an eager little man with pad and pencil. The ruler took a burnt-out cigar out of one corner of his mouth, walked up to an officer at a map marked off in squares, frowned, started to say something, and hesitated. The officer glanced around and snapped to attention. "Yes, my ruler?"

"Nothing." The ruler grimaced. "I was just thinking of something to occupy our friends for the future."

The officer looked impressed. The little man raised his notebook and scribbled rapidly. The ruler looked gloomy, glanced up and spotted Kevv. "Aha!" he said. "You made it!"

Kevv nodded, and watched in alarm as the ruler cheerfully tossed away his burnt-out cigar and pulled out two big black fresh ones.

The little man rushed over, snatched up the cigar butt, and laid it away reverently in a plush-lined case.

The ruler glanced around, glared, started to open his mouth, the lips drawn back from his teeth, took a deep breath, glanced back at Kevv, studied him a moment, and looked relieved. He thrust out a cigar. "One of my own specials. This one's really got a bite." He struck a big match and held the flaring stick out for Kevv to get a light. "Suck it deep into your lungs," he said.

Kevv, half-strangled, the room swimming before his eyes, blew out a cloud of burning smoke and nodded with imitation enthusiasm.

"Aha," boomed the ruler, clapping him on the arm, "follow me back to my office. I'll show you where I make them."

Kevv wiped his arm across his eyes. Live sparks seemed to dance in the air before him. Clutching the smoldering cigar in one hand, he trailed after the ruler down a short hall, around a corner, and past two padded doors hinged from opposite sides of the same doorway to close against each other.

★ ★ ★

The ruler closed and locked both doors, and glanced suspiciously around the little room. He pointed to a small bench with several boxes, a covered jar, and a brush. "That's where I make the cigars," he said absently. He glanced around, took a deep breath, then burst out:

"Did you see that bird out there with the plush-lined

box? What do you make of that? If I spit out a fleck of leaf—Pop. Into the box with it. Why? He says he's a historian. General Krakel vouches for him. All right, but what's this business with the cigars! Is he, maybe, going to analyze the leaf, find out where it comes from, and scatter poisoned insecticide around the crop, to be taken in as the plant grows?" He frowned. "That sounds foolish, now that I say it, but what *is* he doing with those cigar butts?"

Kevv sucked a breath through his nose filters. "Probably try to sell them for historical souvenirs—the ruler's own cigar butts—or maybe put them in a museum with his name on the case as donor. It looks to me like he's getting material together for something on a par with that."

"You think so? Well, it's a stupid thing, but then, the whole business is stupid. Did you see those people out there? Every time I open my mouth to yawn or sneeze, somebody's right there on the spot to say, 'Yes, my ruler.' You should have seen them three months ago. It wasn't 'Yes, my ruler,' then. It was 'No, no! You can't do it that way! That's impossible!' What's gotten into them anyway? I feel like a man who gets set to lift the iron weight and instead it's made out of hollow blackened wood. It isn't natural. Everything I do seems just perfect, but—"

He scowled. "There's a danger here." He squinted and walked back and forth. "Yes. Here's the danger. What if I get used to this? When everybody says 'yes,' and they don't think, *I* have to do it all. And then I won't get it right because I . . . even I—" he glanced at Kevv, looked foolish, and added hastily—"Well, we're all human. What if I make a botch of it? Then they'll come out of their stupor.

Meanwhile, I'll have gotten to think of myself as The Great Ruler. I won't *be* myself. I'll be acting the part of The Great Ruler. Then everything will fly apart and I won't be able to do anything because I'll have lost the threads that make the pattern." He sucked in a deep breath. "Well, I'm glad I see that. When you've got light to see the hole, you've got a chance to put your foot somewhere else." He opened the two doors.

Kevv, dumbfounded, followed the ruler out. As they returned to the main room with the maps, the ruler turned around, and raised his smoking cigar. "Some day I'll show you how I make them."

"Oh," said Kevv. "Yes. I'd . . . er . . . I'd like to see that."

The ruler strode across to the little man with the pad, paper, and box, and thrust a fresh cigar into his hand. "Here. Take this. Then get out."

An officer with a hero-worshiping expression stepped forward. "He is taking down your words, my ruler—for the future."

The ruler fired up a fresh cigar and fixed his gaze on the little man. "It has been not bad to have you here, but now secret events are about to take place and you must loyally get out."

The little man reverently laid away the cigar in the box, seized another discarded butt, scribbled rapidly, and left.

"Now," growled the ruler, "let's see how we're going here. The idea is to find the mistake you make and bash it over the head before it grows up and has a family." He scowled, went over to a big map, and a crowd gathered. He stuck his head through the crowd to take a quick look at Kevv, looked reassured, and vanished again.

Kevv glanced at his half-burnt cigar, pulled over a chair, sat down heavily and frowned.

What do the followers have that the ruler doesn't have?

★ ★ ★

By the time Kevv got back to see Martins, he felt worn out. Martins, however, looked considerably fresher and stronger.

"All right," said Kevv. "I lived through the audience. Now, suppose you tell me what's going on here. What's my function, anyway?"

"What happened?" asked Martins.

Kevv told him, and added, "You know that saying, 'Power corrupts.' Well, I could swear I saw power corrupting when I got here. Then all of a sudden it quit."

Martins nodded. "That's the point of it all. Earth has to safeguard Gurt's quadrite supply. And as far as we can see, the present ruler is the greatest single safeguard that Gurt has—if he doesn't go off the deep end."

"You mean, get delusions of grandeur?"

"Partly. Think of what became of most of our emperors and dictators on Earth in the old days: Secrecy, suspicion, fear of plots, seizure of crushing authority, then overwork, frustration, rage, megalomania, and disaster on a grand scale. We don't want it to happen to Gurt."

"Yeah, but how do we stop it?"

"Well, remember: What do the followers have that the absolute ruler doesn't have? Think of the kind of life they live. You can look on success in their kind of life as a ladder. Once you can get to the foot of it and start up, you don't have to worry about larger questions—like where you're climbing to. The idea is to just get up to that next rung. There's somebody above you, and somebody below you. You just keep climbing and putting rungs behind you. O.K. But what if you're on the top rung? Your head thrusts up into the open air. There's no place higher to climb to. You look down and it's a long fall. Maybe it dawns on you that that fellow one rung below wants to keep climbing, and there's no place for you to go but off. There's no one above to serve as an example, no equal to trust. Nobody you can talk to, and nothing to keep you from going off the deep end but your own self-control."

Kevv frowned, then slowly began to nod his head. "I think I begin to get it."

Martins leaned forward. "Look at it from their point of view. You're the man from the stars. The ladder goes up and up, out of sight, and, if they can't grasp the next rung, you're living proof that it's there."

"Yes," said Kevv. "I think I see. And I can be trusted, because I'm not in the competition." He thought over his meeting with the ruler, then said abruptly. "But it's a strenuous life."

"Well," said Martins, complacently tossing a pair of socks in a suitcase, "it may be a little rough on you, but it's a great thing for Earth. Think of the quadrite." He grinned suddenly. "Besides, you get your reward at the end." He fished through a half-packed trunk and pulled out a small wooden case. "Here. Open it."

Kevv somberly raised the cover and looked in.

"Just as I thought," he said. "Well, I've heard you can stand almost anything if you can get enough sleep, and I intend to try it."

Kevv stood up. "But as for this reward, I'll leave it with you."

He handed back to Martins the box of big, thick, black, custom-made cigars.

SYMBOLS

Colonel Wade Daniels, newly-appointed chief of the diplomatic mission on the planet Knackruth, stood on the snow-covered ledge in the shadows of the evergreens, and looked down on the yellow cannon-flashes and rolling smoke in the valley below.

Mattison, long the mission's communications officer, stood beside Daniels. "Well," he said, "there go the mines. It was a fool setup to leave them to local protection."

Daniels blew out a cloud of breath that slowly drifted away. "The Gurt may still win."

"No, sir. They're caught off-base. Their idea was to hold at that river, bring up supplies and reinforcements, and fight later at better odds. But the river's frozen a month too soon. Now the Ghisrans don't have to bridge the river, or come over in boats, under Gurt fire. Now they can *walk* across. And the Gurt aren't ready for that."

Daniels frowned. His orders stated: "Your primary mission is to secure the safety of the quadrite mines on Knackruth. To this end, you are authorized to treat with any of the local powers—"

The trouble was, only one of these local powers at a time had the mines. But they were always either fighting, preparing to fight, or recovering from a fight. Eventually, the mines were bound to change hands. And while dealing with Gurt was bad enough, the Ghisrans were bound to be worse yet.

"Damn it," said Daniels, "if those mines are overrun a lot of automatic machines, that can't be replaced, are going to get smashed."

"Yes, sir. The Ghisrans will enjoy that. But at least you got the machine operator out."

Daniels grunted and ignored that comment. "Meanwhile, the quadrite supply from here will be cut off, and as I heard it, this is the last developed source in the sector. But our ships have *got* to have quadrite. As a result of losing these mines, we could lose the whole sector."

Mattison nodded. "The mines should have been fortified. We've got weapons that would scare the Gurt and Ghisrans combined out of a hundred years' growth. But no, someone figured that we could save the effort it would take to fortify the mines, and apply that effort elsewhere, by leaving the Gurt technically in control, and paying them for the ore. That way, we wouldn't waste effort. The trouble is, that means we're leaving it up to a weaker power to see that *our* breath doesn't get shut off."

Somewhere behind them, there was a faint thud, and a fainter grating sound.

Mattison glanced around, then said, "It's only Sarge." He turned back to Daniels. "Sir, I'd better go in and see if there's been any reply to your message."

"Go ahead."

Mattison saluted and left, hurrying to the communications cabin.

A bulky, furry form approached Daniels from the right rear, outlined fuzzily for a moment against a moonlit section of the sheer cliff wall that rose out of sight at the back of the ledge. The furry form raised a mittened hand. Daniels returned the salute.

"Sir," said Sergeant Malinowski, "there's a bunch of Ghisrans down on that rock shelf. It's only a matter of time till they find the handholds."

"You lowered the rock into place. They can't get past that."

"They may go up overhead and drop grenades on us." The sergeant's voice held a note of reproach, as if he blamed Daniels that they'd been discovered.

Daniels said dryly, "You think you could have done a better job bringing that mining-machine operator in?"

"Well, sir . . . there must have been tracks—"

Daniels snorted. "Instead of landing her airsled inside the box canyon, so she wouldn't be seen from outside, she came down out on the flats, and *taxied* in. She taxied almost to the big tree where I was waiting, then she jumped out, and fainted. Sure there are tracks. My tracks, from here to that tree, where she was supposed to land. Her tracks, all across the flats and into the canyon, to that tree."

The sergeant blew his breath out wearily. "She must be as fouled up as everything else on this planet."

"And then some," growled Daniels. He took a last look at the moonlit valley, and headed back toward the communications cabin. The sergeant followed.

Underfoot, the snow gritted and squeaked as they walked. Daniels studied the tall trees and the cliff wall, his practiced gaze picking out the camouflaged cylinder that was the rebuilt, dual-drive reaction-and-gravitor derelict they called "The Bucket." This looming weaponless hulk was their only way to get home if the situation on the planet broke up completely, and Daniels was thinking that one good shell hit would finish it. And, if there were Ghisran troops down on that rock shelf—"There aren't any grenades here, I suppose?"

"No, sir. Nothing but sidearms."

Daniels nodded. They reached the cabin, and Daniels opened the door on another form of trouble.

★ ★ ★

Two men, the communications officer and a young civilian doctor, were standing inside, their brows moist with perspiration, their faces twisted in eager attentiveness. Before them, seated in the cabin's one comfortable chair, was a well-curved woman in her middle twenties, wearing dark slacks and slippers, and a tight black sweater that clung to her as if it had been sprayed on.

For an instant, the sudden sight of this femininity struck Daniels with the impact of a warm cozy cabin after the long chill of the outdoors. Then he heard her voice:

" . . .so then I punch a 617 on the Master, trip the override release, and the new matrix test-sorts the bounce-back. If it's O.K., that knocks the 'DIG' light on, and I lock the board. If the 'BALK' lights up, then I punch out a 618 or a 620, and try that."

"Wonderful," said Mattison, his voice oozing sincerity.

"Fascinating," said the doctor, his voice low, intense, and vibrant. "What do you do *then*, Robyn?"

Daniels glanced at the sergeant, who was staring at the woman glassy-eyed.

"Well," she said, putting one finger to the corner of her mouth, "then I usually heat up a cup of hot chocolate—not too much, you know—on account of the figure—and watch the hypnox till the ready-bell goes off again. Then—"

Daniels glanced around. To his left, the tight-beam communicator lit up with flashing lights.

"Mattison!" snapped Daniels.

The communications officer looked around glassily.

"Get that message!"

Mattison sprang across the room.

At Mattison's abrupt departure, the woman blinked, and one hand flew to her lips. Her eyes grew large. She held her other hand out to the doctor, who readily took it. Holding her hand, he looked to Daniels like someone who has taken hold of one of the grips of an electrical demonstration machine, and now can't let go.

The sergeant gave a grunt of disgust.

Daniels cleared his throat. The doctor's face registered such a state of ecstatic pain that it seemed unthinkable to intrude. But with an effort, he said, "Doctor."

There was no response.

"Doctor!"

The man's eyes came to a focus. Daniels said, "Did you see the local ruler before you came back?"

"Yes. Yes, I saw him."

"How did he seem?"

"Medically, or socially?"

Daniels felt a spasm of irritation. "They're two parts of the same thing. Naturally, I want to know both."

The doctor absently let go of the woman's hand. She drew herself together, and sat large-eyed and tense, as if she might explode into a scream at any moment.

The sergeant walked across the room to pick up a folded blanket on the lower half of one of the cabin's two sets of double bunks, walked back from a direction out of range of the doctor's vision, and offered a blanket to the woman. She blinked at him, smiled nervously, and the sergeant smiled back winningly. She accepted the blanket. He helped tuck it around her.

Daniels, momentarily distracted by this maneuver, heard the doctor say " . . .surprisingly well, considering the stress he's been exposed to lately. But the premature freeze seems to have thrown the Gurt military into disorder."

"Their plan was still the same?"

The doctor nodded. "Of course, the freeze wrecked the plans. They'd expected to hold the Ghisrans at the river for a month, and now the river's frozen. When I left, the new plan just seemed to be to fall back as slowly as possible."

Daniels nodded thoughtfully. "If the weather should suddenly turn warm again, the Ghisrans might find themselves with a flowing river between themselves and their supply dumps."

The doctor nodded vaguely, his interest obviously wandering away. He smiled and glanced down fondly at the woman. Her back was turned to him. She and the sergeant were talking to each other, their voices low, their heads about six inches apart.

Daniels was watching the play of emotions across the doctor's face when the sudden tearing of paper announced that the message, whatever it might be, had come to an end.

"Sir," said Mattison, his face pale, "here it is."

★ ★ ★

Daniels tensely took the yellow sheet of paper, skipped the heading, and read:

"Your request for aid has reached us as our resources are stretched to the limit.

"The only ships close enough to reach the planet in time are the superdrive ore-freighter and its tenders. These are all unarmed, and the freighter itself cannot operate within the planet's atmosphere.

"You state that the national forces of Gurt, on which we have relied to defend the quadrite mines, have suffered a series of disasters which have brought a coalition of their enemies within striking distance of the mines. You have not been able to deal with the coalition, or to bring about a truce. You remind us that due to the original agreement with Gurt, your only ship is unarmed, and your mission is without effective weapons.

"In reply, let me repeat that loss of the Gurt mines would be catastrophic.

"Quadrite is essential to fuel our combat ships' drive-units. It is also rare. Loss of these mines would interrupt the flow of quadrite in a large region of space. We are working on a narrow margin. Any interruption in the flow of quadrite will operate on our defensive posture like a cataleptic seizure.

"I do not need to mention that whoever is in charge on

the planet, if this happens, will be held directly responsible, and punished with the severity ordinarily reserved for acts of cowardice in the face of the enemy."

Daniels looked up.

From the valley outside came the reverberating crash of artillery. In his mind's eye, Daniels could see the numerically superior Ghisrans driving the Gurt troops away from the river and back from the mines. What, he asked himself, could *he* do about it? He had three men, plus a female mine-machine operator subject to hysterics—and no weapons but sidearms.

The absence of conversation in the room caught his attention, and he glanced around.

The doctor had his hand on the woman's wrist, and was glancing at his watch. She had a thermometer in her mouth, and was looking up at him worshipfully.

The sergeant was disgustedly shrugging into his fur coat. Mattison, heavily bundled up and nervous, was just going out the door.

Daniels looked back at the message:

"I cannot offer you reinforcements, or even any specific suggestions. However, I will give you a piece of advice that I have found useful:

"Do not operate on the assumption that the situation is hopeless. *Earnestly seek a solution.*

"Remember that our minds normally do not think in terms of reality, but of symbols. The mind selects a few outstanding characteristics of an object, combines them into a symbol, and mentally manipulates symbols to determine what will happen when the corresponding objects act in reality.

"But the symbol is not the object. The mind, in forming the symbol, originally selected certain outstanding characteristics, combined them, and henceforth takes the symbol as a reliable representation of the object. But what was originally a minor characteristic may, in a different situation, become important. Because of this inaccuracy of symbols, an apparently hopeless situation may contain an unseen solution.

"Don't give up. Break the situation down into its component parts, and examine each part in detail. Picture the way the parts fit together as clearly as possible. Imagine this or that element to be changed. Picture a favorable situation related to the present unfavorable situation. What change would bring about—"

Outside, there was a reverberating crash of artillery.

Daniels crushed the message and swore savagely.

Across the room, the woman put her hand to her mouth.

The doctor glared at Daniels, and gestured imperiously for silence.

The door flew open, and the sergeant came on in a whirl of snow.

"Sir, the communications officer wants hot water."

"Then get it." Daniels frowned. "Wait a minute. What for?"

"To unfreeze the hatch of The Bucket. He says we better get ready to clear out."

"All right. And while you're at it, set the internal temperature up from maintenance minimum to standby."

"Yes, sir," the sergeant answered.

"But nobody had better touch those controls."

"No, sir."

"Did you hear anything from that shelf below the ledge?"

"I listened. There wasn't a peep."

Daniels nodded.

The sergeant took a large container of hot water from the big iron stove and went out.

The doctor bent over the woman's chair to murmur soothingly.

Daniels sat down near the communicator, and finished reading the message. Then he dutifully analyzed the situation. The trouble was, the river had frozen, and the Ghisrans could now cross to drive back the outnumbered Gurt. To deal with the problem, he had a communications officer, a master sergeant, a civilian doctor, an hysterical woman, an unarmed escape ship, several handguns, a hideout that the Ghisrans had located, and the highly-specialized mining machines. Which of these things had some quality that he had overlooked?

He turned the problem over in his mind.

Outside, there was a heavy, jarring thud.

★ ★ ★

Daniels went to the door, and looked out.

Light snow was drifting down through the moonlight. Everything looked the same as before, but the artillery fire had again died away, bringing comparative quiet.

From somewhere came a faint rushing sound.

Daniels reached back, pulled the door shut behind him, and glanced around.

Something large and vague blurred down through the moonlight past the edge of the ledge.

From below came a heavy thud, and a rolling, smashing sound.

A shower of small objects flashed past, and a moment later there was a clatter from below.

Daniels sucked in his breath and glanced up.

From somewhere overhead came a low voice, followed by the gritting of metal on rock.

The hatch of The Bucket came open, and the voice of the communications officer floated out:

" . . .just a little artillery fire down there. Nothing to worry about yet."

Daniels called up, "Sergeant!"

"Sir?" came a muffled voice.

"Unlock the control panel. Throw both master switches into the 'on' position. Can you hear me?"

"Yes, sir. Unlock the control panel. Throw both master switches 'on'."

Daniels opened the cabin door.

The doctor was closing a little bag, and saying something to the woman, who was smiling back adoringly.

Daniels said, "Throw a coat on and get out here fast. Both of you."

From overhead came a grating noise, then a heavy rumble.

The communications officer ducked past Daniels, rushed into the cabin, seized hold of a square brown handle on the tight-beam communicator, pulled out a section about six inches by eight in cross section, and bolted past with it.

The doctor's brows came together.

"Shut that door, you fool. You'll chill her!"

From somewhere overhead, came a crushing, grating noise.

Daniels said, "Get her out and into the ship. We're leaving."

"Impossible. She can't be moved."

"Then stay and get crushed."

Daniels crossed through the shadows to the cylindrical base of The Bucket, took hold of the handgrips, and started to climb. He was about halfway to the hatch when some impulse caused him to look up.

Through the light, gentle, moonlit snow, something dark and big plummeted down, straight for the ledge.

Daniels froze.

The boulder struck a projecting bulge of rock, bounded off, and its main mass crashed through the trees beside the ship, taking one of them with it and leaving the ship in full moonlight. A smaller chunk of rock droned past on the other side, to rip away a remnant of the camouflage net that had hidden the ship. Smaller rock fragments clattered down the cliff face to land all over the ledge. From further below came a splintering crash and explosive cracking sounds as the boulder smashed through the forest.

Daniels climbed fast up the side of the ship and in through the hatch.

From below came the doctor's voice.

"Wait!"

Daniels swore, and looked out the hatch. Down below, the doctor was hurrying the planet's solitary Earth female across the ledge toward the ship. As they came, he protectively bundled a heavy coat around her.

"Sir," said the sergeant urgently from the control room, "we're all set to lift off."

Daniels said angrily, "Go get a rope."

The sergeant swore.

★ ★ ★

Down below, the doctor had reached the base of the ship, and was now pointing out the handholds. His voice was a loving, protective murmur. Daniels smiled sourly.

A feminine voice drifted up from below.

"I won't. I can't do it."

"You *can*. Just take hold—"

"No. No, I *can't*."

"Robyn . . . please, dear. Look, put your hand like this, then—."

She jerked back.

Daniels looked up at the cliff face.

The snow drifted steadily down in the moonlight. The cliff loomed vaguely up out of sight.

From somewhere up there came the gritting of metal against rock.

The sergeant leaned through the inner air-lock door and pressed something into Daniels' mittened hand.

"Sir, the rope."

Daniels stripped off his mittens, and quickly tied one end to a brace over the door. He leaned out.

Down below, the woman suddenly broke away, and ran for the cabin. The doctor ran after her, caught her, and pulled her back toward the ship.

Daniels said, "Sergeant, get to the controls and get us out of here the instant I say 'Lift'."

"Yes, sir."

Daniels leaned out the hatch and looked down at the whirling knot of arms and legs. The doctor's voice told of shifting feelings as he and the woman flailed around from the ship to the cliff edge and back again.

"Please, Robyn! Robyn, *look*, dear . . . Hey! WATCH OUT! We're right on the edge—*Robyn!*—Ouch!—*You fool, stop it!*"

A burst of ferocious profanity accompanied a second escape from double suicide, and Daniels, after a hasty upward glance, concluded that the psychological moment had arrived. Cupping his hands to his mouth, he shouted, "*Knock her out!* We'll haul her up on a rope!"

There was a sold thud and grunt.

Daniels heaved out the rope.

"Mattison!"

"Yes, sir."

"Help me here!"

Mattison squeezed into the air lock, and the two men took hold of the rope. Down below, the doctor straightened and called up tensely, "All right. I'll steady the . . . I'll steady her."

Daniels and Mattison pulled on the rope.

From somewhere up above came a grinding crushing noise, a thud, a continuous heavy grinding rolling sound, the clatter of small rocks and gravel falling, a second heavier thud, and then silence.

"Hang on!" yelled Daniels. He turned to shout over his shoulder. "Gravitors only! *LIFT!*"

There was a whine, and a surge of thrust that all but buckled his knees. The rope cut into his hands. Then the cliff was falling away. From somewhere came a heavy solid crash, then a noise like an avalanche.

The whine was rapidly climbing to a scream.

"Sir," yelled the sergeant, "gravitors won't hold the overload!"

Daniels shouted over his shoulder, "Balance on the center engine!"

There was a roar, and a reddish glare lit the snowflakes.

They got the inert form on the rope up over the hatch edge, and the doctor, his face scratched and bleeding, climbed in.

"Sir," shouted the sergeant. "What course?"

Daniels turned to Mattison, "Get that hatch shut, and make sure she doesn't come to and go berserk in here." He stepped through the inner hatchway into the control room.

The sergeant said, "There's no place to go down there, sir. We'll have to take her up, and fast."

Daniels glanced at the outside viewscreen. The screen showed the scene below, the moonlit snow-covered plain, crisscrossed by the tracks of animal-drawn carts and sledges, and alight with the flash of cannon. Through the drifting powder smoke, the river, which cut the battlefield in two, was shown by the sharp black shadow of its bank on the snow-covered ice. In the distance, off to the south, the defending Gurt troops still clung to their positions on the river bank. But below, the Ghisrans were across in force, with the Gurt line driven back toward the foothills, the Gurt troops further north almost cut off, and fresh attackers streaming across where the banks were low, almost directly below the ship.

To land anywhere nearby would mean coming down in a place that might be overrun before the next day was out. Daniels turned to tell the sergeant to take the ship up; then a phrase from the message spoke reproachfully in his ear:

" . . .acts of cowardice in the face of the enemy."

"I'll take it," said Daniels, suddenly determined to take the ship up himself, so there could be no slightest doubt who was responsible.

Another section of the message rose in Daniels' mind:

"Any interruption in the flow of quadrite will operate on our defensive posture like a cataleptic seizure."

The sergeant stood aside.

Daniels thought savagely, "What can I do? The situation is hopeless."

"Do not operate on the assumption that the situation is hopeless. *Earnestly seek a solution.*"

"I have no weapons, no authority on the planet, no troops to command!"

"Remember that our minds normally do not think in terms of reality, but of symbols . . . what was originally a minor characteristic may, in a different situation, become important . . ."

"They're all generalities. I've got about two seconds to decide and then I've got to act."

He slid into the control seat, feeling its surface conform to him, to brace him against the impact of any sudden acceleration.

Regretfully, he reached for the controls.

Another section of the message recurred to him as he gripped the controls:

"Picture a favorable situation related to the present unfavorable situation. What change would bring about—"

Daniels glanced at the outside viewscreen, and was suddenly struck by something obvious, something he could never have overlooked, *except that his mind thought in terms of symbols, not realities.*

"Sir," said the sergeant urgently.

Daniels gripped the controls savagely, and set the ship swooping to the north, and *down*, toward the frozen planet.

The communications officer blurted, "You *can't* set down! They'll get us anywhere down there!"

"He's going after the Ghisrans!" shouted the sergeant. "Sir, you can't get enough of them to count! Beyond the river, they'll take cover in trenches and gullies. On this side, you'll burn the Gurt, too!"

As if to demonstrate the sergeant's warning, the thick clots and masses of troops across the river dispersed, to vanish into numerous trenches and bunkers.

"Sir," cried the sergeant, "you'll never get them. There isn't fuel enough to—"

Daniels centered the ship directly over the river, eased off slightly on the gravitors, and balanced on the rockets.

Whirling clouds of steam and ice-crystals enveloped the ship. The glare from the screen grew dazzling. Then the ice abruptly seemed to turn black, and clouds of fog boiled up.

The communications officer stared.

The sergeant swore in sudden admiration.

Daniels guided the ship steadily down-river, on and on, leaving behind a strip of water that trailed clouds of fog in the moonlight. Then he cut the gravitors in strongly, rose to pass over the Gurt lines, and hovered briefly to look back.

The viewscreen showed the Ghisran troops on the near side of the river, inside a rough arc of Gurt soldiers, with the flowing river at their back. On the far side, the cut-off reinforcements cautiously rose from cover, to find deep water in front of them.

Suddenly perceiving what had happened, knots of Gurt troops began to run forward. Outnumbered by the Ghisrans as a whole, they in turn outnumbered the enemy on the near side of the river.

"They're cut off!" said the communications officer. "By the time it freezes again, they'll be finished. And they won't dare push across there next time, because, *the same thing may happen again!*"

The doctor stared from Daniels to the screen, and vigorously mopped his brow.

Daniels set the ship down gently, well behind the Gurt lines that were now moving forward.

A mental voice repeated to him another piece of the message:

"Because of the inaccuracy of symbols, an apparently hopeless situation may contain an unseen solution."

In his mind, Daniels had seen the ship only as a means of *escape*. Only at the last moment, had it dawned on him that the ship was incidentally an enormous torch.

Daniels drew a long shuddering breath, and silently thanked God.

Then he looked around the control room, with its delicate instruments and complex controls, and abruptly another thought occurred to him.

Mentally, he spoke to whatever it was that under stress had found the solution:

"Don't go away. There's another little problem coming along."

Across the control room, nicely shaped in the slacks and sweater, eyes blinking with incipient hysteria, and surrounded by a general air of solid unreason, their lone female passenger struggled weakly to sit up.

The sergeant relievedly wiped his brow, and felt around for some place to sit down.

The communications officer leaned back and relaxed.

The doctor let his breath out in a sigh and slumped in relief. "That's it. It's all over."

Daniels got up from the control seat and braced himself to move fast.

Robyn screamed.

FOGHEAD

Colonel Stephen Matt knew that the war was going badly. Each major battle began with Earth and her allies inferior in numbers and strength. Only a leadership that delighted in ambush, surprise, and hairbreadth timing enabled Earth to block the enemy advance. And only such a leadership could have lured Colonel Stephen Matt, bruised veteran of innumerable clashes with the enemy and his own head-quarters, to volunteer for something called "detached high-level courier duty."

Matt, seated uneasily in the general's office, wondered why the general found it necessary to give a resumé of the war effort before mentioning what Matt was to do. It occurred to Matt to wonder also just what he was to deliver, and where.

Matt watched closely as the general's pointer of light drifted through a cloud of white dots in the star model.

"Here," said the general, "our star systems and theirs are heavily fortified." He touched, with his pointer, pale silver spheres thickly packed in the far side of the star cloud. "These are the enemy's fortified star systems."

He glanced thoughtfully at Matt. "As you see, colonel, a man would need the farsightedness of a ground mole to attack there. Each of those systems is independent, and separately supplied from the rear. Capture the nearest dozen, and the hundreds behind can put up as violent a resistance as ever."

Matt nodded in agreement.

"Yet," said the general, "all these strong points need supplies." He touched a switch. A cable of bright green ran into the farthest part of the enemy's half of the star cloud, and branched out into a network of fine hairlike lines.

"This," said the general, "is the enemy's main supply route and its branches. The alternate routes are a botch of little-used and wasteful detours. If we could just get at the main trunk of this supply route—"

He swung his pointer around the star cloud, started in toward the green cable, then stopped. "But the distances in this arc are so great that the enemy has ample warning, and can move by shorter routes to block us."

The general put down his pointer.

"In brief," he said, "ordinary military movements can't win the war. Diplomatic measures can't end it, because the enemy won't make peace. We can't settle down to fight it out here forever, because the enemy's larger civilization gives him a cumulative advantage in productivity and manpower. We can't withdraw, because we would merely end up fighting further back and in a worse position. From the enemy's point of view, this boils down to a happy conclusion: the humans can't win the war; they can't draw it; they can't end it; we'll crush them."

The general picked up his pointer, and touched, one-by-one, a number of widely separated stars reaching from the Terran-controlled region around the star cloud toward the green cable.

"A while back," said the general, "we discovered a means for the very rapid transmission of matter from point to point. We should be able to compound this advantage into a first-rate catastrophe for the enemy. The difficulty is, the method can't be applied to a ship as a drive. It has to be used as a station. Do you follow me?"

"I'm not sure, sir."

"The device," said the general, "will throw a ship as a radio throws the human voice. But it's no good unless there's a *receiver already set up where you want to go.*"

Matt nodded, in dawning recognition of what was to come.

"We are," said the general, "quietly setting up a chain of stations. We need *one more.*"

He touched the pointer to a little white dot close to the green cable.

"When we have a station set up here, we can send a fleet through, rip that supply line wide open, seize the star systems nearby, set up more stations around them, and cut the enemy off from his base. With superior mobility, we should be able to throw him into a fog of uncertainties at the very moment when he has to hit hard and fast."

The general paused, and got control of his enthusiasm.

"However," he said, "before we can do that, *someone* has to go in and set up the station."

He looked at Matt.

Matt looked at the little white dot behind enemy lines.

"That," said the general, with enthusiasm, "is *your* job."

While Matt absorbed this, the general added, "We have had to make our preparations in a great hurry, but all necessary care has been used. Actually, the dangerous part will be getting there. Once you're there, everything should be comparatively simple."

He unrolled a big map and went into details. At the end, he looked at Matt.

"Any questions?"

Matt, mentally reviewing what the general had said, in hopes of not finding later that some crucial detail had escaped him, thought a moment longer, then said, "Sir, this could change the whole war, couldn't it?"

The general nodded. "The disruption of that supply trunk could enable us to defeat the enemy in that whole region. Along with some other changes, it could mean the initiative will pass from them to us."

A natural question occurred to Matt, who hesitated a moment, then decided that if he were rebuffed, he would be no worse off than before. "Sir? 'Other changes'?"

The general noted Matt's expression, and smiled. "The biggest change has already happened; that's the elimination of the Out saboteur from his perch in CAP itself. When your enemy has great powers of mental suggestion, the last place you want him is in your Capital between the President and your Chief of the General Staff. To get rid of that one was very expensive, but worth it."

Matt noted that he hadn't been rebuffed. But his question had been neatly sidetracked. He was mentally preparing to leave when the general cleared his throat.

"The most immediate of the other changes, colonel, all involve the return of our command structure to somewhere near normal. Ideas like 'elastic counterdefensive' have been fed to the garbage grinder. We again have a general reserve capable of influencing events. The supplies to the troops now meet their actual needs, or else the Supply Corps gets a change of officers. Offensives rest not on desperate hopes, but on first gaining some strong advantage over the enemy, along with a reasonable calculation that the odds favor victory."

He paused and looked at Matt. "But there is a more indirect change. The development of new devices is back on track—things that can change the realities of the conflict. This device you are to—ah—deliver—is a good example. It will take great skill, but when you do it, it will cut the ground out from under the Outs. It can eventually turn the whole course of the war against them. But there are details in your mission that none of us can know in advance, so you'll need to be alert, and ready to use every resource available to you. We're counting on you to do it. And we have every confidence you will do it."

Matt, who on the basis of experience trusted the high command the way a cat trusts dogs, found himself in agreement, with a sudden total dedication to the job, and a determination to find in advance as many of these unknowable ruinous details as he could.

He came out of the general's office with a thick wad of orders in an inside pocket, and a perfectly blank expression on his face. He walked across the close-clipped lawns, and past the neatly-trimmed hedges and borders of the Base without seeing them. He returned salutes automatically, and when a pretty girl in a print dress stepped out of an ivy-covered arch, saw the look on his face, and brought her hand up in mock salute, he returned that, too, with a deadpan expression that left her uncertain whether to laugh or admire.

Matt was thinking that he had to find some way around a drastic shortage of time. He was to meet his crew and lift ship in less than an hour. The planners of his flight seemed to have spared no pains in working out minute details of course and timing. But the question of the crew was another matter.

Matt showed his pass at the outer door of the Communications Building, went in, dropped his card in the slot of a soundproofed booth, and snapped on the screen. He took out a little pad, and copied a name and serial number from his orders. He dialed Personnel Director, bulled his way past lieutenants, captains, and a major, and left half-a-dozen wounded egos behind him in a little under five minutes. A lieutenant colonel decided to co-operate with him.

"Let's see, sir, you want the most recent available former commanding officer of Captain Andrew A. Decker, O-16R-73472?"

"Right," said Matt, checking the name he'd copied on the pad. "And I don't have much time."

"I'll get the calculator right on it, sir."

"Thank you."

Six or seven minutes later, a scowling colonel appeared. "What's this about Decker?"

"He's been assigned to me. I understand you've worked with him."

The colonel looked wary. "Why?"

"Did you ever have to do a tricky job, in a hurry, with a small heterogeneous crew, and an officer you've never met before?"

"Ah," said the colonel, "I understand. Well . . . Decker. He's efficient, reliable, devoted to duty, only—" The colonel hesitated.

"Yes?"

"Only—Listen, I don't know what goes on in Decker's head sometimes. Maybe the boy's a frustrated scientist. Anyway, *don't let his curiosity get stirred up.*"

Matt blinked.

"I mean it," said the colonel. "One minute everything will be going along fine. You've got a devoted officer in Decker. He's working hard. Then—blam!—a dried green beetle with yellow spots on its wing rolls out of an old report from Procristhus, or something else on that order, and there's Decker with a pin in one hand and a pocket magnifier in the other, bent over the beetle. Work's forgotten. Pretty soon, he's sketching the thing. Next he's prying up a wing. *Phew!* You can take the beetle away from him, true, but then all you've got is a shell. The boy's mind is still on the bug. The only practical thing to do is to shove him into a corner somewhere and get along without him till the fever passes."

Matt combined this item of information with what he already know about the composition of his crew.

The colonel saw Matt's expression and added hastily. "But, aside from this, he's a fine man. An excellent officer. You can rely on him. Generally."

When Matt and the colonel were through, there was

just time to send a few brief personal messages, and get to the spacefield.

At the spacefield, no time was wasted on introductions. But, in a general way, Matt met his crew.

Decker, the communications specialist, proved to be an alert-appearing officer of twenty-some. He seemed courteous and intelligent, and had a glowing look of athletic good health.

The other Terran officer was a tall, wary major, by the name of Andanelli. Matt had known Andanelli before, and noted with smile that the major's left eyelid still drooped in a sad, knowing, cynical look.

Andanelli introduced Matt to the rest of his crew, whose names Matt remembered from his orders as:

Sttongg, Q—Klittsman, 1st, I. K. S. F.

Battokk, D.—Klittsman, 2nd, I. K. S. F.

Klongk, X.—Klittsman, 2nd I. K. S. F.

Rrriffuntarr—M. A. F. L. L.

Stongg, Battokk, and Klongk each had light fur, and expressions of powerful determination on their faces. Each stood slightly under seven feet tall, and each was built with the massiveness usually reserved for armored gun turrets and doors of bank vaults. Aside from this, they looked more or less human.

Rrriffuntarr, on the other hand, had short, dark purple fur, the proportions of a saber-toothed tiger, and a slightly dubious expression while glancing around at the other members of the crew.

Matt said a few suitable words, and climbed in through the hatch.

Andanelli followed, grumbling, "Well, the Kraath and

the Lithian aren't at each other's throats yet. There's plenty of time for that, though."

Decker clambered in next, asking in a low voice, "Do they fight?"

Matt turned to see Sttongg, Battokk, and Klongk drop inside with perfect timing and grace.

After a moment, Rrriffuntarr dropped in, turned, and reached out a paw. Layers of muscle rippled under the close purple fur. The heavy hatch swung shut with a *clang*. The paw flashed out and back. The locking wheel spun tight.

Matt walked thoughtfully into the control room.

Andanelli was feeding tape into the autopilot, his long fingers reaching out to stab buttons and flip switches as he glanced from the tape to the plot-viewer.

Decker was standing by with an absorbed look. " . . .fire hoses wouldn't split them apart?"

Andanelli glanced with a scowl at the tape, then back into viewer. "No," he grunted, "we even spun ship, and that didn't work."

Matt slid into the control seat, glanced at the instrument console, and frowned.

"Andy," he said, "are you familiar with this model?"

Andanelli, scowling into the plot-viewer, said, "Scout cruiser, 2RC3s, sir."

"Any eccentricities?"

"None that I know of, sir. But they've got an awful thin hull. If the countercurrents give out we may have quite a time getting her down."

There was a low whine from amidships.

Matt swung a microphone around. "Ready," he warned,

his voice booming through the ship. "We lift in thirty seconds." He repeated the warning in Kraath and Lithian, snapped the 'Base' switch, and said, "T. S. F. *Drake* to Base. I have twenty-three seconds till take-off. Am I clear?"

"You're clear, *Drake.*"

Matt watched the chronometer needle swing up.

He heard Andanelli say, " . . .eight thousand casualties, just between allies, and never saw an enemy."

The needle swung to zero.

There was a screaming whine from the countercurrent converters.

The ship lifted.

★ ★ ★

Matt maneuvered through the congested flight lanes near Base, carefully checked course and speed, and put the ship on automatic.

Andanelli was still squinting into the plot-viewer. "You know," he said, "this course breaks in and out of subspace at some tricky spots. Take this third jump, for instance. We come out near the center of mass, between the two suns of a binary star. If we're off just a hair in either direction, we could find ourselves working out the three-body problem by trial and error."

"I know," said Matt, "but it can't be helped. We'll be in enemy territory. Every time we break in or out of subspace, it'll show up on their detectors. We have to mask our movements as best was can, and that binary should be a big help."

Andanelli let his breath out in a wheeze, and punched the spacing lever on the plot viewer to get successive images of the course. "This is the trickiest layout I've seen since we almost got cooked raiding their supply base. As I remember, we called that, 'Operation Frying Pan.'"

"This is the same idea exactly," said Matt, with a faint grin. "Better to overheat the hull a little, than to get one of those monster cruisers hot on our trail."

"Only," said Andanelli, staring hard into the viewer, "this route plants us right between their teeth. Then it leaves us." He jabbed the spacing lever futilely. "How do we get out? Where are the alternate escape routes?"

"We *don't* get out," said Matt. "That's the whole point." Carefully, and in minute detail, he explained the general's plan.

Andanelli listened with wide eyes. At the end, his usual gloomy expression was replaced by a blank, considering look. "Hm-m-m," he said, and turned back to the viewer. Matt turned and saw Decker standing just inside the door, his expression thoughtful and intent. Beside Decker sat Rrriffuntarr, lower jaw slightly open, the pupils of its big eyes dilated in a remote gaze.

Behind Rrriffuntarr stood Sttongg, Battokk, and Klongk, their heavy brows contracted in intense concentration.

Andanelli turned from the plot viewer with a look of awe, and said slowly, "Well, by space, it might just—"

Decker blinked and slowly straightened up. "Might just work, at that," he concluded.

The pupils of Rrriffuntarr's eyes contracted to vertical slits. There was a low swishing sound as the dark purple tail thrashed the deck. Then Rrriffuntarr let out a hair-tingling growl of satisfaction.

Sttongg, Battokk and Klongk looked at each other with

grim smiles, and nodded approval. The autopilot let out a warning clang.

"First jump," said Andanelli.

The ship went into subspace.

★ ★ ★

The largest part of the trip went by in a series of hairbreadth escapes as the *Drake* squeaked in and out of subspace under the covering glare of giant suns. To occupy their time between breaks, Matt and Andanelli checked and rechecked their equipment, and carefully studied the details of the final landing.

"What I can't understand," said Andanelli, "is how this planet, that just happens to be ideally suited to our purpose, could be located so close to their main supply route and not be occupied."

"I know," said Matt, studying the enlarged UCF photos. "It's a strange thing. The general said he thought maybe this planet is located at an awkward distance between two other bases."

"Are we sure it really *is* Earth-type?"

"The scout ship that took the photos crash-landed on it," said Matt. He put his pencil on the wide flat top of a bluff overlooking a shelf of land near the edge of an island. "They came down here, on the flat top of this bluff, got out and worked on the ship all night and into the next morning."

"Without suits?"

"Without suits. They were afraid they'd been tracked, and wanted to get out of there as fast as they could. If they wore suits, they'd be clumsy and it would take just so much longer."

"Hm-m-m." Andanelli frowned. "All the same, it isn't natural to leave a planet unoccupied so close to your vitals."

Matt nodded. "I had the same objection. But the fact remains, they *have* left it unoccupied. If we can get down there and set up the station, it won't matter what their reason is."

Andanelli twisted around to look at the photo from another angle. "Say," he said, looking up, "why do we have to set that up on *any* planet? Why not in space? There'd be less chance of our being spotted."

Matt shook his head. "The station gives off enough radiation to show on their detectors. They'd get curious and come out for a look. On the planet, the radiation is masked, and we're spared that. Even if they didn't spot us right away, the fleet has to come through one ship at a time. If they caught us with only part of the fleet through, they could smash us."

"Suppose that planet weren't there?"

"Be thankful it is. Otherwise, we'd have to orbit the station around a sun."

Andanelli picked up the photographs and studied them carefully. "Well," he said, "it *looks* all right. It's too bad the UCF doesn't pick up the fine details of vegetation, and so on."

"Yes, but then every cloud, tree, and momentary patch of fog would hide permanent features of the landscape."

"True, it has its points." Andanelli put the photos back on the table. "Do we have the report of that ship? The one that crash-landed there?"

★ ★ ★

Matt slid around some papers. "Fragmentary enough." He and Andanelli read them together. After detailing a close escape from an enemy's homing missiles, and the resulting damage to the ship, which crash-landed, on the planet, and—

" . . .we almost went over the bluff. Since there was no time to lose, we ran a few quick checks on atmospheric composition while Lieutenant Smith went out in a suit and checked the damage. The atmosphere seemed all right, so we went out without suits, draped the aft section with blankets to hide the light and went to work. It was a cold foggy night but the air was breathable. The job was comparatively simple without the suits to foul us up. The only trouble was that the hit had jammed one of the retaining rings out of shape, and the whole aft section was knocked slightly askew. Everything stuck tight, and we had to jimmy and niggle the units out by inches. We didn't get through till it was starting to get light the next day. Then we got out of there fast. Time of departure was—"

"Well—" said Andanelli scowling, "apparently nothing unusual happened."

"Their medical records were checked over," said Matt. "No unusual sickness."

Andanelli's dubious look gradually cleared way. "Well," he said, glancing at the report, "you never know. That planet *could* be awkwardly located for them, and so far in their back yard that they figure there's no need for a garrison. Or, there might be some jurisdictional squabble between a couple of their generals. You never can tell."

"In any case," said Matt, "there it is." He touched the flat-looking shelf of land below the bluff where the ship had crash-landed. "We're to come down here, plant the relay on the bluff, level a spot down below and set the receiver up under the bluff. The first ship through will be crammed with engineers and heavy earth-moving equipment. In just a short time, we could have a sizeable base right in their back yard."

★ ★ ★

The two men went over the plans for setting up the station and studied each detail, hunting for the flaw that could hamstring them later on.

★ ★ ★

As Matt and Andanelli worked in the control room, they were vaguely conscious of noises in the aft compartment, where Sttongg, Battokk, and Klongk alternately did calisthenics and huddled in concentration over a game called "squeeze." Squeeze was played on a board with twelve squares on a side, each player starting with twenty-four men in the last two rows.

Decker was watching this game with a little black book on alien-race psychology in his hand, and an expression of stupefaction on this face. The two sides in the game quickly got jammed together in the center. Each player moved without hesitation, trying to pile up more men in one part of his line than his opponent had. When this came about, the opponent was forced back a space. However, to get more men in one place meant having fewer men in another, therefore, how—

The game rushed on, one side grinding forward, then the other, with here and there a man next to two opposing pieces picked up, a grant as captured men were traded—why were *those* men captured, and not others?—traded men were fed back onto the last row on the board, apparent slips, errors, and oversight took place in rapid succession, and vanished in new arrangements before Decker could figure out what had happened.

There was a low growl at Decker's elbow, where Rrriffuntarr looked at the board with obvious distaste, turned and bounded to the top of a partition, strolled with delicate balance to a narrow walk over the converter compartment, and thence to a hammock slung up there in the dimness and comparative privacy.

Meanwhile, Matt and Andanelli had finished checking details on paper, and were prying open the solidly-constructed crate of a J-bug, a small earth-moving machine that was to level a site for the receiver. "Where," said Matt, looking around after a struggle with a crowbar, "is Decker? He might as well help us with this."

Andanelli put down a hammer and frowned. "I completely forgot Decker. I'll go get him, sir."

Decker acted as if he were eager to be helpful, but had unfortunately lost the use of his mind. He methodically hammered in a row of nails Andanelli had pulled partway out. He tripped over a projecting brace, and grabbed for support a crowbar Matt was using to pry off a strip of wood. As his two superiors glared down at him, Decker did not get up, but instead pulled from his hip pocket a small black book. Scowling in concentration, he thumbed through it.

"What?" growled Andanelli "is bothering you *now*, kid?"

Decker looked up with a frown.

"It says here, 'the ardent playing of the squeeze game

bears a functional relationship to the onset of *pratha.'*
What's *pratha?"*

Matt and Andanelli stared at each other. "Oh . . . oh,"
said Andanelli. "They *have* started that, haven't they?"

Matt put down his hammer. "This will have to wait," he
said.

★ ★ ★

Matt and Andanelli, with Decker looking over their
shoulders, feverishly hunted through the records of the
three Kraath, then looked at each other in weary disgust.
Matt pulled over a pad and worked out precise calculation.
"That's great," said Andanelli, looking on. "We can't say
'yes,' and we can't say 'no.'"

"Well," said Matt grimly, "there are likely to be these
little oversights when an expedition is made up in a hurry,
and this one was thrown together in a desperate rush.
Now we pay the price."

"But what *is* it?" said Decker. "Sir, what's *pratha?"*

★ ★ ★

Matt started painstakingly checking his figures. "Tell
him," he growled.

Andanelli said, "Once a year, the Kraath have a big get-
together. They play games, pick mates, and so on."
Andanelli shook his head gloomily.

Decker blinked, "You mean, they're likely to go into
pratha while we're setting up the receiver?"

"Yeah. Or sooner."

"What's so bad about that? I mean, what harm—"

"You never saw it. They're like a drunk that isn't happy
unless everybody else is drunk. And we've got Rrriffuntarr
on board."

Matt slapped down his pencil and shook his head. "Why they never learn to keep Kraath and Lithians separated—"

"But," said Decker, "if it comes around regularly, why didn't we know?"

"It hits them," said Andanelli, "in spring on the planet of their birth. They've got more than one home planet; spring comes at different times depending on the home planet, and on whether they live in the northern or southern hemisphere. To make it worse, their years are different lengths, so *pratha* can come any time on our calendar. But the real trouble is, nobody at headquarters knows what it's like unless he's been through it."

"With," said Matt, "a Lithian around."

"Why?" said Decker.

Andanelli groaned.

Matt said, "Can you picture Rrriffuntarr happily playing squeeze with Klongk, and then singing songs all night with Sttongg and Battokk, while Klongk whacks him on the back every few minutes?"

Decker stared off into distance. "No," he said finally, "I can't."

"That's it," said Matt. "Rrriffuntarr wants peace and quiet. Klongk, Sttongg and Battokk went everybody happy. Once that combination gets going, there's nothing to do but dive for the shelters."

"I see it now," said Decker, looking a little awed.

Andanelli glanced around gloomily. "It's a small ship. I hope we make planetfall before it starts."

Matt got up suddenly. "We better check that J-bug."

This time, Decker was a help as they ripped open the crate.

★ ★ ★

Close inspection showed the J-bug to be in good shape. The same seemed to hold true of the rest of the equipment. Everything appeared to have been arranged with forethought. Except that now the three Kraath had taken to singing songs in the evening. Their voices were deep and loud, with a dull booming quality such as might have been expected of giant bullfrogs.

The overall effect was like listening to an orchestra made up entirely of bass drums.

Matt was totally immersed in the effort to find a short cut. The chance, he knew, was small, but it might save the situation if he could. He was checking an unlikely long jump when something jostled his elbow.

Matt looked up to see a massive purple flank. Rrriffuntarr was sitting next to him, back to the wall, eyes glittering in the direction of the booming Kraath trio. "R'r'r'r," said Rrriffuntarr.

"It's a miserable noise all right," said Matt, speaking Lithian.

"R'r'r'r. R'r'r'r'r'r," said Rrriffuntarr, angrily.

Matt forgot about the short cut. The situation wasn't going to hold together that long. Rrriffuntarr was now growling steadily, a monotonous rumble that rose and fell, thick with menace.

Andanelli was standing by the doorway with his eyes shut, and his lips moving, as if in prayer.

Decker came in, saw Rrriffuntarr, and took a hasty step out of the way.

The growl was slowly rising to a threatening whine, a noise that cut at the eardrums as harshly as the Kraath singing battered at them.

Abruptly, Matt had an idea. Matt spoke loudly, his voice rasping and snapping in angry Lithian. "Here we sit, with that noise blasting us out of our senses, and the outlanders are too drugged to see reason. I can't take much more of this racket."

"Neither can I," snarled Rrriffuntarr.

Andanelli squinted hard. "Nor me either," he said.

"But," said Matt forcefully, "if we rip them up to end this awful noise, it wrecks our chance to win the war."

Rrriffuntarr let out a roar of frustration and rage.

From the other room came a new tune—a choppy, crooning noise like a forest of hollow trees attacked by woodpeckers.

"Aieeow!" cried Rrriffuntarr.

"Quick!" yelled Matt. "We can't stand it! We can't end it! Let's howl them down—*War by voice!*"

Rrriffuntarr's glittering eyes widened, narrowed. The huge chest expanded. Rrriffuntarr's sharp-fanged mouth opened wide. There was a high, wavering siren noise like the brash horn at a spaceport.

Rrriffuntarr, eyes shut and head tilted, braced all four legs and cast around with a cutting screech that sawed at the Terrans' nerves, and left them with eyes shut, hands pressed to their ears, and a sensation of dancing spots in their heads.

Time hung suspended.

The terrible noise stopped.

Matt blinked, and suddenly spun to scribble rapidly on a pad.

From the other part of the ship came total silence.

Rrriffuntarr's head was cocked attentively on one side, listening.

Decker stepped into the corridor and called out, "We want to join your singing. Is that all right?"

"*Andy*," said Matt hurriedly, "come here and help me check this."

From the other end of ship came a hollow voice, "Pratha time is not yet."

Andanelli bent over Matt's figures, and sucked in his breath sharply.

Decker translated to Rrriffuntarr, who gave a sort of grin and lay down on the deck, tail thrashing.

"You've *got* it," said Andanelli. "That'll get us there well ahead of time."

"It came to me," said Matt, "just as Rrriffuntarr hit that high note."

There was noise nearby like a big engine running slowly.

Matt and Andanelli looked down.

Rrriffuntarr was purring.

The two men began to tape the new course.

★ ★ ★

Matt spent the last part of the trip explaining every detail about the landing and setting up the receiver to the Kraath and Rrriffuntarr. The three Kraath absorbed the information with relentless concentration. If a point was not clear to them the first time, the second time, or the tenth time, they were prepared to hold their minds fixed on it indefinitely, till finally they understood.

Rrriffuntarr, on the other hand appeared to approach problems by indirection, tentatively testing out first one angle of attack, then another, and seemingly getting nowhere till—*pounce!*—suddenly the answer was clear.

Matt had to admit that both methods seemed to work. As the time approached to make the landing, he was well satisfied that everyone understood what had to be done, and—as possible—why.

Now if they could just make planetfall before Sttongg, Battokk and Klongk went into *pratha* and had a war with Rrriffuntarr. Already, the three Kraath had taken to singing songs in low voices—a sound like distant thumping of cannibal drums. Rrriffuntarr was wandering around, sitting down first here, then there, muttering low growls, tail thrashing, and claws sliding out to bunch the thin plastic sheeting over the steel deck. Andanelli came in tense-faced, "They're playing that game all the time, now."

Matt glanced at the chronometer. "We break out of subspace in about twenty minutes."

He repeated in Lithian for the benefit of Rrriffuntarr, who got up and began pacing back and forth, tail twitching spasmodically.

The twenty minutes till break-out passed like a leisurely eternity. Decker went in to ask the Kraath to please sing in lower voices, and did not come back. Andanelli went to check up, and reported that Decker had been trapped into a game with Sttongg. Soon, Decker's voice drifted out, complaining, "Why *shouldn't* I take that man? What's the *point*, anyway?" Sttongg's voice could be heard, urging, "Move! *Move!* This is *life!*" This was sung, first slow, then fast; first low, then loud; it was crooned and chanted, sung smoothly, then with a hammering intonation.

Rrriffuntarr lay down with a growl, tail stretched out straight and limp, forepaws clutched over forehead.

Andanelli stared uneasily at the Lithian. Matt tensely watched the chronometer. Finally the autopilot gave a sharp clang.

"Thank God," said Andanelli. The ship came out of subspace in the overpowering glare of a sun. Matt hastily checked his instruments, scanned for the planet by UCF, and hurtled the ship away from the sun.

★ ★ ★

The three Kraath came out of *pratha* long enough to help get the tiny signal satellite into its agonizingly precise orbit. Then Matt dropped the ship toward the planet. Everyone crowded behind, watching the screen. The UCF showed the contours of the ground clearly, unobscured by clouds or vegetation. Matt watched as a leaden sea swung up heavily below them. Then a number of islands came into view; two faced each other with wide-flat-topped bluffs overlooking shelves of low land bordering a narrow strait.

Matt snapped a switch, and the projected image of the UCF photo he and Andanelli had looked over appeared on the screen. Matt turned a knob to enlarge it, then spun the image slowly around. The outlines of photo and direct UCF reception matched.

Matt slowed the ship and began to drop.

There was no sign of an enemy base down below. Still, Matt thought it was impossible to know for sure. He became aware of the crowd behind him. "O.K.," he said. "Everyone to his station."

There was the thud of big feet, the scratch of claws,

then a rumble as the turrets of the ship slid open their covers.

Matt threw the recording switch, then kept his eyes on the UCF screen as the ship dropped fast down the side of the bluff.

Decker's voice came to him, sounding a little dubious: "Nose turret ready." One by one, the others reported in, each voice registering uncertainly.

Matt swung the UCF rapidly. No sign of trouble. A lucky thing, he thought. The friction between the Kraath and Rrriffuntarr had already drained their energy. It would, Matt thought, be good to get out in the open again on an earth-type planet, free of the restraint of life in the confined space of the ship.

The UCF spun around again, to show the face of the bluff, flowing up as the ship dropped to a landing. What appeared to be layers of rock, showing an odd weathering effect, rose into view. Matt stopped the turning of the UCF, and said, "Decker—"

"Sir?"

"How does that bluff look to you? Is that rock?"

"Rock? The . . . what? . . .you said, sir?"

"The bluff," said Matt, frowning. "I want to check your impression against what I see on the UCF. Is that weathered rock on the bluff?"

Something appeared momentarily on the screen, a small gray blur against the background of the bluff.

"Sir," said Decker nervously, "all I can see is a dark grayness. We seem to be inside a pretty thick cloud, sir."

The ship settled gently. Matt frowned, checked his instruments, then reached out to snap off the converters.

A section of the screen about two inches across showed a pattern like that of the ripples when a pebble is dropped in still water. The pattern oscillated rapidly, then blurred to a solid gray blot on the screen.

Matt, one hand still on the converter switch, swung the UCF back and forth. The blur moved back and forth with it.

"Can anyone see anything?" he asked.

"Not I," growled Rrriffuntarr.

"No, sir," said the Kraath.

Andanelli said, "Sir, I thought this was a cloud, too, at first. But this is too dense for any cloud I ever saw. And there *seems* to be some kind of layer—"

Decker said, "I see that, too, now. But it wasn't there before."

Andanelli's voice grated. "There seems to be some kind of layer on the outer surface of this turret. Sir, I wonder if they've got a coat of sunscreen on these turrets?"

★ ★ ★

Matt, thinking fast, recalled that the other ship, that had crashed here, had stayed a full night without mention of any deposit that had formed on it. And it would be just like a hurried official to order a coat of sunscreen after a quick glance at the route.

Matt snapped off the converters.

Three widely-separated sections of the screen, each about two inches across, showed an oscillating ripple pattern that blurred to a blot of gray.

"*Decker,*" said Matt, "get down here!"

There was a clang, and a rush of feet, "*Sir?*"

"What's happening to this screen?"

Decker bent over Matt's shoulder. He reached down to swing the UCF. On the screen, the four blots traveled back and forth.

"Sir," said Decker, in a puzzled voice, "I don't know. Maybe a meteor when we—"

"Meteor, nothing," said Matt sharply. "This has happened since we came down."

"Then I don't know, sir," said Decker.

Matt raised the UCF slowly, studying the cliff. What had looked like layers of weathered rock now seemed too regular for normal weathering.

Matt asked, "Could bullets cause those blurs?"

"They might, sir. I don't know, for sure."

Matt looked up. "You're the communications officer. Would they, or wouldn't they?"

Decker hesitated. "I *think* so, sir."

Matt clamped his jaw, and snapped the audio receptor switch. There was a hum as the detector rose out of its well. Matt put on the phones, heard a buzzing noise and a slow dripping sound.

There was an especially loud buzz, and on the screen a gray blur, and oscillation, and another blank blot.

The overall buzz seemed to grow louder.

Matt turned the UCF slowly. The bluff swung past, and there was the shelf, sloping to the choppy gray of the sea. Matt stiffened; the shelf of land had looked flat enough in the photo. Now that they were here, it was plain to be seen that it had definite tilt.

The slanting shelf swung past. Matt had a view of the sea, and of another shelf and bluff on an island about half a mile away.

There was a loud droning buzz in the earphones, and in the background, a steady *drip-drip, drip-drip*.

Their own bluff swung back into view, there was another loud droning noise, the sounds faded and swelled, then two more gray blots appeared on the screen. Matt tilted the viewing angle to look high up, heard another buzz, discovered another blot, and swiftly tilted the viewing angle down. The nose of the ship, seen from behind, appeared on the screen, then slid out of range as the big detector grid swung face down. The screen went blank as Matt lowered the grid tightly into its well.

The dripping sound had stopped, but the droning noise remained. Matt took off the earphones, called Andanelli in for a quick summary of the situation, and checked the atmosphere. Everything looked fine, till Matt noticed the water content; he scowled, and ran another check. Still scowling, he called to Decker to get out a couple of suits.

Andanelli stayed in charge inside. Matt and Decker struggled into the bulky suits, then clambered into the air lock.

Once inside, Matt swung around, reached out for the inner door, and locked it shut. He turned around, saw the equipment locker, and spoke into the transceiver, "Hear me, Decker?"

"Yes, sir."

"Andy?"

"Here, sir."

Matt crossed to the equipment locker, and got out a coil of rope. He carefully fastened one end around a cleat at one side of the outer hatch, spun the lock wheel, and said, "Airlock screen working all right?"

"Yes, sir," said Andanelli. "I see you perfectly."

The lock wheel spun as far as it would go. Matt took hold of the door handle.

Carefully, he pulled the air lock open.

A thick gray blankness looked in at him.

He stood stock-still, then leaned out to look down.

He couldn't see the ground.

★ ★ ★

Matt got a heavy wrench from the locker, tied it on the end of the rope, leaned out, and lowered it like a seaman sounding for bottom. He faintly felt the rope touch, and raised it and lowered it several times to be sure. There was a peculiar springiness when the rope touched. Matt straightened up and turned to look around.

There was a hazy bulk beside him that he realized was Decker. The outlines of the space-lock door were fuzzy and vague. The whole inside of the air lock was gray and indistinct.

Matt said, "Andy?"

"Sir?"

"How's it look on the screen?"

"Like we're underwater off the mouth of a muddy river."

Matt leaned far out and slowly turned to look all around.

He saw grayness in all directions.

He pulled himself back inside, saw the murky blob that was the locker, crossed to it and took out a powerful hand-beam. He went back to the hatch, aimed the beam out the door, and flipped the switch.

The light reached out, lit a length of fog, and seemed

to come to an end several yards away. Matt swallowed, squinted, leaned out, and swung the beam down. He could make out a vague greenish color, but no details.

Matt said, "Decker."

"Sir," said Decker's voice from the earphones.

"I'm going to climb down there. Hold this light, and hand it down to me when I ask for it."

"Yes, sir."

Matt took hold of the rope, started to get out, and realized that the rope hung from the cleat in a supremely awkward position. The cleat was at the side of the hatch. The rope ran straight to the edge of the hatch, bent around the lip of metal, then dropped straight down. To climb down, it was necessary to somehow brace both legs against the curving sides of the ship, and hold the rope up and out to get hold of it. From this position, one might confidently expect to slip, drop, and get both hands jammed against the side of the ship.

Irritated, Matt stepped back and glanced above the door. If there were a cleat there, the rope would hang down where he could get hold of it.

There was no cleat there. He felt outside. The ship was perfectly smooth.

"I think," said Matt, "that I just found the little detail we were afraid of."

Andanelli's voice said, "I completely forgot that. Along with the hull, that's another failing of this boat. To hang the rope so a man can get out in a suit under gravity is something they overlooked."

"Where do they keep the ladder?"

"In the storage. It's collapsible. You want me to get it?"

"No. Wait." Matt studied the rope. Suppose he took it, looped it under and then over, the big hinge of the outer hatch. He was about to try it when Decker said, "Sir, I think I can do it."

"You see a way?"

"I think so, sir."

"Go ahead." Matt stepped back, frowning.

Decker went to the hatch, took the rope, passed it over his shoulder, climbed up in the hatchway, facing out, clumsily started to face in, got the rope down in his hands, and leaned far out, bracing himself with his feet—

Matt caught his breath. "Careful," he said, "the fog may have made it slippery."

"I'm all right," said Decker cheerfully. He leaned almost straight out into the gloom, and started to inch his way down.

Faintly, through the suit, Matt heard something go, "Z'z'z."

There was a sharp *whack* against his faceplate.

Decker made a sound like a man jabbed in the stomach. His suit twisted sidewise, jerked in toward the ship, slammed into it with a rough indrawing of breath in the earphones, then dropped out of sight.

Matt called sharply, "*Decker!*"

There was no answer. Andanelli said in a tense voice, "Want help?"

"Not yet. Have Rrriffuntarr suit up."

"Yes, sir."

Matt shone the light down, and saw nothing but grayness and a vague tinge of green. He gently tugged the rope. It came without resistance. Matt pulled in a loop, passed it over the open hatch, so it hung from the big hinge. He picked up the handbeam and discovered that it had no attachment to fasten it to his suit.

He yanked up the rope, untied the wrench, tied the handbeam on the end, and let it down. Carefully, he clambered up into the hatchway, every movement made clumsy by the suit, took hold of the rope, swung loose, started to slip, and got a loop of the rope around his leg. The rope slipped, and the bulge of the ship ground his hands. He tried to hold the loop against his ankle with his heel, pressed against the ship, and slid his hands down. Then he tried to slide down farther, and discovered that the rope had jammed tight around his leg.

Owing to the thick fog, Matt could not see how the rope was caught, and because of the bulky suit, he couldn't feel how it was caught. But if he didn't get it loose, he would eventually lose his grip and swing upside down, with a good chance of smashing his skull in the process.

There ensued a methodical but increasingly violent struggle, with buzzing things regularly whacking Matt on the faceplate, with his knuckles grinding against the ship, and every muscle aching, and which finally ended when he had almost given up, and then the rope came loose.

He dropped down the rope, his feet hit ground and slid greasily out in front of him.

Matt pulled in the light and snapped it on.

There was no sign of Decker.

* * *

Matt said, "I don't see Decker anywhere. What about Rrriffuntarr—in his suit yet?"

"Yes, sir."

"Just between the two of us, is his style of suit as bad for him as ours is for us?"

"From the looks of it, sir, it's worse."

"Well—Use the remote arms, and haul the rope in. Shut the hatch and disinfect the air lock."

"Sir, the ship that crash-landed didn't have any trouble with sickness."

"No, but what they reported and what we experienced so far bear no relationship whatever to each other. After you've got the air lock cleaned out, send Rrriffuntarr in with the ladder. Have him come down here with another light and about two hundred feet of rope."

"Yes, sir."

Matt felt the rope move, and remembered the light was still tied to the end of it. "Hold it," he said.

"Sir?" The rope stopped moving

"Just another little detail," said Matt, and untied the light. "O.K., pull in the rope."

The rope went up, Matt shone the light carefully around. He saw a foot-thick layer of pale green plants that spiraled up in a mass of interlocked stalks. Near his arm, a thin spiral reached up out of sight in the fog. Matt shone the light on the spiraling stalks, then reached out. Between his fingers, the stalks felt as slippery as if they were greased.

Matt got very carefully to his feet, and shone the fuzzy beam of light around. He saw no sign of Decker. He thought that if Decker had slid in the greasy stalks, or stumbled off dazed, he should have left *some* track. But there was no track that Matt could see.

Matt said, *"Decker?"*

There was silence. Then in his earphones, a voice said weakly, "Sir?"

"*Decker?*"

"Yes, sir." The voice sounded more humble than injured. "I'm sorry, sir. I thought I could do it. But something banged me in the faceplate. It startled me, and I lost my balance."

"Oh. Well, don't worry about that. How do you feel?"

"A little beat-up, sir. But I don't think anything's broken."

"Good." Matt snapped on the light, and said, "Do you see any light, Decker."

"Light? No, sir, I don't."

"Look all round."

"No, sir, I . . . *unh!*"

"*What is it?*"

"Nothing. I just seem to be in the water, that's all. I can't seem to"—the voice had a trace of panic—"get up to dry ground. My feet slip—"

"Can you stay where you are?"

"Sir, in this fog, I can't tell. I seem to be sliding."

"Can you get hold of a handful of grass?"

"I—" There was grunt, then a sigh of relief. "Yes, sir. I've got it. But I'm not sure which way is toward land."

"Don't worry about it. The suit can stand a little water. Just stay where you are and keep a good grip on that grass. If it's like what there is around me, it's greasy."

"I stretched it out and wrapped three or four lengths around my fist."

"Good. How did you get down so far?"

"I don't know, sir. I was out cold."

"Well," said Matt, "it doesn't matter. We'll get you out when Rrriffuntarr—"

Something seemed to slide under Matt's feet. Both legs shot out in front of him. He tried to break his fall with one hand, and clung to the handbeam with the other.

He landed springily, and slid.

He slid as if he were shooting down a steep slope.

There was a splash.

His legs floated. Holding the light out of the water, Matt twisted and grabbed a handful of grass.

He knelt in the water, and shone the light down.

The grass under him was moving in long waves, as if trying to push him farther out to sea.

"Sir," came Decker's voice, "*now* I can see the light!"

Matt shone the light around.

A hazy form was about a dozen feet way, bent over in the fog and water. Matt realized that this was Decker, clinging to *his* handful of grass.

The whole mass of grass seemed to be moving in slow waves running down the slope.

Andanelli's voice said, "Sir, Rrriffuntarr's ready to come out."

Matt said in Lithian, "Can you hear me, Rrriffuntarr?"

Rrriffuntarr's voice, weirdly distorted by the Lithian processes of suit manufacture, hissed, "Yess, but not clearly."

"Where are you?"

"Sstanding by the hatch."

"Have you got the ladder down?"

"No. I am trying to ssnap it open."

Matt scowled, "*Andanelli.*"

"Sir, I showed him how it works."

Rrriffuntarr snarled, "The faceplate of thiss suit ssteams up."

The grass under Matt began to heave up and down violently, so that he sloshed back and forth in the water.

Matt grunted, "Take your time, Rrriffuntarr. It won't do any good to rush."

Rrriffuntarr let out of muffled noise like a string of fire-crackers going off at a distance.

"*Andy,*" said Matt, "see if you can't help him."

"Yes, sir. Rrriffuntarr, if you'll turn to one side, so I can see—"

A hissing noise came through the earphones.

Decker's voice said, "Sir, maybe we could work a little farther up. With the light, we can see a little. If we let go with other hand—"

"That's fine," said Matt. "With one hand, I hang onto the grass, with one hand I hold the handbeam, and with the other hand I reach out and take a new hold. You go ahead, if you want to. I intend to hang onto this light."

Andanelli began giving Rrriffuntarr detailed instructions in unfolding the ladder. This involved as many aggravations and delays as if Rrriffuntarr were blindfolded and Andanelli handcuffed.

The grass surged up and down, backwards, forwards, and sideways. Matt hung on grimly.

Rrriffuntarr let out a violent string of oaths.

Andanelli made soothing sounds and repeated his instructions.

Decker gasped, "Sir, *where is this stuff trying to take us?*"

"*Z'z'z'z!*" Something buzzed around, and whacked Matt's faceplate.

"Don't worry about that," said Matt. "Just hang on."

The buzzing faded.

"*Ugh!*" said Decker. "Yes, sir."

A lengthy stretch of time dragged by.

Rrriffuntarr swore. Andanelli groaned and repeated his instructions. Decker tried out loud to guess what lay out under the water where the grass was trying to sweep them. The buzzing whine droned around their heads and banged them in the faceplates. The grass relaxed as if to throw them off guard, and then surged violently. The water splashed, gurgled, and sloshed them back and forth. The thick gray fog seemed to grow steadily thicker.

The general's comment repeated itself in Matt's head: "The dangerous part will be getting there. Once you're there, everything should be comparatively simple."

Somewhere in the background, Matt could hear in the earphones the three Kraath starting to sing.

At length, Rrriffuntarr let out a hideous oath, and announced that the ladder was in place. "Now . . . what must I do to get to you?"

"Tie one end of your rope to the ship," said Matt. "Tie the other end around you. Climb down and stand ten feet or so away from the ship." He added dryly, "You'll get here fast enough."

Rrriffuntarr could be heard climbing down the ladder. There was a brief silence, then the sound of breath sharply expelled.

Matt snapped on his light.

A writhing figure shot toward them, trailing a rope. There was a mighty splash.

"Now," said Matt, "grab a handful of that grass, and work your way toward me."

Twenty minutes later, they were climbing the ladder back into the ship.

★ ★ ★

After a brief interval made agonizing by the noise of the Kraath singing, Matt sent the Kraath out with an extra length of rope, weapons, and a powerful light on a cable.

Rrriffuntarr climbed dripping wet out of the Lithian spacesuit, and fell into an exhausted sleep.

Decker, who looked as if he had been thrown down a mile-long staircase in a barrel, immediately became curious about the defective Lithian suit. Signs of weariness vanished as he bent over the suit in intense concentration.

Matt checked to see that everything was under control, then lay down for a little rest. He shut his eyes, fell asleep, and someone was gently but persistently shaking him.

"Sir," said Andanelli, "we're in a mess."

Matt sat up. He felt sore, stiff, and drugged with fatigue. "*Now* what?" he said, and the words came out like a challenge to a duel.

Andanelli hesitated, "Well, sir . . . ah—" He held up a bottle. "We found this in the air lock, sir." Matt looked at a thing about the size of the first joint of a man's little finger. The thing was gray, was lying a pool of cloudy liquid, and had several broken filaments thrust up from what appeared to be a coat of thick bristly fuzz.

"Sir," said Andanelli, "I think that's what banged you and Decker on the faceplates."

Matt frowned.

Andanelli added, "I couldn't find any eyes on it at all." He said this in the apologetic tone of one who does not want to tell all his bad news till he sees how the first item is taken.

Matt looked at the thing wonderingly. Then realization hit him.

"I figure," said Andanelli carefully, "that it doesn't have eyes because . . . you know . . . like fish in an underground cave where it never gets light—"

Matt swung his feet to the deck and started for the control room.

Decker was on the floor, rows of neatly-arranged parts spread out around him.

"You think," said Matt, "the fog *never* lifts?"

"At least," said Andanelli cautiously, "not during the season when these things are out."

Matt glanced at all the work spread out around Decker. Matt realized he must have been asleep far longer than he had thought. "What about these bugs? Do you think they see like bats, with echoes, is that it?"

"Well . . . yes, sir, for one thing. And I've studied the UCF records we made when we came down. What looked like weathering on those bluffs is too regular for that. Sir, what if these things have a crowded colony of nests over there. Where the rocks weathered, they might eat in, and . . . the echo from your faceplate maybe sounded more promising—"

Matt said sharply, "What are leading up to?"

Wordlessly, Andanelli handed Matt the outside audio receptor earphones. Matt raised them to his ears.

Z'z'z'Z'Z'Z'z'z'Z'Z'Z'Z'Z

The droning was like hives of swarming bees.

"It's even possible," said Andanelli, as if it were a matter of only academic interest, "that they build outer nests of light tough fibrous material, like hornets; and of course, if they nested in the UCF, that might explain the blurring."

Matt glanced at the screen, which was blank; and thought a moment. Andanelli must have called him for something more pressing that this. "Let's see: Hornets nest in low limbs of trees, and under the eaves of houses, bees nest in hollow—Is the outer door of the air lock open?" said Matt suddenly.

"Yes, sir," said Andanelli, poised like a man in a canoe, with the rapids roaring just ahead.

Matt said sharply, "Can't you close it?"

"No, sir. They've already built in there."

"What about the remote-control arms?"

"They won't move, sir."

"Are the Kraath still outside?"

"Yes, sir. I already tried to have them close it. The bugs drove them away."

"You mean, *they sting through the suits?*"

"No, sir. They squirt a corrosive liquid. It eats holes through the suits."

Matt stood perfectly still. "Where are the Kraath now?"

"Out in the water hanging onto the weeds with one hand."

"We can't have that air lock blocked off. Have you tried the disinfectant spray?"

"Yes, sir. They seem to have the nozzles sealed off."

Matt snapped on the air-lock view-screen. The screen was black, with an occasional flickering of light.

Matt visualized the situation, and stood wrestling with the alternatives.

Decker chose this moment to let out a triumphant yell. "I've got it!"

★ ★ ★

Andanelli looked at Decker severely.

"Sir," said Decker, turning around, "this train of little parts doesn't have enough free play. Sir, every time somewhere along the line it seizes." He hammered the steel deck beside it, "Vibration loosens it. Or, maybe if I—" Decker's eyes focused on the mechanism, and he stopped talking.

"Gone again," said Andanelli. "I've seen people who couldn't hold their minds on anything for five minutes, and I've seen people who kept their minds on something so long nothing else seemed to matter. But here we have an example of the hop-toad mind with the bulldog grip."

"Let him work on it," said Matt. "Rrriffuntarr can work a lot better if his suit's fixed."

"Sir," said Andanelli hurriedly, and with signs of strain in his voice, "there's something else I think I ought to mention about Rrriffuntarr—"

"Now what?"

"Sir, Lithians are pretty enigmatic about some things, and so are their records. I've noticed Rrriffuntarr has seemed to eat quite a lot lately, and seemed to tire pretty fast in that suit . . . of course, it's a bum suit, but—Sir, I was on a ship once where one of the Lithians had cubs. Those cubs can pretty nearly take a ship apart in a single afternoon, and—"

Matt blinked, "Slow down a minute. What reason do we have—"

"Sir, it fits right in with everything else. And the only way I know to tell a Lithian male from a Lithian female is to ask another Lithian. Ask them direct and they take your head off. Sir, I can't forget that awful trip with those cubs—"

Matt looked at Andanelli the way one looks at a trusted associate who has, unfortunately, been exposed to a little too much nervous strain lately. "Well, Andy," said Matt, "let's not worry about that right now. We can figure that out later. Right now, let's get the Kraath inside."

Andanelli seemed to struggle to get hold of himself. "Yes, sir," he said finally, and relaxed a little. "But, sir, if we make a hole somewhere, the bugs will come in and make a nest out of the whole ship."

"The first thing to do," said Matt, "is to make sure everything that should be is strapped in place."

★ ★ ★

After checking the ship, warning Rrriffuntarr, telling the Kraath what he was going to do, and helping Decker put the spacesuit parts in labeled boxes, Matt slid into the control seat and snapped on the converters.

Slowly and gingerly, the ship lifted. The whine of the converters was lost in a heavy threatening buzz.

"The bugs," said Andanelli. "They don't want their nests moved."

Rrriffuntarr came in, eyes large and glittering, and fur on end.

Andanelli said in Lithian, "It's O.K. Just some bugs that have built their nests on the ship."

Rrriffuntarr silently raised one forepaw. This paw had a furry thumblike extension which was cupped against the main part of the paw. The claws of this thumb, and of the rest of the paw were slid out. Pinned by the claws was a fuzzy gray object about the size of the first joint of a man's little finger.

A thought that had been half-formed in Matt's mind suddenly became clear to him.

"Hang on!" he yelled.

He lifted the ship fast and smoothly. There was a warning buzz from outside that rose to a threatening drone.

Mat shifted the converter angle, and the ship slid forward.

The heavy drone rose to a piercing whine.

Matt, tensely calculating distances, heard his own voice say, "Did you plug the hole?"

"Yes," said Rrriffuntarr.

Andanelli said in a low tired voice, "There'll be others. If they can eat through rock, *this* hull won't stop them."

Matt slowed the forward motion of the ship, and shifted the converter angle. The ship slid sidewise.

Z'z'z'Z'Z'Z

There was a purple blur. *Whack!* Rrriffuntarr hit the wall, and dropped to the floor holding up one forepaw. Andanelli picked up his bottle with bug inside, unscrewed the lid, and held it out.

Matt lowered the ship till he felt the resistance of the water.

Rrriffuntarr turned as a buzz approached from the rear of the ship

Whack!

Z'Z'Z'Z
Slam!

Rrriffuntarr growled angrily and unscrewed the lid of the bottle.

"Hang on!" said Matt.

From the rear of the ship came a droning buzz.

Matt shifted the angle of all the converters.

The ship began to spin on its axis.

★ ★ ★

One hour and forty minutes later, Sttongg, Klongk, and Battokk crawled dripping wet into the waterlogged air lock and tore out the soggy ruins of what looked like an enormous partly-finished wasp's nest.

Matt, Andanelli, Rrriffuntarr, and Decker, satisfied that they had plugged all the corroded holes in the ship's hull, helped the shivering Kraath back inside, then put Rrriffuntarr's suit together. All four went outside in the thick fog, and cleaned the dripping remnants of a big nest off the UCF housing.

Rrriffuntarr slipped on a soggy lump of the nest, and slid down the curve of the ship into the water. Matt had three holes in his suit by diehard defenders of the nest. Andanelli tripped over a long ropelike thing that trailed upward into the murk from the audio receptor housing. And Decker found so many interesting things to peer at in the fuzzy light of the handbeam that he was no use whatever to the other three.

By the time they all finally groped their way out of the fog back into the ship, and got ready to get back to work, Matt had almost forgotten what they were on the planet for.

Andanelli seemed to be in the same condition. "Let's see," he said groggily. "We have to scrape out a level spot, set up the receiver, and . . . let's see—Is that it?"

"*And* set up the communicator relay," said Matt. "It will take the signals from the satellite, and pass them down to the receiver. We can also send messages through it." He shook his head dazedly. "Assuming we don't wear ourselves out fighting fog, bugs, and other things you can't get a grip on. Since we hit this planet, nothing has worked out right."

"I could have told you that would happen," said Andanelli. "I always know that no expedition is going to work out right, regardless what it is, and I'm right better than half the time."

"Yes," said Matt, struggling to keep his eyes open, "but now what strikes me is that we can't work on the spiral grass, even if we chop it off. Too greasy. The J-bug will slide sidewise. The *pratha* can do it . . . I mean the Kraath, if they don't go into *pratha*. So we'll have to—"

Matt snapped himself upright, and saw Andanelli with his left eye shut and his right eye shutting.

Somewhere in the ship, there was a grating sound, like rats gnawing in the woodwork.

Somewhere, too, there was a faint hiss, as of gas escaping from an unlit burner in a laboratory.

Matt got up and swung his arms back and forth. He did not wake up, but felt even more heavy-limbed and sleepy.

He barely managed to keep his eyes open while he set the autopilot altitude control for five hundred feet.

He shut his eyes, thinking he had had a hard day, but he couldn't be *this* tired.

Something—He had to—

For an instant, everything went gray, as if a lead sheet had slid over his brain.

★ ★ ★

Matt sat upright, shivering, in a silence broken only by the hum of the converters, and distant grinding and hissing.

Something grated sharply.

There was a rushing splash, and the ship began to settle.

Matt stared at the instruments.

The ship, he realized vaguely, should be rising. He blinked at the altitude reading.

The ship was slowly settling.

He seemed to realize what had to be done, but did not exactly understand what it was. His mind felt as if it were made up of separate parts, each working of its own volition.

Slowly, like the arm of an automaton reaching out to perform its preset task, Matt's arm swung out, his hand struck the edge of the autopilot, drew back, and pressed upward against a switch. The switch resisted, then gave.

There was a click.

The converters whined.

There was a scream like a length of rusty wire drawn through a hole in a sheet of iron.

Matt's eyes shut.

He seemed to be inside a maze of gray rooms filled with drifting fog. Somewhere in one of these rooms, he had lost something, but he couldn't remember where. Now the water was rising, and the fog was growing thick. Someone was hammering on a bulkhead, and he recognized the general's voice, saying, "Hurry, Matt! Hurry! We haven't as much time as I thought. *Hurry!*" And Matt was trying to hurry as he sloshed from one room to another in the thickening fog, but he couldn't seem to . . . couldn't seem to—

Somewhere in the distance, an echoing voice was saying, "Once you get there, it will all be comparatively simple."

The voice faded in the boom of a more distant voice, and Matt seemed to lose his thoughts in the boom of this voice, and then he was not worried, about the general or anything else.

* * *

Matt woke up with a violent headache. The General Action alarm was clanging in his ears. Automatically he reached for his headset, and snapped on the screen.

The screen was blank.

Decker staggered past, his brow furrowed and his teeth clenched, and hauled himself up into the forward turret.

Matt swung the UCF out of its well.

On the screen, a blotchy view of the nose of the ship swung past. A seemingly endless wall of rock stretched out in front.

"Nose turret ready," said Decker. "Only, all I can see is fog."

Matt swung the UCF as the others reported in.

Below and well to one side, a huge black ship hung vertically, a pillar of pale flame raging from its tail section.

Matt jumped for the controls, then stopped.

Andanelli appeared at his elbow.

"Turret's useless," he said. "I can't even get the cover open."

Matt said sharply, "Decker, do you have anything new on the enemy's detectors?"

"Just the usual, sir. Extremely good in space, terrible in atmosphere. They can make out outlines against the sky, and vaguely distinguish land from water. But that's about all."

Matt squinted at the screen. The enemy ship was moving slowly sidewise across a low strip of land at the base of a bluff. It came almost to the end, swung slightly inland, and came back. When it came near the end there, it swung further inland and went back the other way.

A big airlock on the side of the ship swung open.

Matt reached for the controls.

A slim black cylinder shot out, and spun down around the ship in a fast spiral.

The air lock slammed shut.

The black cylinder swung back up, then down, then up. Gouts of pale flame washed over the huge ship from the flying cylinder.

The ship moved slightly inland and started back in the other direction, rockets blazing.

Matt and Andanelli stared at the screen.

"What in *space*—" said Andanelli.

The monster ship moved inland slightly and again started back on its course.

"Andy," said Matt, "what if *we* had this miserable planet in our back yard? Suppose we sent an expedition here, and it got fouled up in bugs, heaving grass, fog and heaven knows what else—what do you suppose *we* would do?"

"Send another expedition ten times as big."

"Sure, but how would we get rid of the grass, and how

would we keep the ship from getting nested over and corroded though by the bugs?"

Andanelli stared at the screen, then nodded slowly. "Now I get it. They're burning the grass, and scorching the nests as fast as the bugs started to build them—But listen, are they over the place where we want to put the receiver?"

"No, but they're just across the water from it."

Andanelli stared at the huge black ship. "Well, this caps it. How can we do anything with *them* breathing down our necks?"

"Maybe," said Matt, "if we're *very* careful—"

The black ship opened a port. Three slim dark shapes followed each other out and splashed into the water. In a moment, there was a boiling of the water, a dull clap, and a ringing noise in Matt's ears. The *Drake* scraped against the bluff.

Andanelli sucked in his breath.

A thing like a huge set of jaws surrounded by slowly twisting fronds, came to the surface at one end of the strait. Slowly, sliding in toward the shore below, it sank out of sight.

"I don't mean to be a pessimist," said Andanelli, "but it seems to me we ought to set that receiver up somewhere else."

"How?" said Matt. "The communications satellite orbits so it hangs right over this spot. We're supposed to set up the relay on this bluff, and nowhere else. The receiver has to be down below, and in line of sight from the extension on the relay. It all sounds arbitrary, but we have to assume there's a good reason for it."

"Sir, how do we even know that satellite is still up there. What if our friends here detected it on the way down?"

"It was designed *not* to be detected," said Matt. He frowned, and reached for the controls. "But we'll have to find out. We'll set up the relay. If it works, we'll know the satellite is still there."

Very gently, he began to lift the ship.

Getting the relay—a bulky object camouflaged to look like a boulder—out the air lock and up onto the cliff, and without lifting the ship so far it might show against the sky on the enemy's screens, proved to be a tricky job. The ship had no equipment that could do the job without a lengthy delay. But the Kraath accomplished it by brute muscle power and total concentration on each step from the ship's hull, up the precarious edge of the bluff to its bare, sunlit top.

As Matt snaked the flat extension cable from the communicator to the edge of the cliff, he was glaringly conscious of the early morning sun on his back, and the scout ship hanging in full view just over the edge of the bluff. Down below, the fog lay like a sea, with another bluff rising up like an island a mile or so away. The fog between the two bluffs was almost black, its surface slowly undulating. In the distance, the fog was lighter gray, and seemed calm, with stray wisps rising from it here and there.

Matt took in this scenery at a glance. Decker started to get absorbed in it, and Matt immediately sent him to watch the screen. Andanelli hardly saw the scene at all. Rrriffuntarr looked warily around and dismissed it with a growl. The straining Kraath plainly had thought for nothing but their burden, and the ground they carried it over.

This ground was thin reddish dirt, with a few sparse plants, and low ridges of red rock showing through. The communicator relay was camouflaged as a dull-gray boulder, that might have fitted in almost anywhere without being noticed. But against the reddish background it stood out like a snowbank in the midst of a desert.

Matt and Andanelli were trying to find some place to sink the boulder into the ground. But the soil was thin, and underlain with rock.

They had no idea how soon the black ship might finish its work and come up out of the fog.

Unable to find any place where the relay was not glaringly obvious, they next tried to hide it by putting the reddish dirt on it in layers. The dirt immediately fell off.

"There's nothing like details," growled Andanelli, rubbing a fistful of dirt back and forth over the gray surface. "In headquarters, they don't think of things like this."

"They have their own troubles," said Matt abstractedly. It was now very plain to him that the rock should have had a rough surface. But it did *not* have a rough surface, and no amount of groaning would fix it.

Andanelli stopped rubbing a moment, and said dubiously, "What about paint?"

Matt frowned in thought, then glanced around. "Rrriffuntarr, go get a blanket and some water."

Rrriffuntarr streaked for the ship.

"If we use paint," said Matt, "we have the problem of getting the right shade and texture. This dirt is exactly right already."

Rrriffuntarr came back with a blanket and water. Matt and Andanelli found a shallow depression in the rock, worked the dirt there into mud, put the blanket in the mud, and walked back and forth on it till the blanket was soaked and plastered with mud. They put the blanket over the imitation boulder, lifted the boulder to put the edges under it, almost squashed their fingers in the process, stepped back to look at the boulder, and found that it looked exactly like a big fake rock wrapped up in a blanket soaked in mud.

Andanelli swore.

Matt studied the rock critically, shook his head, and checked the extension cable to the edge of the bluff. This, at least, they were able to hide.

Then they went back and did what they could to smudge out the worst of their tracks. The reddish dirt, however, seemed ideally designed to take impressions. The Kraath had left footprints that looked, in the slanting rays of the sun, like the tracks of a herd of elephants on their way through a mudhole.

Everyone was quiet and subdued as they got back into the ship.

Matt dropped the ship down into the thick fog, sent everyone but Andanelli to the turrets, and looked at the screen.

Down below, the monster ship still traveled methodically back and forth, blasting the vegetation. The cylinder, belching flame, spiraled about the big ship. The water of the strait had a boiling look. The huge pair of jaws with surrounding fronds was again visible, now lying out of water on the shelf where Matt was supposed to set up the receiver.

The two men stared at this scene, "Something tells me

we'd better use the communicator and let them know back home."

He reached out to a small gray box bolted on the edge of the control panel.

Almost immediately, the communicator began to clack.

★ ★ ★

Matt and Andanelli got up and watched the following message unreel from the communicator:

HELLO DRAKE STP COME IN PLS DRAKE STP DRAKE HELLO HELLO URGENT DRAKE HELLO DRAKE COME IN PLEASE

"It looks," said Andanelli, "as if they might be just as bad off as we are."

With a sensation of foreboding, Matt pressed down the "Transmit" bar, and sent: TSF DRAKE SENDING STP WE READ YOU STP COME IN PLS

There was a short pause, then:

HELLO DRAKE WHERE ARE YOU NOW

Matt sent:

AT DESTINATION STP WHY ARE YOU CALLING

BECAUSE VITALLY IMPORTANT YOU SET UP RCVR WITH ALL POSSIBLE SPEED STP HAVE INFO ENEMY HAS DEVICE SIMILAR TO OURS STP THIS DEVICE EVIDENTLY MORE RIGID WITH RANGE AND LIMITED ANGLE ADJUST-MENT STP BUT INTELLIGENCE EVALUATIONS INDICATE PLANET WHERE WE PLAN TO SET UP RCVR IS INTENDED FOR USE AS ENEMY FINAL TERMINUS STP YOU MUST SET OURS UP BEFORE THEY SET UP THEIRS STP DO YOU

HAVE RCVR SET UP STP WE ARE READY TO
COME THROUGH

Matt read this dully, and sent:

WE DO NOT HAVE RECEIVER SET UP YET.

SET IT UP IMMEDIATELY

THERE ARE OBSTACLES

OBSTACLES DO NOT MATTER STP TIME IS
VITAL STP EXISTENCE OF HUMAN RACE RESTS
ON YOUR INSTANT READINESS TO OBEY
ORDERS STP AND OBEY THEM REGARDLESS
FATIGUE DANGER OR DIFFICULTIES STP IS THIS
UNDERSTOOD STP REPLY IMMEDIATELY

Andanelli groaned. Matt swallowed hard and sent:

I WILL DO MY BEST TO OBEY ORDERS WITH-
OUT HESITATION REGARDLESS FATIGUE OR
DANGER SO LONG AS I HAVE STRENGTH TO DO
SO

There was a short pause, then the printer clacked:

YOUR ATTITUDE HIGHLY COMMENDED STP
BUT TIME IS ABSOLUTELY VITAL STP WHAT ARE
DIFFICULTIES YOU SPEAK OF

ENEMY IS ALREADY HERE AND IN CLOSE
RANGE STP OUR POSITION AND DENSE FOG
CONCEAL US BUT UCF ENABLES US TO SEE
ENEMY STP LOCAL LIFE FORMS ON SHELF
WERE WE ARE TO SET UP RCVR APPEAR SUS-
CEPTIBLE ONLY TO MOST VIOLENT MEASURES

STP VIOLENT MEASURES CANNOT BE USED
WITHOUT ALERTING ENEMY JUST ACROSS
NARROW STRIP OF WATER STP CAN WE SET UP
RCVR ON TOP OF BLUFF

There was a long pause, then:

GRAVITIC CIRCUIT CONSIDERATIONS ARE
INVOLVED IN LOCATION OF RCVR STP RCVR
MUST BE LOCATED FAR BELOW RPT FAR
BELOW RELAY STP THIS COULD HAVE BEEN SET
UP DIFFERENTLY BUT CANNOT BE CHANGED
NOW

Matt frowned, and sent:

CAN COUNTERCURRENT CONVERTERS BE
USED TO SIMULATE GRAVITATIONAL FIELD
REQUIRED

NO BECAUSE CURVATURE OF COUNTERCUR-
RENT FIELD IS TOO GREAT AND WOULD CRE-
ATE DISTORTION

CAN WE GO ELSEWHERE

YES BUT ONLY IF YOU MOVE SATELLITE AND
FIND HEIGHT RELATIONSHIP SIMILAR TO
PLACE WHERE YOU ARE NOW STP YOU MUST
NOTIFY US AND WE WILL TEST TRANSMISSION
TILL SATISFACTORY

★ ★ ★

"That," said Andanelli, "might be the only way to do it.
We'll have to creep around the cliff, get out of detector
range—"

Matt tapped out:

HIGHLY DANGEROUS TO ATTEMPT TO REACH SATELLITE OWING TO HOLING PITTING AND CORROSIVE WEAKENING OF HULL BY LOCAL FORMS OF LIFE

"I forgot that," said Andanelli.

"We'd have remembered it," said Matt, "once the air started whistling out."

The communicator clacked:

INFORMATION HERE INDICATES NO SUCH FORMS OF LIFE ON PLANET AS YOU IMPLY STP STATE IMMEDIATELY AND BRIEFLY ALLOWING ONE SENTENCE EACH DESCRIBE THE APPEARANCE AND CHARACTERISTICS OF THESE LIFE FORMS

Andanelli swore:

Matt drew in a deep breath, glanced at a corner of the room for an instant, then tapped out:

THERE ARE THREE LIFE FORMS WHICH LIVE AT THE BASE OF THE BLUFF OR IN THE STRAIT NEARBY STP ONE IS AN EYELESS NESTING INSECT LIVING AT THE BASE OF THE BLUFF AND CAPABLE OF SECRETING A HIGHLY CORROSIVE LIQUID STP

Matt was about to add that this insect had built its huge nest in the air lock, but realized that he was supposed to give his description in one sentence. Scowling he went on:

SECOND IS A GRAY SPIRAL INTERLOCKING GRASS WHICH MOVES IN WAVELIKE MOTION AND SEEKS TO THRUST OBJECTS INTO THE

WATER AND SUCCEEDED IN DOING SO TO NO
LESS THAN SIX MEMBERS OF THIS SHIP'S
COMPLEMENT INCLUDING THREE WHO
WERE ATTEMPTING TO REMOVE A LARGE
NEST OF INSECTS FROM THE AIR LOCK STP

Now that Matt had tapped this out it was sent and he
could not unsend it. Looking at it, Matt was struck by its
wordiness and seemingly defensive tone. But he was
required to condense all the facts into one sentence and
do it without delay. He went on:

THIRD IS A FORM OF LIFE SEEN ONLY ON
UCF AND WHICH APPEARS TO CONSIST OF AN
ENORMOUS SET OF JAWS SURROUNDED BY A
FRINGE OF TENTACLES

Matt hesitated, looked at this uncertainly. The communicator shoved his message up and printed:

WHO IS SENDING

Matt tapped out his name, rank, and serial number.

With no hesitation whatever, the communicator printed:

COLONEL STEPHEN MATT IS HEREBY
REMOVED AS COMMANDING OFFICER TSF
DRAKE AND PLACED UNDER ARREST STP MAJOR
JAMES J ANDANELLI IS HEREBY PLACED IN
COMMAND TSF DRAKE WITH FULL AUTHORITY
TO TAKE WHATEVER ACTION OF ANY KIND IS
NECESSARY TO SET UP RECEIVER AS SOON AS
POSSIBLE

Andanelli, his face dead white and his eyes glittering,
hit the "Transmit" bar, knocked the preceding message up
two spaces, and rapped out:

ANDANELLI SENDING STP DO YOU READ ME

★ ★ ★

WE READ YOU STP COME IN ANDANELLI

With a look of intense concentration, Andanelli slowly tapped out:

SCOUT SHIP TSF DRAKE NOW WITHIN CLOSE RANGE ENEMY CLASS III CRUISER STP NO ENEMY CLASS III CRUISER EVER KNOWN TO BE SERIOUSLY DAMAGED BY LIGHT ARMAMENT OF SCOUT SHIP STP SITUATION HERE COMPLEX BEYOND ANYTHING CAPABLE OF BEING BRIEFLY REPORTED TO YOU STP EVERYTHING SO FAR REPORTED TRUE BUT GROSSLY UNDER-STATED BECAUSE OF NEED FOR BREVITY STP MY OPINION IS ONLY A MIND CAPABLE OF APPROACHING THIS PROBLEM INDIRECTLY BUT WITH FULL APPRECIATION ALL FACTORS HAS ANY CHANCE OF SUCCESS STP PREVIOUS EXPERIENCE SHOWS ME PLAINLY THAT YOUR ORIGINAL CHOICE OF COMMANDER WAS AND IS STILL ABSOLUTELY CORRECT STP I THERE-FORE USE FULL AUTHORITY DELEGATED ME TO TAKE NECESSARY ACTION OF REPLACING IN COMMAND COLONEL STEPHEN MATT STP THIS ACTION EFFECTIVE IMMEDIATELY STP IF THIS ACTION COUNTERMANDED BY HIGHER AUTHORITY I WILL WITHOUT HESITATION IMMEDIATELY ATTACK ENEMY CRUISER

Andanelli knocked the message up two spaces, and waited, his eyes narrowed.

Matt, standing perfectly still, nevertheless had the sensation that the room was slowly turning around him.

The communicator sat unmoving as if, far away at the other end of the chain of command, nobody dared touch his finger to a key for fear of upsetting the delicate balance.

★ ★ ★

After a long delay, the communicator slowly and gingerly clacked out a message:

YOUR ACTION APPROVED STP COLONEL STEPHEN MATT REINSTATED RPT REINSTATED STP INADVISABLE ATTACK ENEMY CRUISER STP ADVISE GREATEST CAUTION STP REPLY AT ONCE

Andanelli stepped back from the communicator with a look of grim satisfaction. He glanced at Matt, grinned, and bowed, "After you, sir."

The first glimmering of an idea had just come to Matt. He wanted to think, not pass messages back and forth.

The communicator clacked:

COME IN PLEASE

Matt stepped forward, still thinking.

HELLO DRAKE COME IN PLEASE

Matt stopped in front of the communicator, his chin in his hand and his eyes half shut. He almost had it, and when it became clear, he didn't want to lose it.

DRAKE HELLO HELLO PLEASE COME IN DRAKE

Andanelli said savagely, "*Good.* Let *them* worry for a while."

Matt could see the idea in all its connections. Whether it would work, he didn't know. But he had it.

DRAKE DRAKE ARE YOU THERE DRAKE DO YOU READ US PLEASE COME IN

Matt hit the "Transmit" bar:
MATT SENDING

★ ★ ★

There was another pause as the people on the other end considered that they were now talking with the man they had just dismissed, who had been reinstated against their will, and who, it now appeared, very possibly had right on his side. For some time, nothing came from the communicator, then:

DO WHAT YOU THINK BEST MATT STP WE WILL GIVE YOU ALL HELP AND INFORMATION WE CAN

Matt thought a moment, then sent:
IS CASING OF RECEIVER VITAL TO ITS OPERATION

NO STP ITS ONLY FUNCTION IS TO PROTECT INTERNAL MECHANISM

MUST IT NECESSARILY BE PLACED ABSOLUTELY LEVEL

YES THIS AMOUNTS TO ITS BEING CORRECTLY POSITIONED GRAVITICALLY STP IS NOT LEVEL IT CANNOT FUNCTION

COULD IT BE BRACED UPON OR SUSPENDED FROM THE DRAKE RATHER THAN SET UP ON THE GROUND

NO BECAUSE INDUCED CURRENTS IN

CONVERTER OR DRAKE WOULD CAUSE GRAVITIC FIELD DISTORTION

WOULD PRESENCE OF ORGANIC MATTER WITHIN OPEN FRAME OF RCVR CAUSE TROUBLE

NOT IF IT CAN BE BROKEN LOOSE WITHOUT DAMAGING RCVR STP ACTION OF RCVR WOULD THRUST EVERYTHING WITHIN OUT AS SOON AS IT BEGAN TO OPERATE

CAN YOU SEND SOMETHING THROUGH BIG ENOUGH TO FINISH OFF ENEMY CRUISER WITHOUT DELAY STP CAN THIS HAVE SPARE RCVR RPT SPARE RCVR ON BOARD IN CASE FIRST RCVR DAMAGED BY ENEMY ACTION

There was a short delay, then:

YES WE CAN DO THIS

Matt tapped out:

THANK YOU STP THAT IS ALL FOR NOW

OK DRAKE WE WILL BE RIGHT HERE IF YOU WANT US STP TELL US WHEN WE CAN COME THROUGH

★ ★ ★

The fog had faded into blackness and lighted to dark gray again before Matt and Andanelli were satisfied that they had everything ready. By this time, the huge set of jaws had slid back into the water, and the enemy cruiser had finished its trips over the strip of land across the strait, had swung horizontally and blasted the cliffs there, had landed and disgorged an immense quantity of mechanical equipment which speedily and methodically leveled off the strip of land and started to climb back into the ship.

"Nothing like plenty of power," said Andanelli enviously.

"Look," said Matt.

Several small shadowy forms were coming out of the black ship, carrying long thick pipes, and sizable globes.

"O.K." said Matt. "Here we go."

He dropped the ship slowly down the side of the bluff.

On the screen the shadowy figures methodically began to assemble their device.

A buzzing sounded from the audio receptor phones. The buzzing rose to a drone.

Matt swung the UCF into its well.

Watching his instruments, he slowly swung the nose of the ship ninety degrees out from the bluff. He hung there a moment, then slid the ship forward.

The buzzing was continuous, a droning so loud as to seem almost like thunder.

"We must have been right in their nests," said Andanelli, awed.

Matt lowered the ship gently, holding his mind away from the thought of the huge black ship towering just across the narrow water.

Beneath the steady buzz, the converters gave their high-pitched whine.

Matt rotated the ship one-quarter turn right.

Carefully, he lowered the ship.

The buzz stayed right with them, and rose to a threatening drone.

The ship settled, then came to a stop.

In the earphones, Decker said, "Water popped the plugs out of the lower two holes."

Matt increased the converter current.

"And the next two. The plate looks as if it might buckle."

The droning rose to a whine.

Carefully, Matt slid the ship forward. Ahead of him, he seemed to see the black ship, towering ever higher. Below him, he could almost feel the thing they had seen on the screen, lying under the surface, and nursing its bruises. As the *Drake* moved slowly across the strait Matt realized that his mind was split, part of it on calculations and movements that he performed almost mechanically, and part of it in intense and silent prayer.

Decker said, "They're eating through already. I've patched that one. But I see a place I can't get to."

"Do your best," said Matt. He swung the UCF, now half underwater, out of its well.

The half of the screen clear of the water showed him he was almost ashore, and closer to the towering black ship than he had intended. In front of him rose a tall unfinished frame, with shadowy figures standing dead still around it. Then the screen filled rapidly with gray blotches.

"*Now*," said Matt.

He swung the ship smoothly up and forward, the UCF swinging clear of the water, the ship turning on its axis. He lowered the ship. "Let go the coverings."

"Yes, sir."

The ship slid forward. There was a grating noise.

From the black ship, three long slim shapes shot out into the water.

The shadowy figures were running from the half-finished frame, beating their arms frantically about their heads.

The *Drake* was now level.

"Let go the receiver."

"Yes, sir. It's down."

From the direction of the water, there was a heavy dull thud.

Matt swung the UCF around. He saw the receiver's big cubical frame standing on the level ground by the *Drake*. He glanced at his control board. A light was flashing on and off, on and off, then it blinked out entirely. The receiver was level.

"Thank God," he breathed, and threw the ship low and fast across the flat layer of concrete toward the far wall of the bluff. He reversed the converters, stopped the ship, jumped up and jabbed the communicator.

COME THROUGH WE ARE READY COME THROUGH

There was a glare like the sun reflected blindingly from the water.

The black ship stood on a pillar of flame.

A gigantic rim hung in the air beside it.

The screen lit in a blaze of white; the figures blurred in distortion and were gone. A spot on the inner wall of the *Drake* glowed dull red.

There was a ringing clap that seemed to explode inside of Matt's head.

The screen oscillated wildly, then cleared.

The black ship was a shell wilting like a hollow candle before the open door of a furnace.

The huge rim hung unmoved.

Matt swung the UCF to see what had happened to the receiver. But the receiver was gone.

The communicator clacked:

ARE YOU O.K. DRAKE

Matt rapped out:

FINE STP BUT WHERE IS RCVR

VAPORIZED STP WE HAVE SPARE ON BOARD STP IS ATMOSPHERE O.K.

ATMOSPHERE MAY BE BUT THICK FOG CUTS VISIBILITY STP FLYING BUGS NAVIGATE THIS FOG WITHOUT DIFFICULTY STP THESE BUGS SQUIRT CORROSIVE LIQUID THAT EATS THROUGH SUITS AND HULL OF SHIP STP THEY BUILD HUGE NESTS IN SHIP'S AIR LOCK AND ON PROJECTIONS OF SHIP STP ALSO IN UCF GRID THUS DISRUPTING RECEPTION

After a moment, the answer came;

NOT CONCERNED FOG OR LOCAL LIFE FORMS STP STAND AWAY BELOW STP MUST DROP OVERHEATED DRIVE UNIT

Matt swung the *Drake* up and farther inland. On the screen, which Matt realized with a start now functioned perfectly, there fell from the huge Terran ship a glowing cylinder with a length of pipe thrust off-center out of one end. This glowing cylinder hit the water, sent up a splash, and sank out of sight.

Matt turned away as a buzz came toward him from the rear of the ship.

The communicator clacked twice and stopped short.

Matt glanced toward the communicator, then a swift movement caught his eye. He whirled back to the screen.

On the screen, a huge set of jaws rose straight up out of the water and clamped on the giant rim.

Matt sprang to the communicator to see if an order had been sent him. Printed there were two letters:

WH

z'z'z'Z'Z'Z'Z'z'z

"*Sir,*" cried Decker, "spin the ship one-eighty degrees so I can get at the hole. They're coming in by the dozens!"

Matt jumped to the controls.

The next hour passed in chaos. Matt spun the ship. Decker plugged the holes. Rrriffuntarr snatched the buzzing insects out of the air. The three Kraath splattered the bugs against the walls of the ship. One of the Kraath hit so hard he knocked out a fist-sized section of corroded wall, and the bugs came through in hundreds. Matt sent the ship streaking for the open sea; and dove. Something gently caught the ship and there was a munching crunching sound. Matt slammed the ship skyward then dropped it fast. On the viewscreen there hung a big black ship that had just been destroyed. Matt dove for the communicator and found there about a dozen bugs that had set up housekeeping in a small nest they were ready to defend to the death. Matt hit the keys and sent:

LOOK OUT ENEMY SHIP APPRO

z'z'z'z'Z'Z'Z

z'z'Z'Z

z'z'Z'Z
Z'Z'Z'Z

His whole body seemed to dissolve in an agony of fire.

★ ★ ★

Matt came to in the flagship's hospital ward and didn't get out for three weeks.

Once out, he was ordered to the Commanding General's office, and found himself saluting the general who had given him his orders at the start.

The general had one leg thrust out stiffly on a hassock, his left arm in a sling, and a bandaged forehead. He looked at Matt, and growled, "The next time you send me a report, I will believe it."

"I should have put it more clearly, sir. But we were a little shaken up."

"Having been out in that fog," said the general, "and burned by the bugs, and rattled around like dice in a cup when we dropped that drive unit, I can guess what it was like. Since then, I've had two weather stations blown off the top of that bluff by freak winds, a whole ship's crew anaesthetized and almost eaten alive by something that gnaws through the hull of a ship and pumps in gas, and thousands of man-hours lost thanks to that unending fog. What a place! You can't tell where water, air, or land end. It's not a beachhead; it's a foghead."

"Sir, has anyone found out why there's so much fog?"

"They've made noises about it," said the general. "These islands sit practically at the boundary of a warm ocean current flowing north, and a cold current flowing south. I've also been told, part of the trouble comes from the springy plants, that reproduce by thrusting up tall stalks with puffy growths on top; these puffs burst and let out clouds of tiny seed when they're disturbed. The more they're disturbed, the more stalks they grow, the more puffs burst, and the more drifting clouds of fine seed come out. They've been disturbed a lot lately.

"In fact, three of our ships are hung up because some boob got the idea it would ease matters for the air purifiers if they used planetary air instead of recycling. They've got plants sprouting out of the filters, and taking root in any dark spot where there's a stray speck of dust. *Your* ship practically had to be gone over with a blowtorch to sterilize it. And that reminds me." He leaned forward to snap on the intercom.

"How's that final check coming on Colonel Matt's ship?"

"About done, sir."

"Good. Let me know when you're through."

The general leaned back. "Despite the exasperation of this place, things have worked out about as we hoped. But it was close. How did you manage to set up that receiver right under the enemy's nose?"

"Well," said Matt, "they generally rely on a visual system in atmosphere. That was useless here, and their screens are specialized for space. Still, their audio receptors might have picked up our countercurrents. We eased down the bluff, and hung there while the bugs started to nest. We tilted the ship, so the hatch, where the receiver was held on, was out of water. The UCF was half under, so we could see with that part when we swung up to come out.

"The bugs, meanwhile, buzzed and droned, and masked the countercurrents. By the time we got across they were wet and mad, and went for the technicians. We tilted the ship to swing the receiver into position, and let go a cover we had over the base frame to keep the bugs from nesting and throwing the receiver off level. We moved ahead and let down the receiver. We had to use the air lock remote arms to do it, and that meant we had to let the bugs *start* to get settled, but we had to get across before they either corroded through the ship, or blocked the arms. Once we had the receiver set up, we got out of there, and you came through."

The general leaned back and nodded. "And just as we thought we had everything taken care of, we almost got shaken to pieces. That's a peculiar thing about war or exploration. In either one, you have to operate in a fog of uncertainties. When you get involved in both together—"

A buzzer sounded, and the general snapped on the intercom. A voice said, "Sir, Colonel Matt's ship is ready."

"Fine." The general beamed at Matt, and said, "Colonel, I am going to forestall any attempt on your part to volunteer for further service . . ."

Matt, who hadn't even thought of volunteering, tried to look disappointed.

" . . .by sending," the general continued, "you and your crew back to Base immediately. This exploit has entirely changed the balance of the war. You and your men have been cited for extraordinary heroism, have been recommended for immediate promotion, and can expect to be cheered, lionized, goggled at, and sent around on so many speaking tours you'll wish you'd never joined the service. Personally, I want to thank you for getting that receiver up, and I wish you a good trip home, and the best of luck."

"Thank you, sir. I wish you the best of luck."

They exchanged salutes.

Matt went back to the ship and found Andanelli peering though a bandaged left eye into the plot viewer. "Some course we got," he said. "The place is lousy with enemy raiders. We've got to practically hop from frying pan to frying pan till we get back to Station VI. Do you realize they've only got a one-way line between here and VI? They're running the war on a shoestring."

"Just so long as they win it," said Matt. "By the way, we were in the hospital a long time. Did the Kraath—"

Andanelli nodded cheerfully. "They're over their *pratha*. We don't have that to worry about."

★ ★ ★

The trip back was fast and hair-raising at the breaks in and out of subspace. Between breaks, the first part of the trip was so restful that Andanelli shed his cynicism long enough to remark, "This is the life. At this rate we'll be home in no time."

Matt was leaning back in the control seat, contemplating the back pay piled up for him at Base.

"We could," said Matt, "still get smeared at a break point, but it's a relief to be able to get a little rest between times."

Decker came in carrying a small black book, and wearing a puzzled expression.

"Sir," he said, "here's a funny thing. In here, it says Lithians never have more than two cubs at a time. But—"

Matt's feet hit the deck with a slam.

Andanelli froze.

Into the control room padded three purple balls of fluff and claws, their tails waving.

One carried a shoe, which it wrenched and shook, as if to break its back.

One carried a sock, shredded almost beyond recognition.

One carried nothing, and looked all around with hungry glittering eyes.

From the corridor came the rumbling purr of a big Lithian, claws clacking on the steel deck as it indulgently followed the cubs.

From the far end of the ship came the roar of an indignant Kraath.

"Who stole my shoe?"

★ ★ ★

It was a long trip home.

THE GHOST FLEET

Colonel William Beller kept a tight rein on his emotions as he waited in the General's anteroom. The General's feelings toward him were plainly shown by the fact that Beller had waited in this anteroom for two-and-a-half hours while men of lesser rank came and went freely.

Beller became aware that the sergeant at the desk was, for the third time, looking him over coldly. Beller had ignored this twice, out of deference to the ribbons on the sergeant's chest. But now he turned to look the sergeant flatly in the eyes.

For a brief instant, it seemed that a message flowed back and forth between them.

The sergeant's eyes said, "You . . . you're the chicken-livered, yellow-bellied, dirt-eater that turned and ran at Little Orion. You lost us a cluster of stars we'll never take back."

The answering message of Beller's eyes was simpler: "When I command, you obey. It has to be. Right, wrong or indifferent, when I command, you obey."

After a moment of the unequal contest, the sergeant

looked away. A faint expression of puzzlement crossed his face, then he shrugged slightly, and leaned forward as the intercom buzzed.

A small voice reached Beller, which showed that the General in the other room had not bothered to snap up the quiet-switch. "Send Beller in," said the General's voice.

The sergeant glanced at Beller and said, "You can go in now."

Beller looked at the sergeant, and with single-minded concentration willed him to complete the sentence. Save to turn his head slightly, Beller didn't move.

" . . .Sir," said the sergeant unwillingly.

Beller got up, walked through the open door, and down a short hall, to pause at the door of the inner office.

The General, a former classmate and close friend of Beller's, watched him coldly as Beller paused at the doorway. Then the General nodded slightly. Beller stepped in, saluted and formally reported his presence. The General returned the salute, then looked Beller over as if studying him for unpolished shoes and flecks of dust on his trouser legs. Beller stood at attention, waiting, his gaze fixed on the wall above the General's head.

At length, the General said, "I don't suppose there would by any point in asking questions."

Beller said evenly, "Questions about what, sir?" He knew perfectly well what the General meant. But if the General would not state the question plainly, Beller would not answer it.

The General said, slowly and distinctly, "It is generally considered that you lost your nerve at Little Orion."

"Is it?" said Beller, keeping his voice toneless and his eyes fixed on the wall.

The General leaned back, and put his hands behind his head, studying Beller curiously. "I thought you might have something to say."

Beller said flatly, "You have my report, sir."

The General sat up and snorted. "A new weapon used by the enemy. Your ships being destroyed before the enemy came in range. Every green lieutenant thinks the same thing."

"The difference, sir," said Beller coolly, "is that I am not a green lieutenant."

"That's the obvious point," said the General. "*You* are supposed to know better."

"I am supposed to use my júdgment, sir," said Beller. "And if I decide that it is best to retreat, I will so order."

"Regardless of cost, eh?"

"To have stayed where I was would have cost my command, for no purpose. That would have been simple plain stupidity."

"And you prefer cowardice to stupidity?"

For the first time, Beller lowered his gaze to look hard into the General's eyes. "Do you call me a coward, sir?"

Once again, a series of messages seemed to flow back and forth. At last, the General shook his head, leaned back, and made a gesture of disgust. "No, I don't call you a coward, Beller. But if you aren't, you must be a fool."

"You're entitled to your opinion, sir."

The General looked irritated. "Don't be so damned stiff. You know you're going to end up in a general court-martial. Is that going to be your defense—that the enemy had a secret weapon?"

"My defense," said Beller coldly, "is something I haven't thought about. But I will tell the truth, and the truth is that my ships were being destroyed beyond effective range of my own or known enemy weapons. My command was perfectly useless in the situation, and I withdrew to save it."

"And lost us the whole star cluster."

"Would you prefer to have lost the star cluster plus the defending fleet?"

The General waved a hand beside his face, as if to brush away gathering confusion. He leaned forward and said harshly, "In a month, Beller, you may be dead. Shot by a firing squad for cowardice. You'll die with your insignia of rank ripped off. You'll have been provided with a ceremonial sword, which will have been snapped in half, as the troops stand by with rifles reversed —"

* * *

Beller suddenly could contain himself no longer. He whirled, shut the door to the hall, and snapped the lock. In an instant, he was back at the desk, and pinned the General's hand to the desktop as it reached for the intercom. "You fool," said Beller, his voice intense but hardly louder than a whisper, "do you think if you put stars on the shoulders of a jackass, it will make him fit to command a fleet?"

The General's face changed color, but when he spoke, there was only a desperate urgency in his voice, which was also hardly more than a whisper. "You ran. You turned tail and ran."

"Of course I ran. You'd run too with a bear half-a-jump behind you and no gun in sight. Can you think of a better thing to do?"

"You lost us the cluster."

"And saved us the fleet. Try and get it through your thick skull that there *was* a new weapon used. Where do you get the idea it's impossible? Don't you know this whole war is a war of weapons?"

"You got excited—"

"Hogwash. Do you think you can judge a thing like that better than I can? We know each other. Did you ever beat me at chess? Did you ever outrun me? Are you a better pistol shot? In that field problem, the last year at school—"

The General grinned suddenly and pulled his hand loose. "Spare me," he said. He started to laugh, then choked it off. "All the same," he said, "you're in one hell of a spot."

"So will we all be when they get that thing in general use."

"I've got the technical boys working on it." The General scowled. "When I read your report, it seemed . . . I don't know . . . familiar."

"It was unfamiliar to me."

The General shrugged. "Well, they'll find it if there's anything to it." He scowled. "But meanwhile, we've got you to think of."

Beller straightened up and shrugged. "If they want to court-martial me, they'll court-martial me."

"The only reason they haven't already is that they haven't been able to get enough rank together. You realize, they're going to make an example of you."

"If they'd open their minds and listen to me, it would save them a great deal of trouble."

"They won't." The General frowned. "I wouldn't myself, but I know you. The trouble is, this thing fits a standard pattern."

Beller shrugged, "If they shoot me, I'll be no deader than I was bound to be sooner or later anyway. But if they go through that mumbo jumbo with the ceremonial sword and rifles upside-down, they'd better not show it live on 3-V. Have them film it. I'm not sure I can keep from laughing."

The General shook his head. "You've been out of school all these years, and what have you learned? Don't you know raw ability will never take you to the top?"

"I'd rather be myself than be at the top," said Beller. "I like to know what I think when I go to bed at night."

"With a little more tact, you *could* be on top. Then you could do what you want. Let the others change their opinions to suit you."

Beller shook his head. "We've been all over this before. I don't say the system's wrong, or that all considered, it could be done better another way. I don't know. But it seems to me that there are certain solid realities, and the rest is window-dressing. The window-dressing changes, but the reality remains. I want to stick by the reality."

The General nodded. He leaned back, and a look of calculation crossed his face. He got up, and opened a file drawer. "Some of this stuff is silly," he growled, "but it's all almost too secret even to think about. Ah, here we are." He pulled out a bulky folder, sat down, and leafed through it.

Beller stood with feet apart, and hands clasped behind his back, waiting.

The General cleared his throat and leaned forward. "How would you like a suicide mission?"

Beller grinned. The General had spoken as if he were offering a present.

Realizing this, the General said, "I don't mean that quite the way it sounds. In the court-martial, you won't stand a chance. But if you go out on this mission, and come back alive, they won't be able to touch you. The charge is cowardice, and they'll have had it stuffed back down their throats. This is a very dangerous mission. Dangerous enough to be *called* a suicide mission. But in a thing like this, there's nearly always *some* chance. A lot more than in the court-martial."

"Can you send me on it? I haven't been able to make out whether I'm under arrest or not."

The General nodded. "I can send you on it. We're short of men who could do this job, and you're qualified. I can send you on it and wave priorities and classified documents in their faces, and refer to Plan X, and they'll be only too glad to drop the whole thing." He added shrewdly. "There are advantages to understanding human nature."

Beller smiled and nodded. "What's the mission?"

"Well," said the General, watching Beller's face as if nervous about his possible reaction. "Our big trouble right now, you know, is a double one. We're short of ships, for one thing. Since Hauser took over, we've straightened out the imbecilic distribution of forces we had before. But we're still suffering from past losses, and the production program hasn't caught up yet. Then there's this chronic trouble about fuel for the drive-units. We've *got* to have quadrite for combat ships. But the sources we have to rely on are awkwardly situated. For instance, there's the third planet of Ostrago—a place called Knackruth—that supplies us with a great deal of quadrite. We can't afford to lose that source. If we lose it, we'll have to tranship quadrite from halfway across the system. A few months back, Bannister put up a finish fight to stop an Out advance that would have cut off Knackruth. He stopped it. But they wore him so thin in the process that he'll never stop them a second time."

Beller nodded. "Now they're getting ready to try again?"

"We have every reason to think so. They know now there's something valuable to us close at hand, otherwise we'd have been more flexible. What we expect is that they'll go on the defensive elsewhere, switch their heavy forces opposite Knackruth, and smash through Bannister like a rock through tissue paper."

Beller nodded, waiting.

"Ordinarily," said the General, "we'd wait till we thought they had their arrangements about two thirds ready, then we'd hit them hard in another sector, fall back where they advanced, and try to get in behind their main attack. But we can't do that now. We can't afford to lose Knackruth. We don't have the strength for a serious attack. We have to try a hoax."

The General glanced at Beller uneasily, looked down for a moment at the folder from the file, stiffened his jaw, and said, "The name of this plan is 'Operation Ghost.' The force to be used consists of three fleets, each consisting of

twelve simulated Class-A battleships, forty simulated
Class-A and 1A cruisers, and one hundred and twenty-six
simulated smaller ships. Your flagship will be an R-Class
dreadnought—unsimulated, with new communications
and detector equipment."

Beller winced. Mentally he groped back through
remembered lists of specifications. "R-Class" How far
back in antiquity was that? He grinned suddenly.

The General, watching his face, relaxed a little. "Your
mission is to attack the main enemy force head-on. You
will move through Bannister's defensive screen as if you
intended to crush the Out attacking force by the sheer
power of numbers. The main thing is to act like a man
with half a thousand ships at his back."

"You figure if I tried a feint attack elsewhere, this simulated fleet could never make it through their defenses?"

The General nodded. "Ordinarily we'd spare you
enough real ships to get through their outer shell, but we
can't afford it now. What we hope to do is to disjoint their
forces opposite Knackruth. When they see this fleet coming, they'll start multiplying their defenses. They'll pull
back their own main forces, either to back up their
defenses or attack elsewhere in the hope of throwing us
off-balance. In either case, they'll scream for help from
other sectors, and that will mean a great many of their
ships pulled out of action all around the perimeter."

Beller nodded, then said thoughtfully, "How do we
know this hoax will fool them? What if they just decide we
couldn't spare such a force, and therefore it can't be real?"

"You have to consider their frame of mind. We know now
that they operated for many years with a saboteur planted in

our capital. We know that they have extraordinary powers of mental suggestion. For years, they got by with this, because we ordinarily just won't believe such a thing is possible. The last messages out of the capital show that during a change of administration the new Defense Secretary uncovered the whole thing. Before the saboteur could get to him, the Secretary brought down Hauser and the general reserve and blew the capital to bits.

"Once a new team took over at the auxiliary capital, it dawned on them that all our arrangements were wrong. Defenses were rigid and badly organized. Warship design was antiquated. Supplies were routed so as to take the longest possible time in shipment. Contracts were let to the most inefficient contractors. The worst available equipment was procured, with incessant halts in production to change this or that insignificant detail. The whole thing was a mess.

"In spite of this," said the General, "they hadn't beaten us. We had a terrible time in their next attack, but before it was over we hit them so hard they were glad to get out with a whole skin. Since then, they can't predict us. We've made the most of our remaining resources, and if they have any sense at all, they know what's being gotten ready for them. If it comes out at them five months before they expected it, that just proves they miscalculated again."

Beller nodded thoughtfully. "It might work, at that."

"It's worth a try," said the General. He added dryly, "Do you wish to volunteer for this assignment?"

Beller and the General smiled at each other. Then a question occurred to Beller, but he was afraid to ask it:

Where could the General have dug up a crew qualified to run the ancient dreadnought?

★ ★ ★

Beller boarded the dreadnought carrying a newssheet that had been spat at him out of a printer during breakfast in the lunar commissary. This sheet contained optimistic interpretations of the news from all sectors, plus a number of features and columns. Part of one of these columns had interested Beller personally:

"And then there's an ugly little item from out Little Orion way. It seems the local brasshat defending a vital cluster lost his nerve when the Outs arrived, turned tail and ran, dragging his fleet behind him. The story has it that he didn't stop till he reached Aux Cap and had the general reserve to hide behind, and then he let out a yell that the enemy had a secret weapon. Their only weapon is ordinary courage, but it took this brasshat by surprise.

"Cowardice is an ugly word. It's an ugly charge to brand a man with. But we'll brand this man with it, gladly. He's already branded himself. With the future of the race hanging in peril, the only treatment for this sort of rat is the firing squad or the rope, and we'll keep right after the Space Force till they give it to him. We'll have more details on this later . . .

"Now a note for you showbirds. Sheila Wister, who performed so beautifully in 'Sellout,' is back again—"

Beller shut the lock of the little courier boat behind him, and stepped away as the hydraulic lifts raised and slid the boat sidewise to lock it tight in its cradle.

He glanced around, puzzled by the general atmosphere of the ship. Everything seemed in unusually good order.

That the air purifiers were functioning perfectly was evident from the forestlike freshness of the air. Deck and bulkheads were neatly painted, with no sign of rust anywhere. The brass handle of the inner air-lock hatch was polished and coated with a protective film. Beside the hatch stood a very elderly man in the uniform of a major of the Space Force Reserve. He saluted stiffly, and Beller returned the salute.

"Bovak, sir," said the major, in a rusty voice. "I'm your executive officer."

Beller said, "Glad to meet you, major." He glanced around at the excellent condition of what he had seen so far, scowled and cleared his throat. "Could you tell me where this ship has been kept? I wasn't aware we had any of this class in reserve."

"We didn't, sir," said Bovak dryly. "This ship was Exhibit C in the Arts and Sciences Museum on Landor II. Across the fairgrounds in the crystal dome back of the pool."

Beller felt as if a case of ammunition had been dropped on him. The major, who had looked elderly before, suddenly appeared two-hundred years old to Beller. He didn't like to say what he said next, but he had to know how things stood.

"And you, Major?" said Beller gently.

"I, sir, was chief of the maintenance crew that cared for the ship." The major said it with pride. "My crew, sir, is now your crew."

"Ah," said Beller, trying to appear appreciative. It dawned on him that he was going into space against the Outs in a museum exhibit manned by janitors, with a dummy fleet behind him, while he himself was a pariah on temporary leave from a general court-martial. "Operation Ghost" was well-named.

"Well," said Beller, "let's look the ship over."

"Yes, sir," said Bovak.

★ ★ ★

The tour of inspection showed Beller the massive lines on which the ship was built, along with the excellent condition in which it had been kept. At intervals, he was introduced to an elderly reserve captain or lieutenant, who turned out to be his gunnery officer or drive-unit engineer. There was not an enlisted man on board. It was only after he'd reached the control room that it occurred to Beller to wonder if these ranks were real or simulated. He had forgotten that he himself had been made—for the purpose of commanding the simulated fleet—a simulated lieutenant-general.

Well, there was nothing to do now but hope and pray.

He turned to the eighty-five-year-old pilot, and said, "Let's go, captain."

The pilot smiled faintly, and reached out past a little placard reading: "Control Board: At this panel are grouped the master controls for flying and fighting the ship. Many of the secondary controls are completely automatic.—Exhibit C, *Science and Industry.*"

There was a very faint vibration as the giant engines came to life. Lights winked on the instrument panel in a fashion strange to Beller.

The museum piece turned its nose in the direction of the enemy and began to move.

★ ★ ★

The days fled past as the huge insubstantial fleet hurtled

toward Knackruth, the quadrite-rich planet of the sun Ostrago. The fleet was halfway there when word came through that Bannister, blocking the way to Knackruth, was under heavy attack. A little later, Bannister himself was on the screen. Beller knew that all Bannister had been told was that a "force of considerable size" was approaching, and would attempt to pass out through his defenses on a certain day.

On the screen, Bannister eyed Beller's uniform, and his eyes widened. A lieutenant-general ordinarily commanded very considerable forces.

"Sir," said Bannister, "I'm sorry to trouble you, but my orders said I might get in touch with you if necessary. I'm under heavy attack here, and I don't think I can hold." He added sharply, "I'll do my best. But I'd be a liar if I said anything else."

Beller nodded. "What do the Outs have?"

"Counting only large ships, there's a dozen battleships, and eighty big cruisers. They have smaller ships in proportion." Bannister hesitated, then said, "I can't hold them. I've tried everything I can think of, and they've just got too much of everything."

Beller nodded coolly.

Bannister's eyes moved slightly back and forth, searching Beller's face and noting the total lack of surprise or excitement. Suddenly Bannister looked at Beller's insignia again, glanced at what few details of the ship could be seen through the short-focus screen, and said, "I don't mean to presume, sir . . . but if you will forgive my asking . . . what force do *you* have, sir?"

Beller had been afraid of this. The latest information,

however, was that the enemy was intercepting just such conversations as this. Beller reminded himself to act like a man with "half a thousand ships at his back."

He scowled, and said coolly, "As a matter of fact, Bannister, you *do* presume. But I know you've been under a great deal of strain lately."

"Yes, sir," said Bannister stiffly. "Sorry, sir."

"Therefore," said Beller, "I will freely forgive you."

"Thank you, sir." Bannister squinted at him curiously. "I asked, sir, so that I might know whether to place my remnants under your command as we pull back."

"I wasn't intending to pull back."

Bannister blinked. He opened his mouth, and hesitated.

Beller said, "As a matter of fact, I doubt that this will make any change in our plans whatever."

"But, sir . . . twelve battleships and eighty cruisers . . . plus auxiliaries—"

"They make no more difference to me than one battleship and half-a-dozen cruisers." This, Beller thought, was literally true. One properly handled cruiser could blow up the whole fleet, with the possible exception of the dreadnought. But Bannister plainly put a different interpretation on it.

"Sir, you don't mean—"

"I mean nothing. However, Bovak—" Beller turned to his executive officer, out of reach of the screen. "Take a detector sweep of the first division and transmit it to General Bannister."

"Yes, sir," rasped Bovak, reaching for the coupling switches.

Bannister blinked, and turned from the screen. A

muffled exclamation burst from him as the traces appeared on his auxiliary screen. He whirled to stare at Beller, who said dryly, "Sweep the second division, Bovak."

"Yes, sir."

Bannister returned to the screen. "We'll chop them to mincemeat. They've got some kind of funny weapon, and we may have to look out for it, sir. But they can't stand up to this."

Beller felt like a traitor, but he smiled and said, "We'll do our best."

Bannister, obviously lifted into a state of exaltation, saluted with glowing eyes.

Beller returned the salute, and the screen blanked.

The ghost fleet swept on.

★ ★ ★

They were a little beyond Ostrago when the first trace of the enemy fleet showed up on the long-range detectors. Seriously cut up, Bannister was still hanging onto a sun-system at their flank and rear, hoping to hit the enemy remnants as they fled.

Beller said, "Form plane on axis of attack."

Bovak, doubling as Beller's division commanders, manipulated three levers on a control box. The dummy ships, their large light volume driven by light engines, moved slowly apart, like a giant metal flower blossoming from its bud.

Immediately the enemy traces on the long-range detector screen did the same.

The two fleets opened up, forming giant lattices only one layer thick. In this position, each ship would be best situated to bring its maximum power to bear on the enemy.

The two fleets continued to open up, each trying to reach out further than the other, lest the other be able to send an unopposed detachment forward to curl over the thin edge of the opposing formation and wither it with an overpowering concentration of fire.

Now, Beller saw, the distant Out fleet had reached its utmost extension, and was adjusting the positions of its ships to best advantage.

The ghost fleet, however, continued to open up.

Watching the symbolic representation of the positions develop on the battle screen, Beller was amazed that the enemy fleet refused to pull back or slow its pace. The two fleets had fallen into a perfectly standard pattern, which, if the ships of each had been equal, would have meant the total ruin of the enemy. Of course, there was still time. It could be that the enemy commander was trying a test of wills. The communicator buzzed, and Beller snapped it on. Bannister, looking fatigued and utterly hopeless, was watching him sorrowfully. "I've had a chance to evaluate all my battle reports, sir."

Beller nodded.

"Sir," said Bannister, "there's no doubt of it. We've had chance reports before and now there's proof. The enemy's using a secret weapon."

Beller nodded dryly. "There *have* been reports of a new weapon."

"Well, the reports are true. This Out fleet hardly had to really exert itself to finish us. But they're being clever. They mask the effect. All the same, this thing, whatever it is, just touches the ship, and—blooey—it blows apart."

"What do you mean 'touches'?"

"I don't know, sir. Let's say, they merely aim it. It operates beyond our effective range. They merely aim this thing, pull the trigger, and by what process I don't know, we're finished. The ship blows apart."

"How is it, then, that any of your force is left?"

"I'm small fish. If they slaughtered me, you'd withdraw. To fool us, they only mauled me, and used the weapon at less than maximum range, and they used it cleverly. When an ultrafast missile was just starting out from one of our ships, they'd hit the missile. The explosion of the missile would wreck the ship, and we'd take it for a strike by one of their missiles. But on correlation of all the data, we find that we were destroyed by something that set off our own weapons, save for one or two cases where we got too close, and they used the thing direct."

"IIm-m-m," said Beller, nodding. "You'll report this as soon as possible."

Bannister's eyes widened. "Yes, sir. But I assumed you'd pull back."

Beller nodded. Unfortunately, he was counted on to create a diversion. If he pulled back, he would have slowed the Out fleet by only the delay it cost them to maul Bannister rather than evaporate him. He couldn't split his ghost fleet into fragments moving in all directions to confuse pursuit, because the whole thing was centrally controlled from the dreadnought. Any maneuver that merely delayed contact would provide that much more time for the enemy fleet to discover the nature of the hoax. However, Beller thought, there was still the possibility that the enemy might intercept this conversation. Cause for future hesitation and uneasiness might still be given them.

Beller said, "There have been rumors of a new weapon. Now we'll test it and see."

Bannister blinked. "But . . . sir . . . they'll destroy the fleet."

"That may be. But, believe me, Bannister, when I say that this fleet represents a very minor fraction of the production power that is now coming into play. We'll see what this new weapon can do. And then we'll see what hits them when they get in a little farther."

Bannister swallowed. His expression wavered between dread and hope. Finally, he said "Yes, sir," and saluted. The screen blanked.

The battle screen showed Beller that the ghost fleet had now reached its fullest extension. As the two fleets began to close, Beller said, "Increase acceleration to fleet maximum."

"Yes, sir," said Bovak.

The battle screen showed the two fleets, rushing together.

★ ★ ★

They were still beyond the ordinary maximum range when Bovak said, "Strike. Battleship in the first division. Strike—Second division 1A-cruiser. Strike. Three A-cruisers, third division. Battleship, second division. Cruiser, first division. Three cruisers, second division—"

Beller watched the battle screen, where the symbols winked out like checkers picked up and tossed off the board in mid-play. This was what Beller had experienced at Little Orion, save that here there was nothing to gain by withdrawal. As he watched, great holes began to appear in the ghost fleet.

Somewhere in the rear of the old dreadnought, there was a warbling sound that rose, and died away.

Beller glanced at Bovak, who looked blank. Bovak had given up relating the losses, as it was impossible to keep up with them. Almost a third of the fleet was gone.

Beller said, "Decrease acceleration of the center."

On the battle screen, the outermost ships began to draw ahead, as if to overlap the edge of the enemy formation. This bid vanished along with the outermost ships.

The ships were not yet in range, but Beller thought it unnatural for a fleet in this position not to try something, however disorganized.

"Dreadnought hold fire. Fire all weapons on simulated ships only."

In the rear of the dreadnought, the warbling began again. It rose to a peak, then died away again.

On the battle screen, the lines reached out, as the ghost fleet fired its scatter of puny weapons. Beller felt gratified. This had the look of discipline breaking down, with here and there a controller losing his nerve and letting off a weapon at hopeless range.

The warble started up again, low this time, and died away.

Now two thirds of the fleet was gone. Only now were they starting to come into range.

The warbling began, died away, rose, died away, rose to a peak of twanging that seemed to vibrate the whole ship, died away, rose again.

Bovak was talking to the engine room. He glanced at Beller, puzzled. "Nothing wrong there, sir. I don't know what makes that noise."

The dreadnought was now alone on the battle screen, coming into conventional range of the enemy fleet. Beller was struck by the situation that had come about. The dreadnought was approaching the enemy fleet like a dart flying at a huge target. At any moment this target might erupt in a concentration of destructive energy that would vaporize the dreadnought in a fraction of a second.

Bovak pulled down a large red lever. "Controllers, select targets."

The dreadnought was now within maximum range. Nothing happened.

Then dazzling lines reached out from the dreadnought, to converge on an Out battleship. The battleship vanished.

From a different set of batteries, another set of dazzling lines reached out. The controllers, Beller realized, were coolly conserving the ship's energy at this range. He saw the lines converge. Another Out battleship vanished.

Still there was no return fire.

But all around Beller, the twanging was so continuous that it seemed almost solid.

A third Out battleship vanished under the power of the dreadnought's weapons.

Beller, partly dazed by the continuous noise around him, stared at the battle screen. The situation added up to nothing he could understand. Unless—

Beller stepped up beside Bovak, and took another glance at the battle screen. The Out fleet still did nothing but rush on. It retained its formation, extending it slowly as the dreadnought approached. The formation was like a disk with an almost perfect circular rim. Beller said to

Bovak, "Fire on the ship in the geometric center of that formation."

Bovak relayed the order to the controllers.

Again the dazzling lines reached out, to converge on a large cruiser at the center of the enemy formation. The cruiser vanished.

Abruptly, the twanging sound was gone.

The other enemy ships continued on their courses, unaffected, dumbly.

Another Out battleship followed its predecessors.

Beller said, "Cease fire. Decelerate."

Bovak shoved up the red lever.

The two men stared at each other.

★ ★ ★

The General said wonderingly, "A *second* ghost fleet?"

Beller nodded. He was back in the office where the General had first unfolded the plan. But the difference between this visit and the last was enormous. Symbolic of the difference was the attitude of the sergeant in the anteroom who had looked at Beller with something approaching awe.

The story had, of course, been told over the communication web, but the General wanted it first hand.

"So" said the General, smiling, with a look of calculation, "at the end, it was just your ship versus the whole Out fleet?"

"Yes, sir."

"You didn't run. You didn't crab sidewise to get out of there. You didn't scream for help. You just went straight for them, head-on."

"The inertia of the ship, sir," said Beller dryly, "would

have thrown me into their lap sidewise or backwards, regardless what I'd tried to do."

"Oh, I know; but I'm thinking how it's going to sound if they go through with that court-martial. Well, then, next you figured the action of the Out fleet was peculiar."

"It dawned on me," said Beller, "that they were acting exactly as I had acted a little earlier. Then I remembered Bannister saying that they'd hardly exerted themselves to beat him. Of course, it would seem that way if he was up against dummy ships with only a few real, remote-controlled weapons for deception purposes. Next it dawned on me that the Outs might be stretched to the limit, too. Naturally, they want to finish us before the tide turns too strongly against them—and we've been coming up lately. The obvious place for the control-ship, if this was another ghost fleet, was in or near the center. We blew it up, and the rest just drifted on. It was then that we started to hunt for whatever had made that terrific twanging noise."

Beller handed the General a small placard, such as is used in museums to explain exhibits:

DISRUPTER COUNTERVAIL

The disrupter countervail was used during the period of the Early Space Wars to counteract by split-phased resonance the action of the nuclear disrupter. The nuclear disrupter was in this period used to unbalance the binding forces of the atoms, causing a rapid collapse of the structure of the attacked ship. The disrupter, however, required the use of such large and complex equipment, and its action was so easily countered, that it soon fell out of use. For many generations, the countervail was carried on ships as a matter of routine precaution, though the disrupter itself has seldom ever been used since the early space wars.—Exhibit C, Science and Industry.

The General looked up.

"Orders from the capital removed all remaining countervails on the older ships several years ago, to save space and weight. No one raised a question. We'd never had any use for the things. When the trouble you mentioned started, first it fit the standard pattern of . . . excuse me . . . a frightened man making an alibi for himself, and then it looked as if it might possibly fit the standard pattern of a brand-new weapon. It never occurred to us it might be an old weapon revived. We were victimized by too much reliance on standard patterns."

"When you think about it," said Beller, "that's something we're up against all the time, isn't it?"

"How do you mean?"

"We're likely to end up confronted with one solid fact—a real truth—at the center of a huge formation of conjecture, opinion, and all manner of things, dependent on that one central thing that's real. The sheer size and volume of the total may seem overwhelming."

"Yes," said the General, "but if you can avoid being dominated by it, and deal with the real fact—"

Beller nodded.

"Then," he said, "you've got a chance to knock out a Ghost Fleet."

CARGO FOR COLONY 6

Colonel David Nevv watched the hands of the chronometer line up for the sixth break-point, and remembered General Lawson's warning as if he heard it anew.

"You've got twenty days to get there," said the general, "and for safety, you should make it in twelve. Red Base won't answer our signal, and the last incomplete report from *Vanguard* was that the Flats were sending a big 'friendship delegation' aboard. Now Blue Base tells us the Flats are making overtures," he looked at Nevv wryly, "to send down a geological expedition *with its drill rigs and other heavy equipment*. I've ordered Blue Base to refuse permission and to open fire if the Flats try to come down. Green Base and White Base are on full alert, so for the time being Colony 6 is safe."

"For twenty days?"

"If the Flats are cautious. In twenty days Green Base will be too far around in its orbit to give any cover. Blue Base won't come into position for another week. The Colony's only overhead protection will be Red Base, and there's every reason to think the Flats now own Red Base.

You've got to get there before Green Base is out of range. We're giving you an AA dreadnought stripped for speed, and the best control-room crew you could possibly have. If you can get in there and get your cargo to Hunsinger before the Flats move in, the Colony's saved. If you don't make it, the Flats will sew it all up before we can get our fleets collected together from all the places that were supposed to be more dangerous. And once they get that far the Flats will cut off everything we're just starting to develop from the Colony outward. The reverberations will shake us for a hundred years."

"Sir, I never thought the Flats were *allies*, but—When did they turn into enemies?"

General Lawson exhaled sharply. "They aren't enemies, damn it."

Nevv said, "If they're attacking Colony 6—"

"They're calculators. As long as we were fighting the Outs, and getting our heads kicked in, the Flats saw us as no danger to them, while the Outs were a real danger. So the Flats stayed formally neutral, let us do the fighting, and helped us on the side. We took this for friendship. Colony 6 was a possible long-range problem, some day, because, despite its nearness to Flat territory, we were the ones to discover that nearby cluster of breakpoints into subspace, opening up promising routes for future colonization. Routinely, we set up the colony. It was a good routine move; but we should have seen it would make trouble, and been prepared."

"Yes, sir. I see that. But . . ."

"Try to see it from the Flats' viewpoint: Bad enough that they didn't find it first; now do they really want someone else to control it? But, in fact, as long as we were up against the Outs, we wouldn't be pouring warships and streams of colonists through there any time soon; so there was no big hurry about that problem. Well, we got rid of the Out saboteur; our overall plans now make some sense; our recruitment and training are going well; our production is way up. In that last fight, we outclassed the enemy. We are now beating the Outs. This changes all the calculations."

Nevv followed the reasoning, and the general went on, "The Flats figure they better take care of Colony 6 while they still can. They know we don't want to take on another war while we're entangled with the Outs. So the Flats are using every trick and subterfuge to avoid giving offense as they make believe they're still our buddies, and at the same time finish off Colony 6. It all makes sense from their viewpoint. But we can't let them get away with it. Colony 6 is the gateway to a big chunk of our future."

Nevv stood motionless, thinking. "Sir, if they're not actual enemies . . ."

"Colonel, they don't hate us, if that's what you mean. But if they squeeze the trigger, we're just as dead."

"But we don't have any backlog of enmity with them. Except for this one source of annoyance . . ."

"This one bucket of red-hot rivets down the backs of their necks."

"H'm . . . Yes . . ."

"I don't know what the devil you're trying to get at. We can judge how important it is to them by the fact that they're risking war with us by trying to take the colony."

"But you say they're trying at the same time to avoid an open break—by all kinds of subterfuge?"

"Yes. What of it?"

"Well, then, can't we expect a little hesitation—"

"I sure wouldn't count on it."

"But they don't want a war with us, do they?"

Lawson frowned. "No. But they don't want our colonization convoys passing through their back yard, either. The problem is very simple: Colony 6 is a big bone with a hungry dog on either end."

"They don't know what our present fleet strength may be, do they?"

"H'm'm . . . No . . . What do you have in mind?"

"I'm just trying to see what there is to work with."

"If you can get that cargo to Hunsinger before the Flats get control of Colony 6, they won't be able to get control. Hunsinger is one of the few to understand that cargo. That's our main chance. The rest of this stuff is just speculation. I think it's accurate. I hope it gives you a picture of what we're up against; but the main thing is to get that cargo to Colony 6 ahead of the opposition."

Nevv stood straighter. "Yes, sir. We'll do our best."

"All right," said the general, "but bear one thing more in mind. The Flats were supposed to be friendly, and our manpower in Planning is always limited. We have only a partial set of alternate routes to Colony 6. If the Flats got Red Base intact, they probably got the route maps, too. Every time you break out of subspace, expect a reception committee. If you can't get away, depress the switch for nose turret ten on the firing console. That will destroy the—cargo. We can't let that fall into their hands."

★ ★ ★

Nevv had saluted. The general had returned the salute

and gripped Nevv by the hand. And now Nevv watched the chronometer and felt a tightening of his stomach muscles. He glanced to his left, and saw Lieutenant Colonel Randolph Hughes, his head invisible in the pilot globe, his hands steady on the manual controls. He glanced over his right shoulder and saw no sign of Lieutenant Colonel Philip Mannin, his astrogator. Nevv spoke into the microphone. "Phil, we've got just twenty-one seconds till break-point."

In Nevv's earphone, Mannin's voice said, "Coming. I was just looking over the cargo."

"Nineteen seconds," said Nevv in warning. He heard the metallic click of the latch as Mannin came in. Nevv turned and saw Mannin start to strap himself in his acceleration couch.

"Ready," said Nevv. "Fifteen seconds."

Hughes' voice said, "Ready, pilot." A moment later, Mannin said, "Ready, astrogator."

The narrow second hand swung up to join the minute and hour hands on the chronometer. For an instant, all three hands were in line. A bell chimed softly. A wash of colors swept away Nevv's view of the control room. He heard the heavy distant clang of the breakpoint gong down in the empty crew's quarters. He felt something cold and soft press on his shoulders, and realized that the command globe had settled in place. Abruptly he seemed to be alone in a blackness lit with brilliant pinpoints of white.

Hughes' voice said, "Here we go. One to the left foreground high. One to the left foreground low. One to the *far* left foreground high—"

As Hughes spoke, bright target disks showing detected

spaceships began to spring into view, and gently-curving fine lines traced out to show the ideal potential tracks of projectiles to be hurled against them.

"To the far left background low," said Hughes. "To the far left background high—"

Mannin cut in to say, "Alternate courses." A green line, a yellow line, and a red line appeared as if hanging in space before Nevv's eyes. Each line represented a course to a new breakpoint into subspace, red being the longest course in normal space and green the shortest.

Mannin said, "Green course, eighty-three hours in subspace, minimum; yellow, eighty-six, minimum; red, forty-three minimum. Green, five alternates; yellow, four alternates; red, two alternates. Final breakpoint: green—"

Suddenly Hughes said, "Near right background high! Near right background low!"

Two glaring orange-red marker disks showed up close below to the ship's right rear and close above to the right rear.

"Sewed-up," growled Hughes.

A short purple line appeared directly in front of Nevv's eyes.

Mannin said, "Backtrack route for return to the last breakpoint. We might try another route from there."

Nevv said, "Don't move the ship at all." He swung his hand up and hit the trip-release at the bottom of the command globe. The globe spun up out of the way.

★ ★ ★

Directly in front of Nevv, the viewscreen flared and lit up, showing a remarkably broad-shouldered individual, with a wide head and wider neck, wearing a bright blue uniform with a yellow sash draped across his broad chest, with three tufts of red on the yellow sash, and a cluster of golden spikes on each shoulder. This officer had small triumphant eyes under bushy brows, and a head of short bristly hair that ran down his neck on either side and vanished under his collar. He watched Nevv like a cat with a bird in its paws and said nothing.

Nevv recognized the insignia of a Flat admiral, and immediately brought his arm up in a precise salute.

A faint frown crossed the Flat's face, and he returned the salute.

Nevv said, "Colonel David R. Nevv, commanding T. S. F. Dreadnought *Prometheus*, requests permission for T. S. F. Vengeance Fleet One to pass in column of dreadnoughts, shipwise."

The Flat's mouth opened slightly and shut again. His eyes darted once to either side of the viewscreen, as if hastily checking instruments, then returned to Nevv. His mouth began to move, and a moment later the translated version of what he said came though: "Colonel, I have received word of no such fleet. Where are the rest of your ships now?"

"Still in subspace, admiral. *Prometheus* is the lead ship in this column."

"May I ask—as the interested representative of a friendly power—what is your destination, and what is your mission?"

"Our ultimate destination is secret, sir," said Nevv. "As for our mission, there have been certain difficulties far out-world of our Colony 6. The flag has been insulted, sir. Low forms of life have attempted to take a mean and treacherous advantage of us. I am sorry, but I am not at liberty to give details. I can only say that our answer to the insult has been long planned and is being carried into effect with the utmost secrecy. Again, sir, I formally request you to give permission for T. S. F. Vengeance Fleet One to pass, in column of dreadnought, shipwise."

The admiral scowled, squinted, then blanked his face and gave a good imitation of earnest sympathy. "I am very sorry, colonel. This region is being used as a . . . er . . . practice mining exercise region, and we simply cannot allow your fleet to go through. If your supreme commander wishes to consult with me when he arrives—"

"Sir," said Nevv earnestly, "I, too, am very sorry. My instructions on this point were explicit. Perhaps I haven't explained myself fully and clearly. Our flag has been *insulted*. This is T. S. F. Vengeance Fleet One. The supreme commander is not with this fleet. This is a combined operation, admiral, timed to the second. If *this* fleet is out of timing, it will affect the operations of the others. We have spent too much time and material in preparation to allow this to happen. When the steel blades of the trap slide shut, admiral, they must all bite in at once; otherwise some of the vermin may get away. Admiral, this is an affair of honor. I must tell you, sir, we are going through. And now, admiral, *again* I ask your permission."

The Flat officer took a deep breath, looked directly at Nevv and said in a low hoarse voice, "I am very sorry, colonel, this is a practice mining region, and our ships here constitute, as it were, a region of our own territory. You can understand, colonel. Our own . . . ah . . . honor? Yes, our own honor is involved."

Nevv shook his head. "I'm very sorry, admiral. We've had such good relations with your people before. But we've spent too much time in preparation. We can't sacrifice the timing and the secrecy." He reached out and brought his hand down hard on the "Prepare" bar of the firing console. The battle-stations' gongs back in the empty crew's quarters let go with a tooth-jarring clatter that reverberated in the control room.

Nevv turned to Mannin. "Set up alternate Fleet course to avoid this obstacle." He glanced at Hughes. "Send signal fourteen, 'Sacrifice to avoid delay.'"

Hughes, his face the color of freshly-sliced unripe onions, hit the beam-signal keys twice, then twice again.

Mannin spoke up briskly. "Send Alternate 20-25-25 orange."

"Right," said Hughes. He struck the keys again.

Nevv flipped over the public address switch and pulled the microphone to him. "Men," he said firmly, and multiplied echoes of his voice boomed back to him. "Men, this is the C.O. speaking." His voice roared and reverberated in the empty ship. "Men, we have been slightly delayed, but we are going to blast out a diversion so the Fleet can go through unhindered. There are a number of ships to deal with, but remember, follow your saturation procedures carefully, and don't be overeager for the kill. We want to get the full benefit of these new weapons, and we don't want anybody hogging a target. This is all going down on film, so everyone can be sure he'll get full battle-credits for good square hits and methodical controlling. And lastly, men, remember, every ship burst neatly open here, every clean suckout, every well-placed sun-shot, will put us just that much closer to the *real* enemy. That's all, men. Listen for the signal, and no jumping the gun."

On the screen, the Flat admiral put a finger inside his collar, puffed out his cheeks, started to say something, and hesitated.

Nevv put his hand on the firing switch for nose turret ten. He turned to Hughes.

The Flat admiral, speaking rapidly, said, "One moment, colonel. I have just received special instructions from the high officer commanding in this region. You may proceed, but only along a specially marked route—to avoid the mines. One of our ships will mark the route—"

Nevv said courteously, "Thank you, sir, But if you do that, we will be late at our rendezvous. We'll just have to take our chances with the mines." He turned to Hughes. "Course red, colonel."

"Yes, sir," said Hughes. He pulled down the pilot globe. There was a roar and a trembling, and the big ship began to move.

On the screen, the Flat gave a weak smile, nodded with imitation briskness, and broke contact.

★ ★ ★

All the way to breakpoint into subspace, Nevv could feel a sensation like a faint cold wind across the back of his neck and shoulders.

When they were well on their course in subspace, Hughes ran his fingers over the automatics settings, then shoved up the pilot globe. He looked at Nevv, grinned feebly and said, "I used to think we should make these ships *fully* automatic. But what machine could have gotten us out of *that* mess."

"We aren't home yet," said Nevv dryly. He glanced at Mannin. "How many more breakpoints on this route?"

"Two in, three out," said Mannin.

Nevv considered that. If the Flats were planning a big seizure of space in this direction, and if—as now seemed clear—they had the route maps to Colony 6, no doubt the breakpoints ahead would swarm with warships. Messages would already be snapping back and forth through subspace, and even now, Flat technicians would be hastily setting up sensitive detectors by the thousands. Flat intelligence experts would be huddled over maps and grids, sending hurrying messengers with slips of paper to Flat calculating machines. Sooner or later, some Flat computer was going to flash its lights and unroll a string of symbols that boiled down to, "It's a bluff, probability such-and-such."

The thing to do, Nevv told himself, was to keep that probability from verging on certainty. He drew out a message form and wrote:

"T. S. F. *Prometheus* to T. S. F. V. F. I.: Breaking primary subradiation ban as per Directive Seven rpt Seven B rpt B. Obstacle passed. Advise not repeat not use Reserve Killer Groups this sector to cleanse obstacle-markers. Do repeat do suggest preparatory shift these groups in event unexpected exigency. Entire complement this ship volunteers bait duty at next mousehole.—D. R. Nevv, Colonel, Commanding."

Nevv handed the message to Hughes, and said, "Send it in the old code. If they've got Red Base, they've probably got the code books, too."

"What if they haven't?"

"We've got to take the chance. If we send it in clear, it will be an obvious fake."

Hughes nodded and went to get the old code book.

Mannin said, "I didn't want to trouble you with this before, but what do we have for a cargo?"

"About forty medium-sized crates. What's in them is none of our business."

Mannin scratched his head. "Well—Could you at least tell me if they were specially loaded on?"

"No, the same as usual. In a cargo web. Why do you ask?"

"Do you have a few minutes?"

Nevv scowled and studied his astrogator for a moment. He glanced at the chronometer and saw that he had three hours and twenty-seven minutes till the next breakpoint. "Sure. If it's important."

"It seems important. I don't know, but I think you ought to get a look at that cargo."

Hughes looked up from the code book, and Nevv told him where they were going.

* * *

The ship, aft of the control room, was a reminder of their desperate need for speed. The bulkheads had been cut out, leaving little but the structural frame of the ship. And in some places, where heavy internal loads had apparently been removed, only short thick stubs of beams remained.

Nevv, climbing down past the chopped-off beams, wondered uneasily if the ship had been pared a little too closely.

Mannin called back. "There. Take a look at that."

Nevv stopped and looked. Further to the rear, the cargo hung in its separate crates, each crate in its own net of strong ropework, each net held by ropes branching out like the spokes of a wheel to the heavy cables of the cargo web. The cargo web stretched across the axis of the ship from one side to the other, fastened by massive coiled springs to the ship's outermost structural frame. The idea was to cushion the effects of sudden shocks and shifts in acceleration. Nevv, holding to a heavy post, studied the cargo web from overhead. "Looks all right," he said.

Mannin shook his head. "Come closer," he called.

Nevv glanced at his watch, then climbed down ladders past a solitary spaceboat and several stripped-out floors of the ship till he stood beside Mannin on a little inspection platform near the empty center of the web. Then he saw it.

The web was bowed above them, like the arch of a low dome, or a sail stretching ahead in the wind.

Nevv glanced down at the platform. The ship's increasing forward motion held his feet against it. The web *should* be bowed slightly downward, toward the rear of the ship. Instead it arched upward toward the control room and the ship's nose.

"What have we got here?" said Mannin wryly. "Antigravity?"

Nevv shook his head. "I don't know. But I checked this after the first and third breakpoints. It was all right then."

"It isn't now."

Nevv dropped to his knees and opened a trapdoor in the floor of the platform. He climbed down a ladder with Mannin following closely, and walked out a narrow catwalk till it ended at the wall of the ship. He looked up. The massive coiled spring overhead was drawn well open.

Nevv looked at Mannin, and Mannin shrugged helplessly.

"Well," said Nevv, looking back up at the spring, "if we climb up there, maybe we can find out what's wrong." He turned to go up the steel ladder at the end of the catwalk, reached out for the first rung and stopped.

A track of sheared-off stubs ran up the wall where the ladder had been removed.

Nevv opened his mouth to say something, then cut himself off. He glanced at his watch. With a sensation of relief, he said, "I'm sorry, Phil. I've got to figure out what we're going to do when we hit the next breakpoint. I can't spare any more time for this."

Mannin shook his head. "I'm sorry, Dave. But as astrogator of this ship, I have to ask you to do something about it. It's throwing off my calculations."

Nevv stared up in frustration. "How long has it been like this?"

"This is the first I've seen it like *this*," said Mannin. "The last time I looked at it it was warped too far *down*. I had to go up, take a sight-fix, and reset the chronometer guide. Then when the Flats had us under their noses, the ship showed first a slight forward, then a slight backward movement, with *no power applied*. Next, we made the run through normal space in about four-fifths the time it should have taken us."

Nevv took out his handkerchief and passed it across his forehead. He was trying to think but he was aware that his mind was working as sluggishly as a ship that has gained headway in one direction, and now has to be slowed down, turned around, and started off on a new course. "Can't you take sight fixes and just feed in corrections to allow for this?"

"Yes," said Mannin dryly, "so long as this uncontrolled thrust happens to be applied along the ship's axis. But what am I supposed to do if it's suddenly applied at right angles? Or . . . say . . . circularly, to spin the ship? I don't have much experience plotting courses for a flying gyroscope."

Nevv stared up at the net for a moment, then looked at Mannin. "We've got to get up there somehow. Then maybe we can figure out what's wrong."

"That suits me," said Mannin. "How?"

"Follow me," growled Nevv.

★ ★ ★

They turned around and strode back along the catwalk till they reached the ladder to the inspection platform. From here, other catwalks branched out under the web.

Nevv glanced at Mannin. "You don't happen to have a flashlight, do you?"

"No," said Mannin.

"All right," said Nevv. "You take the first catwalk, and I'll take the second. If a ladder is still there at the end of yours, call out."

Mannin squinted down the catwalk, and shook his head in disgust. For the next five minutes, they strode up and down long branching catwalks that invariably ended in blank walls where ladders had been ripped out. They met at the center and peered around at the yet deeper gloom down below. Nevv shook his head, turned and climbed back up the inspection platform ladder with Mannin following close behind.

They climbed back up through several stripped levels, and Nevv made his way cautiously to the spaceboat, rotated it in its cradle, and glanced down. The boat was over a large empty cell in the cargo web. "Go relieve Hughes," said Nevv. "I think we can get down to the web in this thing, but Hughes is the best man to pilot it."

"You want me to stay in the control room?"

"Yes, just in case something else goes wrong."

Mannin climbed out of sight. Nevv leaned out with one hand on the spaceboat, and squinted down at the net. The net sprang down suddenly, and Nevv involuntarily rose on his toes with a feeling of lightness. He grabbed at the spaceboat, felt his weight come back and shoved hard away from the gap between flooring and boat.

The clang of a hatch overhead told of Hughes starting down the ladder.

Nevv told Hughes what he wanted, and the pilot glanced down at the net. "Well," he said, "these boats are built for maneuverability, but with the bulkheads out, we'll pollute the whole atmosphere down here." He glanced around. "It looks to me like they tore out most of the recirculators. This is practically stagnant air. If we pollute it, we'll have to put on spacesuits to work down here."

Nevv nodded thoughtfully and glanced down at the net. He crossed to the spaceboat and found in the emergency kit a big coil of half-inch rope, a flashlight, a claw hammer, and a hatchet. He handed hammer and hatchet to Hughes, who followed him down the ladder.

Nevv crawled out on a beam over the net. The beam crossed directly above one of the catwalks that branched out down under the net. Nevv lowered the rope down through the net, till it reached the catwalk. Then he made a series of hitches around the beam, tested the rope, gripped it with one hand, gripped the beam with the other, slid his feet down, and barely made it from the beam to the rope; then he slid slowly down in stages, the rope wound around one leg and clamped by his feet. When he reached the net, he crawled out onto a crate. He looked up and saw Hughes, pasty-faced, embracing the beam overhead. Nevv studied the crate, then called out, "Tie the hatchet and hammer on the other end of that rope and send them down. Be sure that rope doesn't slip."

Hughes lowered the rope, and Nevv chopped away part of the knotty net holding the crate. The crate itself turned out to be made of stiff splintery wood closely fitted together. Nevv pried at it uselessly with the hammer, then enlarged the gap in the net and chopped a hole in one edge of the crate. He pulled back the boards and shone the flashlight through the hole, stripped back a stiff wrapping, and saw a dark green, crackle-finished cylindrical surface. He pulled away more wrappings and saw on top part of what appeared to be a control panel. A corner of white caught his eye.

Mannin's voice echoed down from above. "I need Hughes up here. We've got to make a course correction."

Nevv twisted around to look up at Hughes.

"Go ahead. I think I've got everything I need."

* * *

Hughes inched cautiously back along the beam, and

Nevv took hold of the white corner of paper and pulled it out. It was a thick instruction manual, stamped "Deadly Secret—P. M. Corp, Propulsion Unit."

Nevv looked at the manual with considerable awe. "Deadly Secret" was a classification he had never even heard of. He listened as Hughes started up the ladder, then knelt carefully on the crate. He suffered a brief pang of conscience for looking at such exalted material without proper clearance, then opened it up. He flipped through it with one hand, shining the flashlight over a large number of electronic diagrams and technically-worded descriptions. He paused on a page headed "Operating Instructions." He read:

"Due to the unconventional character of the equipment, considerable care and patience may be required before perfectly satisfactory results are obtained. It is advisable to carry out initial practice and testing using only Pilot Sub-Circuit A."

Overhead, a hatch slammed shut.

Nevv read on:

"This is highly important.

"Pilot Sub-Circuit A will reproduce perfectly the phenomena to be anticipated from activation of the Main Drive Circuits; but the average continuous energy release will be of the order of 10^{-9} that of the Main Drive Circuits.

"As the underlying nature of the phenomena involved is not perfectly understood, great care must be exercised until such time as the characteristic action produced by Pilot Sub-Circuit A is perfectly responsive and reliable."

Nevv frowned over the last sentence, flipped toward

the back of the manual, and suddenly experienced pressure like that of a high-speed elevator starting upward. He jammed the manual in his pocket, grabbed for support, and felt the whole cargo web balloon under him, almost flinging him loose. The crate he clung to shifted around and strained up against the weakened net.

Nevv let go and grabbed his rope.

The crate abruptly yanked away, and the whole web snapped downward like the inside of a bowl.

The rope quivered and dropped about a foot, and Nevv suddenly became aware that what he had hold of was the relatively short length Hughes had lowered. Holding his breath, Nevv swung gently out, then back, and managed to grab and swing to the other rope. He looked down. The net suddenly ballooned up again, almost touching his feet. Then the net sprang down and up and fell part way again so it was flat.

Overhead, a hatch clanged open. Hughes' voice called down, "You O.K. down there, Dave?"

Nevv ran his tongue around the dry inside of his mouth, studied the motionless net for a moment, then slid quickly down the rope. He landed on the catwalk with the feeling that all his life would be anti-climax after this.

Then he remembered what was waiting for him at the next breakpoint.

"Dave!" called Hughes' voice. There was a clattering on the ladder.

Nevv took a deep breath, managed to clear his throat, then called out, "I'm O.K."

Then he felt in his pocket for the manual, and started up the ladder to the control room.

★ ★ ★

At the next breakpoint, Nevv found himself looking at an even more broad-shouldered individual, with an even wider head and neck, with four red tufts on his yellow sash, a head of grizzled hair, and small crafty eyes that looked at Nevv as if each and every little cell of Nevv's brain was wide-open to view. This officer fixed Nevv with his eyes, said nothing, and looked at Nevv with a perfectly expressionless, waiting face.

Nevv said, "T. S. F. *Prometheus* requests immediate permission to proceed."

The officer on the screen appeared to move his head the tiniest fraction of an inch.

"Thank you, sir," said Nevv courteously.

The officer made no reply.

Nevv put his hand on the firing switch for nose turret ten. Keeping his eyes focused on the Flat's eyes, he said, "Course green, colonel."

"Yes, sir," said Hughes.

The Flat officer kept his gaze unwaveringly on Nevv's eyes, and Nevv in turn kept his eyes focused hard on the Flat's eyes. It took nineteen minutes to reach the next breakpoint, and in this time neither Nevv nor the Flat blinked once. By the time the Flat vanished from the screen, Nevv felt as if his eyes were coated with dust.

Mannin cleared his throat.

Nevv, massaging his eyelids with his fingertips, turned to see Mannin pull his head out of the astrogator's globe. Mannin's face looked unusually sober and thoughtful.

"Did I miss something?" asked Nevv.

"Nothing worth thinking about," said Mannin.

"What?" said Nevv.

"When we came out, the foreground was loaded with red and orange markers."

"Yes?"

"As we went on, the markers blinked out one-by-one. It looks to me as if they were sending a whole fleet into subspace to backcheck."

Nevv glanced at the chronometer. It showed twelve hours fifty-two minutes till the next breakpoint. He pulled out a message blank and wrote:

"T. S. F. *Prometheus* to T. S. F. V. F. I.: Per Directive Seven rpt Seven B rpt B. Second obstacle passed without incident. However, spacing of obstacles this route appears highly significant. Sending visual records this encounter via sub-sub code eight-bee-eight repeat eight-bee-eight. Phasing out one-zero-six repeat out one-zero-six. Request alternatives. Suggest reply spaced silences before phase in. —D.·R. Nevv, Colonel, Commanding."

Hughes shoved up the pilot globe, and Nevv handed him the message. "Send it in the old code."

Hughes nodded.

"Oh," said Nevv, "one more thing. How does the ship seem to handle?"

"Fine," said Hughes. "I don't know whether it's because she's stripped-down or what. But I have the feeling I could pilot her into springing somersaults if I tried."

"That's nice," said Nevv. He turned to Mannin, who was looking sharply at Hughes, and said, "Let's go below for a minute."

Mannin stepped to the hatch, glanced at the pressure dial by the door, looked back hard at Hughes and went out.

★ ★ ★

They climbed down past stripped-out levels to the cargo web inspection platform. The web dipped slightly around them.

Mannin and Nevv looked at each other, then glanced up toward the control room. They waited.

Abruptly the web sprang up like a dome.

Nevv started back up the ladder with Mannin right behind him. They went into the control room.

Hughes was in the pilot globe, his hands on the manual controls.

Nevv and Mannin looked at each other, then climbed back down again. They looked up from the inspection platform.

The web was bowed far up overhead.

Nevv took a deep breath. "What will that do to your calculations?"

Mannin said heavily, "Well, it's along the ship's axis. I may have to take sight-readings till I'm blue in the face. But just as long as it's in line with the rest of the thrust." He glanced up toward the control room. "Just so long as the ship doesn't start—springing somersaults."

Nevv glanced at his watch. "Let's see what time you've got. Here, let's set them both the same. O.K."

"Now what?"

"Go up and pry Hughes out of the pilot globe. Ask him if he can try some trial accelerations and decelerations later on. And glance at your watch to see just when he comes out of the globe."

Mannin nodded and started back up the ladder.

Nevv looked soberly up at the ballooning net, pulled up

the trapdoor and climbed down onto the catwalk. He strode to the end of the catwalk, and looked up at the massive spring. Its heavy coils were pulled considerably farther apart than before. Nevv walked back and started up the ladder. Part way to the platform, the net suddenly dropped back and hung with a shallow dip. At the same moment, Nevv felt lighter.

Nevv glanced at his watch.

The hatch clanged far above. There was a sound of shoes against metal, then a pause, more sounds, and another, lighter sound of the hatch.

The cargo net sprang upward. Nevv clenched his teeth, braced himself as his weight increased. He glanced again at his watch. He fished a pencil from his pocket, located a scrap of paper in his wallet, and marked down the times when the web had moved.

Overhead, the hatch shut. There was a faint scuff and rattle of descending feet. Mannin came down with a pencil stuck over one ear, and handed Nevv a message blank. "There's the time he got out from under the globe. I asked him if he could do some trial accelerations and decelerations. He said, 'Sure.' I started down, then sneaked back up and watched him settle the globe in place. That's the second figure."

Nevv compared these figures with his own. Within a margin of a few seconds, they coincided.

Nevv glanced at Mannin. "Can you work out a test series that won't throw us too much off schedule? One you can correct for easily?"

"I think so."

"Don't make it too drastic. I want to watch it from here, and I don't want to be thrown out through the hull."

Mannin nodded, looked hard at the net, and started up the ladder.

"Wait a minute," said Nevv suddenly. "Help me get that rope first."

The two of them retrieved the rope Nevv had climbed down on to the cargo net, then Mannin went on up to the control room. Nevv roped himself flat on his back on the inspection platform. He lay still, warily watching the cargo.

★ ★ ★

The web began to inch yet higher. Nevv felt himself pressed harder against the floor of the platform. The heavy cables of the cargo web creaked.

Abruptly the web dropped down. The platform fell away from Nevv's back and the ropes bit into his chest, midsection and thighs.

The web sprang up again. Nevv was pressed hard against the floor.

Nevv lay still and rose up, watching the web alternately spring high above, then fall far out of sight. Eventually the hatch clanged, and Mannin came down the ladder. He helped Nevv up. "Did you find out anything?"

"Just that we've got the first pilot in history to fly the ship by means of the cargo. How did the tests work out?"

"Well, the ship's initial acceleration was about thirty per cent above normal. The deceleration was fifty-one per cent above normal the first try, and inched up to about fifty-eight per cent above the last try."

Nevv frowned, glanced at the net, and started up the ladder. They entered the control room, shut the hatch, and looked at Hughes, his head in the pilot globe. Nevv got out the "Deadly Secret — P. M. Corp. Propulsion Unit" instruction manual. Nevv and Mannin huddled over it intently.

They went through it once rapidly, skimming quickly over bristling tracts of terminology, and pausing to study circuit diagrams and detailed drawings of the unit's exterior. Then they went back over it again and forced their way through the tougher parts like men chopping thick under-growth with machetes. At the end, they looked at each other blankly.

"Well," said Nevv, "let's try it again." His mind swum with sentences like: "In the following Tentative Operating Instructions, a number at the beginning of a paragraph refers to a dashed arrow in figure III b at the top of page six herein, except where Experimental Models X-2a or X-2b are under consideration, in which case the aforesaid number refers to a dotted arrow in figure IVa at the bottom of page one of Supplemental Leaf 6a, unless otherwise stipulated elsewhere."

Mannin suddenly got up and said, "I've got to take a sight fix. You see what you can make of it."

★ ★ ★

Nevv looked up to see Mannin start across the room with an expression of relief. Nevv looked at the manual with exasperation, then began leafing through it slowly. When Mannin came back, Nevv was reading one part over and over.

"Find anything?" said Mannin hopefully.

"I don't know," said Nevv. "Look at this." Mannin bent beside him and they read:

"The controls of the Propulsion Unit are unusually

simple, and, after sufficient skill has been acquired, may often be operated with a minimally light touch. It is highly important for the unpracticed operator to have clearly in mind a precise mental image of the action the Propulsion Unit is intended to perform. It is at first necessary that this correct mental picture be thoroughly understood and borne in mind to obtain the maximal level of performance consistent with the operator's skill and personal qualifications."

"Hm-m-m," said Mannin. He glanced over at Hughes with his head in the pilot globe. He looked down again at the manual. "'Minimally light touch,'" he quoted.

Nevv followed Mannin's gaze to Hughes, then thought of the cargo web alternately billowing up and sagging down as Hughes' mind concentrated on accelerating or decelerating the ship. "It's an uncanny idea," he said.

"It sure is," said Mannin.

"Still," said Nevv, certain possibilities beginning to occur to him, "if it *does* work that way—"

"Yeah," said Mannin, nodding agreement.

"Pry Hughes loose from that globe," said Nevv, and looked back at the manual. Again he read the paragraph.

Hughes came over and grinned. "What a ship. We should strip them all down."

Nevv and Mannin explained to him about the cargo, then Nevv said, "It seems to me that by the time we come out the next breakpoint, the Flats will have spent thousands of man-hours convincing themselves we've fooled them. They'll be in no mood to be bluffed all over again. What we need is something completely unexpected—"

Hughes, perspiring uneasily, said, "Wait a minute, Dave. Are you trying to tell me the ship goes even faster when I think it will go faster, and slows down more when I think it will slow down, *just because I think it?*"

"Well, in effect, with this cargo—"

"What happens if I can't convince myself? I mean, this whole idea is pretty fantastic, but just suppose—"

Nevv glanced up at the chronometer and felt a fine perspiration forming on his brow. He leaned back and forced a bleak smile.

Mannin said earnestly to Hughes, "You just did it. It should be no trouble at all to do it again." He added, "If we're going to get an edge on the Flats, you've *got* to do it again."

"Yeah," said Hughes, "I did it unconsciously. How do I know—"

"Look" said Mannin determinedly, "We've *got* to get this stuff through to the Colony. To say nothing of our own skins."

Nevv forcibly relaxed his suddenly tensed muscles and tried to ease his mind away from the problem for a moment.

Hughes said, "On *faith*, you want me to do it. O.K., I'll try—"

Nevv thought that now that it was too late he could see it plainly enough from Hughes' point of view. Show a man a twenty-foot hurdle over a pit of snakes and say to him, "If you believe, our device here will get you across safely. But if you *don't* believe—well . . . But, on the other hand, you must get across. You've *got* to, because—"

Hughes was starting to turn away. Nevv could see

Mannin's tenseness, and a sort of angry resentment on Hughes' part.

Nevv said, "Wait a minute. I think we've got all the parts of the puzzle, but we're trying to jam a couple parts together that won't fit."

Hughes said, "I'll fly . . . or try to fly . . . any ship made that runs by controls. But you stick me in an empty cubicle and tell me to *think* I'm flying, and I don't promise you anything at all."

Mannin said, "We saw it. You've done it already! You can't say you can't do what you have done."

Nevv took a deep breath. "Well," he said quickly, "what we've got to remember, of course, is that what we're talking about is only the supplemental part of the thrust. The main drive of the ship, of course, supplies most of the thrust, and that isn't affected at all by what we're talking about."

"No?" said Hughes. "Suppose I should try for maximum thrust from the ship, and then it should occur to me to think about going slower? Then what?"

"Holy—" began Mannin, his voice grating.

Nevv could now clearly feel the perspiration on his forehead. He glanced unhappily at the chronometer, thought a fervent prayer, then launched back into the conversation. "Splendid! That would be wonderful! You'd cut the forward motion while the radiation from the drive units remained constant. The idea is to throw off the Flat gunnery computers. Practically any unpredictable action will do."

Hughes looked a little dazed. "Wait a minute—"

Mannin started to say something, then cut himself off.

"Now," said Nevv firmly, "the control factor you have to use at first is precise visualization—"

"How could that affect the cargo?" Hughes demanded.

Nevv looked surprised. "Through the resonant q-wave receiver in the unit's control circuit, of course. Didn't we explain that?"

"No, you didn't. What in space is a resonant q-wave receiver? And who thought that up?"

"It's all here," said Nevv, tossing across the manual. "You read that, and you'll know as much about it as we do."

Hughes scowled and picked up the manual. He started to read it, then flipped back through it slowly. His face began to relax. "Well," he said, handing the manual back to Nevv, "that looks scientific enough. What's all this business about doing it on faith?"

Mannin made a choking sound, and Nevv said quickly, "If we said that, we just expressed it badly. The correct procedure is the visualization, with the regenerative action of the pilot globe coupling the q-output to the q-wave receivers in the Propulsion Unit control circuit. You look at diagram VIII b, there, I think it is . . . about the middle of the book."

Hughes reached out, then yanked his hand back. "What do I want all that stuff for? I'm a pilot, not an electronics technician. What I want to know is, what do I *do*?"

"Well, you visualize the action desired. The q-waves, transmitted by the—"

"Hold on," said Hughes irritably. "I don't want to go through all that. All *I* do is to visualize it, is that right?"

"That's it," said Nevv.

"Then," said Hughes tentatively, "the q-radiations activate the control circuit. But I don't have to worry about that. All *I* have to do is visualize it. Correct?"

"Absolutely," said Nevv.

"O.K." Hughes looked thoughtful. "Listen, what if I visualize a sudden rotary motion?"

Nevv felt that he had to say something. "My understanding," he said, "is that the Propulsion Unit is perfectly multi-directional." He was about to add some vague qualification when Mannin cut in hotly.

"Listen," said Mannin, "I can plot a course for a spaceship, but I'm not checked out on spinning tops."

"Never mind about that," said Hughes. "You just wait till we come out in normal space, and lay down your course as usual. Leave the rest to me." He started back across the control room, then stopped. "I'm going to get in a little practice, then get some rest. You guys scared me for a minute. I thought I was supposed to work some kind of hoodoo."

"It's all right there in the manual," said Nevv, feeling a little weak.

* * *

Mannin, Nevv, and Hughes, all got at least a little fitful sleep before the next breakpoint arrived. When it did come, and Nevv's eyes adjusted to the blaze of white pinpoints against deep black, there was a space of perhaps two seconds when Nevv thought they might possibly have no trouble, this time, at least.

Then the glaring markers began to spring into place. Hughes' voice began to drone. "Near right background high, near right background low, near right foreground high—three of them, near right foreground low—"

A single green line hung in front of Nevv's eyes. Mannin said, "Just one route this time."

" . . .far left foreground high—two of them, far left foreground low, near left foreground high—one, two, three, four, five—" His voice cut off abruptly. "The place is full of them."

The short purple line marking the backtrack appeared before Nevv. He pushed up the command globe. Before him, the screen flared and lit to show a huge, broad-shouldered officer whose yellow sash bore tufts of red from one end to the other. In the clusters at his shoulders, each gold spike bore at its tip its own cluster of long shiny gold needles. Nevv's eyes rose from the tufted sash to the immense shoulders, broad neck and wide head. The officer was white-haired, with his eyes fixed thoughtfully on Nevv's, and something approaching a compassionate expression on his face. He shook his head ever so slightly as he watched Nevv. "Very clever, my boy," he said, "but of course you were bound to be stopped sooner or later. The odds were far too great. Don't move your ship now."

Nevv reached out for the firing console.

The Flat's pitying expression was having a worse effect on his morale than anything before, and he had a little trouble keeping his face expressionless.

The Flat said quietly, "Don't give us the Vengeance Fleet business, now. We know better."

Hughes hissed, "Shall I let him have it?"

Nevv said mechanically, "Sir, I am aware now that for

some reason you doubt the word of a Terran officer. I am astonished."

The Flat smiled. "No doubt your 'honor' is touched. I must tell you, colonel, that our sense of boggleglobble is similarly affected by your whole story. Moreover, all this chasing around has had a bad effect on our budget."

"I am very sorry, sir," said Nevv, grimly holding to his story. "The apparent lack of belief of your subordinate officers has been conveyed to my superiors."

"Who are still in subspace?"

"I cannot disclose their whereabouts—"

"*We* can't find them anywhere."

"Sir, secrecy was one of the prime considerations when this force was readied for action."

"It must have been. How is it that *you* turn up again every time we look around?"

Nevv had a sensation of blood rushing to his head.

Hughes' voice said, "*Ahh.*"

Nevv said quickly, "Sir, further secrecy on my part would be pointless. The mission of *Prometheus* has now become, first, to determine by your actions whether any collusion exists between your people and the miserable vermin who have insulted out flag." The whole foreground was acquiring a pinkish tinge. The Flat's huge form began blinking on-and-off on the screen. "And, second," said Nevv, "to warn you by primarily defensive maneuvers of exactly the sort of unknown factors you are now up against."

The whole ship sprang forward, ramming Nevv far back in the acceleration couch and choking the breath out of him. There was a high, squeaking screech, and his

insides seemed to twist sidewise and up. A nauseous sense
of being wrenched two ways at once gripped him, and he
was swallowed in a rush of blackness. His last dwindling
sensations were of a heavy crash and an abrupt silence.

★ ★ ★

Nevv came to with the impression that he was strapped
to the arm of a big clock, and the arm was swinging
around and around. He heard Hughes say, "This control
room is just a trifle more off-center that I thought it was."

. Mannin, speaking in gasps like an exhausted runner,
said, "I've always had . . . good feeling towards you,
Hughes . . . but just exactly what . . . did you do just then?"

"Spun the ship like a gyro," said Hughes proudly,
"jammed on full forward acceleration, then gave her
everything I had to jerk the tail sidewise and around in a
new direction. She really jumped, and then I improvised
a little." He chortled. "They never came near us."

Nevv opened his eyes painfully. His head was throbbing
and he felt sick and weak. His mind went in feeble circles
grappling with Hughes' maneuver: If the ship were spinning
clockwise, and its long axis was suddenly swung in the arc
of a circle—Well, the ship might be considered a uniform
hollow cylinder—Wait, what about the armor belt?
Consider the simplified case of a short cylinder—

Suddenly Nevv came wide awake. He spoke and heard
only a hoarse whisper. He swallowed hard, took a deep
breath, and managed to say, "Where are we?"

"Subspace," said Hughes triumphantly. "I whipped her
back on course and slammed her though right at the
breakpoint."

Mannin said, "Spinning?"

"Yes, pretty hard," said Hughes. "Why?"

"It seems to me"—Mannin paused, and Nevv heard him take a breath—"the spin would induce an electromagnetic field—What that would do in subspace, I don't know."

"Well," said Hughes, "anyway, we're here. *Boy* what a ship!"

"Sure," said Mannin feebly. "But where is here?"

Nevv unbuckled himself from the acceleration couch and looked dizzily around. "Phil," he said, "if you can manage it, take a sight fix, will you?" He turned to Hughes. "I haven't figured out what you did yet, but I'm glad we're still alive." He remembered hearing the crash, and wondered if anything had broken loose. "How's she handling?" he said.

"Beautiful," said Hughes.

Nevv decided he had better take a look anyway, and walked carefully to the hatch. He hauled back on it and nothing happened. Nevv thought that he must be weaker than he had imagined and gave a hard tug. The hatch remained as solid as a section of wall.

Mannin said sourly, "To be perfectly honest, I don't see anything here I can identify."

Nevv put one foot on the wall, both hands on the hatch handle, and heaved back with all his strength. His arms felt like they were pulling loose at the shoulder joints, but aside from that, nothing moved.

The communications receiver went *ping*, and Hughes said soberly, "I'll get it."

Mannin said, "If we stop right where we are and cast around, I think there's about a twenty per cent chance we can find out where we are. It may take us a week to do it."

Nevv gave a little yank on the hatch, then stepped back. His gaze chanced to fall on the air pressure gauge by the door. The black pointer of the pressure gauge was resting on its pin, its point at the zero mark.

Hughes said, "This message is in the old code."

Nevv growled, "Unscramble it." He whacked the pressure gauge with his hand. The pointer didn't move. He turned around, walked over and picked up the microphone. "Men," he said. No answering boom came from the direction of the crew's quarters. Nevv hit the "Prepare" bar on the firing console, felt a faint vibration in the deck underfoot, but heard none of the jarring clatter of the Battle Station's gong. Plainly, there was no air back there to conduct the sound. He walked back to the hatch and pushed the emergency air-lock button. A little warning light lit up red, there was a hiss, and Nevv waited for the light to turn green. The hiss ceased, but the light remained red.

Mannin said, "That just could be Sclythes VI over there, and if so, it will take us at least an hour-and-a-half to get back on course."

Hughes said in an unhappy voice, "I've got the message decoded."

"Let's hear it," said Nevv grimly.

"Supreme High Command to All Ships in Volume Twelve," read Hughes, "Relay the following: To Terran ship T. S. F. Dreadnought *Prometheus*: Kindly return to pick up upper segment your fuel feed mechanism, one Mark XII oversize coil spring, and large quantity unnamed small parts and pieces recovered by our salvage detectors. —Cordially, Sasram Vannaf, Supreme High Admiral, Commanding."

Mannin said, "On closer observation, that couldn't possibly be Sclythes VI."

Hughes started for the hatch. "If that really *was* the upper segment of the feed mechanism, we're in an awful mess."

Mannin pulled his head out of the astrogator's globe, snapped a little spool in the viewer, and said, "If it doesn't turn out to be Epinax or Castris, we might as well start saying the last rites now." After a moment, he added, "It isn't Castris."

Hughes tugged at the door.

"No use," said Nevv, "the air out there is gone. We've got atmospheric pressure at about one ton to the square foot on this side holding it shut."

Hughes stepped back, looked at the air-pressure gauge, whacked it a couple of times with this hand, then shook his head wearily.

Nevv said, "Send this in the old code. 'T. S. F. *Prometheus* to T. S. F. V. F. I.: Your assumption correct. Will comply.—D. R. Nevv, Colonel, Commanding.'"

Hughes nodded.

Mannin said, "Well, maybe we'll make it yet. That's Epinax, and it's going to cost us a five-hour delay."

In a low voice, Hughes said, "If we've lost the upper segment of the fuel feed, we can't afford *any* delay. The only fuel we've got left in that feed is on the lower parts of the mechanism."

Nevv said, "What about the reserve?"

"We'd have to lock it in place manually. And I'm not sure the reserve fuel isn't one of the things they stripped out to save weight."

Nevv looked at the emergency air lock with a sudden unpleasant thought. "Did anyone happen to notice if we've still got the air lock here?"

Mannin said, "We've got the base and the hinges. I noticed that the last time I came in. The lock door itself is stripped out."

Nevv felt as if he had been hit in the pit of the stomach.

The communications receiver went *ping*.

Hughes trudged over to it. After a moment, he said, "This is in the new code."

"Decode it," said Nevv.

Mannin said, "Did somebody say something about the air being gone from the aft section?"

"Yes," said Nevv. "We apparently lost the upper segment of the fuel feed right through the outer wall the last time we got away from the Flats. With all the bulkheads stripped out, the air just went out through the hole."

"Oh . . . Oh," said Mannin. "Well, there's at least one spacesuit in the emergency locker there."

"That's good," said Nevv, "but the point is, this hatch opens *in*. There's no air pressure on the other side. On this side, there's normal pressure of about 14.6 pounds to the square inch. That's around a ton to the square foot. You'd need a man with an iron arm to haul that hatch open. Once it was open, the air in here would blow out into the aft section and diffuse into outer space. If we weren't in spacesuits, that would be the end of us. If we were in spacesuits, the air supply wouldn't last forever, to say nothing of trying to run the ship from the inside of one of those things."

Mannin exhaled sharply, turned around, opened a square cabinet and pulled out a thick volume.

Hughes said wearily, "I've got the message, Dave."

"Let's hear it."

"'Blue Base Colony six rpt Six to T. S. F. *Prometheus*: Under heavy attack. Need help badly. Your messages intercepted here. At first dismissed as Flat hoax, but that not comprehensible. If you have force available as indicated, urgently request your aid. Please advise at once. Use latest code delivered by courier. Red Base is captured and old code with it. - T. B. Smith, Lieut, col., Commanding.'" Hughes looked up. "That was all in the new code except the sentence, 'Use latest code delivered by courier.' That was in clear."

Nevv nodded slowly, and turned to Mannin. "Did you notice about the reserve fuel supply?"

Mannin looked up with one finger holding his place in the book, "I think it was there, Dave. When I was helping you get the rope hauled up, I noticed something bulky overhead in about the right place for it."

Nevv said to Hughes, "How long will the normal fuel supply last, exclusive of that in the upper segment?"

Hughes glanced at the chronometer. "It might just last to the next breakpoint—If we don't have to detour."

Mannin said, "We've *got* to detour."

"Is that," said Hughes, "actually going to take us five hours?"

"Yes, it is."

"We can't do it," said Hughes. "We just don't have enough fuel. Unless the Flat was bluffing."

"We can't assume he was bluffing," said Nevv. "I don't see how he could have guessed that the control room air lock had the door stripped off. And that's all that keeps us from just going back and checking." Nevv frowned. "Is there any way to get the reserve fuel to the feed mechanism?"

"Only by taking it out and locking it on manually. We can't do that without first getting out of the control room."

"Well—" Nevv turned to Mannin. "Is there an earth-type planet listed that we can reach from here?"

"Two," said Mannin. "If we break out of subspace in forty minutes, we can reach Blackwall III, an Earth-type planet with an aggressive alien mechanized culture. If we break out in a little over two hours, we can reach an unnamed Earth-type planet with a nomadic humanoid culture. And that's all there is, unless we want to wait half-a-day more."

"What's the humanoid planet like?"

"It was surveyed about a hundred and sixty years ago. Quite a load of exotic diseases, but I think we've got the shots for them in the emergency kit. The language of the most advanced race is on file in the General Hypnoculture Index. The planet's code is 'D'—suitable for emergency landing for minor repairs. It says here the local food is edible; but then a man can starve while he figures out whether the bark, bud, root, leaf, or fruit is what he's supposed to eat."

"I hope," said Nevv, "we don't stay there that long. All we want is to raise the air pressure in the aft part of the ship, get this air lock open, and put the reserve fuel in the feed mechanism."

"Well," said Mannin, "it looks like we ought to be able to do that, all right."

"Good, then plot a course to it." Nevv turned to

Hughes. "Is there anything you know of that could delay us once we get *that* done?"

"No," said Hughes.

"All right." Nevv took a message blank and wrote:

"T. S. F. *Prometheus* to Blue Base Colony Six rpt Six: Am instructed to inform you Reserve Killer Group One rpt One, Reserve Killer Group Two rpt Two, Reserve Killer Group Three rpt Three now being detached to destroy enemy forces operating against you. Projected time of arrival: eighty-four hours following code-date this message. You are instructed hold out with all possible grip and tenacity. Vital situation hinges on you. —D. R. Nevv, Colonel, Commanding."

Hughes took the message, looked at it, swallowed, looked at Nevv and said, "What code?"

"The new code."

"Yes, sir." Hughes bent over the code book.

Mannin said, "I've got the course plotted. It'll take us one hour and fifty-seven minutes to get to breakpoint. Landing on the planet should be a perfectly routine matter. That leaves me personally nothing to do for over two hours. Just as a safety precaution, I wonder if I should go under hypnoculture and learn the local language."

"We'd both better," said Nevv.

Hughes looked up. "Shall I?"

"If you think you can trust the automatics."

Mannin said, "What about shots? We're bound to be exposed, and a good high fever could put the lot of us out of action for a week."

"We'll have to take the shots in turn," said Nevv. "I'll take them first so we can see what their effect is."

Mannin nodded, grinned suddenly, and hauled out the bulky medical emergency kit. As Nevv looked on, Mannin opened the kit, took out a thing like a needle-snouted machine pistol, went over and got the manual, glanced alternately at it and the kit, and began clipping small vials into a magazine that slid into the grip of the gun. As if to himself, he murmured, "Let's see, paratyphoid outvar. gamma six, contagious prothrombinopinex, graymold fever, toxic enteromycosis, chronic infectious hypoxemia, stumprot, nicterine hypsophobis, osnithosis outvar. beta three—" He stood up, holding the gun. In a businesslike manner, he said, "All right, remove your shirt." He gave a routine-looking smile. "This won't hurt a bit." He swabbed Nevv's arm, and swung up the bulky, needle-tipped pistol.

Nevv felt his arm go numb. He turned so that his eyes were straight ahead. "This is no time to start unfolding your latent talents," he said grimly.

"Stand still there," said Mannin. There was a *thug* sound, then another, and another, *thug, thug, thug.*

Nevv felt a wave of heat, a sudden chill, and an overpowering dizziness. He felt hands steady him, he tried to catch his balance, then everything went black.

Nevv gradually became aware of a lazy swirling dizziness, and a ringing in his ears. He drifted a little further awake, and realized that his mouth felt dry and his head felt hot. He tried to sit up, and felt so faint that he had to lie down again. He lay still for a long time. Eventually, he opened his eyes and looked up. It took him a moment to focus his eyes. Then, very carefully, he swung his feet to the floor and stood up.

Mannin and Hughes were both stretched out unconscious. The gun lay on the floor at Hughes' side.

Nevv stepped to the hatch and glanced at the pressure dial. It read "14.2" The pressure in the aft part of the ship was almost normal. Nevv walked back across the control room, and pulled down the command globe. A scene appeared of brown grassland, low distant hills, and small clumps of trees and brush. Far away, what looked like a wispy column of smoke drifted skyward.

Nevv pushed up the globe and glanced around the control room. The thought came to him that he could switch the reserve fuel to the fuel feed mechanism while Hughes and Mannin were still unconscious. But he wasn't sure just how the immunization injections would affect either of them, and he still felt weak himself. He decided to stay, get out the hypnoculture records and learn the local language.

Mannin came to before Hughes, and sat up with his brow knotted, his eyes tightly shut, and his lips drawn away from his teeth. He made a gagging sound, and Nevv said, "Water?"

"No, I'll be all right." Mannin opened his eyes, gradually uncrossed them, put a hand to his head and carefully got up. "How's Hughes?"

"Still out."

"I must have passed out on him. He gave me the shots, and I was going to give them to him. Did you see we'd landed?"

"Yeah. I've been learning the language. Not that we should ever need it."

Hughes groaned. Nevv turned around, and saw Hughes open his eyes and carefully sit up. "O.K.?" asked Nevv.

"Yeah, I think so," said Hughes. "Boy, I dreamt the Flats had me."

Mannin said, "Let's hope that doesn't happen."

Nevv walked to the hatch and back. He felt reasonably strong. "Have we tested the air?"

"The analysis equipment," said Hughes disgustedly, "was apparently stripped out."

Nevv turned to Mannin. "How was it a hundred and sixty years ago when the survey was made?"

"Fine. A trifle high on oxygen, but that's no problem." Mannin got to his feet, and walked carefully around the room, and Hughes did slow cautious knee-bends and gentle loosening-up exercises.

★ ★ ★

Nevv went to the hatch, and checked the pressure gauge. He pulled back on the hatch. The hatch opened, and Nevv felt as if a miracle had happened. He started down the ladder, with the others following. He paused at the level just above the cargo net and looked up. There, well out of reach and heavily braced in place, was a bulky, solid-looking case marked in red:

**CAUTION
EMERGENCY
FUEL**

There might once have been some natural way to approach this case, but none was visible now.

Mannin growled, "A ship like this needs a crew of man-sized spiders to run it properly."

Nevv could think of nothing to say at all, and Hughes

let out a snort of disgust. "Let's check the feed mechanism first."

★ ★ ★

They climbed down the ladder, paused at the inspection platform to look at the cargo web, sagging slightly out-of-shape, then climbed on down to the catwalk. In the wall to the side, above them, was torn a sizable hole, with the blue of the sky outside showing through.

"That," said Mannin, "looks like where the spring went through."

Nevv leaned over the side of the walk and stared into the gloom below. To one side was a very large, jagged-edged hole through which light shone onto the floor below. For a fleeting instant, it looked to Nevv as if the shape of the hole, and the light on the floor, shifted and changed. He blinked his eyes, and watched. Through the hole, he could see the brown of the grassland outside.

Hughes said, "There's a trapdoor in the floor here somewhere."

"Sure," said Mannin. "But is there still a ladder?"

There was a rusty creaking as the trapdoor came open, "Don't feel any—Wait. Yes, here it is."

"Be careful," said Mannin. "You can't tell. They may have sawed it off halfway down to save weight."

Nevv said, "Hold on a minute. Do we have a flashlight? Shut that trapdoor a minute."

Mannin said, "What's wrong?"

"I don't know if anything's wrong. But if we can get a strong flashlight, we can look down there first without having to go down. What happened to the one I had? Did I bring it up to the control room?"

"I don't know," said Mannin. "I'm surprised there was a flashlight on the ship."

Hughes said, "I don't mind going down, Dave. We might just as well find out since we're here."

Nevv's eyes were gradually becoming accustomed to the dark. It seemed to him he saw a faint movement on the floor at Hughes' feet. Nevv bent forward.

A vague shape, light and fast, swung up at Nevv's side. The catwalk swayed underfoot and Nevv's neck was clamped in a grip like a vise.

"Look out!" yelled Hughes.

There was a solid *crunch*, and a sudden silence.

A low, almost whispering voice spoke in Nevv's ear. "Glawarmish, *Vilna*." The words resolved themselves into, "Welcome, *Friend*." "Friend," was spoken in a cold, ironical tone.

From below came a soft voice. "Destra vilna sosso hottig." Nevv heard it partly as a foreign tongue, and partly as its meaning: "Bring the dear friends down here."

The next time the voice spoke from below, Nevv was scarcely aware at all of the unfamiliar words. This time the voice said, "Two of you sneak up there, and see if there are any more of them at the top."

There was a very faint sound on the ladder, going rapidly up. A second followed.

Nevv considered the chances if he were to bring his heel down hard on the instep of whoever had him from behind. There were already two up near the control room. But if he could get the spaceboat—

While Nevv was making his decision, a rope tightened around his hands, a cloth dropped over his head and yanked into his mouth, and a rope jammed hard around his ankles. He was upended and lowered head first over the catwalk.

He wanted to shout to Mannin or Hughes but he discovered that the gag so jammed his jaw and tongue, that it was impossible to make a meaningful sound. Then he felt the noose at his ankles starting to slip, and all his attention was drawn to bending his feet as sharply as possible to keep the rope from slipping loose and dropping him on his head.

A voice called down from far above. "No more of them up here."

"Good. Come on down, then."

* * *

Strong hands gripped Nevv by the shoulders, and a deep voice behind him said, "What did you have to lower him by the feet for? Suppose the rope let go?"

A hissing voice answered from above, "I would gladly have put the noose around the other end of him, but that isn't allowed yet."

A third voice spoke out of the gloom. "Enough of that. Put them all outside in the sun, where we can get a look at them."

Nevv was bundled out through the hole in the side of the ship, and lowered by a rope passed under his arms and across his chest. He was dropped on the brownish grass, and Hughes and Mannin were dumped beside him.

"Go get the Inspector," said someone, and Nevv involuntarily twisted around. The word "Inspector," had been spoken in Terran.

Now he was in daylight, Nevv could see his captors.

They were muscular hairy sunburnt men, with furry skins tied about their waists. They had shrewd eyes and an erect bearing, and were looking from the ship to their prisoners thoughtfully.

Beside Nevv, Mannin groaned miserably and twisted around.

One of the fur-clad men shifted his short, thick club. "Lie still, you. You will get what you deserve."

Someone said, "Here comes the Inspector."

Nevv turned his head and saw a man with a white band at his forehead striding briskly forward, followed by two men carrying a box with long handles. "Where are the suspects?" asked the Inspector. "Suspects" was in Terran.

"Right over here."

The Inspector came over, folded his arms on his chest and studied Nevv, Mannin and Hughes. The Inspector frowned. "Roll them on their sides a minute. Hm-m-m. Stand them up. I see. Well—Turn them sideways. All right, now tilt them forward. Hm-m-m." The Inspector turned to the men carrying the box. "Get out the front view."

The two men set down the box, opened it up, and removed a large piece of thin grayish stone. Handling it carefully by the edges, they held it up. Drawn in white on the stone was an excellent likeness of a man with remarkably broad shoulders, a broad head and a broader neck, with small crafty eyes, bushy brows, and a head of bristly hair that ran down his neck on either side and vanished under his collar.

The Inspector looked from this drawing to Nevv, and back at the drawing again. A crowd gathered around, and followed the Inspector's example. The Inspector went over to the box and lifted out other thin slabs of stone, glancing first at them and then at Nevv, Hughes, and Mannin. Scowling, he disappeared into the crowd, and came out with a gnarled, white-haired man. "You took care of one when he was sick," said the Inspector. "See if these are the same."

The white-haired man put his ear against Nevv's chest, first on one side, then on the other. He put his ear against Nevv's midsection. He pushed Nevv's head over on one side and ran his hand down Nevv's neck.. He stepped around and looked at Nevv from several angles. He did the same for Hughes and Mannin, then shook his head decisively. "These are different."

A little murmur went up. The Inspector said, "Take the gags out of their mouths." He looked at Nevv and asked, "Where do you come from?"

"Up there," said Nevv, glancing at the sky.

The Inspector scowled, and nodded his head at the drawing. "These others said they came from up there, too. Are you, perhaps, related to them?"

Nevv hesitated an instant, then said firmly, "We are fighting with them."

The Inspector's eyes glinted. "Who's winning?"

"At the moment, they are. If we can fix something that went wrong with our"—he hesitated, groping for a word—"wagon there, we should be able to win."

The Inspector glanced at the ship. His gaze rested on the hole torn in one side. He turned around and snapped orders. "Go get Netsil and all his scientists." The word "scientists" was in Terran. "Go tell the king, and ask for two hundred sturdy laborers. Let them rush here like the wind. Send a signal to the missile-testing ground"—this was in Terran—"and bring the Big Arm in case the others should come down before we're ready."

★ ★ ★

Men darted through the crowd, and from a distance there were shrill whistles. "Here, Boy! Come, Runner!"

An instant later, the ground trembled underfoot. A long brown blur shot into Nevv's field of view, swung around in a haze of dust and flying bits of turf, and streaked for the horizon.

The Inspector raised his arm and said solemnly, "The enemy of our enemy is our friend. Let the ropes holding our friends be cut and burnt in the fire. Let all men deal with our friends fairly."

A murmur of assent went up. The ropes were undone, a short piece was cut off of each and tossed on the ground. Someone dropped some sticks and began to arrange them. The Inspector came over and said, "I knew you were honest the instant I saw you, but we can't take chances." He glanced at the broad-chested drawing. "Those vermin came down in their sky-wagon, got sick and our cousins to the west cared for them like their own. When they got well, our cousins shared the great wonders of our science with them, and tried to convert them to our way of living. But they stuck to their . . . no offense . . . wizardry, and when they left, they carried off with them four of our most beautiful women, a newly-made suit of silver temple armor, two sacred gold incense burners, and sixteen haunches of fresh-cured swamp-ox."

Nevv shook his head. "Our experience with them has been much the same."

The Inspector looked up at the sky. "We'd help you fight them, but we don't have any way to get up there."

"Don't worry," said Nevv fervently, "you just let us get back to work and we'll take care of them."

Mannin said, "We'll shake them till their teeth rattle in their skulls."

The Inspector's face suffused with pleasure. He let out a bellow, and men came running. "Help our friends back into their wagon. If they want anything, get it. If you can't get it, tell me right away."

Nevv, Mannin, and Hughes were hoisted back up through the hole in the ship. They clambered in and stared at each other in the murky interior. Hughes let out a half-hysterical laugh. "Well," he said, "what did we come down here for, anyway?"

They went to look at the fuel feed mechanism.

★ ★ ★

The upper segment of the mechanism turned out to be completely torn away, and Nevv and Mannin climbed up for another look at the reserve fuel supply case. This case squatted with safelike massiveness well out of their reach and was solidly fixed in place. With the help of their new friends, Nevv and Mannin were hoisted and swung over to it, and by stages managed to get the reserve fuel down to Hughes, who at last locked it onto the feed mechanism.

Nevv again climbed down onto the cargo net, and very carefully examined several of the crates and their contents. Comparing with the manual, he looked over their controls carefully, then called to Mannin to come down. "Look here," he said, "when they packed these things, each wrapper apparently had a thick fold over the controls. When the cover was packed in place, it threw the switch. But look here. It was the switch to Pilot Sub-Circuit A."

Mannin stared. "Then what's the main circuit like?"

"I'm afraid to try it here," said Nevv. "Wait till we lift ship."

They climbed down.

By this time, successive shouts from outside told of new arrivals, and when Nevv and Mannin looked out, they saw at a distance heavy long tables and benches, a big fire with a glowing bed of coals. Another glance showed men swinging huge mauls to drive stakes into the ground around a massive square of logs. On the square rested a platform bearing a low upright framework with a large heavy case thrust out in front, and a series of things like short thick giant spoons thrust out behind. A man stepped forward and tugged on a rope. One of the spoons snapped up and around, and slammed against a padded beam. A streak shot out, and a swirling puff of dust climbed up about a hundred and fifty yards away.

"Look straight down," said Mannin.

Nevv looked down and saw men working on a scaffolding that was rising fast at the base of the ship.

Nevv's mouth opened and shut.

Down on the ground, a man with a mallet walked over and struck a big, yellow-metal gong. People began to run toward the tables.

The Inspector walked over and looked up. "The victory feast begins," he called. "We will celebrate your coming destruction of the thieves. You must sit at the head."

Nevv glanced desperately at his watch. "*Our* custom," he called down, "is to celebrate *after* the victory."

The Inspector looked shocked. "You might be dead then." He glanced down and said something that sounded like, "Why, that's barbarous!" He looked up again and loudly called out. "You must be our guests now, otherwise we will *have* NO FEAST!"

A silence fell over the hurrying people, who stopped and began looking first at the feast being carved from the spit, and then up at Nevv. There was a low, swelling mutter.

Nevv glanced up and saw several men by the log frame. They were walking slowly around it, pushing on a long pole. The frame with attached spoons was swinging slowly around.

Nevv did a fast mental calculation: Two hours in subspace to get back to where they were when they'd decided to come here. A five-hour detour to get on course. Twenty-seven to twenty-eight hours more till the last breakpoint. He glanced at his watch. Well, they had time left, but what if they needed it later on?

The muttering down below had turned into a waiting stillness.

Nevv looked at the big frame. He glanced inside at the fuel feed mechanism. He looked around the interior of the ship and saw some eight to ten muscular figures swinging down from overhead struts and beams. He let his breath out sharply and said to Mannin, "Have you got any ideas?"

"Not a one. I only hope this feast doesn't last all night."

Nevv suddenly remembered the Inspector's pronouncement about the ropes that held them being cut and thrown in the fire, and the prompt action to cut off just a small length and throw *it* in the fire.

Nevv leaned down and called out, "Let your custom be our custom. We will come down and join you at the feast."

A scattered cheer came up. The Inspector looked relieved. The rush for the tables picked up where it had left off.

* * *

Nevv had expected to escape from the feast after a comparatively short time. The feast, however, went on and on, darkness settled down, torches were lit, and as the copious gallons of drink poured out began to affect the revelers, they showed such a capacity for involved hair-splitting discussions that Nevv began to wish he had never heard the language. To Nevv's right, for instance, sat Netsil, the famous scientist. It was Netsil who had designed the Big Arm, which had just helped Nevv to decide whether or not to stay for the feast. Just beyond Netsil sat the Inspector, and beyond him sat Mansen, an elderly man, still considered a great scientist but now thought second to the younger Netsil. Mansen, Netsil, and the Inspector grilled the Terrans on all phases of their life, and uncovered countless inconsistencies.

The Inspector, swinging a big gourd full of liquor, finally said belligerently, "You wizards, why don't you come down to earth and live like honest people?" He took a drink. "No offense." He took another drink. "But what have you got? Oh, you whiz through the air by magic, appear and disappear, materialize huge huts of no earthly substance. But what does it all mean?" He jabbed out a finger. "Do you *really* know what you're doing?"

Netsil took a draught from his own gourd, and leaned forward. "We *would* like to know some more details," he said persuasively. "We don't get to talk with sorcerers very often. You know, I have a favorite theory. I think there's a solid substructure of science somewhere under your magic, even though you may not know it."

Nevv, exasperatedly trying to see his watch, growled, "*Everything* we do is science. That's what we've been trying to tell you."

"How," said Netsil gently, "can that be? A scientific process, you admit, is perfectly reproducible. Now, from what you've told us, many of your processes work, or don't work, unpredictably."

"That," boomed the Inspector, "is just what I say. They don't know what they're doing. No offense." He drained his gourd, and scooped it into a big bowl at the center of the table. He fixed Nevv with one eye while the other roamed around at random. He took another sip.

Nevv glanced at the ship and tried to calculate just what would happen if they quietly got up and headed for it. He didn't think the Inspector was quite drunk enough yet.

Mansen leaned forward. "I have my own theory. And perhaps Netsil and I can both learn more if you will concentrate on one scientific device of yours."

Netsil drained his gourd, got up, refilled it, and swaying slightly, came back. He bowed to Mansen, "Exactly what I was about to suggest, Professor." The word "Professor," was in Terran. Nevv considered that one hundred and sixty years ago the people on this planet were just nomads. Now they had "professors."

Netsil took a long sip from his gourd. Mansen and the Inspector were watching attentively. Netsil said, "One scientific device—let it be a practical one."

"Well—" said Nevv, and was suddenly brought up short by the thought of what his hypnotically conditioned vocabulary was likely to do when he came to unfamiliar scientific terms. He glanced at the Inspector, who was now waving his gourd like a baton, with only an occasional glance at Nevv and his companions.

"Well?" said Netsil. "Your practical device?"

★ ★ ★

It suddenly dawned on Nevv that "practical" was in Terran, too. Nevv wondered briefly just what frustrated Terran professor had gotten marooned on the planet some time in the dim past. He collected himself, thought for a moment, and said, "All right. Let's take the case of simple device we use to power light . . . er . . . carts, boats and so on."

"Can you," said Netsil, taking a sip from the gourd, "explain it so others could make one and use it? That's an important point."

"Yes. At least, I can explain it," said Nevv belligerently. "It's a simple gasoline engine. Basically—"

Netsil and Mansen looked at each other. Netsil cleared his throat. "Gasolinen djinn," he said.

"Basically," said Nevv, feeling himself redden slightly, "it's a cylinder . . . a hole . . . and a piston that moves up and down inside of it. Gasoline is squirted into it. The gasoline—"

"One moment," said Netsil, putting his hand gently on Nevv's arm. "The gasolinen djinn is a hoop, and a magic wand that flies up and down inside. A potion is sprinkled over it—"

"No, no," said Nevv exasperatedly. "It's all perfectly scientific. This gasoline isn't a potion. It's a liquid—like water. There's a flash—like a little bolt of lightning. It ignites the gasoline. The gasoline catches fire. There's an explosion. That is, a big bang, like thunder. It drives the piston down. This gives the power. The strength. Then we attach it to a . . . say," Nevv groped for a word, "a winch. It's the winch that does the work. There—" He mopped his brow. "It's all scientific."

"AH-h," said Netsil, rolling his eyes. "Ah, yes. Scientific. Let's see now. You have a hoop—"

"It's not a hoop. It's a hole. A space. An emptiness. The wand—I mean the *piston*. The piston fits tightly inside of it."

"Ah, hm-m-m. You have an emptiness, then. The wand fits tightly inside the *emptiness*. Water is sprinkled over it. Lightning flashes. The water—*water*, mind you!—bursts on fire. There's a roar like thunder. The wand flies down. This gives strength to the—did I hear you correctly?—to the witch. And you say it's the witch that does the work."

Nevv shook his head and groped for words.

Mansen said, "Now, my theory, Netsil, allows for this. These people, who we call 'wizards,' *were* scientific once. Observe the logical reasoning from point-to-point. It's the content that seems meaningless. Even here—"

"Gibberish," snapped Netsil, "hoops, wands, witches, thunder and lightning, burning water—"

"It may all have some meaning we don't understand," said Mansen insistently. "My theory is—partly, of course—that a science and perhaps a scientific people—like everything else, has a rise and a fall. A peak is reached, then, as it were, it bears fruitful offspring; these offspring grow—"

Netsil, red in the face, glared at Nevv and snapped, "This djinn of yours, does it . . . he . . . whatever it is . . . always work?"

"Always? Well, no. Not right away. Sometimes it takes a while. It takes a knack—"

"Aha! A *knack*. Some can do it better than others?"

"Well, yes."

"*Why?*"

"I don't know. Some people seem to have a way with them."

"Will it work for the same person at some times and not at others?"

"Yes, on cold days—"

"Aha!" growled Netsil, swinging around to glare at Mansen. "When the moon Skybird is over the moon Bright-One, and the night brings frost to the valley, dance three times around the toadstool and the thing will work. Otherwise—"

Nevv felt his ears get red. He started to interrupt, then saw the Inspector stretched out on the table, snoring.

"Science," said Netsil very firmly and finally, "*Always* works for *anybody*, and it *always* works *anytime*."

Nevv kicked Mannin under the table and jerked his head toward the ship.

"Science," said Mansen, "may be in different stages. Now a bowman practically always hits a fair target, Netsil—when he's grown up. As an infant or as an old

man, however—or when not at his best—or with an
unfamiliar bow—"

Nevv eased carefully away from the table.

"*That*," roared Netsil, "is an unscientific comparison,
professor. For instance, the infant isn't a bowman till he's
grown up!"

Nevv and Mannin cautiously got up. Hughes swung a
leg carefully over the bench.

"Where," asked Mansen, "are you going to get bowmen,
if you kill the infants, Professor?"

Nevv whispered, "Walk fast, but don't run."

Sounds of violent argument dwindled behind them as
they wound past festive tables toward the ship.

They clambered rapidly up inside, checked to see they
had no unexpected guest, then Nevv hastily explained his
plan.

The take-off, once they managed it, was uneventful.
Nevv, in the spaceboat, listened as Hughes and Mannin
discussed matters in the control room.

"We might," said Hughes, "be able to speed things up
when we go into subspace by trying a fast spin. After all, if
it threw us *off* course—"

"Nothing doing," growled Mannin, "we'll just have
time to get things done when we said we would if nothing
else goes wrong."

Finally Hughes said, "Dave?"

"Yeah," said Nevv.

"We're free of the planet. If you want to try that now, I
can cut the acceleration."

"O.K." said Nevv. "Open the space doors in the hull."
Very cautiously, he began to work the spaceboat controls.

Hughes, up in the pilot room, swung open the ship's big space doors, and Nevv could look down and see the stars outside.

Slowly, the spaceboat began to move.

★ ★ ★

Once Nevv had brought the spaceboat back into the ship, and they were on their way through subspace, Nevv's mind began uneasily sorting things over. He mentally went through the steps of his plan, picturing his actions carefully and vividly, till he thought he could carry them out, if necessary, with hardly any conscious attention at all. The trouble was, he thought, that some thorny little detail might sift in unseen and ruin everything. He twisted around in his seat and spoke into his microphone. "Phil—"

Mannin's voice said, "Yes, Dave?"

"Are you sure you can bring us out near that asteroid belt?"

"Near," said Mannin, "but not at. If I try to bring us out *at* it, we're too likely to have a collision."

"O.K." said Nevv. He sat back and wondered, first, whether the Flats would detect and blast them the instant they came out; and second, if they didn't, whether Hughes' lightning bolt maneuvering would get them into the asteroid belt without at the same time ripping the ship to pieces.

A comparatively small amount of this speculation put Nevv in a frame of mind like that of a man on trial for murder, waiting while the jury deliberates.

It took a hard effort to put his mind on the problem of finding something he could think about till the ship came out at its last breakpoint. For a while, he thought about the argument between Netsil and Mansen, and Mansen's question: "Where are you going to get bowmen if you kill the infants?" Sleepily, Nevv thought, "Where are you going to get new sciences if you deny the first unexplainable facts?" His mind went around and around on the question, and his head slumped sidewise on the padded acceleration seat of the spaceboat.

Nevv dreamed that a giant with a great bow and a sheaf of arrows was crying out in pain, and when Nevv went close, the giant was just a little baby crying.

There was a din in Nevv's ears that started to shake him awake, and it seemed that he was standing side-by-side with a giant who drew back his bow and sent shafts of pure energy out into space.

"Dave," cried Hughes' voice, "it's breakpoint! Can you hear me?"

"What?" Nevv sat up. "It can't be."

There was the soft chime of a bell over the earphones, then a wash of colors. Then a violent slam back into the acceleration chair as the ship sprang forward, swung head-for-tail, then braked hard.

★ ★ ★

Nevv's hands went to work automatically. He swung the spaceboat carefully through the stripped frame of the ship, dipped down through a large empty cell in the cargo web, came gently up again, and watched the net grow slightly larger above him. He loosened the wide belts of the acceleration chair, and put on the bulky spacesuit.

Beside him, the big space doors of the ship swung slowly open.

The spaceboat pressed gently into the net, and began to spring back.

Nevv swung his arm forward, feeling clumsy in the suit, and pushed down the evacuator stud. He heard the *chug* of the spaceboat's compressor sucking air out of the cabin and passing it back into the tanks. The *chug* grew fainter as the pressure dropped.

Nevv glanced out, saw that the boat was starting to spring away from the net. He opened the hatch, checked to see that he had the rope, which he could hardly feel, in his hand, and pushed gently away from the spaceboat. He drifted to the cargo web, caught hold, and clumsily tied the rope to the web. Then he pushed off of the web toward the spaceboat, which was drifting slowly away.

Nevv tied the rope to a ring on the side of the space-boat, got the hatchet, and pulled back on the rope toward the web. He made his way to the side of the web away from the space doors, and chopped the big cables free of the springs. The springs on the other side contracted, pulled the net toward the space doors.

A sudden intense white light lit the inside of the ship for a moment. Nevv glanced out through the doors and saw a distant asteroid glow white. The Flats were in action.

Nevv went carefully around the inside of the ship, till he had completely freed the web at the edges. He pulled himself back to the spaceboat, rechecked a small oxy-acetylene torch, went back, and cut free the ladder that passed down through the center of the net. He got back into the spaceboat, and very gently applied the power. He glanced back to see that the net was trailing, and swung out past the big doors.

In front of him, he could make out a cluster of dark slowly turning objects about twenty to forty feet thick. There was a wide empty space, then he thought he could see other, larger, objects turning in the distance. He had the impression of being rushed along in a giant stream of widely separated bits and pieces.

To one side, there was a brilliant flash of light, then another, and another.

Nevv crawled out the spaceboat hatch and pulled back along the rope to the web. Holding the torch and trailing the hatchet on a short length of rope, he glanced around for the two crates he had used to test with. He saw the web was hopelessly tangled, switched on the suit's headlamp and one after another carefully cut loose the two nearest crates he could reach. He ripped the crates open with the hatchet, managed to get the cylindrical drive units separated from the boards and wrappings. He concentrated on a mental picture of the two units swinging base to massive base.

Before him, the two units tipped slightly, and like two magnets, turned and swung together, base to base.

A brilliant wash of light lit them, and Hughes' tense voice whispered in the earphones. "Ready?"

"Almost."

Nevv pictured the drive units coming closer to him, then blanked his mind as completely as he could. He reached out, the suit-light shining on the control panels, switched off Pilot Sub-Circuit A, and switched on the Main Drive Circuits. Nevv pushed off gently for the web.

"O.K." he whispered.

* * *

The units spun as one, wavered, swung together in a narrow cone, then dove down at an angle away from the ship.

Nevv pulled along the rope and began to cut loose another crate.

Mannin's voice spoke in his ears.

"Attention all ships, Killer Group One: Bombardment Division: Fire by Salvos. Light Units Two and Three: Torpedoes ready. Prepare to close."

A brilliant blaze lit the cargo net. A burst of blue-white lines starred out and streaked past to his right.

He tugged at another crate, pushed the tangle of ropes and cable away from it, and began to chop at the edge of the case.

A thing like a long, oversize oil drum shot past him, paused, sprang away, hesitated, lit by the dying glow of an asteroid, sprang up, appeared hovering near the nose of the ship, shot down and out of sight.

Nevv glanced up again from the crate. Far in the distance, a brilliant point of light flared into view. Not far away, there was another bright flash. Then another.

The drum shot into view, paused by a brightly-glowing red asteroid fragment, dropped and vanished. Where the glow had been, was a narrow red streak, stretching out and away to a tiny red dot far-off.

A series of brilliant flashes lit up in the distance.

A half-hysterical garble sounded in Nevv's earphones. Mannin's voice said steadily, "No terms whatever. We don't want your surrender. Just get out. And you'd better make your peace before the Main Fleets get back."

Nevv took a deep breath of the stifling metal-and-rubber-smelling air in the suit, gagged, and began working the tangle of ropes back around the case. He tied them clumsily, started back toward the spaceboat, then stopped. He glanced toward the ship, formed a mental picture of the crates and net moving back toward the space doors, and felt the rope to the spaceboat tighten. He glanced back, looked ahead, and piloted the boat back into the ship by means of the cargo. As he passed through the big space doors, an elongated cylinder shape moved through behind him.

Hughes' voice, shaking with strain, said, "Put them back on the pilot circuit, Dave."

Nevv pushed away, caught hold of the cylinders, and carefully set their switches.

Prometheus began to move. Nevv got the spaceboat in its cradle. He let the air back into the boat, and with a sense of great relief, got out of the suit and took a deep breath. He glanced back and saw the cargo bunch itself in the center of the aft section of the ship. He stripped open an emergency food packet and settled down. He felt the ship swing forward fast, and sank back in the cushions. He was wondering uneasily just who had commanded the Flats outside.

Hughes said, "Where to?"

"Contact White Base and tell them we have a slightly damaged ship to bring down. Tell them our hull's punctured and our fuel feed's hurt, and ask if they can take care of us."

In a moment, Hughes said "Yes."

"White Base, then," said Nevv.

★ ★ ★

White Base had the look of a fortress that has had the upper works so pounded into rubble that they serve merely as a buffer to protect the parts underneath. But the bulk of the grimy men who greeted Nevv, Hughes, and Mannin could not have seemed much happier. Each wore a grin of fierce delight and went to work on the ship's hull as if possessed of supernatural strength.

The moment the hull and the feed mechanism were repaired, Nevv glanced at Hughes. "O.K., back to the asteroid belt."

Hughes had his head in the pilot globe. "By the drive," he said, "or by the cargo?"

Nevv stared at him. "By the drive."

The ship lifted, and Nevv said to Mannin, "Who was in charge of the Flats here?"

"Somebody with four tufts on his sash, a collar full of hair, and a gold cactus on each shoulder. I was so nervous that's about all I saw of him. I hope he thought I was mad."

Hughes said, "You want me to contact the colony?"

"Stay right where you are," said Nevv. "Phil, get in touch with the colony. Send 'Have cargo for you. Shall I bring it down?' Send it in the new code."

"Right," said Mannin.

Hughes said, "Do you have something in mind for me?"

"Yes. I'm going to reactivate those two drive units. Then I want you to get them outside."

"Wait," said Hughes. "I think I can do it myself by swinging one of the others down. I didn't think of it before." After a moment, he said, "O.K. You want them outside?"

"Yes, as soon as you can get them there."

There was a faint rumble, and a trembling underfoot as the space doors opened. "O.K." said Hughes.

Mannin said, "The Colony answers, 'Keep cargo. You're doing fine.'"

"Send 'Will keep cargo.'" Nevv glanced toward Hughes. "Did you have any trouble back there?"

"Just sheer nerves, that's all. I was afraid a chance hit might get us before we got into action. Then I thought I might do something wrong."

"How was the aiming?"

"Not bad. The pressure of the two units locked them together. As the detectors spotted a target I lined the drive unit up on an asteroid, chunk, or fragment along a target track, then jammed on full acceleration. The drive units stood still, balanced. The drive played on the fragment in a narrow beam, kicked it forward, accelerated it, and I guess built it up to somewhere near the speed of light before it hit. The impact must have been terrific."

"Could you work better with another set of them?"

"No thanks. One's enough."

Mannin said, "Anything more for me to do?"

"Not just yet. Keep your eyes open and tell me if any Flats show up. Hughes will be too busy."

★ ★ ★

Hughes abruptly sucked in his breath. "Very far right foreground high. One ship."

Mannin sprang across the room.

Nevv stiffened and watched the viewscreen.

"Shall I hit him?" said Hughes.

"Not yet."

The screen flared. The white-haired Flat, his many-tufted sash drawn taut across his chest, looked at Nevv with his face cool and immobile.

Nevv looked back at him.

Finally the Flat said, "If this isn't a bluff, none of it makes sense."

"If it is a bluff," said Nevv, "it's a painful one. Do we have to bluff you again?"

"Where are your ships?"

"Not *my* ships, Admiral."

"You seem to be the spokesman."

Suddenly Mannin said, "Near right foreground high, low, dozens of them—"

Nevv said, "Fire at will."

Hughes' tense irregular breathing was the only sound Nevv could hear in the room. Then there was a light *ping* sound, such as a light fragment might make bouncing off the wall of the ship. Nevv kept his eyes on the white-haired Admiral. Abruptly, the Admiral said with his face slightly twisted and the corners of his mouth drawn down, "Enough."

Mannin said, "They're gone. All but one. Very far right foreground high. That's gone. Near right foreground high."

On the screen, the Admiral flickered off, then on.

Nevv snapped, "Hold fire, all Groups."

The Flat looked at him steadily. Then he vanished from the screen.

"Gone," said Mannin.

Nevv said, "If any Flat shows up again anywhere in range, obliterate it."

Hughes said, "Why not that last one?"

"I don't know," said Nevv, feeling his shirt cling to his chest and back.

Mannin said, "Why didn't he take us?"

"Again I don't know." Nevv took a deep breath. "Send to the Colony: 'Request suggestions for disposition of cargo.'"

A few moments later Mannin read: "Return cargo your base immediately." He looked at Nevv.

"That's the message."

Nevv, Mannin, and Hughes looked at each other.

"Plot a course," said Nevv dryly.

Hughes sucked in his breath and said, "You want the . . . cargo back inside?"

"Yes," said Nevv, "as soon as the course is ready."

Hughes said in a tense voice, "Do you mind if I deactivate the Main Drive Circuits now?"

"Go ahead."

★ ★ ★

The trip back was so totally uneventful that when Nevv, Mannin and Hughes stood before General Lawson, none of them could think of anything to say about it.

"We just came back," said Nevv. "We caught up on some sleep, that was all."

The general said, "You'll each be advanced one grade in rank, with full seniority as of the date of your first encounter with the enemy. You'll each be given the highest decoration that we can bestow. Other than that, what you've done must pass totally unnoticed. We're trying even now to find out some way to maintain this secret that won't be unreasonably hard for you."

"Sir," said Nevv, "this must have been a hard secret to keep."

"It has been."

"Sir, *why* keep it? With this, our colonists could do anything."

The general smiled faintly and looked steadily back at Nevv.

Nevv stiffened suddenly, and felt very cold.

Mannin said, "Sir—" then abruptly cut himself off.

The general looked at Hughes. "What was your reaction to it, colonel?"

"After a few minutes of it," said Hughes, "I never wanted anything more to do with it. Suppose I should make a mistake?"

The general nodded and glanced at Nevv. "If that were the universal reaction, why, of course we needn't keep it secret. But consider the possibilities. The destructive power of new developments goes up and up, but where is the defense? Suppose *one careless or ill-intentioned person should get hold of this?*"

Mannin said, "And yet it could mean so much—"

"That's just it," said the general. "It could and perhaps some day it will. The race evolves. You three men, for instance. You took it out; you used it as best you knew how; you brought it back sheathed and safe." He cleared his throat. "We could trust *you.*"

He raised his hand in a brief salute, and said:

"We'll share the secret, but heaven help us.

"Some things can't be shared till you can trust *everyone.*"

ACHILLES'S HEEL

Supreme Interstellar Marshal John von Eckberg Lindt knocked the ash off the end of his cigar onto the floor of Supreme Headquarters, and shifted his powerful body into a more comfortable position in the padded swivel chair.

Across the room, from floor to ceiling and wall to wall, lights winked and relays clicked as Combat Forces Master Integration Computer changed the dispositions of the Fleet to counter the latest Wij-Wij probe. At the foot of the enormous bulk of Combat Forces Master Integration Computer was a cot. On the cot lay a man, with one hand trailing on the floor. This man was James Edison Martell, recognized as the greatest pragmatic scientist since his namesake, Thomas. In the hand of James Edison Martell was a somewhat battered silver flask, from the cap of which a clear brownish liquid leaked out to stain the floor.

Supreme Interstellar Marshal von Eckberg Lindt was considering the philosophical implications of Martell, the computer behind him, and the flask, when the Immediate Action buzzer sounded on his desk.

Lindt put his feet on the floor, and glanced alertly at the desk top. A hole opened up, and a sheaf of papers jumped out. Lindt picked up the first sheet, noted that it was an Allocation of Supply order, signed it and set it aside. The rest of the papers were lists of promotions, demotions, classifications, transfers, appointments, adjudications and evaluations. Lindt glanced rapidly through them and signed all but the demotions and strategic evaluations. He stacked the signed papers neatly and set them on a faintly outlined square on the desk. The desk top opened and the paper vanished like laundry down a chute. Lindt gave his attention to the strategic evaluations:

OSD 6: All Sectors Overall situation at present critical. Density of stellar systems under enemy (Wij-Wij) control great, enabling high order of productive capacity. Adaptive Wij-Wij physiology apparently enables use of most planets in their systems. Though impossible to verify this, as no Wij-Wij prisoners have yet been taken alive. Nevertheless examination of enemy dead reveals complex nervous structures whose function appears to be internal adjustment to the external environment. For whatever reason, Wij-Wij military productive capacity has increased at a violent pace since our initial armed clash, and is expected to surpass human productive capacity in the near future.

Estimates of enemy psychology indicate brittle superiority feelings underlain by dread of unknown origin, coupled with severe strain due apparently to adaptive stresses on unlike planets; together with these seem to be feelings of inferiority, due to superior tactical and strategical handling of human fleet and resources. There may also be a lack of psychological adjustment to "emptiness" of spaces occupied by humans. In any case, there is clearly an indisposition to send any but very heavy forces into these regions of space.

The expected enemy action is a violent single thrust with all forces united in one massive fleet.

The planned human counteraction is: Resistance to the last possible moment at selected points and belts in line of attack. Leapfrog withdrawal to new strong points and belts in line of enemy penetration. Pinching counterattacks against sides and rear of enemy penetration. Simultaneous counterattacks directed toward vital enemy communications centers in the region of the star, alpha-Primorus.

The anticipated result of the action is uncertain.

In summary, the Wij-Wij enemy appears to be acting under some powerful compulsion, possibly the dread of a supposed innate human superiority. Whatever the cause, study of captured armaments and observed enemy military activity clearly indicates a rapid increase in military strength and its underlying productive capacity. Coupled with the fanatical Wij-Wij hostility, this strength is expected to be used in one single-minded deadly thrust whose outcome cannot be predicted.

Lindt frowned thoughtfully, reread this paper, signed it, and dropped it down the waiting hole in the desk top. He picked up the list of demotions, read down them, snorted suddenly and crossed one off. On the back of the sheet, Lindt wrote:

"Re: BVIII Decision 0-624. The girls on the planet

mentioned—I say this from personal experience—heave mats over electrified guard fences to get into fortified camps; they dig tunnels under roboticized guard lanes; when the wind is right they drop into camp on specially built one-woman kites. The crime mentioned is, on this planet, no more likely than murder committed by pushing a suicide long after he jumped. The officer's punishment is reduced to a fine of one dollar. He is not to be demoted; he is to be reassigned. J. V. Lindt, S. I. M., Comgen B."

Lindt read through the rest of the list, made a few notes, dropped the papers down the hole, which snapped shut, and put his feet back up on the desk. He tossed his cigar stub on the floor, and watched as a long low thing like a miniature alligator on wheels slid into the room, scooped up the cigar and ash, gave Martell's leaking bottle a quick wipe, and vanished through a low hole in the opposite wall.

Lindt settled in the chair, moved his feet around to a more comfortable position, then stripped the wrapper off another cigar, lit it, and blew out a cloud of smoke. He looked across the room at the clicking, clacking, flashing monster which was theoretically a member of his staff, and spat a fleck of cigar leaf onto the floor.

What, he asked himself, gave the Wij-Wij their fanatical drive? He thought back to the first time he had heard of this problem, and saw in memory the strong build and rugged features of the Operations Chief, General Vernon Hauser, as Hauser reset the glossy wall-sized display and rapped a pointer against a portion of the display thick with stars.

"We first ran into them," said Hauser, "when we hit this

region. We had no doubt we had the Outs on the run, and
we thought there was a good chance we could finish them.
Instead, a counterattack threw us back in disorder. But
heavy reserves were on hand, and we put them in to crush
the Out counterattack. The enemy committed reinforcements that at once renewed his attack. It was then that we
discovered we were fighting a new enemy. The Outs had
withdrawn—'fled' would be more accurate—in this
direction. We had no reason to think this was anything but
Out territory. But a close-quarters fight on an asteroid
showed that this was a different race entirely."

Lindt said, "But, to a degree, the Outs can alter their
physiology."

"Which fooled us for a while. But if you'll picture a
thing like an upright man-sized caterpillar, you'll have
some idea of the difference. We tried to communicate
with their high command, but couldn't get a message
across. We still don't understand them. And we've had
no prisoners to question. We have yet to take one single
individual alive. Their psychology is a total mystery to us,
though there are guesses."

Lindt studied the display, the shiny surface of which
reflected the image of both men, their insignia of rank
identical, but Hauser's uniform bearing also the small
glittering star of the General Staff. Lindt glanced at the
display thoughtfully. Hauser held out the control box,
"Here. The sooner you understand what we're up against,
the better."

Lindt adjusted the display, to enlarge the enemy
regions. "When they counterattacked, what did you do?"

Hauser said, "We withdrew, since obviously we were

fighting the wrong people. They continued to attack, regardless."

Lindt studied the display. "Is this accurate?"

"Location of the star systems is very accurate. The faint violet border that shows the limit of alien control of the star systems is as accurate as we've been able to make it. But bear in mind, we thought the Outs owned this region just a little while ago."

"It's like a citadel planted in someone else's territory."

"At the very least, it's a damned distraction. We don't want to fight these people. But we can't get loose from them. If it were not for this, we could almost certainly force the Outs to give up. Our production and tactics have reached the point—thanks to the absence of their sabotage—where we outclass them. But this complication puts everything in doubt. To top it all off, the Wij-Wij have their damned weapon—we don't know how it works—what you hear is a kind of noise—Wij-Wij-Wij is what it sounds like, and if you can't get away from it, it knocks you senseless. A crew or garrison subjected to this is useless. The ship or fortification has to be operated by computer control, and even that takes special shielding."

Lindt said thoughtfully, "All this is news to me."

Hauser nodded. "Security clamp-down. We are not eager to spread the information. We could do with fewer varieties of aliens, all watching and figuring their own advantage. If they get the idea we're in a mess, they'll try to get some use out of it."

"Is there coordination between the Outs and these—what do you call them? Wij-Wij?"

"Right, Wij-Wij. As far as we can tell, they're separate."

"That's something, at least."

"What it means is, we have two separate wars on our hands. The Outs, we want to finish. These other people, we merely want to keep at bay, till we settle with the Outs. Then we make peace if we can; if not, we'll have to fight them, asinine as it seems. We want you, Jack, to deal with this unappetizing mess."

"I was afraid that was coming."

"You don't know the half of it. There is a theory that this Wij-Wij apparatus that knocks people unconscious is a mind-reading device and gathers intelligence. If so, we need to provide confusing information."

Hauser added thoughtfully, "Your job so far has been to watch our back, keep the aliens on the far side of our territory from getting too restless. An unusually independent command, requiring flexibility, originality, and daring. We want you now to do the same against this actively hostile enemy, keeping him off our neck so we can deal with the Outs undistracted—unless someone else should deal himself in, that is. What do you say?"

"Vern, you're the Opchief. You only need to give the order."

"I'm happier with willing associates."

"It's an interesting proposition, all right. But with an active opposition, I'll need more troops. This can't be all bluff."

"We'll give you the forces you'll need. This sector is, as I said, heavily computerized. Since we got the damned saboteur out of the system, incidentally, we've found it possible to make much more progress in computerization. As there is a real risk that this present enemy, who makes long-range penetration attacks as a regular thing, may get some of our documents, or in one way or another get information dangerous to us, we are planting misleading information at the very beginning. The computers are to be programmed as if your sector is a much larger part of human territory. Your rank will be accordingly higher. We will use more automatized spacecraft to increase the size and striking power of your command."

Lindt frowned. "What's the rank?"

Hauser looked uneasy. "We—ah—are making you a Supreme Interstellar Marshal. The same pay and allowances as full general, of course."

Lindt laughed. "With that title, you could forget the pay."

"It fits with an overall set-up designed to confuse the enemy. But the rank is real enough. Within your sector, you have complete control. Just keep these damned inchworms off our backs. We don't want to have to think about them while we settle with the Outs. We believe you can handle this better than any of the rest of us."

★ ★ ★

Lindt now remembered the words of praise, and ached with the urge to rap the Wij-Wij where past experience told them they were safe. But he restrained himself. He had tried that once before. He had got a resounding victory. At the same time, supply schedules were unstrung from here to the Border, the Wij-Wij redoubled their efforts, and he ended up right where he'd started. Lindt glowered at Combat Forces Master Integration Computer, sucked on his cigar, and began going over the problem again.

The computer meanwhile clicked, murmured, chortled, and twinkled.

On the cot at its foot, James Edison Martell rolled over and put the bottle in his mouth.

The alligator-shaped robot slid through the wall and wiped up the brownish stain.

Inside the wall, a bimetallic spring adjusted slightly to keep the temperature at a cozy seventy degrees.

Supreme Interstellar Marshall John von Eckberg Lindt fell asleep and dropped his cigar.

The alligator-shaped robot snapped it up.

Martell groaned.

Combat Forces Master Integration Computer droned competently, clicked, hummed and flashed securely. Its drone climbed to a roar, subsided to a tremor, rose to thunder—its lights bright like the eyes of a maniac, then dim with the exhausted flicker of a weary invalid. The walls of the room flared in the glare of the overhead lamps, grew dim in their dying glow, then blazed again to dazzling brilliance.

Lindt landed on his feet. For an instant he knew neither who he was nor what the scene around him meant. Then he heard it.

Wij-wij-wij-wij-wij-wij-wij

Lindt sprang for the locker, yanked out a chute suit and threw it to Martell. Lindt climbed into one himself, pulled the fastening strings tight, and glanced at the computer. Useless. With the current varying wildly from instant to instant, the computer was no more fitted to live than a man in a vacuum without a suit.

Lindt glanced at Martell. "Hurry up and follow me."

"Where to?"

"Chute. Turn left in the hallway."

"Coming."

Lindt trotted out the door and into the hall. *Wij-wij-wij-wij-wij-wij-wij*

He dove through an oblong black hole, felt the leathery surface of his suit catch and slide, then catch. He shoved back hard with his hands. The chute dipped and he dropped fast on the oiled slide.

Wij-wij-wij-wij-wij-wij-wij

The wind blew back hard on his face. Thick layers of rock and metallic ore fled upwards past him. The next time the sensation came it was milder.

Wij-wij-wij

The slide dropped him fast, curved gently, hissing against the hot surface of his suit. Then he was sinking into thick, deep foamy layers, air bubbles trapped in thin plastic. The bubbles burst as he sank, down and down, slower and slower, to come up angrily, his reflexes eager to trigger the counter-punch, his muscles aching for the word—

Wij-wij-wij

He went out into a lighted hallway, the yellow glow of oil lamps varying slightly, lighter and darker, as the Wij-Wij attack hit the gravity compensator and changed the lamp draft even at this depth.

Wij-wij-wij-WIJ-WIJ-wij

Lindt stumbled. Everything seemed to go dark. He almost fell, then sprinted down the hallway. Ahead the corridor narrowed, the ceiling coming low. A sign read:

COMMAND AREA—SHIELDED

Lindt strode around a corner, into the suddenly bright

glare of steady electric lights. He shrugged out of his suit. Martell stumbled into the room behind him.

"Boy," said Martell, pulling off his suit, "they've got that thing directional now. They nearly put me out on the way down that hall."

Lindt grunted. He was looking the room over, noting that it was, as it should be, a duplicate of the room above. Only it was too close a duplicate. Down here, the duplicate Command Forces Master Integration Computer was supposed to run from its own shielded supply, receiving reports micro-angled through sub-space to the huge manifold in the next room. But the gigantic face of the computer was silent and unlit.

"What," said Lindt, "is wrong with that computer?"

Martell scowled, stepped to the face of the computer and glanced at a dial. He threw a switch over and back.

"Current supply is O.K." he said. He stared at the face of the big machine, glanced at Lindt. "How bad is the situation?"

"Very bad," said Lindt. "Orders issue from this place direct to seven sectors of the B shell. We're expecting an all-out attack any time. The attack will probably be simple and massive. Our reply is so complex that it has to be perfectly coordinated or we'll get ground up piecemeal."

Martell grunted, and went behind the computer. There were sounds of metal sliding on metal.

Lindt became aware of the continuing silence in the room. Unless this local surprise attack was worse than he'd thought, his staff should be here now. He stepped over to the communications screen and set it to receive only. He dialed Weapons Evaluation. The screen flickered, and showed three men slumped at desks. Beside one of the desks was a creature something like a giant furry inchworm. Lindt stiffened, switched the scene to Supply. A pile of men lay one on top of the other near the doorway. He switched to Monitor, selected Corridor I, and saw a file of giant inchworms with packs on the middles of the backs, carrying T-shaped weapons. Each of them seemed to be watching and aiming in a different direction. Their stance and hasty bobbing walk gave them a look of terrific urgency.

Lindt switched from corridor to corridor, finding some empty, but most containing at least a few of the inchwormlike creatures on guard.

From behind the computer, Martell's voice brought a muffled string of oaths. Lindt looked up. Martell came around the corner carrying something like a drawer from a file cabinet. He held it up for Lindt to see.

"Look at the label," said Martell. "Read it."

"P-06-XLVPT-201J-12LVBXc."

"It's supposed to be, 'P-06-XLVPT-201J—12LVBXb,'" said Martell.

Lindt glanced back at the screen, stepped aside and pulled a lever set into the wall nearby. A very light detonation made the room tremble. "What of that?" he said. "Because it's VBXc, it won't work?"

"No," said Martell. "Because it's VBXc it won't work *right*. The b is the standard model. The c is supposed to be for a larger experimental computer. Somewhere some man or supply machine slipped up. Since this component is replaced every three months, every military computer in the system probably has a c in it. The effect isn't to stop the computer. The effect is inaccuracy."

"In that case," said Lindt, "why won't this one work?"

"Internal cutout," said Martell. "This computer and the one upstairs have the same design, receive the same information. All the computers are connected by direct cable or through subspace manifolds. They all come to the same conclusions. This sudden raid is obviously something unexpected, at variance with the calculated possibilities. When anything at variance with the calculated possibilities arises, the computer has to run an internal check. A special circuit is cut in, a complex many-stage problem with known data and known answers is fed to the computer circuits and simultaneously to the memory banks. The results are compared, and if there's any variation whatever, the computer knows it is inaccurate. Then it checks itself circuit-by-circuit till it finds the trouble. The defective assembly pops out and the computer won't operate till the check finally gives the right answers for known problems."

"This happens to all the computers?"

"All. They're all connected together. The communications lag through subspace is insignificant."

"Who thought of this?" asked Lindt abruptly. "A human, or another computer?"

"I thought of it," said Martell. "And I pushed it through despite engineers who thought they had the Perfect Machine."

"Then," said Lindt, "every Combat Forces Master Integration Computer in the system is out of action?"

Martell nodded. "And will be, till that circuit is replaced."

The communications screen buzzed. Lindt snapped it

on. A tense group of oversize furry inchworms was there, clearly trying to see. Lindt let them squint in vain. He glanced at their weapons, which were T-shaped, the same fore and aft, like two revolvers with a common grip. One muzzle aimed toward Lindt's screen, and the other toward the Wij-Wij using it. The creatures had four fingers, two around the grip and one on each trigger. Lindt stared at this arrangement, then looked up.

"Herro," came a flat even mechanical voice, sounding l's and r's the same. "Herro, cerrs remaining of superbeing rogicar. Your prexus dying is. You we detected. Resistance hoperess is. Actions you predictabre. Come harrway six surface to. We you harm cannot. You we onry information want. Since resist hoperess is, no choice you. Come harrway six surface to. *Now.*"

Lindt frowned at Martell. "That computer has apparently done every thing so according to the odds they think we're perfectly logical."

Martell was scowling. "Where did they learn to translate with a German accent? And what is that about our 'dying plexus.'"

Lindt squinted. "It sounded more Japanese to me." He glanced at the screen, and switched to the shattered room he and Martel had left during the attack. "As for our 'dying plexus,' I detonated the emergency mine inside the computer upstairs. The Wij-Wij sound as if they think of us as one big creature. You and I and everyone else is a 'cell,' each computer is a 'plexus,' and I suppose our chains of command are 'nerves.'" He frowned again and switched back to the intent group of giant inchworms with their double-ended guns.

"Well," said Martell abruptly, "that tells us something about Wij-Wij. But will we live to use it? Come on. Let's get out of here."

"There's no way," said Lindt. "But can you use this computer to get some information out?"

Martell was walking back to the computer. "We can do better than that," he said. "Stick right with me." He opened a tall panel in the side of the computer and stepped in. "Pull that shut behind you."

Lindt frowned, followed, and found himself in a tall narrow corridor. He pulled the panel shut, and followed Martell.

"Access corridor," said Martell. "We have to be able to get at the inside of this thing somehow. And at these cables overhead."

Martell wound his way expertly among the narrow branching corridors, and Lindt followed closely. The corridor they followed widened, and the overhead cables and wires increased in number. They stepped out into a room where big branching ducts led to a single giant conduit that passed into the wall. "Recognize it?" asked Martell.

"It's out of my line," said Lindt, "but of course it must be the subspace manifold."

"Right." Martell began carefully working at a section of the largest conduit, which was about five feet in diameter. "You know what's in here?" he asked.

Lindt said, "The micro-angle mechanism, whatever that may be."

"Exactly," said Martell. "And now I'll tell you. Wait—" The section of conduit, a rectangular piece about two feet by three, suddenly came loose, and Martell set it down with a grunt and a clang. "Inspection plate," he said. "We usually do the inspecting with a mirror or a stick, or an X ray on the overhead trolley. Some brave souls go in. When I was a brash youth, a friend of mine in Section A used to toss wadded-up messages along the floor of the conduit, and twenty feet away in Sector B III, I would fish them out."

Lindt blinked. "Twenty feet—"

Martel nodded. "Twenty feet. The micro-angle conduit is a tube of normal space twisted around on itself and bent through subspace. 'Micro-angle' refers to the sharp curve of space in the cross-section of the tube."

"Why don't we use these things for supplies, transport of personnel—"

"Too expensive for supplies, and when you get in there, you'll see why we don't use it for personnel," said Martell, stepping back. "You go first. Cling to that big thick cable in the center. Just keep your mind on moving steadily ahead. When you come to a junction, go any way at all. I'll follow right behind you."

Lindt frowned, took hold of the edge of the rectangular inspection opening, put his leg over and got in. The conduit stretched out before him, dimly lighted. Lindt felt uncomfortable but not uneasy. He moved forward, slowly, bent sideways, with an arm on the thick cable.

The awkward part was that of moving ahead through a five-foot pipe with roughly a two-foot cable taking up the center. A little ahead, he noticed that the wall of the tunnel seemed made of a different material. He reached that point.

Gravity went.

Lindt seemed to be falling. Not down. Not up. But in on himself.

His head was shrinking. His limbs spread in all directions like the arms of a starfish. He was collapsing like a balloon with a stone tossed on the center. His legs and hands were enormous.

"Keep moving," said Martell, his voice coming at Lindt from all directions at once, like the rays of the sun going backwards, and not all striking home at the same time.

Lindt pulled on the cable. Tugged and pulled in an automatic motion he remembered from sometime, but that had nothing to do with him now, except that he knew he had to try to do something.

His legs and arms were enormous, long and stretching longer. His body somehow was spread out around his head like a flapjack around a pat of butter. And stretching farther, thin and—

Snap

His legs were touching each other, all their feet together. His head in its finite but unbounded size rimmed the edge of eternity.

He kept his hands moving.

Snap

His heads were flying apart, his arms around each head like wheel spokes, his long thin bodies pinwheeling out and away from his distant feet. His hands groping along the cable wall around him.

Snap

Like a thousand-mile-long cable himself, equipped with a pin-size head and two stubby arms at one end, and tiny feet far out of sight at the other end, he crept like a stretched-out dachshund toward a faraway forgotten goal, past a strange wavy line of demarcation in the wall of the endless tunnel he was in, and—

Snap

He was himself.

Hanging on to a two-foot thick cable in a five-foot conduit, in a dim light, with his memories coming back thick and strong.

The noise Lindt made brought the technician who let them out of the conduit.

"That," said Martell, "is why we don't use the conduit for personnel transport."

Martell led the way back, with Lindt grimly following. Behind came fifty genuine volunteers, heavily armed, their teeth gritted, and hooked together by a rope. They were coming out of the manifold shaking and cursing just as six big inchworms came in through the inspection corridor.

The nearest volunteer snapped his gun to his shoulder, said "Ahhh," and fired.

The shot hit home.

Lindt, his own gun snapping to his shoulder, saw both the Wij-Wij's fingers contract. Simultaneously, the others jerked in unison, then snapped up their T-shaped weapons.

Wij-wij-wij-wij-wij-wij-wij

Lindt was sure he got two himself. But that was not what occupied his mind. He bolted down the corridor, twisted and turned. The corridor narrowed.

Three big inchworms turned to face him. Their T-shaped guns swung up.

Lindt took a flying leap for the nearest one, drove his fist hard into the fur and rubbery flesh beneath. He knocked the gun to the floor. His foot trod and ground on the feet of the Wij-Wij. His hand, seeking, found what he was looking for—a joint. He bent one of the creature's forearms sharply back, and twisted.

A soundless shriek split the air around him.

He grinned like a bulldog with its teeth set in solid flesh, and prepared to hang on till the clock of the universe runs down and stops.

He looked up, his mind still closely attending to the job of grating that forearm, twisting, bending, and almost but not quite snapping.

"What in space—" came a voice.

The two other big inchworms were leaning weakly against the wall, their weapons on the floor and plainly forgotten.

Martell came around a corner, his eyes wide.

"They're all out on their feet," he said, then looked sharply at Lindt. "Oh," he said, "then they're—"

"Telepathic," said Lindt, "fully telepathic. Get out there and tie them up."

The place was secure again, and Lindt had his feet on a new desk.

Martell was sitting on the edge of his cot, grinning. "You're sure they won't commit suicide, or get murdered?"

"How?" said Lindt. "And does a man's finger commit suicide, when someone bends it back? True, at the time the man might want to chop it off to get free, but that's hard to do in that situation. Nobody's likely to get through to these prisoners now unless they try a full fleet action, and as soon as they try that, we'll turn the thumbscrews. Live and let live."

Martell burst out laughing. "And telepathy's supposed to be an advantage."

"It was," said Lindt, "so long as they fought actions where they got killed, not captured. If one got painfully hurt, he pulled the other trigger so the rest could fight on. No wonder they avoided little skirmishes. A man can take a lot when he's part of a tremendous attack. The sharp pains and the impact don't bother him then. It's the steady nagging pain that wears him down. The pain that just gets worse when he tries to get loose. That's what their telepathy does to them, and we've got their collective finger bent back. But it *was* a help to them before. No wonder they expanded so fast, with that co-ordination. And no wonder they were scared of us. They think of themselves as all one big creature. They must think of us that way, too. But pain and defeat in one sector doesn't stop us or make the whole human race wince and fall back. They must have thought of us as we think of a fanatic who can't be stopped by ordinary fears or pains, who'll lose a limb or take a wound and just keep on coming. No wonder they were frantic and thought they had to do away with us."

Martell nodded and lay back. "I hope we've had an end of that." He glanced at Combat Forces Master Integration Computer, clicking and flashing with a bland assumption of superiority. "Now I have a new viewpoint of that thing, too," he said. "It's mankind's habit-mind, that's all. We can turn it off and do without it, if necessary. We can think of better things. I've got a friend down the conduit in Sector AXIV, who thinks we ought to do away with these integration computers entirely."

"No thanks," said Lindt. "Habit has its limits but it's useful. You need habit and originality both." He took out a cigar and began to peel off the wrapper. "Somehow, you, me, and the computer have to get what's happened across to the Wij-Wij. Making them jump with pain every time they turn a fleet our way is good, but not good enough."

Martell nodded.

Lindt wadded the cigar paper.

The little metal alligator on wheels trundled in, its receptors on the paper, and waited.

Lindt tossed it aside, lit the cigar and sent out a cloud of smoke.

OF ENEMIES AND ALLIES

Yklon 138(3), Commander of the Wij-Wij War Horde, glanced moodily around his headquarters, and tried to estimate the likelihood that, somewhere in this latest message from the hostages, there was some element of usable truth. Yklon had just finished an unusually bad evening meal, and his disposition was suffering with his digestion. Sourly, he listened to the message machine emit its recorded whistles and squeaks, to give a weirdly phrased account only partly clarified by the interpreters who huddled around the machine and mentally passed on their edited version:

"From Agbar 221(1) in the enemy-presumed-was neutral-is ally-would-be armed forces headquarters, to Yklon 138(3), Commander of the War Horde. The communication referenced in your request for information is, I repeat, *is* true. I and three members of my unit were captured, rendered unconscious, and deprived of all suicide-weapons. We are still being held hostage, along with others, in the presumed-enemy headquarters.

"The presumed-enemy has provided us with food,

water, and the chance to rest. He has refused us the means to carry out the defeat-penalty, and explained that he is not at war with us, and so we are in fact not defeated, but only detained for purposes of communication, and of enforcement of non-war by causing us severe discomfort and pain, and hence creating by mental transference the non-approach of the War Horde.

"We realize this may be somewhat difficult to understand, but it is nonetheless entirely true.

"This presumed-enemy, you argue, is in fact a unit of large size and great destructive capability belonging to the traditional Enemy of our race, who recently attacked our territory. Hence you command us to use every means of destruction and, if unable to overcome or escape the enemy, to immolate ourselves as a penalty for defeat, and to prevent the enemy gaining information from us.

"The presumed-enemy, however, insists that the attack on our territory was not made by him, but that he was pursuing the Enemy, entered our territory by mistake while trying to get at the Enemy, and was attacked by our forces in error. He has pointed out convincing differences in his equipment and devices from those used by the Enemy, and moreover creates at close range none of the perception-gap typical of the Enemy.

"In short, revered Yklon, this presumed-enemy is, regardless of superficial appearances, of a different race entirely, and identifies itself as 'human'—a name we know from intelligence operations to be applied by the Enemy to one of *their* most formidable opponents.

"This represents, not as you seem to argue, a problem, but an almost unbelievable opportunity.

"I again urgently request that you recognize the clear facts, cease your antagonistic posturings, and form common cause with the enemy-presumed-was neutral-is ally-would-be so that the very clear advantages of this realignment of forces can be realized, and the destruction or neutralization of our true Enemy can be brought about.

"Cordially,
"Agbar 221(1)
"Head of Clan"

Yklon, particularly irked by the expression, "antagonistic posturings," swallowed hard as the queasiness from supper merged with his reaction to the message. He grappled with the wording "enemy-presumed-was neutral-is ally-would-be" and scowled at the Chief Interpreter as he thought: "That's the best you can do?"

The Chief Interpreter's integument, under his sparse bristles, was a dull gray, and he avoided looking at Yklon as he thought, "Sir, we had trouble even to detect this audio replay. The enemy—if they are enemy—took us for a possible raiding party and hit Agbar and the captives on the digits to cause pain and warn us off. It wasn't remotely lethal; it was just a little warning; but we had no idea what might come next. And neither did Agbar and his people, and all their fear and dread came across, too. And our electronics units are way behind the enemy's—if they are enemies—so not only did we have to get close, but our reception was horrible even then. And, sir, you wanted the message quick, so we haven't had any chance to rest, and—"

"Yes, yes," snarled Yklon mentally. "Now summarize the whole message, and strain out all the self-pity, both Agbar's and yours."

"Sir," thought the Chief Interpreter. "Agbar, highest ranking of the captives held by, apparently, the 'humans' he claims we've been fighting since the Enemy retreated through our region—this Agbar, Head of Clan 221, reports that the humans who captured him are distinct from our traditional Enemy, and are not inimical to us. Agbar urges us to make common cause with them, and argues that they cannot be a faction of our Enemy, regardless of their physical resemblance, because their equipment is different, and they do not have the Enemy's unmistakable psychological characteristics. Agbar warns that, as he and the other captives are being held by a non-enemy, neither he nor they may validly be ordered to commit suicide."

"H'm," thought Yklon. "Well, there is some sense in it, after all. That is a good comprehensible summary, Chief Interpreter—much better than the original."

"Thank you, sir. This Agbar must be under a lot of strain, sir."

"Yes. No doubt. But there was something about his message . . . let's see . . . Run through that part near the end again."

He scowled as the message came through: "I and the rest of us would remind you that suicide . . . is not required in the face of a non-enemy, however formidable, and the attempt to force it is in plain defiance of the Code of Proper Action, *and punishable as such*."

Yklon's irritation led him to momentarily forget that

representatives of possibly half the Clans were doubtless listening in, and could readily share his more intense thoughts. That piece of amnesia, in turn, led him to express his reaction in a clear and unmistakable way:

"Surely a gross exaggeration," he thought.

"Not so," came an instant answering thought. "This is Onson 230(4), Assistant Head of the Tribunal of Custom Enforcement. That statement of Revered Agbar, Head of Clan, is quite true, my dear Yklon. And should we receive from Agbar a request for enforcement, the Tribunal will bring this matter before an Assembly-in-Thought of the Clans United. This, Revered Commander of the War Horde, is no light matter, and it is certainly not 'gross exaggeration.'"

Yklon winced, and this time suppressed his response. With some officials, his position as Commander of the Horde could rouse an automatic antagonism, a form of jealousy praised by historical scholars as a defense against any single individual seizing the overlordship of the State. Yklon, any lust for power glutted by the problems of leading the Horde, was unimpressed by the argument; but he was stuck with its practical application.

Above a general background mumble of half-articulated thought, Yklon now heard another sharp mental voice:

"Etkal 320(19) speaking. As a Chartered Consultant on Customs, I am, of course, thoroughly conversant with this subject. I am therefore shocked, revered Onson 230(4). Are you speaking for the whole Tribunal? Or just for yourself? Do you know this is their view? Have you actually asked them? And, above all, have you—or they—researched the question? If so, are you actually unaware of the well known case of Irlop, Head of Clan, vs. the Tribunal at the turn of the present aeon? Not only was that case quite similar, revered Onson, but it ultimately resulted in a Reversal of Verdict, no small humiliation for the entire Tribunal. So, if I were you, I would approach this matter with some discretion.

"And, to the revered Commander of our War Horde, let me say that I and my Consultant Group will be honored to place ourselves at your service, to turn any such difficulties as this to the embarrassment and cost of your foes. All that is needed is to simply agree now to our very reasonable fees, and we can begin work at once. What say you, Revered Commander Yklon?"

As other thoughts clamored in the background, Yklon experienced a cold shudder. All he needed, on top of his other miseries, was a breach-of-custom suit before an Assembly-in-Thought of the Clans. The usual duration of such a suit was 'nearly forever.' It would lead naturally to the enrichment of Etkal, his heirs, assigns, and associates, and the impoverishment of everyone else bogged down in it.

Yklon suppressed his natural reaction, and strained to keep his detectable response cool and courteous:

"Many thanks, Revered Consultant Etkal. But, at the moment, I would prefer not to complicate the execution of our war plans by personal matters. The safety of the State is and must remain paramount. For all of us."

This came out sounding a little more superior and condescending than Yklon intended. And the dead silence following it could mean anything. He wasted no time to get things moving in the right direction:

"Regardless of personal feelings, what matters is that the request of Agbar be dealt with fairly and speedily."

But, damn it, thought Yklon, damping his thought down to a level hopefully undetectable by anyone outside his immediate presence, *Is it really possible there is something to Agbar's picture of this shambles? And—Worse yet?—What if he's right?* Forcefully, he thought, "Chief of Signals—"

"Sir?"

"At once, by electromagnetic communication, inform Agbar, Head of Clan 221, that the command to remove himself from the enemy's control by suicide is rescinded. I repeat, the self-immolation order is canceled. Inform Agbar that we will give his request the most immediately useful response: Let him at once invite the head of the hopefully-to-be-allied power to join us in discussing actions we may both take to embarrass—fatally, if possible—our mutual Enemy."

A background murmur of approval swelled to the level of applause, causing Yklon to cling tightly to the awareness that this situation could be catastrophic if Agbar turned out to be wrong. All he, Yklon, had to do to get swept over the edge of disaster was to be drawn into resonating synchrony with that enthusiastic mental applause. He would then forget what he had to remember:

The whole miserable situation with these hostages could be a trap.

★ ★ ★

As Yklon examined this from the Wij-Wij viewpoint, the human commander, Supreme Interstellar Marshal John von Eckberg Lindt, was staring at a thing about the size of a very large footlocker stood on end. He looked up to say to his technical chief, James Edison Martell, "If you're serious that that footlocker-sized box is its replacement, maybe you'd better explain how this—" He gestured to the room-filling monster known as Combat Forces Master Integration Computer—"got shrunk down and compressed into something a reasonably strong individual could drag around in a duffel bag."

Martell said dryly, "You put someone not too bright in charge of our headquarters and you'll be surprised how much damage he can do. Let someone brilliant, who is deliberately sabotaging us, have the chance to put *his* foot in our affairs, and it will be worse yet."

Martell paused, glanced around, then went on. "What we have here is a combination of two effects: First, the rapid progress in computers; second, getting rid of the Out saboteur, who managed to get it established at Headquarters that only full-sized vacuum tubes—the bigger the better—are reliable enough for military purposes. This replacement here uses miniaturized tubes and transistors, which both are very much smaller."

Lindt started to ask a question, considered the technical nature of the reply he would get, and gave a noncommittal grunt. "Well, let's try the thing and see what it can do."

There was a sharp rap on the door, and Lindt glanced up.

"Come in."

A sergeant came in, bearing a length of yellow message paper. "Sir, this is a translated copy of a message from Wij-Wij headquarters to the captured commander of Wij-Wij prisoners here, who wants to talk to you."

Lindt read the message.

"So, they finally agree to recognize the facts? Tell the Provost Marshal I'll be right down. Tell him to let the commander of the Wij-Wij prisoners know I'm coming."

"Yes, sir."

Martell waited till the door closed, then glanced at Lindt. "Good news?"

"The Wij-Wij want to parley."

"That is good."

"Maybe. It could also be pure confusion—or a trap. After all, their territory is completely surrounded by Out territory. These big inchworm look-alikes may be some kind of tributaries of the Outs."

"Well," said Martell, "the Wij-Wij are certainly bullheaded and pugnacious. Still, if the Outs wanted a conference, I'd be nervous. But these overgrown caterpillars don't seem very tricky to me."

"Don't forget, they're telepaths. And telepaths of a different race. 'Talking' with them is an experience. There's plenty of opportunity there for 'misunderstandings.'"

"Yes, true. Well, good luck, anyway."

"Thanks."

★ ★ ★

Yklon 138(3), Commander of the War Horde, feeling better after a night's rest and a day contending with nothing worse than the known problems of preparing for a conference, was surprised at his own reactions as he faced Supreme Interstellar Marshal Lindt across the conference table. The human, seated upright in a chair, looked like the Enemy, but instead of looking frightening or evil, he seemed as enigmatic as a block of granite. Yklon, reclining

on his wide leather-padded board that had one end on the
floor and the other clamped to the edge of the table, tried
to sense some kind of mental response from the Marshal,
found nothing, then glanced around. Interpreters and other
experts of both races packed the room.

Yklon, both arms bent and stubby hands casually gripping the edges of his board, murmured to the Chief
Interpreter by his side, "This fellow across from us—Do
you get anything from him at all? Don't answer with a
thought. Vocalize."

The Chief Interpreter made a low throat-clearing
noise. His voice sounded rusty. "Nothing. No thoughts.
And no perceptions, true or false."

"What do these people call the Enemy?"

"Externals, I think. No. 'Outs.'"

"You remember that captured Out we questioned? He
radiated visual effects. Every time we asked a tough question, reality would seem to waver, start to fit what must
have been some false picture he was trying to project,
then snap back to what it really was. He apparently couldn't
synchronize his power of illusion with our nervous system.
Do you get any of that with this fellow?"

"Nothing as yet, sir. He seems to have the illusive
talent of a sack of gravel. You remember, Agbar claimed
there was none of it in his experience, either."

"But it could be exceptional mental control."

"True, sir. Very exceptional."

"Yes. Exactly."

"How would we check—"

"Say to him now, vocally, through the interpreters, that we
agree in principle to take part in the attack on the Enemy."

"Sir, that will surprise him and everyone else. We haven't led up to it yet."

"I want to surprise him. Let's jolt him. Let's see if he drops his mask, for so much as an instant."

The Chief Interpreter emitted a series of sharp squeaks and whistles. There was an audible stir in the room. The other side, clustered around a large black overgrown box with wires and cables that snaked under a table and all around their side of the room to other pieces of apparatus, looked up wide-eyed, then translated to the Interstellar Marshal, who, despite his unexpressive face, somehow looked interested, and at once gave a series of mumbling growls that appeared to be the human method of vocal communication.

The Chief Interpreter translated the Marshal's answer:

"I'm glad to hear it. Let's waste no time. Our main forces are already in action."

Yklon growled, his voice low, "Well, there's no perception-gap at all. But what he says doesn't fit our picture of their forces." He thought intensely, "Command Council, what is your view of the present 'human' war activity?"

There was a murmuring mumble that quickly faded to one strong mental voice:

"Ygban 210(2), Head of Council, speaking. The bulk of these people are disengaged and evidently refitting, we aren't sure in what way. But by no means are their main forces grappling with the Enemy."

"So. We've exchanged one meaningful comment, and already they are lying to us. What is the Council's suggestion?"

"String them along and let's see what other stench they emit."

"Has anyone noted any visual falsification of reality?"

There was a mental murmur and mumble, followed by, "Nothing yet. But the whole crew look physically like the Enemy."

"Do you detect any telepathic thought?"

"Nothing so far."

"Perhaps then these *are* 'human.' And humans are liars." Yklon growled to the Chief Translator, "Say vocally, 'We admire your warlike energy and tenacity. How goes the battle with the foe?'"

This produced visible confusion amongst the human interpreters—assuming they were humans, not Enemy. The Interstellar Marshal, however, appeared to brush aside the suggestions of his crowding assistants, to look directly at Yklon, and snarl out a string of rasping noises that produced a corresponding uproar amongst Yklon's interpreters.

"Now what?" said Yklon aloud.

His Chief Interpreter spoke with a tremor, signifying shock. "The Interstellar Marshal said:

"'If you want us to fight on your side, spare us the sarcasm. I repeat, our main forces are in action against the enemy. If your Intelligence operations are so faulty you think our local forces are our main forces, that is your fault, not ours.'"

Yklon, jolted, considered this response, and abruptly noted that now he *was* picking up some kind of faint mental radiation—it seemed like impatience—from the human across the table.

The Interstellar Marshal now gave more snarls and growls. Yklon's interpreters consulted, then the Chief Interpreter translated:

"Let's not waste any more time. While we doodle around here, the Enemy has produced a form of mass illusion so powerful as to confuse our observers at a distance from the action. Are you familiar with this?"

Yklon gripped his board hard with both hands.

A strongly articulated thought came from the Command Council:

"Ygban 210(2) speaking. We resent the human's attitude. Our suggestion is to deny his question. It is obviously a probe for information."

Yklon thought, "Yes, but why?" Aloud, he said to the Chief Interpreter, "Say we are familiar with that Enemy tactic, but have run into it only once—when we penetrated deep into Enemy home territory."

The Interstellar Marshal said: "Do you have a way to counter it?"

"Yes," said Yklon. "Withdraw."

"We don't intend to withdraw."

"Then you will fight at a disadvantage. If you withdraw, the Enemy in our view will not use this weapon in following you. It is our belief that the weapon requires a very wide-based installation to produce its effect, and for some reason the Enemy does not reproduce the installation outside his home system. We have no idea why."

Yklon could sense the disapproval of the Command Council, apparently because he revealed this information readily, and contrary to their advice.

There was a growl from across the table. The Chief Interpreter translated: "The Interstellar Marshal says: 'In your opinion, we have penetrated to their home system?'"

Yklon said, "Yes. I may be mistaken. They may have reproduced that effect elsewhere. But I doubt it."

"We have a question you may not care to answer: Why is your territory embedded in the Enemy territory? Are you under their protection in some way?"

Yklon noted wryly that this question stopped the thoughts of the Command Council. Their growling disapproval of him seemed stunned into silence by the probing audacity of the human.

Yklon, however, could feel a surge of admiration and the beginnings almost of trust. Instead of slogging around endlessly through a swamp of false answers, half-truths, and mutual deception, the Marshal was striking directly at the uncertainties.

Yklon said, "Far from it. They would eliminate us if they could. But our nervous systems are so different from theirs that they cannot effectively mislead our perceptions— though they can, apparently with ease, disrupt many of our electronic devices. There is one aspect of this that I personally did not understand until recently, assuming I do understand it now."

"What is that?"

"They seem to be especially hampered upon entering any territory we hold in large numbers. We thought this resulted from a cumulative reaction to our nervous systems. But we have found it is technological. A line-of-sight communications device of ours, in itself none too satisfactory, but very widely used, evidently temporarily damages their capacity to inflict illusions when, by accident or design, we focus it on them."

This statement roused the council from its silence. A

strong thought reached Yklon: "That was a military secret. You have the right to decide what to say, but you are revealing too much. Remember you are our representative, not our ruler. You command at our pleasure. Pay attention to our advice."

Yklon at once replied mentally, "If you want to replace me, do it. Just remember, you chose me for a reason. I will not contentedly murgle and slodge in this confusion we've been stuck in since the Enemy retreated through our territory—apparently in flight before these Humans. If I see a chance to strike at the Enemy, I will seize it. Our guest here has the clear desire to end this mess. Now either remove me, or trust me. But keep watching."

The Interstellar Marshal was saying, "We appreciate your frankness."

"Then reciprocate it. Can you penetrate our mental communications?"

"Possibly some of us can. If so, they haven't told us. So far as I can answer the question: No, we cannot."

"And—if you will excuse the question—is that a strictly truthful answer, or a wording to avoid the need to give a strictly truthful answer?"

Yklon could sense the Command Council's dismay; but the Marshal didn't hesitate:

"Sure, I'll excuse the question. That is a strictly truthful answer."

Yklon grappled with a very brief impression—he didn't know if it came by telepathy, or by some fleeting expression on the human's face—of amusement. Yklon went on:

"How did you know that our congratulations on your progress against the Enemy was sarcasm?"

This question produced, in Yklon's mental background, a gasp of shock, as at a serious social misstep. But again there was no hesitation or disapproval in the Marshal's response:

"First, in translation, it sounded sarcastic. Second, in your Chief Interpreter's voice, there was a special tone, which our interpreters have identified as indicating 'lack of sincerity, possibly sarcasm or insult.'"

"How did you know this? Are you receiving mental summaries from your translators as we talk?"

"No. We have explained in the past that we are not normally telepathic. Certainly we are not routinely telepathic, as you seem to be. But I need to understand the translations, and had already talked all this over with our interpreters. And are you receiving mental summaries from your specialists?"

"Constantly," said Yklon. "Except when they are too shocked to think by my disregard for the proprieties."

There was a peculiar sound as of some breathing difficulty on the part of the human. Yklon thought intently, "Chief of Alien Physiology, what is the significance of that strangling noise of the human leader?"

"We cannot explain it, sir. Possibly it adjusts to some minor change in atmospheric pressure."

The Marshal, shaking and with his head bowed, straightened up, took a fresh breath, and spoke aloud. Yklon's interpreters translated: "I have similar difficulties, myself."

"May we ask," said Yklon, creating another impression of shock from his superiors, "what is the reason for your enmity with the 'Outs'? We do not get along with them.

But, in our view, they have a strong resemblance to you; one might expect you to be allies, not enemies."

The beginnings of a warning thought, "Yklon—" reached him, but faded away at the enormity of this intrusion.

The Marshal, however, said thoughtfully, "I suppose, if things had happened differently—" Then he started over. "To begin with, the Outs moved into territory we planned to settle. There was a clash, and a freak individual dogfight led to the capture of one of them, severely wounded. At this time, we had no clear idea of their power of illusion, or of how rapidly they could recuperate; so the 'body' of this supposedly dead enemy was shipped to our Capital for examination, and ended up at our military headquarters."

Yklon winced. "And this captive—supposedly dead—"

"Supposedly dead, but really alive, with great powers of deception, and for practical purposes indistinguishable from us, was now in our headquarters. From that time on, unwise decisions, and disastrous orders, came down to us. Any emissary sent to protest came back convinced the orders were correct. We began to lose the war, and the losses were becoming more extreme, when there was a change of control at the Capital; external records indicate that one of our new leaders found that this Out captive had infiltrated the command structure, and was using his power of suggestion to sabotage us. Before the Out could stop him, this new official ordered down the reserve fleet and destroyed the Capital—and the saboteur. Since then, we've done a little better in the war."

There was a murmur from the Command Council,

apparently as surprised as Yklon, who began to speak, then realized he did not know what to say. Then the Marshal said, "Well, what do you say we get down to specifics on how to wreck the Outs?"

Yklon didn't hesitate. "Yes. But do we, even combined, have the force to do it?"

"If you and we combine, we will together make a striking force we believe the Outs cannot cancel out."

"Are you certain that if we attack with you, we will not be leaving our territory wide open to Enemy attack?"

"There are very few certainties in war. But we have this portion of space electronically saturated with warships and signal devices, and we see no sign of the Outs anywhere beyond their territory. And, in their territory, our main forces have them by the throat."

"You are using detached units here?"

"Yes. Sometimes individual warships."

"In large numbers overall?"

"Yes."

"We have evidently not detected some of them."

"Good. We are doing our best to conceal them."

"Unlike you, who operate in widely separated cooperating units, we do best in one united fleet. I have the authority to join in a concentrated attack, as you suggest, but it would be best if our full command structure agrees. For this, we need to know if we have been misled as to human strength and numbers."

"You have been, to the best of our ability."

"We have?"

"Of course."

"Why?"

"Your attacks were disrupting our war with the Outs. We felt we had sufficient strength to defeat the Outs while a fraction of our forces independently held off your attacks. But we didn't know if you were somehow allied with the Outs, so we had to mislead you."

"Are you misleading us now?"

"Not to my knowledge. Have you used your communications device on us—the one that hampers the Outs' illusions?"

"Certainly. We thought you were part of the Enemy. And our device works against you; although, where it merely blocks the Enemy's illusion-making power, it renders you unconscious. That, together with baffling intelligence reports, only cleared up when we realized you might be a completely different race."

"We're glad that's settled."

"There is another question here. We have captured documents indicating that you personally control the main force of humans."

A fresh upheaval in the background of Yklon's thought told him what the Command Council thought of this revelation.

The Interstellar Marshal said, "We have deliberately planted misleading information. I control possibly twenty percent of our forces against the Outs."

"Twenty percent?"

"Yes."

"But you are the Supreme Commander?"

"Only here. The overall Supreme Commander is a general by the name of Hauser. My job is just to prevent your interrupting our attack against the Outs."

"But this is the wrong use of force against them! You should not divide your strength!"

"Theoretically, you're right. But we had the Outs on the run. We didn't want to break off our attack on them; but we were unable to make peace with you, apparently because when we entered your territory, you took that for an attack. You weren't the real enemy, so we left just enough force to—hopefully—keep you out of the main battle against the Outs."

The astonishment of the Command Council came across to Yklon, who said to the Marshal:

"In that case, our united strength—yours and ours— would heavily increase the attack on the Enemy. And do you indicate that that fight is now in balance, not favoring either side?"

"No. We still have the edge. But this new trick of theirs slows us down."

"As your twenty percent roughly balances our strength, we, also, must have a relative force of about twenty percent. Your twenty plus our twenty equals forty. As the current human force in actual action against the Enemy equals one hundred percent minus your twenty, and the Enemy is losing, then the Enemy has perhaps seventy-five percent, while you have eighty percent in action against him and twenty percent watching us. The arrival of your and our united strength in combat should change that balance from—say—eighty vs. seventy-five to one hundred twenty vs. seventy-five. That could be decisive."

"Yes, but relative force can be deceptive. We need to make the most of this advantage."

"Yes. Let us not try to crush out a victory by force alone

and end up bled dry. The Enemy is in his own territory. He may resist desperately. Let's first unhinge him by striking in a direction where he is weak. And he must not know ahead of time that we are coming."

Yklon could sense a faint telepathic radiation from the human commander. It seemed to be approval combined with the beginnings of enthusiasm.

The Marshal leaned forward and spoke directly to Yklon:

"There are signs the Outs intercept some of our communications. So while we hit their weak point by surprise with everything we've got, it might not be too bad an idea to have a heavy traffic in messages to tell nonexistent units where to hit next. We want to give the Outs every chance to make mistakes."

As this comment reached the Command Council, Yklon suddenly received their mental response: "Ygban, Head of Council. We like this fellow's style, Yklon! If you agree, join with him! Now is the chance to *end* these cursed illusionists."

Yklon opened and closed his grip on the edges of his board. "Yes. Yes!"

The Marshal said, "We're agreed?"

"We're agreed. Now let's work out the details. If we scant the details, they might still wreck us."

★ ★ ★

The battlespace was huge, comprising the enormous distances between the stars and the planetary systems, in which floated the detached space fortresses, the individual scout ships, manned or automated, and the warning devices whose main function was to tell of the approach of an enemy, the whole knit together into a defensible unit by the formidable fleets, the solar beams, and the communications net that carried the information on the actions of the opposing forces, and the orders to the defenders.

Supreme Interstellar Marshal Lindt, in the Combined Forces Command Ship, studied the greatly condensed visual image of the battlespace—which appeared to hang suspended as Lindt moved the controls, causing the image to turn in the air before them, then lift slightly and roll over and backwards. Then he paused. From this angle, the tiny lights, of various colors and degrees of brightness, representing the location of the defenses of the Enemy, seemed spread out and faint.

Yklon growled through his Chief Interpreter, "Let us strike them hard from this angle."

Lindt said, "They should have some difficulty to reply. If they have anything left but strictly local reserves, we haven't found them. They are almost totally committed."

"And our simulated fleet?"

Lindt shrank the image to a yet smaller representation, which showed the combined real fleets swinging up from "below," while a ghostly force of blurs came down from "above."

"Our communications ships," said Lindt, "can make enough noise to seem like an armada coming in to hit them from another angle."

Yklon stretched out a stubby hand to take the control box, and played back the past images, noting the changes which had led to the present position. He then progressed to the coming changes, to note the most probable positions, and gave a low murmur of gratification.

"If our past experience is still a reliable guide," said Yklon, expanding the representation to its normal size, and handing the control back to Lindt, "their detectors should pick us up very soon. And then they should pick up the deception fleet."

* * *

The Enemy's forces, though already stretched to the limit, suddenly seemed to multiply visibly, becoming enormous in their total numbers, as huge beams of searing light swung through the battlespace, and images of human ships exploded before Lindt's eyes.

Yklon said, "This is their deception device. This is why we withdrew."

Lindt said, "It's all visual. There are audible signals from the display when a ship or unit of ours is actually destroyed. There are no such signals now, regardless how it looks."

"We know this. But it is hard to function effectively when deceived by our own detection apparatus. Normally, we can brush their illusions aside. This is much more forceful."

Abruptly the distorted effects were gone, and the display showed the Outs turning toward the deception force.

Lindt watched the movement of the now superior human and Wij-Wij forces. Then for an instant the display again showed Out forces that were massively superior crushing puny human and Wij-Wij fleets. A moment later, the display showed the enemy being beaten by powerful fleets converging on his ships and strong points. Then the display showed new forces of the enemy intervening, and the attacking fleets being annihilated.

From the background, a voice said, "Marshal Lindt, we have a message from General Hauser: 'Continue attack using computer control and non-visual signals. The enemy is rotating this sham from one of our units to another. *He can't keep it up.*'"

Lindt said, "Send to Hauser: 'It's what we're doing already. Do you believe this effect can get any worse than it is now?'"

Briefly, the actual scene on the display showed him the Outs in a terrible situation, being destroyed wholesale.

Yklon said, "That, too, is inaccurate. It is too sudden. It exaggerates the effect of our attack."

For an instant, the entire scene before Lindt went black, showing nothing—neither the display, their own ship, the interpreters, nor anything else. Lindt realized that either all power to the lights had been cut off, or his vision itself.

Then abruptly, the display was there before him, and the scene on it showed the Outs at a severe disadvantage. The interpreters of both races, and Yklon himself, were all there, looking, despite their differences in appearance, badly shaken.

Yklon said, "This is something else they can do. This is why we withdrew. Will you persist, or withdraw?"

"Aside from making illusions, I don't think there's anything they can actually do. But if we try to withdraw now, we'll make mistakes and we may get whipped."

"I am in contact with my unit commanders," said Yklon. "When this happened to us before, all of our units were affected at once. This time, there are breaks in the illusion from one unit to another. It is possible to form a consistent picture of what is actually happening, though the sources vary from moment to moment. I think you are right."

Their surroundings again went black. Then there was a whirl of light in the blackness. In this, black shapes began to form. There came to Lindt a sense of dread and horror that was beginning to move out from the shapes in the center of the blackness. With an effort, he looked away. The sense of foreboding grew and strengthened.

Lindt felt a surge of anger. He focused his gaze directly at the white swirl with its foreboding shapes. Exactly what he thought or did was not clear to him, but the shapes abruptly vanished, as if in response. Then there was again the blackness there had been before; then it disappeared, again showing the inside of the ship.

A voice spoke from the background, "Marshal Lindt, General Hauser has answered your message. He says: 'It evidently can get worse. But they aren't letting up every few seconds because they want to. They're overloaded.'"

The display now showed the Out warships nearest Lindt's and Yklon's combined fleets falling back, severely damaged. As the Outs were driven back, a very large, apparently artificial space installation of some kind was attempting to withdraw with them, but was too slow. The fire of the attacking fleets began to register on this installation.

Again, there was blackness. Then, after a brief delay, the display was visible in front of them. A series of dazzling flashes, from the place where the installation had been, showed briefly the results of the heavy fire of the approaching fleets.

Lindt waited, the afterimages of the brilliant flashes still visible, expecting the blackness to blot out the display, but trying to see the part farthest from his and Yklon's attack. If this display was accurate, the Outs were suffering heavily. Where Lindt and Yklon had hit, the enemy was all but wiped out, and the effects were ripping the battlespace into two huge separated parts. On the far side of the display, a scatter of Out warships was enjoying a brief victory, as the human deception fleet, made up mostly of communications ships, having done what they were supposed to, fled the combat.

Looking over the display, surprised that it was still visible, Lindt could see no way the enemy could make sense of his own dispositions. And there was no way the Outs could know in which direction Lindt and Yklon might turn next, while the immense size of their attacking force guaranteed ruin for any of the ragged defenders who should try to stop them.

Lindt turned to Yklon.

"The system in the center of this display is their home system?"

"That is our belief. We may be wrong."

"But that system well to the 'right,' in the display, has the only really solid looking defense."

"Yes, but it would not be able to hold against our attack."

"Unless everything beyond it moved in to reinforce it."

"Yes."

"So let's head for their home system instead."

As the combined fleets of Lindt and Yklon swung at high speed toward the distant system that seemed to contain the home planet of their enemy, the enemy struggled to disengage from Hauser's attack, to reinforce their home system as best they could. But then the aim of the attackers changed, to attack another target entirely—one that could have given serious trouble if it had received the reinforcements.

The overwhelming attacks continued, with no repetition of the Out interference that had caused Yklon to suggest withdrawal. Remorselessly, the Out positions were overwhelmed, and collapsed. And then, the attack against their home planet and its fellow planets and their star was resumed, smashing through complex sets of mutually reinforcing roboticized space fortresses, to seize the satellites of several outer planets. With bases established on these satellites, with a number of the space fortresses under their control, a steady supply of Wij-Wij troops, workers, and industrial equipment began to move in, methodically seizing more and more of the Out home system. At a clearer and clearer disadvantage, the enemy fought on, making increasingly desperate, and more and more futile, counterattacks. The possibility of the total destruction of the Outs began to seem a reasonably likely end of the war.

Lindt was examining wreckage from the space installation destroyed shortly before the last use of the Out's special device when a message came from Hauser:

"The Outs are asking for peace terms. They apparently begin to see where this could end."

Lindt replied, "How do we make peace with a bunch of illusionists? They can fool us without half trying."

"They can fool *us*. They normally can't fool the Wij-Wij."

"They want peace *now*. Wait until they've had it for a while. They'll get rested up. They'll recuperate. They'll realize that they, the proper masters of the universe, have given in to a bunch of weak minds with no illusion-making powers and their inchworm/caterpillar allies. This will be offensive to them. Revenge will be called for. They'll harangue each other. They'll make a plan. The next thing you know, they'll figure out how to stab the Wij-Wij in the back, recover the basis of their former power, and erupt out at us."

"What do you suggest?"

"I can only think of two suggestions. First, if we can manage it, wipe them out completely."

"That's apparently possible, but it won't be quick or easy. We've bypassed part of their territory. We'll have to go back and take care of that. And individuals and small groups could still exist in places we regard as ruined. It could take us a thousand years to finish them off completely. And centuries more to make sure of it."

"Yes," said Lindt, "and the whole process would be horrible. But it might still be worth it."

"What's your other suggestion?"

"The Wij-Wij can knock us unconscious with a device of theirs. This device, used against the Outs, *temporarily stuns the Outs' ability to create illusions*. I have this from Yklon himself; but we need to know a lot more about it. If we can develop this, we might severely limit the Outs' special threat."

"This device is what makes that 'Wij-Wij-Wij' noise we hear when they attack?"

"As I understand it."

"Okay. You check on that. Be sure we have the right information. And see what Yklon thinks. If you can, get a sample of the device. If you can't, let me know, and we'll go at it on a higher level. Meanwhile, we'll offer the Outs a temporary truce while we work out the details for them to pull back from their more advanced territory, which threatens our own and Wij-Wij territory. If that device is workable, and if it hits the Outs anywhere near as hard as it hits us, it should help solve this mess."

Lindt said uneasily, "Look, I know I just suggested this myself. But it strikes me as too easy; you know, germs become immune to medicines; new weapons beget new defenses. We don't want to go through all this again a hundred years from now."

"We don't intend to rely on this and nothing else. But if you'll just figure the cost to us of continuing this war on an extermination basis, which incidentally will hold back our own exploration and settlement in space, then a strictly fair peace looks a lot better."

"I agree. But making a fair peace with the Outs might strike them as just weakness on our part. And some of our own people think if there's no threat staring you in the face, you should disarm completely and save a *lot* of money."

Hauser gave a short bark of a laugh. "There's a point you may be overlooking. On the far side of the Outs' territory, there's a bunch of aliens called the 'Stath.' Not far from them, there's the 'Ursoids.' You've been in another part of our territory, with other neighbors. Don't worry about there being no threat staring us in the face. Anyone who wants to disarm just hasn't looked around yet. Wait till they get a good look at the Stath and the Ursoids."

"I think," said Lindt, "I have heard of them, in some briefing or other. But it was all a long distance away and just background when I heard it. What are *they* like?"

"Well, the Stath are a lot like overgrown weasels. They'd slit your throat for the entertainment value. But if they make an agreement, they *will* honor it—so long as they respect you. And the Ursoids are the kind of people the Stath respect. The Ursoids will bash your brains in if they think you've gone back on a deal. And they're both the same in one respect: They only want all the territory that adjoins theirs. If you see what I mean, nobody can happily disarm with them next door."

Lindt thought it over, and suddenly smiled. "So—From another angle, we aren't the Outs' only worry, then?"

"Oh, no. We're just the one most susceptible to their power of illusion, and outwardly the most like them."

"Supposing we should completely wipe out the Outs, then these other beauties would move in?"

"To the best of their ability, you bet they'd move in. Our intelligence reports suggest they'd do it now, only that might drive us to join forces with the Outs, and then they'd be in deep trouble. They're leery of taking either of us on without a big advantage. And, of course, they don't really trust each other, for good reasons."

"Somehow," said Lindt, looking thoughtful, "I suppose we aren't the perfect neighbor, either, looking at it from their viewpoints."

"No, and while our beating the Outs will increase their respect for us, our ruthlessly exterminating the Outs might drive them into each others' arms."

"Yes." Lindt could feel the situation mentally rearrange

itself. "Maybe we *could* reasonably make peace with the Outs, after all. Provided we keep our eyes open."

"I think so," said Hauser. He paused, then added, "There's more than one side to having interstellar neighbors, especially if they're all a little less less than perfect."

Lindt nodded ruefully. "Knowing the details about the others makes each of us look better."

BEWARE OF ALIENS BEARING GIFTS

THE KINDLY INVASION

He sat at the solid oak desk where he had sat for forty years, and methodically went through correspondence as the cheers drifted up from the avenue below. His back stayed turned to the window where the confetti and ticker tape fluttered down. Below, in the street, the cheers rose to a wild crescendo, but he looked up only when an urgent tapping sounded on the door.

"Come in."

It was one of the new girls from the office, with several others behind her.

"Oh, Mr. Peabody, *could* we look out your window?"

He looked at the girls' eager faces, slid a personal letter back into its envelope, and growled crustily, "Go ahead."

The girls were delighted. "Oh, *thank* you, Mr. Peabody." They rushed to the window as Peabody devoted himself to routine correspondence. Behind him, suppressed gigglings, murmurings, and sighs told him the girls wished to join their screams with those of the crowd below. Under his breath, Peabody growled, "The damn fools."

Down in the avenue, the cries finally began to die away

into the distance, and Peabody frowned at the last letter, wrote in the margin, "Tell him, no. Let him get a patent first." He glanced up and cleared his throat, and the girls turned guiltily and left the window, to troop out, saying, "Thank you, Mr. Peabody."

He smiled dryly. "You're welcome. But what did you see?"

"Oh," said one of the girls excitedly, "we saw the envoy's car!"

"And," said another, "we could see him waving!"

"A green arm?" said Peabody, "—or a white or brown one?"

The girls looked thunderstruck.

"Well," said one, "it must have been someone *with* him. It could even have been the President."

A small, beautifully built girl said urgently, "Didn't you *want* to see him, Mr. Peabody?"

Peabody's eyes gave a frosty glint. "I'm not interested in interstellar shell games. Or confidence men, human *or* alien."

The girls looked shocked. The girl who'd asked the question said earnestly, "But the *serum*, the—"

Peabody waved his neatly trimmed square hand. "All humbug. Never put a hook in the water without bait on it."

"But," cried the girl, "I *know* the Shaloux would never—they're *sincere*. Have you watched, on the TV, when they told about—"

"I seldom watch television. I get my news from the papers, where I can take it in at my own pace, and pick out the bones, instead of swallowing it all whole. No, I don't trust the Shaloux. What's their motive? *Why* do they offer us this 'life-serum'? What do *they* get out of it?"

The girl blinked at him, plainly incapable of following his line of reasoning, or even of crediting the possibility that anyone *could* reason that way. She started to speak, but Peabody cut her off.

"No, that's enough." He smiled. "While we chatter on company time, business is going to the dogs."

The girls laughed dutifully, thanked him again, and closed the door gently.

Peabody took out the letter he'd been reading before they came in. He finished his reply, then sent the lot out to be typed, or sent on at once to the company officers who would deal with the problem as directed.

He sat back, put his hands behind his head, and waited. One reply was bound to bring a lightning-fast response.

The phone rang.

Peabody picked it up.

"Hello?"

"Mr. Peabody? This is Charles Lathrop. I have your memo on pricing here. I—ah—I realize you like all major company decisions and differences in writing, but the price you want us to set on this new .30 Recoilless Repeating Sharpshooter—" Lathrop hesitated, as if groping for suitable words. "I just want to be certain there's no *error*. This price—"

Peabody snapped, "What about it?"

"Well, sir, it's—it's pretty fantastic—"

"Don't you think they'll sell at $37.50?"

Lathrop made a kind of desperate gobbling noise.

"Sir, they'd sell like wildfire at a hundred thirty-seven fifty. Sir, this gun uses a completely new principle, and—"

"I'm aware of it."

"No one else can match it. We've got a temporary practical monopoly."

"Good. We can do what we want."

"Yes, sir, and that's exactly why we should charge $137.50. This would rob no one. It would benefit everyone. Here we've got a gun that will punch a hole through eight feet of pine boards, and it's got the kick of a pussycat. A ten-shot magazine, with Lightning Reload Guides, a flat trajectory, minimum maintenance, maximum reliability, tough, rugged, dependable, accurate beyond belief. Sir, the *right* price for this is $199.95, and that's dirt cheap at the price."

"We're charging $37.50."

★ ★ ★

There was a silence. Finally Lathrop said, "Could you tell me *why*, sir?"

"Are we going to lose money on it?"

"N-No. This way we'll still make a bare profit. But we *could* make a mint."

"But this way we'll sell more guns."

"Yes, there's no doubt of that."

"And this is quite an effective gun."

"It certainly is."

"And it can take surplus ammunition."

"Yes, but after you use enough of any kind of steel-jacketed ammo—"

"One thing at a time, Lathrop. Now, how popular is this gun going to be?"

"Very popular. But I still don't see why—"

"Won't it be the most popular gun Peabody Arms and Ammunition ever produced?"

"Yes, sir. I have to admit, it certainly will be. We've already been swamped with inquiries. This gun will be a household word for excellence inside a month."

"All right. Now, every man likes to leave some monument behind him. Something to be remembered for."

"But, Mr. Peabody!" Lathrop's voice advertised his astonishment. "All you have to do is take the serum—"

"I'm not anxious to remain my present age for the next thousand years, Lathrop. Moreover, I don't trust the Shaloux."

"But all you have to do is to let them open their minds to you! You'll see that they're kindly, benevolent, loving. All they care about is to help others!"

Peabody looked at the phone as if he smelled rotten fish. He said coldly, "The price of the gun will be $37.50."

There was a sigh of resignation.

"Yes, Mr. Peabody."

Peabody hung up. Now, that was taken care of, and he had a nice plausible reason for his action. Anyone could understand it. No one could confine him to an institution for it. He shoved the phone back, reached into the bottom drawer of his desk, and pulled out the morning edition he'd glanced through on the train. There were the huge headlines staring at him:

SHALOUX OKAY EARTH!
FULL MEMBERSHIP NOW!

Peabody snorted. "Humbug. Silly claptrap." He read on:

New Serum Shipment
100% Inoculation
Is Shaloux Aim

"Sure," growled Peabody. "But why? What's *their* aim. What do *they* get out of it?"

He read further:

Open-Mind Conference Held

Peabody slammed down the paper.

"Open-mind! Everybody's supposed to have an 'open mind'. Humbug! Open it far enough, and *who knows* what will come in? The whole thing's a trap. Leave the door open, to prove you trust everyone. Then the thieves can strip the house and put a knife in you while you sleep."

Cautiously, he began to read the paper, conscious of the article's bias, opening his mind just a little slit at a time to bash the unwelcome ideas over the head as they entered:

Washington — Miliram Diastat, the benevolent (How the devil do *they* know he's benevolent?) plenipotentiary (Hogwash. He may be just a messenger boy.) of the Shaloux Interstellar (They could come from Mars, for all we know.) Federation, met with the President today, and in solemn rapport (What's "rapport" *really* mean? Maybe it's hypnotism.) concluded the mind-exchange (Or brain-washing) which is a precondition for entry into (defeat by) the Federation.

Mr. Diastat (Why call him "Mr."? The damned things are neuter.) assured reporters afterward that all had gone well (For the Shalouxs, that is.) in the mind-exchange (brain-washing). He said (*It* said), raising his (its) hands (extremities of upper tentacles) to heaven (over its head—that is, over the end of the thing with teeth in it.), that our peoples will be joined as one (eaten up) with (by) theirs, in a final ceremony next year. At that time, travel throughout the vast extent (*They* claim it's vast.) of the Federation will be free to all (Economically impossible.), and Earth's excess-population problem will be solved (Everybody will be killed.), while at the same time (never) personal immortality will have been granted by universal (Humbug. There must be *some* people with sense enough to keep out.) inoculation with the serum (slow poison).

★ ★ ★

Peabody read on, scowling, about the heaven-on-earth that would come about with the wonders of interstellar science, about how everything was to be free, all the work was to be done automatically, and everyone in the Shaloux Federation was invariably happy. He snorted, growled, cursed under his breath. The Shaloux, the paper went on, were loving and kindly, because that was how they were educated to be; and in their Federation, advanced methods of production rendered the satisfaction of every ordinary desire not only possible but practically instantaneous. The abundance of space in the universe cut friction between differing ways to a minimum.

Peabody rejected the whole line of argument, then angrily turned the page, and studied a photograph of Miliram Diastat, the Plenipotentiary of the Shaloux Federation, who was shown "shaking hands" with the President. The paper also showed a view of him head-on, so to speak. The caption compared the plenipotentiary to a "large mint-green teddy bear," but to Peabody the creature looked like a giant cucumber with a lot of teeth in one end, stood generally upright but with a forward tilt, and equipped with two sets of tentacles, top and bottom, and a tail with a barb-like sting ray. Beneath the picture, the paper quoted a speech in which this entity was referred to as "Our Brother from the Stars."

Peabody threw the paper down in disgust.

Grant the *possibility*, he thought, that all this *might* be true. After all, nearly anything *could* be possible. But was it likely? Did it fit in with experience? Did it add up?

He jammed the paper into the waste basket, and sent for one of the new girls.

"Have you," he demanded, "taken the serum?"

Her eyes widened. "Oh, yes, sir. I don't want ever to get a day older."

"What happens if you fall down in the bathtub?"

"Well—" She blushed. "I intend to be careful."

"I mean, accidents could end immortality pretty fast."

"Yes, sir, but I'm *sure* the Shaloux have some answer."

"You've—ah—'exchanged minds' with them, and that convinces you?"

"Oh, yes, sir. They're perfectly straightforward and well-intentioned. All you have to do is to let them *show* you. You just open your mind to them."

"There's a machine involved, isn't there?"

"Yes, sir, but that's just because we aren't developed far enough to do it direct. It's just a *little* machine anyway. It's not much bigger than a hat box."

Peabody shook his head. An atom-bomb was just a comparatively *little* thing.

This whole business, he told himself, stunk. Aloud, he said, "It's all hogwash."

The girl smiled. "Sir, excuse me. If the experts all believe it—"

"The experts all have open minds."

"But isn't an open mind the best?"

"That depends on who's trying to put what into it."

"But you *can't prejudge*."

Peabody snorted. "If I see somebody, who would profit by murdering another man, secretively sift a powder into this other man's drink, I'll prejudge him. I may go wrong this way, but not often. What you have to consider is, *what's their motive?*"

The girl looked at him almost with pity. "Sir, honestly, you really *should* let them show you their minds. And you should open your mind to them. They could help you, so much."

Peabody instantly closed his mind to that suggestion, and to the girl's almost loving kindly tone.

"I have my weaknesses," he said crustily, "but I hope walking into boobytraps isn't one of them. You talk about these monsters as if they're angels. They don't look angelic to me. The devil with it. Take a letter."

★ ★ ★

The next six months passed in what, for Peabody, was equivalent to a siege. Hosts of fantastic ideas clamored at the locked door of his mind, seeking admission. His own brother "exchanged minds," took the serum, saw the light, and tried to convert him. Peabody added another bar to his mental door, and installed bolts at top, bottom, and on the hinge side, just in case. He didn't rest content with having closed the main entrance to his mind. He watched alertly for anything that might have figuratively sneaked in through the cellar window; and when he found it, in the form, say, of a grudging thought that it would be only fair to the Shaloux to *try* their mind-trading—when he found such a thought, he ruthlessly broke it down to its essentials, rejected the bits and pieces, and held the fort secure. As the press, radio, TV, and ordinary everyday conversation praised the Shaloux and their selfless Federation, the urgent ideas bounced off Peabody like BB-shot off a locked safe.

Meanwhile, the Peabody Miracle-Gun, as the new 30-caliber rifle came to be called, was making a hit on its own. Sales began to skyrocket. Profits crept up sedately. The exasperating rumor spread that the gun was Shaloux-designed, which infuriated the actual designer, but didn't overly trouble Peabody, as it increased sales. Sales, in fact, rapidly climbed to such a point that anti-gun fanatics grew virulent. Peabody pointed to his low profit-margin and bared his teeth in a grin like the Shaloux. The critics pointed to the gun's unprecedented power, range, accuracy, and the murderous effect of the specially shaped Shock bullet when it hit its target. Peabody put hand on heart and pleaded that in the coming age of Federation-inspired universal peace and understanding, no one would even think of using the guns against other *humans*; the gun would be just a memento of old Earth, and a merciful, quick-and-painless defense against unFederated monsters that might be run into occasionally on new worlds. On this piece of hypocrisy, the criticism foundered and expired.

By now, eleven months had gone by. A fever of expectation began to seize the world. In one more month, Earth would be a Federation member. When half of the last month was gone, a new rumor suddenly exploded into a stated fact: The advanced science of the Shaloux had discovered a new type of universal antigen that would make any human who took the treatment proof against all known human diseases.

Peabody's office staff was amongst the first, locally, to take the treatment, and for two solid weeks they glowed with health as Peabody suffered with a miserable cold.

Peabody's mind stayed closed, but, apparently from inside, the thought was germinated: "Suppose I'm wrong?"

In response, he thought coldly, "It wouldn't be the first time."

"But I could be giving up a lot out of sheer bullheadedness."

"*Somebody* has got to keep his head, and I won't quit now."

* * *

With the nucleus of an inner revolt threatening to erupt out of hand anytime, Peabody clamped himself under tight control, and devoted himself to stimulating the sale of his gun, an activity which, in flashes of another viewpoint, quickly suppressed, seemed almost childish.

Angrily, he told his errant thoughts, "When I'm convinced a thing like this is genuine, maybe then I'll cut loose from common sense. Not until."

By now, his incredible wrongheaded obstinacy was legendary among his acquaintances. Only a lingering wonder at the success of his gun kept them from kidding him mercilessly.

By now, too, everyone around him, with only rare stubborn exceptions, blazed with apparent health and well-being, while he crept around sniffling, sneezing, and muttering, "Hogwash. It's humbug. All of it. There's a catch somewhere."

On the day before the admission of Earth to the great Shaloux Interstellar Federation, a new announcement rocked the world. Shaloux science had discovered how to reverse the human aging process. This was to be done by reinforcing "cellular memory," reversing "colloid crystallization," and "regenerating" nerve-cell tissue. The means of stimulating all this had been reduced to a few "key compounds" and "pseudo-viruses," that could be packed into a few pills. Anyone who had taken the life-serum, could now take the pills, and be seventeen years old into the indefinite future. Best of all, the whole process would take only a week or so to complete.

Wherever Peabody turned, men and women of all ages were now munching pills, and dutifully feeding them to children, who were thus guaranteed never to get older than seventeen.

The next day, when formal admission to the Federation was to take place, started off normally, thanks to the Shaloux request that through the city and the offices people go as usual to their places of business. But a little after one o'clock, a number of celebration parades began winding their way through the city, and the offices promptly emptied into the streets. Peabody, his back turned to the window, ignored the screams and shouts, and dictated to Miss Burell, a young, somewhat plain, but highly efficient secretary. As the noise from the street below reached its climax, he glanced at her curiously. "Are you sure you don't want to go down there?"

She shook her head. "I don't like screaming crowds. Besides, this whole business reminds me of the Pied Piper of Hamlin. And I don't believe in their life-serum."

"What about their universal cure?"

She looked unconvinced. "It may be just what they say. But it doesn't ring true to me. And this latest thing—the pills that will make everyone seventeen—"

"Certainly," he said, smiling, "you understand that our wise elder brothers and their magnificent science—"

She looked at him as though he were insane—which made his smile grow wider—and said:

"It's awfully odd that we're supposed to eat this latest pill just a little before their big ships come down to carry out the so-called 'ceremony of admission.'"

"But if you've 'exchanged minds' with them under their hypnosis machine, you realize that they're perfectly sincere and benevolent, don't you?"

"I wouldn't let them use that machine on me for a thousand dollars. All this something-for-nothing benevolence of theirs reminds me of a finance company. They'll put cash in my pocket, all right. But *then* what?" She poised her pencil to take dictation.

Peabody grinned, brought his mind back to the letter, started to speak, and paused.

★ ★ ★

From below, the only sound was a low grinding noise, followed by a repeated scraping sound.

He listened, heard a few distant, oddly inflected voices, then a harsh grating noise.

Frowning, he got to his feet, quietly slid the window up, and glanced down into the canyon between the buildings.

Down below, the sidewalks were heaped with motion-less figures. In the street, bright-green Shaloux pulled the bunting and gay decorations off their stopped parade floats, to disclose the mud-colored vehicles beneath. With the brightly-colored cloth and paper gone, the first vehicle looked like an armored car, and the others like open amphibious personnel-carriers.

Peabody looked it all over, and nodded sourly.

"Miss Burell, in my coat closet you'll find several of our new rifles, and three big boxes of ammunition. If you'll bring out a rifle, and drag one of the boxes over here—".

She was gone in a flash, came back with one of the guns, and then slid out a large cardboard carton. The rifle fit neatly in Peabody's hands as he raised it, felt the two little pins that showed the gun was loaded and the magazine full, moved the selector lever to semiautomatic, made sure the safety was off, and then paused as there came a tinkle of glass from across the street, where the windows were sealed shut for all-season air conditioning.

A quick glance showed a man one floor down, taking aim with a rifle just like Peabody's.

Pam-pam-pam came the familiar sound, for the first time actually musical to Peabody's ears.

He looked down at the street, raised the gun, made due allowance for his height above the target, and squeezed the trigger.

The gun moved in his hand like a kitten batting lightly at a ball of yarn.

Down below, the control box of an open personnel-carrier erupted in a blaze of sparks.

Peabody adjusted his aim slightly, squeezed the trigger.

A large Shaloux exploded in a green haze of teeth and snakelike arms.

An amplified voice boomed out, "We are your Elder Brothers from the Stars! This is all a mistake! We—"

There was a quiet businesslike *pam-pam* from across the street, and that took care of the amplified voice.

From somewhere else came the sound of methodical firing. A line of holes stitched their way across the first of the line of Shaloux vehicles, suggesting that someone was trying the effect of the steel-jacketed ammunition.

Peabody sighted on the door of the vehicle, and plugged two Shaloux as they burst out. A third erupted through a trapdoor in the vehicle's roof, went off the top in a flying dive, and got around the corner so fast that there was no time for Peabody to even take aim. Nevertheless, the wall repeatedly exploded in flying fragments just behind the Shaloux as it streaked for cover.

Peabody was vaguely aware that Miss Burell was using one of the other guns to good effect, and that up and down the street, the occasional *pam-pam* had become an almost continuous murmur, suggesting that a small but definite percentage of humanity felt uneasy when offered the universe on a silver platter. He grinned.

★ ★ ★

A shadow slid over the face of the building across the way. Peabody realized this must be some kind of aircraft, stepped back from the window, and abruptly there was a dazzling blaze of light, a clap that shook the building, a clattering of broken glass, and then a long interval of swirling sickness.

When he came to, aching and dizzy, with ringing ears

and a cheek that felt like ground meat, he was with a group of other people, being held upright before a large green creature at a curving desk.

It took Peabody a few moments to get used to the sight of Shaloux hurrying past in the corridor outside, Shaloux standing respectfully behind the creature across the desk, and Shaloux entering to bob briefly before the desk, exchange short bursts of gobble, and then back out into the corridor and hurry away.

Peabody could feel his hair prickle and his flesh crawl; but he kept his jaw stiff, and waited patiently. Eventually, some chance might present itself to do the Shaloux some more damage.

In due time, the creature at the desk realized that his captives were conscious, and turned toward them.

Speaking with great care, using a clear understandable pronunciation, the Shaloux said, "I am Miliram, Plenipotentiary of the Interstellar Federation."

Peabody's head throbbed, and he was faintly dizzy, but he paid close attention as the voice went on:

"We Shaloux wish to express our sincere regrets for what has happened. We are very sorry. You see, the molecular composition of the human body is somewhat exceptional, and reacted rather strongly with our life-serum. This whole unfortunate incident, which we deeply regret, has come about because of the unusual allergic response of human tissues. We want you all to understand that we Shaloux meant no harm to you and your people, but were motivated only by the broadest and most humanitarian of reasons. You *do* understand that, don't you?"

In his mind's eye, Peabody could again see the

unconcerned Shaloux ignore the prostate humans, tear the bunting off their vehicles, then grind forward.

Someone said, "Allergic response? You mean all this was *accidental*?"

The Shaloux didn't hesitate. "Entirely. We are prostrated with grief."

Out of the corner of his eye, Peabody could see the Shaloux briefly hurrying past in the corridor.

The plenipotentiary went on smoothly:

"Brothers of Earth, believe me, we Shaloux *love* humans."

★ ★ ★

The words came out with such sincerity that Peabody almost forgot what he had seen with his own eyes. Around him, there was sickly sympathy. Peabody made a murmur suggestive of a kind of the same noise himself, as soon as he got control of his vocal apparatus.

"Then," said the Shaloux sincerely, "you, like we, all wish to make amends, to wash the misunderstanding away, once and for all?"

"Of course," murmured Peabody, adding to the mumble of agreement.

"You realize," said the Shaloux, "that we wish to make amends for the damage that has unfortunately been done to our human brothers? All the things that we promised will be yours, though it will take a little longer, since we must, first, improve the serum."

The last words "improve the serum" came out with a peculiar emphasis, and it dawned on Peabody that the plenipotentiary must still think that all humans had taken the drugs, but that a certain percentage, for some reason, had been unaffected and would just need stronger medicine. In that case, the Shaloux had no idea what they had accidentally done to the human race.

In a wishy-washy voice, someone near Peabody was saying, "Certainly we *must* do what we can to spread the word that all this is just a *dreadful* mistake. But surely, Mr. Plenipotentiary, if you merely *tell* them—"

"Unfortunately, before our—ah—information and assistance teams can get really near the survivors, who are equipped with truly vicious weapons, your countrymen shoot our—ah—aid men—and prevent us from clearing up the misunderstanding."

There were murmurs of shocked incredulity, even though everyone Peabody could see had a look that didn't quite fit the sound.

"This is terrible," said Peabody, speaking above the murmur, and putting sincerity in his voice. "How can we *stop it*?"

The plenipotentiary said earnestly, "We thought, perhaps, if their *own* people told them, they would be more likely to listen, and to accept our sincere apologies."

"Yes," said someone, "that certainly seems very likely."

"And then," said the Shaloux, "perhaps you could have them all gather together in one spot, where we could care for them better, and give assistance to the survivors."

Peabody waited a few seconds till he trusted his voice. At that, he recovered before the rest could find anything to say. He murmured, "Yes, that certainly *would* be more efficient."

"Exactly." The plenipotentiary added sincerely, "If you people would like to exchange minds with me, to prove—"

Peabody did his best to nip that in the bud. "It isn't at

all necessary. What you've said has completely reaffirmed our beliefs about the Shaloux Federation. We are anxious to get started."

The plenipotentiary beamed with what appeared to be satisfaction, murmured a few gobbling noises, and the guards released them.

An hour later, Peabody, Miss Burell, and the others were standing at the base of a hill looking back as the Shaloux aircraft that had brought them there dwindled into the distance.

Miss Burell said unbelievingly, "I never expected to get out of *there* alive."

Peabody felt as if he might pass out anytime. Still, he was better off than he'd been a little while ago. He cleared his throat. "They out-suckered themselves."

The ex-prisoners were glancing at each other. "Well," said one of them, "we must end this resistance to our wise Brothers from the Stars. Did anyone notice how thin that hull was?"

"Yeah. Half-a-dozen good men, with the Super-V steel-jacketed ammo, in Peabody rifles—"

Miss Burell was looking around blankly, "Didn't *anybody* fall for that Shaloux?"

Peabody, despite his aches and pains, was starting to feel better.

"Consider," he said, "the Shaloux didn't kill people *at random*. Instead, they baited a trap, which *only attracted certain people*. What do you suppose they've done to the human race?"

"You mean, they've carried out something like natural selection, only faster?"

"Exactly. And who do you suppose they've selected as survivors?"

* * *

Back at Shaloux headquarters, Miliram Diastat, the plenipotentiary, was having uneasy second thoughts. The possibility had just occurred to him that conceivably the human survivors had never taken the Shaloux life-serum in the first place, but had successfully resisted that bait. And in that case—

"Queasal," he said to a nearby psychological-warfare officer, "Ah, a question of theory has just occurred to me."

"Yes, sir. You wish to know?"

"Ah-h'm. It is correct, is it not, that our standard Fast Conquest Procedure is based on the victim's desire to get something *free*?"

"Absolutely, sir. The Prime Bait is based on the invariable, universal SFN-trophic psychological reaction. Offer the victim Something-For-Nothing in a sufficiently alluring form, and you invariably suck in the whole local population, and can clean out one planet after another at very modest expense, without maintaining a burdensome planetary combat-force."

"Yes. Now—ah—as a hypothetical question—*if* we should ever run into a bunch, some of whom *lacked* this standard response—then what?"

"It would be a nasty situation, sir. After one of our operations, there is always an abundance of weapons, shelter, stored food, and so on; but, of course, it does the locals no good, because dead locals shoot no guns. But, in the hypothetical situation you mention, the survivors could make use of them, and would be very hard to root out.

Worst yet, they would doubtless reproduce, and *h'm*—the characteristics of a *whole race* of such people would be frankly unpredic—" He paused. "Of course, this is all purely hypothetical, but as far as I'm concerned, I can tell you *I* would hate to experience—" He paused again, staring at the door through which the human prisoners had been led out. He swallowed uneasily, producing a characteristic reflex clicking of teeth that did not signify confidence.

The plenipotentiary cleared his breathing ducts, and spoke loudly. "Of course. Well, now we'll want to get ready to exterminate the rest of this present batch." He coughed, wheezed, and glanced back at Monolar Oia, his second-in-command.

"Monolar, my boy," he said, "you know, I've been thinking about your advancement. A successful planetary occupation such as this present one could really help your career." He coughed painfully. "Personally, I've been feeling rather off my feed lately, and if you'd like to take over, why—"

Monolar looked as if he'd been doing some furious thinking, too. Before Diastat could finish his offer, Monolar said piously, "Sir, with me, you come first. This planet is the crowning jewel of *your* career, sir. I couldn't possibly excuse myself for being selfish about it."

Diastat squinted at the next officer in line, who was staring with foreboding out a porthole at the planet, sucking his teeth, and plainly readying some unctuous reply. There was no hope there.

The plenipotentiary turned from his officers to the large globe that showed an overall view of this planet where things had started out so promisingly. His face showed the hopeful expression of a crook with a nice confidence scheme, in need of exactly one thing to put it over—an eager and trusting sucker.

But as he looked at the globe, the plenipotentiary's expression gradually turned to gloom.

No matter how he approached the problem, there just wasn't a sucker in sight.

MISSION OF IGNORANCE

Second Lieutenant Jack Smith, at attention before the weird-looking entities, asked himself why *he* had to represent Earth at this second visit of the Galactics. Their first visit, marked by a jovial presentation of gifts, had been handled by the highest officials on Earth.

Across the legless table that hung before them with no visible support, the Galactic Emissaries appeared to be pondering the same question. The one seated directly before Smith, more or less human in appearance, and acting as a spokesman, made a throat-clearing noise. His voice was extremely cold.

"Excuse me if I seem repetitious. Did you say you were a *messenger* from the Earth representative? Or are you some kind of functionary attached to his staff?"

"I *am* the Earth representative."

"I find that difficult to understand."

Smith was inclined to agree, but there was no use dwelling on that. He considered his scant but explicit instructions, and said, "I have written authorization to that effect."

"I suggest you show it."

"I will show you my authorization, *if you show me yours.*"

The asininity of this was clear to Smith, who didn't know two words in any Galactic tongue. But—He had his orders.

The Galactic spokesman stared at him a moment, then acquired a peculiar inward-turned expression, as if he were trying to remember a long-forgotten name. At the same time, the Emissary's lips moved very slightly, and Smith had the eerie sensation that the Emissary was talking to someone inside of his head. The Emissary looked sharply at Smith, turned away, and called over his shoulder. From behind one of the curved gray screens, that blocked Smith's view of whatever was in back of the Galactics, came a respectful low-voiced reply.

The spokesman put his hand behind the screen, then placed on the floating table a thing that looked like a small book, followed by what appeared to be a strip of cellophane tape, then a child's block with rounded corners and edges, two dominoes of varying colors and designs, and several pieces of thick paper covered with symbols suggestive of Egyptian hieroglyphics. The Emissary turned toward Smith, and made a slight bow. He spoke ironically:

"Here is our authorization. Please feel free to satisfy yourself that everything is in order."

Smith took a brief look at the things. "I'm prepared to take your word for it." He reached into the inside pocket of his jacket, selected the first of three long envelopes, took from it a crisp white sheet of paper, checked to be sure it *was* his authorization, and handed it over. As he stood waiting, Smith was again struck by the farcicality of giving a second lieutenant the job of representing the planet. There must be *some* reason for it. But what? And why hadn't it at least been explained to him before he was sent here?

Meanwhile, the Galactic, on looking over the authorization, frowned in irritation, and turned it around.

Smith, faintly puzzled at this error, said politely, "You've got it upside down."

The Emissary changed expression, swung around in his seat, called to someone behind the screen, and handed the paper back out of sight. He turned back toward Smith with a cold stare, then sat looking once more like someone intently trying to remember a forgotten name.

Smith studied the Galactic's face. At first, his lips seemed to be moving, very slightly. Then the motion vanished. The Galactic glanced sharply at Smith.

From behind the screen came a click and a snap, then a puzzled voice.

The Galactic reached back, dropped the paper before him on the desk, and looked flatly at Smith.

"What language is this?"

"English."

"You lie."

Smith stiffened, then remembered he was supposed to be a diplomat.

"You are mistaken."

The Galactic held out the paper.

"Suppose you read this to us."

Smith turned the paper around, and read:

"To whoever it may concern: This is to certify that Jack

Smith, Second Lieutenant, E. S. C. F., is duly, officially and in accord with all relevant usages and requirements, appointed Representative of the Special Governing Council of Earth, for the purpose of meeting, consulting with, and carrying out any necessary preliminary negotiations with, the entities known as Galactic Emissaries . . ."

Smith read through to the end, lowered the paper, and directly opposite him, the spokesman for the Galactic Emissaries was looking at him with a distracted expression.

Exasperatedly, Smith asked himself, *Now what? Why that look? It was a simple matter of reading what was written, wasn't it?*

The Emissary leaned forward. "May I see that paper again?" After looking at it, he folded it vertically down the center, so only one side was visible at a time.

"Please read the left side, half-line by half-line, from top to bottom; then turn the paper over and read the other half-lines, on the right side."

Frowning, Smith began to read. This, he decided, must be a check, to make sure he actually was reading. If, for instance, he had spoken from memory, he would now have the problem of mentally dividing the remembered words into as many groups as there were lines of words on the paper, then dividing each group of words roughly in half, and then calling off all the left halves in order, followed by all the right halves. Happily, since he *was* reading it, his only problem was an occasional word or phrase cut apart by the fold in the paper.

When Smith finished, a low voice spoke from behind the screen.

The Emissary looked at Smith wonderingly.

"This, then is written in some form of . . . ah . . . official cipher-script?"

Smith looked blank. Apparently someone hidden behind the screen had checked, and found that he'd read the authorization correctly. Nevertheless, the Galactic Emissary seemed almost as much in the dark as Smith himself. Smith looked at him wonderingly.

"It's just standard shorthand."

The Emissary jumped as if someone had touched him with a hot wire.

"*Shorthand?*"

"Yes."

Smith looked around in amazement.

This harmless comment had created the same effect as a sackful of snakes turned loose at a garden party.

When the clack and jabber finally died down, the renewed quiet was again broken as all the pale-green strands crowning the head of one of the Galactics rose up on end and vibrated with a shriek. Meanwhile, the spokesman was saying anxiously to Smith, "This . . . shorthand . . . is it just taught to a few men selected for the . . . ah . . . diplomatic corps, or is it taught *widely*?"

Smith stared at him. "It's taught widely. Why not?"

The Emissary didn't answer, but turned to talk earnestly to several of the others. When eventually this came to an end, he looked back at Smith.

"Our computer didn't recognize this . . . ah . . . shorthand. This document, then, is written in a formerly obscure form of shorthand?"

Smith thought it over. It was just standard everyday shorthand. But wait a minute now. It was sometimes called "Burdeenite Fastwrite." And the Burdeenites hadn't come into existence till *after* that first visit of the Galactics.

"Not obscure, but fairly new," said Smith. "New, that is, since your previous visit."

This created a scene like chickens in a henyard when a rat runs through.

Frowning in perplexity, Smith reminded himself of the size of the huge Galactic ship, and how it hung easily clear of the ground, its huge mass supported on nothingness. The power represented by this ship was self-evident. Yet, the Galactics themselves were thrown into confusion by a few scratches on paper. Why?

The spokesman was suddenly silent, his head oddly tilted. Then he spoke very firmly to the others, and faced Smith.

"If this paper is in a script unknown to us, how are we supposed to *read* it? And if we cannot read it, how do we know what you have said is true?"

And, thought Smith, considering that the Galactics *wouldn't* be able to read it, why had his superiors sent him with it in the first place? He shrugged and thought over his instructions: "If they refuse to accept your authorization, open *the second long envelope*, and take out Sheet One."

Smith felt in his pocket, and drew out the second long envelope. He got out Sheet One, unfolded it, and found that it was the same authorization, but in ordinary print. He handed it to the spokesman of the Galactics.

Why, he exasperatedly demanded of himself, *hadn't he just been given* that paper *to hand over, to begin with*?

The spokesman looked up.

"This authorization for Lieutenant Jack Smith appears to be in order. However, we have no proof that you *are* Lieutenant Jack Smith. Kindly let us see your identification."

Smith perfunctorily slid up the curving zipper on the left sleeve of his battle jacket, undid the button of his left uniform cuff, and turned the sleeve back to reveal, apparently either tattooed or indelibly stamped, a blue-outlined oblong on the inside of his left forearm, bearing the name "Jack Smith" and several groups of smaller letters and numbers.

There was a stunned silence.

The spokesman sat back, and said dazedly, "I see."

Smith, baffled, rolled down his shirt sleeve, buttoned it, and ran the zipper back down the sleeve of his battle jacket.

He was gradually coming to feel as if he were serving as a stand-in in some kind of alien poker game, laying down cards passed to him by the real player, who was out of sight. It was supposed to be just a friendly little game, but actually everyone in it was out for blood, and every play had implications that he couldn't fathom.

Around him, the gigantic ship clicked and murmured, while the Emissaries, as if they had just been dealt some unexpected and formidable rebuff, sat around in a daze. Finally they roused themselves, exchanged brief low-voiced comments, and glanced almost fearfully at Smith. The spokesman finally drew a deep breath.

"Ah . . . On mature consideration, Lieutenant Smith, we feel that, while you evidently *are* the Earth representative, still, out of respect to your own highly-esteemed planet, we feel that someone of higher rank and greater experience should be sent here, to deal with the weighty problems that may arise."

Smith nodded agreeably. That certainly was what *he* thought. However, his instructions on this particular point were perfectly simple. He reached in his pocket, reopened the second long envelope, and got out Sheet Two.

Sheet Two proved to be folded around a somewhat smaller envelope, with unequivocal instructions written on the face. Smith read the instructions; then, feeling foolish, he opened the envelope, shook out a little plastic bag, and stuck it temporarily in a side pocket. He unfolded a long sheet of thick paper adorned with seals, crests, silver and gold ribbons, official stamps, and illegible signatures over imposing titles. There were also three blank spaces for him to sign, so resting the paper on top of the envelopes, he got out a pen and scrawled his name in the blank spaces. He then handed the paper to the Emissary, put the envelope away, and methodically got out the little plastic bag.

The Emissary, meanwhile, stared at the paper.

Smith tore the end off the plastic bag, shook out a kind of bronze X, a glittering silver circle, and a crown-shaped pin set with tiny rubies and diamonds. One by one he pinned these emblems onto his uniform jacket, then dropped his gold bars into the plastic bag, and put it away. He was still the same person, but no one in any of Earth's armies would have known it.

The Emissary looked up from the paper.

"So, this document, when signed, gives you the temporary rank of Field Marshal, Member of the Special Governing Council of Earth, and Prince Imperial of the Royal and Imperial House of Mogg?"

"That's what it says," said Smith. He was unenthusiastically aware that he had just experienced the first half of the most meteoric rise and fall in Earth history. The paper specified that his rank lasted while he was on the Galactic ship—and was revoked as soon as he set foot on Earth again.

"Why," asked the Emissary, "didn't they send someone of this rank in the first place?"

"I don't know."

"Why, if they were going to give you this rank, didn't they give it to you before you came on board?"

"I don't know that either."

The Emissary showed a glint of frustrated peevishness. "Why, exactly, *did* they send *you*?"

Smith said irritatedly, "Don't expect *me* to read their minds."

This, after it was out, had a hint of an insubordinate tone that Smith wasn't happy about. It also seemed to stun the Galactics.

Yet again, Smith was treated to the sight of a collection of alien entities, with few familiar features to judge by, somehow projecting an appearance of disordered stupefaction. And the spokesman once more looked as if he were earnestly trying to remember a forgotten name.

Finally, down the table, an entity that resembled a set of joints of bamboo, of various lengths and diameters, topped by a kind of flattened giant clamshell, bestirred itself, opened the clamshell a crack, and emitted a series of grating squeaking noises.

The spokesman seemed to receive some message from this, cleared his throat, and said something over his shoulder.

After a moment, there was a murmured reply.

The Emissary turned to Smith.

"I don't believe we have heard before of the Royal and Imperial House of Mogg."

Smith doggedly got out the third envelope. As the Galactics watched anxiously, he drew out a large folded sheet of paper marked "Env. 3, Sheet 2, and read aloud the first sentence:

"The House of Mogg is one of the many startling results of the precedent-shattering first visit of the Galactic Emissaries."

Smith paused, and glanced at them, wondering if this simple comment would have an effect.

The Emissaries showed a variety of expressions, which ranged from resignation to faint hope.

Second Lieutenant Smith read on:

"The House of Mogg, closely allied to the Burdeenite and certain other faiths, controls roughly one-fourth of the land surface of the Earth, and possibly one-tenth of its populace. It is headed by a monarch whose actual name is unknown, the name 'Mogg' having been adopted in the early days when the Burdeenite faith and allied political movements were outlawed.

"The main distinguishing characteristic of the House of Mogg is its unalterable opposition to the use, within its own territories, of the remarkable gifts presented by the

Galactic Emissaries during their First or Preliminary Visitation.

"These gifts, by the widespread and unselfish use of which the fitness of Earth to join the Greater Galactic Community is to be decided during the Second or Determining Visitation, include:

"1) The marbus plant. This plant is pest-free, and hardy in all but the most extreme polar regions. All parts of it are tasty and nutritious. It is prolific and fast-growing, requires little care, and may be grown in a variety of forms, depending on cultural practices. The effect of the marbus plant, properly used, is to enormously increase food production, thus offering the total elimination of famine at the present population level.

"2) The drug popularly known as 'Superpill.' A minute quantity of this drug, taken orally, permits family planning, with no known side effects, for up to two years at one dosage. The effect of this drug is to permit easy stabilization of the population at current levels.

"3) The 'condensed-circuit' computer. This device, based on the 'polyphase crystal,' provides an unprecedented number of switching elements per unit volume, at extremely low power-drain. The computer is composed to two basic parts, the 'crystal' and the 'control.' The crystals were grown originally from seed crystals provided by the Galactics, in baths prepared according to their instructions. The controls are manufactured according to the Galactic patterns. The precise mechanism by which the condensed-circuit computer operates is, for Earth scientists, still a matter of conjecture, although it has been suggested that the control, by a very rapid three-dimensional scanning process,

alternately determines, and detects, certain finely-balanced
fundamental properties of the individual atoms of the
polyphase crystal. The practical effect of this very compact
low-drain computer has been to obsolete all former
computer technology, enormously accelerate already-
existing trends in industrial and transportation control,
and revolutionize many phases of human activity, including
education. With the aid of a pocket-sized, relatively
inexpensive computer, a child of eight can now easily
perform abstruse calculations far beyond the skill of the
professional mathematician of pre-Visitation days. Dates and
events of history are readily available from the computer, as
are chemical and physical facts in enormous abundance.
By proper use of the computer, numerous relationships
between seemingly isolated facts can readily be discovered.
Hence the new computer has come to be a tool of thought
comparable to the old-time 'slide rule,' but on a far greater
scale, and, for this reason, much present-day education
is actually training in the skillful use of the condensed-
circuit computer.

"To all of these developments, the House of Mogg, and
the Burdeenite and allied faiths, are unalterably opposed.
In their territory, former types of computers and control
devices are in use, and undergoing continuous and rapid
development; old-style Earth plants provide food; and the
'superpill' is banned on pain of death.

"The Burdeenite territories have highly irregular
borders, and many are seemingly-indefensible enclaves.
But they are not molested. Following the original secession
of the Burdeenites, the Governing Council strove to compel
obedience by force, and strengthened its human combat

forces with newly-developed unmanned combat-machines controlled by their own internal computers, and programmed to track down and destroy armed rebel forces. The Burdeenites argued that they themselves were fighting for the cause of humanity against 'alien-inspired devices,' and refused to fire on human troops unless seriously attacked. The combat machines, not yet perfected, malfunctioned, and committed a series of incredible atrocities against both sides, with the result that the human combat forces went over to the Burdeenites *en masse*. The Governing Council, fearful to commit its remaining troops, agreed to a prolonged truce, during which it rapidly developed improved combat-machines.

"During this truce, however, large numbers of engineers, scientists, and technicians, disliking the trend of events, joined the House of Mogg. They were at once put to work in the industrial and research facilities under Burdeenite control. The cause of what happened next is a state secret of the House of Mogg, but the outer facts are clear enough.

"The Governing Council, determined to bring the Burdeenite regions back under control, worked to create formidable forces of improved and thoroughly tested types of combat-machines. The Burdeenites labored to multiply and strengthen their fortifications, and to create a unified industrial whole of many of the regions under their control. Both sides were apparently successful.

"The Governing Council then delivered an ultimatum, on the rejection of which the Council attacked, using tremendous concentrations of combat-machines in the effort to achieve a quick and decisive victory. The result was a smashing success of the Burdeenites on all decisive fronts, the combat machines being somehow destroyed in enormous numbers. In the resulting sudden peace, the Burdeenites exacted only modest territorial gains, insisting instead on their religious, intellectual and political freedom. This peace has proved durable.

"The Burdeenite territories offer numerous perplexing features to the outsider. One is the incredible depth and strength of the fortifications, the works often completely concealed by remarkable skill in camouflage. These fortifications, though formidable beyond belief to the outsider, and stocked with enormous quantities of food and other supplies, never satisfy the Burdeenites, who labor constantly to further strengthen and improve them, though no enemy is in sight.

"Another baffling feature is the paradox, frequently seen in Burdeenite territory, of advanced research and development carried out along lines already eclipsed by the Galactic gifts. A related feature is 'backsearch'—research to uncover *past* methods and devices, already eclipsed by Earth's own progress; such discoveries are greeted with as much rejoicing as completely new facts, methods, and devices; the Burdeenites do not necessarily place even the most antique device, for instance, in a museum, but study its principle, and often improve the device *along the lines it would naturally have followed if new methods had not displaced it*. Peculiarly enough, some of these antique devices have been improved to such an extent that they have returned to daily use even *outside* Burdeenite territory. The achievement of such a feat is always cause for a patent of nobility in the House of Mogg.

"These eccentricities have proved valuable to the Burdeenites, in that an enormous trade in novelties has sprung up. The Burdeenite 'Never-smoke Catalytic Long-Burning Efficiency Lamp,' for instance, is an extremely popular item, because of its intriguing design, and also because of its surprising effectiveness as a portable emergency light source. Numerous Burdeenite invented games, such as 'Bash,' 'Guerrilla,' and the ever-popular, 'Invasion From Outer Space,' enliven interests dulled by excessive leisure. A peculiar feature of this last named game is that it has grown into a cult, and its devotees actually stock many of those goods and devices that might be useful in an actual 'invasion from outer space.'

"To the Burdeenites and their curious ways must also be credited the development of Fastwrite, the standard shorthand now taught in grade school, which for many uses has displaced the somewhat cumbersome computerized Voiceprint based on Galactic technology.

"Government in the Burdeenite territories rests largely with the House of Mogg. As nearly as an outsider can comprehend, the House is a nonheredity monarchy and aristocracy, with a minimum of laws. One oddity is that property taxes increase when property value is permitted to decline. Another is that the Chamber of Confusion, or Legislature, is permitted to put only a certain fixed number of laws on the books. Beyond that number, a previous law must be revoked, or somehow consolidated with others, for each new law added. No new or changed law can become effective until it passes examination by the Board of Dunces, a seven-member panel whose function is not to pass on the *fitness* of the law, but on its comprehensibility; the

Board of Dunces is made up entirely of men with no legal training.

"The House of Mogg, and the Burdeenites, represent a curious development in Earth history. While incomprehensible by ordinary standards, their influence, despite the amusing eccentricity of their ways, cannot be denied."

Smith finished the paper, turned it over, folded it up, slid it into its envelope, and put it away. Then he looked up.

The Galactic Emissaries were sitting there like so many vegetables.

Finally, the spokesman forced himself to sit straight behind his floating table. He drew a deep breath, and looked Smith in the eye.

"Inform the Governing Council, and the House of Mogg, that we will recommend to the Central Executive that, in due time, Earth be admitted to the Great Galactic Community as a Full Member. Please express our regrets that we cannot stay longer on this occasion; but urgent matters have been reported to us, and we must leave at once."

★ ★ ★

Smith repeated the whole thing in the Council Chamber, answered questions of the Governing Council of Earth, and of high representatives of the House of Mogg, and finally found himself drained dry of information. By this time, he felt thoroughly worn out, fed up, and exasperated.

The chairman of the Council looked around, and said thoughtfully, "I believe that answers *our* questions."

The Leading Crown Prince of the House of Mogg

thought a moment, and nodded. "It covers what we wanted to know."

Smith said, in as polite a voice as he could manage, "Sir, could you tell me whether I will *ever* find out what actually happened?"

"Why," said the chairman of the Governing Council, "haven't you worked that out by now?"

"No one has bothered to tell me about it, sir."

"You were *there*, weren't you?"

"I was a kind of ignorant bystander, I suppose. I spent a good part of my time wondering why someone qualified hadn't been sent."

"You *were* qualified, or we wouldn't have sent you."

"Sir, I didn't know the first thing about the situation!"

"*That* was one of your chief qualifications."

Smith blinked. Why would they send someone who knew nothing? Abruptly he thought again of the Galactic Emissary's odd habit of sitting with his head to one side, occasionally moving his lips very slightly, as if he were talking to someone out of sight.

The chairman said, "Those people ran rings around the Earth representatives the first time they were here. The amazing part of it was, the better informed *our* representative was, the better the Galactics looked. On thinking it all over afterward, it dawned on us that, impossible as it seemed, this would make sense *if they were telepathic*, or if they had a device that served the same purpose.

"Moreover," said the chairman, "while we couldn't be sure what their setup was, they insisted that custom and ceremonial required them to do important business at a particular floating desk on their ship, so it seemed *likely* that the telepathy was carried out by the aid of a good deal of equipment that they preferred not to move, and that was located somewhere near that desk.

"Now then, what were we to do? Apparently, the more capable *our* representative, the more the Galactics would learn. How could we deal with them, granted they had this advantage? The only way we could see was to send someone who was levelheaded and self-controlled, but *who knew practically nothing whatever about what was taking place.*" He smiled at Smith's expression. "Of course, you were, in effect, a puppet. But that was what we *had* to have to deal with them on an equal basis. We weren't quite sure of their purpose, and it would have been unwise to reveal our hand."

"But, sir," said Smith, "why did nearly every piece of information *jolt* them? What should such advanced races care about our shorthand, our identification stamps, and the House of Mogg's refusal to accept their gifts? Granted, the Galactics might choose not to accept us into their organization. But . . . I got the impression some sort of *fight* was going on, and, without knowing what I was doing I was somehow delivering heavy blows."

"You were."

"But how?"

The chairman leaned forward.

"These benevolent Galactics, with their marvelous gifts, weren't here to uplift us, and welcome us lovingly into their Great Galactic Community. They were here, plainly and simply, *to conquer us.*"

Smith felt as if the ground had shifted under his feet.

"But, sir—to conquer people, do you give them gifts

that actually make them better off? That increase their ability and strength?"

"Yes," said the chairman dryly, "if you're slick enough. If you can read minds and see which poison your opponent thinks would be beneficial to him. If you're technologically advanced, and have had enough practice, so that it's simply a matter of varying your standard procedure to fit the victim."

The chairman turned, and nodded to a Burdeenite wearing sword, pistol, and some kind of translucent chain mail. The Burdeenite crossed the room, and took away a screen before a table set against the wall. This revealed a large crystal lying on the table, a cage of mice beside the crystal, and, in a tub beside the table, a *marbus* plant, with its spray of slender green leaves, out of the center of which grew a tall leafy stalk covered with buds and small pink flowers. The Burdeenite returned to his seat.

The chairman looked at Smith. "Thanks to the so-called 'condensed-circuit computer,' of which such crystals as that on the table are the heart, we now have a remarkably complex civilization based on extremely precise timing. Our air travel, for instance, is as complicated as a series of split-second ballet maneuvers, changing and interlocking without letup. Chaos would follow the slightest misjudgment. Everything rests on the computers that control the system."

The Burdeenite coolly raised a thing like a small radar antenna, and briefly aimed it at the crystal.

There was a singing note, followed by a sound like a tossed handful of sand.

In the crystal's place was a pile of tiny grains.

The chairman said, "Without the crystal, the condensed-circuit-computer is useless, and without the condensed-circuit computer, our Galactic-based technology would collapse. But that is only part of the story. Near the remains of the crystal, you see a cage. You'll notice that it's divided in half by a vertical partition. On the left side, we have mice treated with the Galactics' ultimate birth-control Superpill. On the right side, we have mice that are not treated."

As the chairman stopped speaking, the Burdeenite leaned forward and tossed a small capsule that smashed on the floor halfway across the room.

The mice in the right half of the cage continued to hop leisurely from food dish to water dish, to and from a box in the corner where they popped out of sight.

The mice in the left side of the cage began frenziedly to mate.

The chairman said, "Observe that, provided the active agent of the so-called Superpill is already in the system, this effect is created by a minute concentration of another substance *in the air.* The larger the mass of the animal, for a given concentration, the less dramatic the immediate effect. But the ultimate result is the same—a *drastic increase of the birth rate to far above normal.*"

As the chairman stopped talking, the Burdeenite calmly raised a small jeweled atomizer, aimed it across the room, and squeezed the bulb.

Smith, momentarily dazed, stared at the shattered crystal and the two halves of the mouse cage. In each case, the change had been made so *easily.* Then he turned, to glance at the atomizer.

From behind him came a sound like a loose coil of rope tossed on the floor.

Smith whirled.

The tall stalk of the marbus plant lay outstretched, so flat it almost looked as it had been painted on the floor. Around the ring of the tub, the slender leaves hung straight and limp.

"Just suppose," said the chairman, "that you were in charge of a great spaceship—perhaps belonging to a great Galactic organization (never mind about it being a *benevolent* organization) and let's just suppose your job was to subvert Earth and make it obedient to that great Galactic organization—what could be nicer than to get Earth *totally dependent* on certain technological developments *that you could withdraw at will*? At a mere snap of your fingers, Earth's whole technological civilization could collapse, to leave, for practical purposes, a planetful of ignorant savages with no relevant skills, whose reproduction rate could be altered at will, and, if you chose, whose main food supply could also be wiped out with a snap of your fingers. Think how cooperative such people would be once they saw what you could do. Suppose that, having delivered the necessaries to bring about this situation and having seen the fools rushing to their own destruction, you then went away to take care of other business and returned when your calculations showed the situation would be ripe.

"Then," said the chairman, "suppose you summoned to your ship the Earth representative, planning perhaps to give him the same little demonstration we have just given here, and suppose you discovered: first, that a mere *second lieutenant* had been sent to deal with you; next, that in your absence, instead of dependence on computerized voice typers, a new, *completely nontechnological* system of rapid writing had been developed; third, that a *completely nontechnological uncomputerized* system of identification had come into use; fourth, that one-quarter of the Earth's land surface was in the hands of a sect which, *for religious motives*, rejected the gifts, and in their place was developing Earth's own technology at a fever pitch; fifth, that the sect was armed to the teeth, dug in, stocked for a long fight, seasoned in battle, and so situated that you couldn't count on striking at the nonmembers without hitting the members of the sect, or vice versa, and, sixth, to top it all off, suppose you had no way to judge whether this was *all* the bad news, or whether this was just the tip of the iceberg showing above the water, with a lot more underneath? *If you had been in that situation, would it have jarred you*?"

Smith gave a low, involuntary whistle.

The chairman smiled.

"Any further questions?"

"Just one, sir, if I won't be taking too much time."

"Go ahead. Ask what you want."

"Well—*are* the Galactics beat? Considering, that is, their technology, and the fact that part of the Earth, and a large part, *is* dependent on their gifts?"

"It depends on what you mean by 'beat.' If they wanted to destroy the whole planet, who knows? But short of that, they're confronted by a situation that offers, so far as we can see, no sure solution for them at all. Different races, and different animals, have different systems of conquest. Tigers spring on their victims from concealment, spiders ensnare them, foxes trick them, wolves run them down. Each selects the particular game suitable for its purposes. The Galactics' system apparently is to find races in a certain stage of technological development, conceivably by detecting incidental electrical signs, and then offer them a free ride on a technological flying carpet. Once the victim steps on the flying carpet, they jerk the rug out from under his feet. Who knows what equipment it takes to find the victims and tailor this technique to suit them? Maybe that ship of theirs is equipped with things we've never conceived of—*and has very little actual armament*. But even if it's heavily armed, and they *could* kill a lot of humans, how does that help *them*?

"If an elephant turns up at a water hole, a big cat *can* attack the elephant; it will hurt the elephant, all right, but what does the cat get out of it? Just some unwanted excitement, some sore muscles, and the possibility of getting flattened into a rug. There are not many calories in war for its own sake. When an oversize bumblebee gets in the web of an efficient spider, the spider cuts it loose. Better to get the thing out of there so something can get in. No fox in its right mind is going to sink its teeth into a bear. A sensible predator attacks creatures it can hope to digest, without the risk of being finished off in the attempt.

"Now that we're on guard, if the Galactics want to conquer us, I think they can only hope to do it after a long struggle, requiring endurance, discipline, and courage— and not just the advantage of their technology. And yet, a technology like theirs will tend to relieve them of much of the need to *use* those other traits. And, for lack of some means of exercising them, traits tend to disappear."

The chairman shook his head. "No, I imagine the Galactics—or that bunch of them, anyway—have found their specialized confidence technique too profitable to get themselves entangled in a profitless unpredictable situation calling for traits they aren't particularly strong in anyway."

Smith thought back to the Galactics' reaction. There had been *some* trace of endurance, discipline, and courage in evidence—but not much.

He glanced across at the Burdeenites, and was struck by the evident cross-grained tenacious independent quality of those who would pit seemingly antique methods against the newest of the modern, *and win*.

Looking at those faces, Smith could suddenly see things from the predator's viewpoint:

When the victim manifests *those* qualities—better hunt up another victim.

BRAINS ISN'T EVERYTHING

After an hour inside the gigantic spaceship, Steven P. Winters, US Delegate to the Interstellar Mutual Love Conference, had a few doubts about his host.

Winters, uneasily seated on his perch, peered around the curving bulk of what had introduced itself as "Friendly Hug and Clasp Osher Diomak." As much as anything, Friendly Hug and Clasp Diomak resembled a kind of leather flying saucer equipped around the rim with good-sized octopus tentacles. There was one large round dark eye above the base of each tentacle, with a sort of disklike membrane that evidently served as an ear to one side, and to the other side a similarly-sized slit which opened from time to time to emit reassuring words in a tone of soothing confidence.

As far as Winters could see ahead, around Diomak, there sat other Earth delegates—G. Malik of Russia; Madame Kuo from China; K. Ngusi, an African delegate. Behind Winters was Lord Orban of Britain, and behind Orban was the delegate from France. Each was uneasily seated upon a limb—that is to say, a tentacle—that twisted up at an angle to serve as a backrest, and then reversed itself to pass across the delegates' shoulders and provide a friendly squeeze from time to time.

Several feet from Winters' ear, to the side of the tentacle that was serving as Winters' seat, the slit now opened up.

"Winters, my boy," said a sincere friendly voice, "what I want to bring to you and yours, I repeat, is the choice of fellowship, understanding, long life, health, vigor, vitality, plus—ah—*involvement* in the—ah—wonderful world of interstellar civilization. *Your* happiness is *my* happiness. I realize from what you say that such offers are legendary amongst you—but now, at last, the legend becomes reality. The wonders are all yours to choose from. You have merely to make your choice."

Winters, Orban, Malik, Kuo, Ngusi, and the other delegates adjourned to a "conference room" set aside for them by Diomak. This "conference room" resembled the flight deck of an aircraft carrier adrift in the Pacific on a foggy day. From the misty surface below, twenty-foot lengths of tentacle thrashed into view, and big saucer-shaped bodies, streaming water, broke the surface and then vanished again.

The delegates looked around somberly.

"M'm," said Winters.

Orban peered over the edge. "How do they travel with all *this* inside?"

"Gravity control," said Malik. "What a technology!"

The French representative sardonically eyed the tentacles erupting from the water.

Malik added dryly, "Although, technology aside, Diomak seems not completely *sincere*."

Winters grunted his agreement.

Madame Kuo said, "But think what he offers:

"Perfect health.

"Long life.

"Great mental development.

"Universal friendliness.

"Mutual understanding.

"Great vitality . . . *And so on.*"

Malik nodded. "We can't ignore that."

"Remember," said Lord Orban, "Diomak offers us these marvels *as capsules*, to be taken once every three weeks."

"Miracle drugs," said Winters, ironically, "to end all miracle drugs.—Nevertheless, all Earth is waiting to find out what we've picked."

"And this," said Madame Kuo, "raises a curious point. Each of us may select *one* capsule. This means that China, which practically constitutes the entire human race, with only little bumps of others around the outer fringe, may select only *one* type of capsule—*for her whole people.*"

Lord Orban cleared his throat.

"I should say we need a solid front against this alien and his trinkets."

Malik, eyes narrowed, said, "How will Diomak stop us from *trading* capsules?"

Winters, groping for some approach that made sense, came again to the same conclusion:

"It seems to me we've got only one choice. Whatever we do with these pills afterward, for *now* we've got to accept. So the problem is, who takes which kind of pill?"

Lord Orban shook his head. "These capsules could be disastrous."

The discussion went on, traveled in a circle, went around again, and continued until finally even the sequence of the repetitions became monotonous. Winters and Malik wanted an agreement as to who would get which capsules, so as to make trading easier. Madame Kuo became mysteriously noncommittal. Lord Orban argued for an agreement to refuse the pills entirely. K. Ngusi wanted to question Diomak further. The Japanese representative felt that there should be more time for consultation. The German delegate was impatient to do *something*.

Disgruntled and disunited, the delegates returned to talk to Diomak.

Diomak slid his tentacles around them like a friendly big brother.

"Well, Winters, my boy—did you decide?"

"I—uh—do you mind if I ask you a couple of questions, Mr. Diomak?"

"Call me Osher, Winters. *All* my friends call me Osher."

"All right . . . do you mind if I ask you one or two questions, *Osher*?"

"Not at all, Winters. Go right ahead."

"Well—ahh—you see, there's been a certain amount of—well, mutual distrust, on Earth, and—"

Diomak put in quickly, "That's what we want to get rid of. Exactly, Winters. You are entirely right. I agree with you wholeheartedly."

Winters groped around mentally for the thread of his thought. Before he could find it, Diomak spoke, his voice radiating good fellowship:

"So, that's taken care of, eh, Winters? Now, did you decide what you wanted?"

Winters hesitated, still couldn't remember what he had intended to say, and shrugged. "Yes, it was—"

"No, no, don't tell *me*. We will make the choices so *all* can hear. Just sit back, and we will decide, with—ah—witnesses—so everyone can trust everyone else, eh? Ha, ha.—Isn't that right?"

Winters swallowed and sat back. He now had the impression of dealing with some kind of interstellar salesman of stolen cars, with transactions in hashish and opium thrown in on the side.

"Now, dear friends," said Diomak, his multiple voice purring in many tongues, "we are all met here together in free will, no coercion or duress used to freely agree that I, Osher Diomak, will freely give to you, periodically, *and without charge*, and will *deliver* to you, also without charge, enough capsules to last two years—of whichever kind each of you publicly agrees on—one kind for the inhabitants of each political group or unit, known as 'nation' or 'country,' as followed:

"USA?" In a low voice, Diomak asked, "What will you have, Winters, my boy?"

Winters was wishing he hadn't known so many languages as to be picked for this job, or had been brought up as a trader in some tricky competitive business. As it was, he had the sensation of knowing *something* was going on—but *what?*

"Perfect health," he said.

"Excellent, excellent. *Fine*. A *wise* choice, my boy . . . Russia?"

"Long life."

"Long life, eh? Excellent . . . and what does China choose?"

"Great mental development."

"Good, good. Splendid choices. Next . . . Republic of France?"

The French representative stood up.

"France *refuses!*"

"What?—ah?—*Monsieur?*"

"*What* you are doing, I do not know. Until I know, I will have nothing to do with this!"

Diomak spoke earnestly, soothingly, persuasively:

"You have your people to think of. Surely, you wouldn't *deprive*—"

The French delegate turned on his heel and headed for the exit.

Lord Orban stood up. He glanced at Winters. Winters evaded his gaze. Orban leaned over.

"Would you buy bonds from Diomak?"

Winters shuddered. "At the moment, I wouldn't buy chewing gum from him!"

"If now we both walk out—"

"What would they do back home?"

Orban straightened. His voice was cold and clear.

"The United Kingdom declines every part of this proposition."

He strode toward the exit.

There was an uneasy stir in the room.

Diomak clucked regretfully.

The door banged shut behind the British and French representatives.

Winters sighed. It was an impressive exit; but when they got *home*—

Winters stayed where he was.

No one else walked out.

Diomak went down the long list of nations.

Winters braced himself to report to the President.

★ ★ ★

The President listened closely, and at the end said, "Did you find out whether these capsules *can* be traded?"

"No, sir. That was one of two questions I tried to ask. But Diomak got my mind off the subject."

"What was your other question?"

"What is *he* getting out of this?"

The President nodded.

"It all *looks* generous. But no living creature survives on generosity *alone*."

"All that interstellar brotherhood stuff *may* be what he's after. But that isn't how he struck me."

The President picked up a closely printed sheet of paper.

"I'm told that, on analyzing this situation, the following appear to be plausible reasons for Diomak's offer:

"1. Drug entrapment—the pills are addicting.

"2. Slow poison—Diomak wants our planet.

"3. Hypnotic drugs—the pills increase suggestibility, and Diomak makes suggestions.

"4. Psychological dependency—the pills work, and we won't *want* to do without them. Then he'll name his price.

"5. Side effects—the pills' side effects will tie us in knots. Same purpose as 2.

"6. Overeffectiveness—the friendliness drug will make

people easy to fool and cheat; the health drug will make people so active they can't stop to think. Same effect as 5.

"7. Fakery—the pills were camouflage. Diomak planted plague by infecting the delegates during his conference.

"8. Anaphylactic shock—the first pills will set up an allergy. Later pills will trigger a violent reaction. Same as 2.

"9. Plague inoculation—the pills contain deadly germs. This has two variants: (a) all pills are infective; (b) to make it harder to detect, only one pill out of ten thousand or so is infective."

Winters shook his head.

"Maybe I should have followed Lord Orban out the door."

"What do *you* think?"

"For whatever it's worth, I think the capsules will be useful—probably not worth what Diomak claims, but still useful. And I think he aims to make a profit some *other* way."

"You don't think he aims to finish us?"

"No, sir. I think he aims to get what *he* wants."

"And he wants?"

Winters shook his head in exasperation.

"I can't imagine what it is that he wants."

★ ★ ★

In the next few days, the pills were delivered to each nation's capital, and the US found itself with hundreds of millions of little yellow capsules, packed in six-sided drums with flat tops and bottoms. The delivery was simplicity itself. The fun started with the distribution.

One and only one capsule had to be somehow gotten to

each and every individual, out of all the increasingly impatient millions of individuals. And each capsule, offering three weeks of perfect health, obviously could be robbed or stolen.

The government, at least, showed no hesitation. Paratroops controlled the roads leading to the sites where the pills were landed. Armor backed up the paratroops. Marines ringed the site itself. The Treasury Department handled the pills, roughly along the lines of gold bars. The Internal Revenue Service, supposedly best acquainted with who lived where and had how many dependents, mailed out the capsules in special containers. The containers, designed by the CIA, proved to be waterproof, shockproof, corrosion resistant, heat resistant, child-proof and almost adult-proof. Meanwhile, the Food and Drug Administration, testing random capsules, announced that they contained only a mixture of salt, starch, sugar, gelatin, and baking soda, and could not possibly cure anything—although harmless, they were a fraud.

The government, with an election coming, paid scant attention to this announcement, and kept putting capsules in the mail under the watchful eye of the postal inspectors, with the FBI backing *them* up.

With the capsules at last distributed, the Internal Revenue Service smilingly offered to pass out extra left-over pills to adults who could prove they had never made out an income tax. One measure of interest in the capsules was the number of people who came forth to accept this offer.

Soon, as capsules were rushed to sick relatives, word came that the hospitals were emptying.

Winters found himself reading the headline:

MEDICAL SOCIETY SUES!
ALIEN PLOT AGAINST MD'S
CLAIM PILL FRAUD!!

He skimmed the article, to find that "mental suggestion," "mass hypnosis," and "interstellar chicanery" were
ruining medicine:

*"Hospital occupancy in this state is down by sixty-nine
percent. This is a devastating blow to the hospital industry, and there is no end in sight."*

Winters eyed a little plastic box containing a small yellow capsule that he carried around like a good luck charm.
What did Diomak want in *return* for this?

The phone rang.

"Georgi Malik," said the voice on the other end.
"Madame Kuo and I would like to see you."

"Fine. At my place?"

"Ah—it's such a nice day—why don't we go for a ride?"

"A taxi?"

"Why not?"

They picked the second taxi after the one Malik was
agreeable to, following the one Winters wanted. Madame
Kuo had expressed doubts about earlier selections.

"Possibly," said Malik, as they pulled out into traffic,
"they are *all* bugged. Besides, the things are so small
now—ah, well—who knows?" He studied Winters alertly.
"Your health—pardon me for prying—appears good but
not extraordinary."

"I haven't swallowed the thing."

"Ah."

"Are your people living longer?"

"Well—of the people given the actual capsule, there have been no deaths. Some were in severe automobile accidents, and are having a painful recovery. But they are *living*."

Winters blinked, started to ask a question, and changed his mind. He glanced at Madame Kuo.

She smiled briefly.

"If I seem no more intellectual than before, do not be surprised. I—what is the expression?—'chickened out'."

"You didn't take it either?"

"I look at it now and then. It is an odd shade of blue." She hesitated. "One of my superiors ate his, however, and for entertainment now works out calculus problems in his head."

The taxi slowed for a light. On the sidewalk, a man in his eighties jogged past. A man of forty or so turned handsprings. A policeman, beaming and swinging his club, strode along whistling.

Malik said, "You have heard of the upheavals in Britain and France? Diomak refuses to allow them any capsules of whatever kind."

"Yes," said Winters. "But I thought that was on account of some regulation Diomak is stuck with."

"The result is the same. Ah—did Lord Orban recover from that mob attack?"

"I've heard he's living on a small island in the Caribbean. I couldn't locate it on the map."

Madame Kuo said, "Mr. Malik and I felt we three might—ah—mutually equalize the distribution of the capsules."

Malik nodded. "One of the automobile accident victims happens to be a high official of the Party. Such is his suffering that even euthanasia has—h'm—received consideration. But it didn't work. We would like to restore him to perfect health."

Madame Kuo said, "We have a similar situation—a brilliant theoretician, made more brilliant by the capsule. He is, however, well along in years. But if he could spend his last days *in perfect health*, there is no predicting what he might accomplish."

Winters nodded. "Why not buy some capsules from a dealer? There seem to be about twenty million Americans who don't trust these pills, and millions of others who want to be sure of a second one when the first wears off. So there's a natural market for them."

Malik looked unenthusiastic. "*Those* capsules are unreliable."

"Sometimes," said Madame Kuo, "they are good. Our people here used some that were effective. Those shipped home were worthless."

Winters said hesitantly, "There is a rumor that certain capsules from—ah—other countries—have found their way here, and been totally worthless. Though they worked *there*."

Madame Kuo looked startled. "Could it be?"

"Diomak," said Winters, "may have some way to deactivate them."

"Then," said Malik, "we will have to try bringing the patient to the medicine. Though I cannot conceive how Diomak could do such a thing."

★ ★ ★

Several weeks passed, and soon Winters had *two* little capsules he hadn't taken, then three. Most of his friends were glowing with health, but there were still a mysterious twenty million who refused to take the pills. Yet the only such people Winters knew were the President himself, the Vice-President, all the members of the cabinet, several senators, and—Winters paused. Could there be *twenty million* distrustful people in the *government*?

As for himself, Winters had now been debriefed, interviewed, and present at so many hearings that he fell asleep still struggling with questions, and woke up giving answers.

Malik and Madame Kuo appeared to be suffering from the same difficulty.

"What," she said, "is Diomak's *motive*? What does *Diomak* receive? *Why* is he doing it? How am I to say?"

Winters said, "Do the health pills work for your people *here*?"

They both nodded. "Diomak's *motive* is the problem."

Winters nodded. "That's my problem, too."

Winters' ears hurt as vigorously healthy interviewers demanded, "*Why* is Osher Diomak doing this for us?" "Is there an interstellar civilization based on love and generosity?" "*Why* can't *our* government be selfless?" and "Does pure generosity rule all the *other* races in the Universe?"

As the pills accumulated, Winters hoarsely talked his way through "Face the People," and then found he was scheduled for a double-length session of "Meet the Nation."

So far, no one had shown any sign of poisoning, allergy,

strange illnesses, unusual suggestibility, drug addiction, or even so much as mild stomach acidity. The only signs even of strain appeared to be amongst doctors—who were leaving for less healthful climates—and travel agents, who were laboring overtime to accommodate the gigantic tourist trade generated by people who wanted capsules other than those their government had officially chosen.

Winters moodily added another pill to his collection, and turned as the phone rang.

There was a meeting at the White House, and Winters was wanted.

* * *

The room, as Winters went in past the guards, had that silence reached when everyone has said everything he has to say, and what everyone has said adds up to something no one present can even so much as get in focus.

The President, at the far end of the crowded table, sat with his chair tilted back, frowning. Around the table, people slumped, leaned on their elbows, vacantly exhaled smoke, massaged their eyelids, massaged their temples, sat back staring at the ceiling, or sat chin on chest staring at the tabletop.

Winters, alarmed, pulled his chair out a little incautiously, and banged the leg of the table.

The President looked up.

"Have a seat, Winters. Maybe *you* can clear this up."

Everyone at the table glanced dully around.

Winters kept his face expressionless.

"Anything I can do, sir—"

"We have reached an impasse. Around this table sit administrators, whose physicians, biochemists, intelligence experts, military men, physicists, statistical analysts, and computers have been focused on Diomak since he showed up. To make a long story short, every scrap of objective evidence suggests Diomak is being perfectly fair with us. *But there is not one of us here who doesn't think we are being manipulated*."

Winters, under the weight of watching eyes, spoke carefully. "I think, sir, he could be a *trader*."

"How does that fit in?"

"Then the evidence of his being fair would be consistent with the idea that he is manipulating things for his own advantage. A trader, in the right circumstances, can give everyone a good deal, including himself. It's all a question of what's scarce in one place and plentiful in another."

The President nodded.

"The trader pays a good price for an item that's cheap *there*. He brings it here, where it's expensive, and sells it cut-rate. He takes our cheap surplus item in payment, because it is worth more elsewhere."

"Yes, sir."

The President leaned forward.

"But *what* have we got to offer?"

"I've been thinking about that, sir. Obviously, this free gift is to demonstrate *his* merchandise. He must be going to offer eventually to buy something from *us*. Well—what have we *got*?"

Everyone around the table, as if by some signal, sat up, to listen alertly.

The President said, "This is where we got stuck. What could *we* offer Diomak? Consider the access to raw materials that space travel must give to Diomak's people. For manufactured goods, consider Diomak's spaceship, and the techniques *that* implies. So far as intellect is concerned, consider the ease with which he learned our languages. For good measure, do you know that those pills evidently contain tiny 'seed-organisms' that are scarcely more than molecules—and yet, when absorbed through the walls of certain tissues, they build up structures that act almost as factories to turn out things *like* viruses, but the action of which reinforces certain bodily functions? These 'viruses' are useful. Then there is a mechanism apparently activated by limiting factors involving gravitation, inertia, and the Earth's magnetic field, and that deactivates the capsules. We still don't have *that* worked out. Now—consider a civilization that can do *that*—and then you tell me exactly what *we* can offer *them*."

Winters nodded. "Yes, sir. But"—he glanced around at the shrewd and knowledgeable eyes focused upon him—"with apologies to present company, sir—*brains isn't everything.*"

"What do you mean?"

"It's the *scarce* item that's most highly valued. If gold lay around in chunks, but copper were scarce, which would be higher-priced? Since the human race is a—ah—a trifle short in brain power now and then, it follows that learning, degrees, and reputation for brains, get great credit. We assume that, *with enough brains*, everything *else* will follow. But suppose you have a place where brains are commonplace, and something else is in short supply? Then what?"

There was a stir in the room.

The President said, "What *could* they lack?"

Winters shook his head.

"All I can say is, it must be something we take more or less for granted, and don't appreciate the value of."

★ ★ ★

It was about two pill-deliveries later when Winters got another call:

"Diomak wants all the original delegates on board his ship. You have to be ready to go by five p.m."

★ ★ ★

This time, Diomak was not so cheerful. Some of his tentacles lay stretched out limp. Others were wrapped around his central "head." All his numerous eyes were either shut or half-shut. He had the look of an octopus on Monday, after a little overindulgence on Friday, Saturday, and Sunday.

When everyone was settled, Diomak made a visible effort to pull himself together.

"Wonderful, wonderful," he said dully. "We are all here, just like before. This time, we have a—a thrilling surprise. A wonderful—ah—heh—friend has come to make sure everything is the way it *should* be."

Winters glanced around.

Through a doorway across the room stepped an entity vaguely suggestive of a tall stork that had been dipped in India ink, dried off, and provided with a thing like an eight-sided attaché case, a pocket calculator, and a microphone.

Diomak shuddered.

"It is Gentle Corrector Vark, *Himself.*"

Winters strained to get Gentle Corrector Vark in focus. Part of the trouble was that the Gentle Corrector's knees worked in reverse, the lower leg swinging up almost at a right angle on each step. Another problem was the long black bill, which appeared slightly flexible, showed no visible lengthwise opening, but had a great number of regularly spaced perforations. It suddenly dawned on Winters that this "bill" might be some form of filter or gas mask. Winters made a mental note of the possibility, then watched Vark raise the microphone.

"*AAaaahhkkk!*"

A series of complex twanging noises made the air hum and vibrate.

Winters' ears hurt.

Diomak's voice trembled as he translated:

" 'I. Subject: Possible infringement of Regulation Z of the Office For Legal Regulation of the Correction and Controls Department of the Alien Consolidation Administration.'"

Winters leaned over to Diomak's ear membrane.

"Does Gentle Corrector Vark always talk in paragraph headings?"

"Always. They all do."

"Why?"

"They rule as a legal bureaucracy, and it is they who make and interpret the law. They always talk to us in regulations, for our convenience in obeying them."

A light was slowly beginning to dawn on Winters. It was almost blotted out as, across the room, Gentle Corrector Vark spoke again:

"*Ssnarrr!* Eeeyee—eeeyang—"

Winter's teeth buzzed. His hair tingled at the back of his neck. His eardrums vibrated to selected tones from auto accidents, fire alarms, untuned pianos, and mosquitoes passing overhead at midnight.

Diomak's voice quivered:

"Gentle Corrector Vark states:

" 'II. Classes of Possible Corrective Action

    " 'A. For Infringement

        " '1. Intentional

        " '2. Unintentional

        " '3. Indeterminate

    " 'B. For Non-Infringement

        " '1. With Prejudice

        " '2. Without Prejudice

        " '3. Indeterminate'"

"Gllll . . . Snnarrrr!" said Gentle Corrector Vark, as the air hummed, shrieked, and twanged. "Yik—eeeeeyyokk—*vakkkkhh!*"

Diomak trembled all over.

    " 'C. Applicable Corrections

        " '1. Dismemberment

        " '2. Acid

        " '(a) Dip

        " '(b) Spray

        " '3. Tongs . . .'"

There was a tap at Winters' shoulder

Lord Orban, tanned where he wasn't bandaged, growled, "Look there."

A column of more or less stork-like creatures was coming in through a rear door. Each carried a sort of large heavy bat.

Diomak was now translating the various ways in which tongs could be used for corrective purposes.

Winters leaned close to Diomak's ear membrane.

"What's this gang coming in the back door?"

The tip of Diomak's tentacle clutched Winters' ankle.

"Those are Corrective Healers!"

Winters took another look. They were adjusting their clubs as they came. Nozzles thrust out the ends of some. Steel claws slid out of others.

Diomak tremblingly started translating again:

" ' . . . and all alien entities are hereby advised that constructive collusion in violation of Regulation Z requires immediate restitution of all items wrongfully appropriated, without exception.

" 'B. Failure to comply with "A" above, whether voluntary, involuntary, or indeterminate, will mandate application of one or more of the following Corrective Entitlements:

" '1. Extermination

" '2. Decimation

" '3. Compulsory fratricide

" '4. Exile

" '5. Sterilization

" '6. Other

" 'C. Appropriate entitlements shall be determined by the Gentle Correctorship. All decisions will be final.

" 'D. Manner of—'"

Winters leaned over to Diomak's ear membrane and spoke urgently.

"What's Vark talking about now?"

"He's saying you will have to return all the pills."

"What? We've already eaten most of them."

"Those, too."

"How do we accomplish *that*?"

"It is impossible, but you must do it anyway."

"Why?"

"The Gentle Corrector has spoken."

"Oh, I see. And just what was wrong with our accepting the pills in the first place?"

"Vark hasn't yet announced that anything *was* wrong. What he would be punishing you for would be *obstructing the investigation.*"

"Because we don't cough up the pills?"

"Certainly. He has *ordered* you to do it. Not to obey is obstruction."

"Did you know this would happen?"

"I—er—there is no way to tell what they will do next. But they were extending their exploration in this direction, and I thought I should get here first."

Winters cast a glance over his shoulder at the Corrective Healers, who had split into two lines, and were marching along the walls of the room toward the front.

"Didn't you know Vark would tell us to give back the pills?"

"No."

"Why?"

"The Gentle Correctors have rules for everything, and the rules can all be interpreted in different ways. Only the Gentle Correctors can decide which way to interpret the rules."

"Well, that fits. And what's a Corrective Healer?"

"One who specializes in quick cures for mental confusion. He is a Pain Expert."

At the head of the room, the Gentle Corrector twanged and buzzed. From the side walls of the big room, the Corrective Healers closed in with tongs, claws, nozzles, and electrodes.

Winters growled, "What's this long cone-shaped thing they all wear on their heads?"

"That is their air-filter. There is little dust or smoke on their home planet, and their air passages are extremely sensitive. As there are many impurities in the air here, they are wearing filters."

Winters snarled, "Tell the other Earth delegates about the filters." A Corrective Healer was coming straight for him, bat outstretched. At this distance, Winters could hear as well as see the snappy spark jumping between the bat's electrodes.

In front of Winters, Malik leaned over to listen to Diomak—then twisted around to observe a Corrective Healer coming at him with outstretched nozzle.

Winters jerked his foot free of Diomak's clinging tentacle, and dove for the nearest set of long slender legs. As he slammed the creature to the floor, Winters got a grip on the air filter and yanked. The cone, which felt like some kind of stiff rubberized fabric, came partly loose.

There was a mind-stopping screech, a gagging, then a sneeze that seemed to jar the room. Then Winters' opponent took a swing. The bat grazed Winters, and the effect was like walking into an electric fence. Winters got a fresh grip, yanked the filter completely loose, and as the creature doubled up in a sneeze, Winters got the bat. He turned it around and tried it on the Corrective Healer, who made a noise like a piano with all the keys hit at once, took a flying jump, collapsed in a heap, then lifted up in a heavier sneeze.

Winters glanced around at his colleagues.

Lord Orban was straightening over an inert heap on the floor. Malik was bent over using the baton like a hammer. Madame Kuo was grappling with a Corrective Healer equipped with a set of steel claws. Winters politely stepped over, yanked the "Healer's" filter loose, and threw him headfirst into the wall.

At the front of the room, Gentle Corrector Vark, eyes wide, hands spread on the bulkhead behind him, had stopped talking.

Diomak was flushing various shades of pink and blue. Winters bent close to make himself heard above the sneezes and screams.

"Vark," said Winters, "doesn't look happy."

"This is unthinkable to him! Only *Vark's* people are allowed to use force! It is their *law!*"

"And just how do they enforce that?"

"With hideous threats and tortures!"

"Why let them?"

"They use force!"

Winters frowned.

"Do they have many spaceships?"

"Hundreds."

"How many warships?"

"Almost a dozen."

"Are these to fight other spaceships, or to bombard planets, or what?"

"They have some of each—those to destroy spaceships and those to bombard planets."

Winters said uneasily, "How long will it take them to get a warship of either kind here?"

"They could have one here in less than a decade."

Winters blinked. "*Ten years?*"

"Yes. They are almost as fast as light, but we are far from the center."

"I see." Winters straightened. Around the room, the screams were dying down, but the sneezes continued. He said, "Are such ships hard to build?"

"Not," said Diomak, "once you have the engine designs and the proper alloys—both of which I can offer."

"How *long* do they take to build?"

"Several of your planet's years—when you have the designs."

The great light finished dawning on Winters.

"I see. And what is it *you* want from *us*?"

Diomak explained.

At the end, Winters said soberly, "We'll see. That is usually an expensive proposition."

★ ★ ★

As Winters, back on Earth, reported what had happened, everyone listened intently.

The President said, "What *is* it he wants?"

"He wants us to *free his home planet*. And from what he says, and from what we wrung out of Vark and his crew, we evidently could do it."

"And in return—?"

"In return, he offers us his race's *complete technology*."

A murmur went around the table. The room filled with smiles. There were even a few administrators to be seen briskly rubbing their hands.

The President said, "So *that's* what he wants?"

"Yes, sir. A little of Vark goes a long way."

"But this still doesn't make sense! Are Vark and the rest of these overseers ahead of Diomak's people technologically?"

"Diomak said—and Vark didn't dispute it—that his race is ahead of Vark's race. Vark's race is the *governing* race—that's their specialty."

The President frowned.

"Are they more *numerous?*"

"No, sir."

"Then—why look for somebody *else* to do the job? That *is* what Diomak was doing here, wasn't it?"

"Yes, sir."

"Well—Diomak's people have the technology, they've got the numbers, and they've got the brains. What can anyone else possibly offer that they haven't got already?"

Winters shook his head moodily.

"They've apparently lost or mislaid something."

"What?"

"Well, sir, *we've* been lacking in technology, so we rate it above other things. But there's a lack that's worse yet."

The President said impatiently, "What *is* it?"

Winters shook his head.

"Winston Churchill said it, sir—but I don't remember the exact wording."

"Never mind that. Let's have it."

Winters cleared his throat, and around the crowded table they leaned forward.

Winters repeated slowly:

"Of all the virtues, the father of the others is *courage.*"

The President straightened.

"They're *afraid?*"

Winters nodded. "And the result sure shows that brains and technology aren't a cure-all. They got stuck with Vark's kind several generations ago, and ever since they've been looking for a way to get rid of them. They've got the technology, they've got the numbers, and they've got the brains, but—"

The President smiled.

"But they aren't *belligerent* enough."

"No, sir," said Winters, suddenly smiling himself. "But they *are* good traders. They kept hunting—till they found a place with an oversupply of exactly what they need."

THE UNINVITED

THE CAPTIVE DJINN

Guard Captain Skeerig Klith looked up as Senior Guard Lieutenant Ladigan Grul came in looking smug.

"Sir," said Grul, holding out a sheaf of papers, "the combat crews just dragged in an outworlder." Grul smiled, baring canine teeth an inch-and-a-half long.

Klith reached out for the report, and in his excitement ran his claws completely through the papers.

"It seems too good to be true," he said, flattening the report on his desk. "The cowardly vermin always use their magic powers to get away."

"This one slipped up somewhere. And with due respect, sir, it isn't 'magic'. The best opinion is that all they've got is a more advanced science than ours."

"When it gets that advanced what's the difference?"

"Sir," protested Grul, "no matter *how* advanced it gets, Science is not sorcery."

Klith snorted. "These outlanders came down out of the sky. They go through the air at 16,500 laps to the sneeze. If they want something, they aim a rod at it and it comes. To get rid of it, they point a rod at it and it goes.

We've seen them control their machines by *voice*. That's not sorcery?"

"By a perfectly natural process of scientific development, one step at a time—"

"Maybe wizards *get* their powers by a natural process of development, one step at a time. Anyway, what's the difference to me? If you don't understand something, it's magic, right?"

"Sir, in that case, basically everything is magic."

"Exactly," said Klith, "and in *that* case, as I said, what they use is *magic*. Now where's the prisoner?"

Grul opened his mouth, then shut it. In a choked voice, he said, "The prisoner is in the Central Cell Block, New Tier, sir."

"Hm-m-m." Klith glanced through the report. "The vermin was captured at the foot of Mount Daggeredge. His vehicle had apparently malfunctioned, and was taken to the District Technological Laboratory for study." Klith looked up. "I suppose you know, Grul, that our offensive to smash the main nest of these clawless cowardly outworlders has run into a little embarrassment?"

Grul's ears swiveled around. "No, sir. All I know is that our bombardment is so intense it can be heard a hundred and twenty laps away."

"Unfortunately, it makes just as much noise when you miss as when you hit."

"But their base is in clear sight."

"And there's something like thick, elastic, invisible armor-glass between our artillery and their base."

Grul shook his head in disgust. "There's always something."

"This prisoner may be very useful to us."

"You mean, we can question him about the barrier?"

"Exactly. In fact, we can question him about *all* their arrangements. Possibly we can find out why they're really here. That business about the goroniuk mine is obviously a cover-up."

Grul nodded. "Who would want such worthless stuff? Merely to be around that goroniuk makes a man sick, and his fur falls out in patches. Shall I bring the outworlder up now?"

"Play zango with him for a while. It will put him in a co-operative frame of mind, and if Higher Headquarters should send for him, he's unhurt."

Grul grinned and displayed his canines. Zango was played with a dozen pieces on each side. All the men moved by jumping, and all the jumps were long.

★ ★ ★

Hedding was sitting in the cell sourly eyeing the furnishings. The cot was so short and wide he could only rest on it curled up. Beside the cot was a scratched-up post, obviously convenient for sharpening one's claws. In the corner was a box of sand. In the back wall of the cell was a neat round hole six inches across, covered by a small iron door. The function of this was a mystery to Hedding. For food, he'd received a small piece of some kind of ground-up fish and cheese, called *sznivtig*, with a powerful odor. He'd also been handed a bowl of water. Hedding drank the water, looked the food over closely, and buried it in the sand. He lay back on the cot with his feet hanging over the edge, and noticed the small dull bulb in the ceiling. The metallic deposit on the inside of the bulb suggested the stage of the planet's science. It occurred to Hedding that there ought to be some kind of opportunity there. But what?

Just then, there was a rattle at the door.

A creature with large round pupils twitched its whiskers and pointed a gun at him. The gun had a bayonet that curved down at the end, like a claw.

Hedding, despite his conditioning, could barely understand the grating voice:

"Did you eat?"

"Not yet. I wasn't hungry."

"You had good luck, then?"

Hedding squinted around the cell. "Good luck? Not that *I* know of."

The jailer looked blank, then shrugged. "Bring your *sznivtig* and follow me."

"Where to?"

"Cell block 'C'. Get your claws out of the mat, and let's go."

Hedding followed the jailer through half-a-mile of dim corridors, and wound up inside an identical cell with exactly the same fittings. Fifteen minutes later, there was a rattle at the door and a new voice:

"You in there! Follow me!"

Grumbling to himself, Hedding followed the guard down a winding staircase for ten minutes, and found himself inside an identical cell fitted in exactly the same way. Twenty minutes later, there was a rattle at the door.

"Prisoner! *Attention!* Follow me!"

"What's wrong with this cell, for Pete's sake?"

"*Silence!* You will not question! *You will obey!*"

Cursing to himself, Hedding trailed off after the guard, tramped for twenty minutes along corridors lit with dim bulbs, then went around and around and around and around up a circular staircase, along another corridor and into a new cell, where the door clanged shut behind him, and fifteen minutes later a fresh voice spoke jovially:

"Prisoner. Ears up! We are taking you to a new cell. Get your *sznivtig* and follow me!"

★ ★ ★

Guard Captain Skeerig Klith shoved the message across the desk to Senior Lieutenant Grul, who read aloud, "Imperative prisoner be interrogated by scientific methods. Dismemberment, red-hot irons, hauling over the walls, and similar methods that impair clarity of mind are contraindicated. Only preliminary questioning is permissible pending my imminent arrival. Queel Snnorriz, Staff Psychologist."

"That boob," said Klith. "Obviously, he's going to baby the outworlder. You remember when they put the cretin in charge of that gang of hardcase prisoners? He was going to 'unlatch the bound memories that caused their amoral and antisocial behavior.'"

"Who could forget it?" said Grul. "The prisoners made Central into a fortress, had this grass-eater Snnorriz hung up by his tail, and threatened to slice the guards up an inch at a time if they didn't get their way."

Klith nodded gloomily, "And then, when the Iron Division went in and straightened the mess out, the boob complained that his *therapy* had been interrupted."

"They should have accidentally finished him off in the fight."

Klith shrugged. "There's no getting around the fact that he's the Emperor's cousin, and also way up in the Scholastic Hierarchate."

"Regarding which," said Grul, "I say, get them all together in one place, and set off a good strong—"

"*Sh-h*," said Klith, glancing around nervously. "None of that." He cleared his throat, dropped off the bench, and exercised his claws on the nearby sharpening post. "Our immediate problem is this prisoner. How's he coming along?"

Grul's lips stretched in a grin. "He was patient the first four or five . . . ah . . . moves in the game. But then he disarmed a guard, got laid out by the guard's mate, and is now trailing around in a bad frame of mind."

Klith nodded. "Except for that fight—which he started himself—none of it will leave any marks. Run him on down to the bottom floor of the Old Tier. Let him get a look at where we can put him if we feel like it. I'm going to take a nap. After I wake up, I'll want to have him up here."

★ ★ ★

Hedding, feeling of the bump on his head, followed the dim figure down the faintly-echoing corridor past the rows of silent cells. He cleared his throat, and tried to remember if this guard was friendly. There had been so many guards, and so many cells, that they were starting to run together in his mind.

"Say," he said, "are these cells occupied?" An echo bounced back from somewhere, then another, fainter, echo.

"*Arnh*?" said the guard.

Hedding waited till the echoes died down, and repeated the question.

The guard grunted. "Oh, most cells in this block are empty. Watch your head. We're going down lower."

They started down a spiral staircase, going around and around and around and around, and they went down so far into the gloom that Hedding began to suffer from the illusion that the staircase was circling upward under his feet and all he was doing was to move his legs and stay in the same place.

The guard coughed apologetically. "No need to put your *sznivtig* out down here. They'll come right out after *you*."

Hedding, traveling around and around in a daze, said stupidly, "They will?"

"Sure as death and demerits," said the guard. "See you don't go to sleep. Pick off a few now and then, snap their necks, and toss them into the pack. Keep them busy. If it gets too thick in there, climb up the clawpost and take a breather. Be sure you get your tail up. These things can jump."

A little of this seeped through into Hedding's consciousness. He came awake, aware of the gritty rust underfoot, and the change in the occasional lighting fixtures. Down here, they had gas lamps, with wavering luminous flames.

Suddenly, there was a scuttling noise, the guard bent over, there was a squeak, a *snap*, a *thud*, and a multitudinous scurrying sound.

"Just a few levels more," said the guard.

By now, cold dew was dripping from the steps overhead,

the air was dank, and lights showed dark walls trickling moisture.

"Careful," said the guard, "watch this next step."

Hedding edged down warily. From up above came a thump. Behind them, the guard's mate was following, just in case Hedding should try anything.

The guard in front said, "Inside this tier of cells—what we call the Old Tier—the lights are gaslights. Watch your footing."

They stepped off the staircase with a splash. Directly in their path, a black hairy thing the size of a man's hand slid up on a thread.

The guard ducked aside, and led the way to a cell with water on the floor, a dead thing covered with orange mold in the water, a bare squarish cot with toadstools growing out of the wood, and the post leaning against the rear wall. Here and there in the dimness, eyes glowed. A cold dank draft smelling like garlic blew in the direction from which they'd come, and made the overhead gas flames waver, so that long shadows flickered over walls and floor.

Hedding looked around incredulously.

The guard scratched at a metal plate affixed to the bars, and glanced at a slip of paper. "It's the right cell, all right. But that's the worst mess I've seen since Snnorriz took over Central Prison."

The second guard was now standing just inside the corridor. "Stick him in, and let's get out of here."

"Look at those stobclers with their eyes glittering in the light."

"What do you think I *am* looking at."

"If we leave him here, what'll be left when we get back?"

"That's *his* lookout, not ours. We got our orders: Put him in Cell 6t42e, Old Tier. There's Cell 6t42e, Old Tier. Orders are orders."

The first guard frowned, and reluctantly shoved a large key in the lock. He turned it, to the squeal of rusty metal.

Hedding was now fully awake. A quick glance at the guards showed that he could only hope to overcome one, and would have to fight the other at a disadvantage, since their weapons were long knives and he was unfamiliar with them. Victory would leave him inside a labyrinthine prison, where he could be recognized on sight. Escape didn't seem in the cards, but maybe talk would help.

"Sure as death and demerits," he said reasonably, "they're going to want to question me later."

The second guard had a knife out, and was looking around nervously.

"That's not *our* worry."

"No?" said Hedding. "If they want to question me and can't, who will they pin the blame on?"

There was a thoughtful quiet, in which could be heard the scratchings of many small claws.

Guard number one looked at number two. "What then?"

"We got our orders."

"To lock him up, not execute him."

"If we *don't* we're disobeying orders to lock him up."

Hedding said, "One of you stay here. The other go up and tell them."

"Regulations say we stick together. Otherwise, you might overpower one of us, get the short-sword and uniform, and get out."

"I'm an outworlder. I could never get past the guards."

"It wouldn't matter if you were a sixteen-legged crab with eyestalks. It's what regulations say, and you don't argue with regulations."

"Regulations must say something about putting prisoners in cells unfit for occupancy, and killing prisoners wanted for interrogation."

The first guard swore. He shoved Hedding into the cell, clicked the lock, and turned to the second guard. "Go out and start up the steps."

As soon as the second guard was out, the first grunted. "Ah, these stobclers are all *over* the place! I better kill a few to keep the rest busy." He whipped out his long knife, slashed here and there, then shouted, "There it goes! *Run for it! Here come millions of them!*"

As a matter of fact, the glowing eyes were at almost the same distance as before, though in continually increasing numbers. The knife, however, now lay inside Hedding's cell.

The guard shot out the door. The clatter on the staircase told Hedding the other guard needed no urging.

Gratefully, he picked up the knife and looked around.

Slithering wetly over each other, the things began to move in on him.

* * *

Guard Captain Skeerig Klith kept his hands flat on the desk, and sought to keep his claws from biting into the wood.

"Yes," he growled. "The prisoner is roughly our size, and has the same general build."

Senior Guard Lieutenant Grul added, "His fingers are

longer and thinner, Learned Sir, and without retractile claws. But he seems to handle things well just the same."

"I see." Their guest sprawled on the bench, hind paws thrust over the edge, holding in one forepaw a fume-generator stuck on the end of a large silver pin. This fume-generator was a black, waxy-coated cylinder, about as long and thick as a man's first finger. Wound around the outside were spiral strips of decorative silver and gold fabric, which burnt up slowly as the generator was consumed, and added their own peculiar fragrance to the general smudge.

Guard Captain Klith edged his bench back from the desk, and glanced around at the windows. They were open, but there wasn't the slightest suggestion of a breeze.

Klith cleared his throat.

"If you'd prefer to enjoy your generator outside by the parapet, Psychologist Snnorriz, we'd be glad to continue this later on."

Snnorriz didn't answer at once. Instead, he applied his pursed lips to the near end of the fume generator. A look of exquisite refinement appeared on his face as the far end glowed red, and silver and gold strips burned away in clouds of gray smoke.

Klith glanced around desperately. The room had a ventilator chimney, left over from the days when it, like the cells, was lit by acetylene, and the fumes had to be drawn up and out. But the ventilator got most of its draft from a jet of flame burning in the chimney. And this flame had to be lit. Klith groped under the desk till one extended foot found the dusty push-pedal that, assuming it was in working order, would ignite the ventilator flame.

The psychologist, meanwhile, with a look of ineffable wisdom, slowly exhaled a boiling gray-green cloud at the guard captain.

Klith shoved down hard on the pedal. There should be a little *pop* followed by a faint roar. Nothing happened. The valve might be stuck, or, worse yet, the valve could have opened, but the worn flint might have failed to strike the scratch-plate. He shoved again harder.

There was a flash.

BANG!

The room jumped. A cloud of dust particles intermingled with chips of stone and bits of mortar showered down, followed by a flaming nest the size of a man's two fists, and filled with odd bits of tin, old rings, and shiny coins, from which a small purple bird flew screaming out the nearest window. By a stroke of supreme good fortune, the burning nest and its load of trash landed on the psychologist's head.

In the chaos of the next few minutes, with Snnorriz bounding around the room like a madman, it was a simple job for Klith to get rid of the fume-generator, pin and all.

As he was congratulating himself, a guard corporal appeared in the doorway, regarded the screaming Snnorriz with amazement, then faced Klith and saluted.

"Sir, we've got a couple of guards out in the anteroom. According to them, that outworld sorcerer is down in the Old Tier getting eat up by hordes of stobclers. You want I should give 'em what-for for bothering you about it?"

Snnorriz hit the floor and screamed, "You *barbarians!* You prehistoric *reptiles!* You'll get that prisoner up here unhurt, or *my cousin the Emperor will hear of it!*"

★ ★ ★

Hedding by now was up sidewise on the bars, resting on the cross-piece of the heavy doorframe, his left arm and both legs hooked through the vertical bars, his right arm reaching down with the long knife as he picked off enough of the vermin to keep the rest happy.

Somewhere outside, he knew, the expedition would have automatic monitoring devices hunting for him. A tiny transmitter inside his body-cavity was giving off a faint signal that should be detected sooner or later. The trouble was that even after they found him, they had to *reach* him. If he could get outside, his chances of being spotted and picked up would be much better.

Just then, out in the stairwell, the shouted warnings and clank of metal told of the cautious descent of a sizable body of guards.

"Back there!" shouted a familiar voice. "You four in the rear, hold the entrance. In the lead, there! Shove past the sixth cell in the tenth row, kill as many of these vermin as you can reach, and pitch them down the corridor. Keep moving!"

The clank, splash, and jangle drew closer. Then, peering down the corridor, Hedding saw the feline guards in the wavering glare of the gaslights. His urge to escape took on urgency as he saw one of the guards pause to eat a large stobcler. Those holes in the cell walls were beginning to add up for Hedding.

"All right," shouted the familiar voice, "step out down that corridor!"

There was a rattle of keys, and the creak of the cell door.

"Now, where in—"

Hedding dropped to the floor. His cramped muscles nearly gave way, as he whispered, "Thanks for your knife," and handed it back.

The guard gave a quick glance around. "What a place," he muttered, and stepped forward to clang a small rusty door shut over a hole where several pairs of beady eyes were gleaming. "Agh! It's enough to spoil a man's appetite. So many at once make one's hide quiver. In the corridor there! Back toward the stairs. *Move!*" He guided Hedding out of the cell by the arm, and locked the door. "All right, mates, we've got the prisoner, and we may get out of this without a demerit. But nobody better panic on those steps, or I'll turn him in myself! Let's go!"

Hedding looked overhead curiously.

"What do you use in those gas lamps. What kind of gas is that?"

"Glow-gas," said the guard. "They ship in drums of gasrock, and the engineers sink the stuff in big water tanks. When water hits the gasrock, it boils off glow-gas. They used to light the whole prison that way. You there, up ahead! Are you stuck to the steps? *Move!*"

The procession wound up toward the top floor.

There, in the guard captain's office, Queel Snnorriz flared up again.

"The Empress, herself, gave me that platinum pin. She's going to be *distressed* if I show up without it. Of course, I *can* tell her the circum—"

Guard Lieutenant Grul said earnestly, "When you jumped up, Learned Sir, it seems to me the generator and pin went out the window together."

Guard Captain Klith was relievedly breathing fresh air again, but Snnorriz's hints and threats about the Imperial Court were starting to get on his nerves.

The psychologist cleared his throat. "I was in the Throne Room the other day, when His Imperial Majesty was accepting the Semi-Annual Efficiency Lists from the Heads of Service. The Emperor put his thumb by one of the names and said, 'What do you think of this fellow?' I turned to him, and—"

A guard corporal stepped in, cast a fishy look at the psychologist, and saluted Klith. "Sir, they've got that outworlder out here."

"The Crown Prince," Snnorriz was saying, "admired that pin—"

Klith, normally a patriotic man, had never felt more like an anarchist. Angrily, he jumped to his feet, looked out the window, and pointed.

"Lying on the parapet there, one floor down, is your precious pin. I'll just send a guard down to—" Klith blinked.

The pin, its faceted silvery head glittering, was obscured by a small purplish blur. A triumphant squawk sounded and the parapet was bare.

"*Where is it?*" shouted Snnorriz, at Klith's elbow. "You said—"

"A pack-bird just flew away with it. Can I help that?"

"Do you expect me to believe—"

In the background, Senior Lieutenant Grul could be heard speaking urgently to the corporal. "Get him in here, quick!"

Klith and Snnorriz were now shouting at each other.

"*Sirs!*" said the corporal, in a voice suited to an outdoor amphitheater, "*here is the ALIEN SORCERER, under guard!*"

Snnorriz and Klith turned as if on pivots.

Hedding was trying to deduce what was going on when the guards suddenly shoved him forward.

"*The ALIEN SORCERER,*" roared a voice, "*under guard!*"

Hedding stared at a tough-looking feline in leather tunic, accompanied by an overbred dandy in scorched black velvet and white ruff, a slender dagger with jeweled hilt at his side, his whiskers upcurled at the ends, and a faint wisp of smoke drifting up from the fur just over his right ear.

Hedding glanced around the many-windowed room, looked up at a faint roar emanating from the ceiling, and was about to speak when a droning noise passed overhead. Hedding would have given a good deal to get to the window, but a guard had him by either arm.

The tough-looking feline glanced at the window. "What's that noise?"

A guard presented himself at the door. "The skywatch lookout just yelled down the voice-tube, sir. There's one of the outworlders' flying machines making slow circles high overhead."

Hedding congratulated himself that he'd been located so quickly. But the device couldn't come in and get him. He had to show himself.

The feline in leather tunic said, "Tell the lookout to let us know if it comes lower. You see, gentlemen, the outworlders are searching for this one here. The fact that they're just circling overhead shows they don't know exactly where he is. We want to keep it that way."

"That should be easy, sir," said a second feline in leather, with different insignia. "The fellow has no tools equipment, or weapons. He doesn't even have claws, sir."

"Remember. He is a *sorcerer*."

This time, it was the feline in velvet who spoke, after delivering himself of a condescending laugh. "You of the military may, of course, use such inaccurate terminology if it suits your natures. We of the Priestly Hierarchate of Scientific Wisdom speak more accurately." The thickening of the atmosphere following this little speech seemed to be lost on the speaker, who went on, "All that these outworlders have is merely our own knowledge, carried a bit further. They've just refined it some more. 'Sorcerer.' There is no such thing as a 'sorcerer'! Why I wager you that this fellow here, common as he looks; would fit right into one of our own Lesser Guilds. Come, fellow, to which Great Branch of the Mother Tree do you cling—Matter, Energy, Body or Mind? Speak up, now."

★ ★ ★

Hedding decided a mining engineer was closer to matter than to the other three, and said obediently, "Matter, sir."

"And what might be your specialty?"

"Goroniuk mining."

The feline in velvet looked indulgent. "So you say. But what would anyone want goroniuk for?"

High overhead, there was a rumble. If Hedding could attract attention, the controller at his distant board would bring that spotter down. Each spotter had a roomy passenger compartment, and carried food, water, and weapons.

But first he had to get its attention.

The tough-looking feline in leather tunic pulled out a length of strap with steel studs on one end.

"You are being questioned, Prisoner. The question was, 'What would anyone want goroniuk for?'"

"Tush," said the feline in velvet. "Spare me this crudity. I have come prepared to handle this my way."

"You don't get anywhere by coddling prisoners. Raise a few welts, and they'll listen closer the next time you speak."

"Nonsense. That way you consolidate their opposition, or drive it underground. *My* method raises the submerged resistances to the surface where we can deal with them psychologically." He glanced at Hedding. "Which method seems more scientific to *you*?"

"Yours, unquestionably."

The feline in leather snorted contemptuously.

The feline in velvet turned to Hedding, a brotherly smile displaying his teeth to great advantage.

"Come with me, fellow. Regard me as your friend."

Guard Captain Skeerig Klith spent the next hour in a state of profound boredom. As he worked at his desk, he could hear Snnorriz carrying out his interrogation in an adjoining room. It was unlike any interrogation Klith had ever carried out. Instead of snappy questions and answers, with occasional screams from the prisoner, there was comradely laughter, and endless conversation. In short, Snnorriz was a good deal more friendly with the prisoner than he was with Klith. At one point, when Lieutenant Grul was with him, Klith commented on a peal of laughter from the other room:

"Listen to that. The fop is happier with an outworld alien than he is with us."

Grul grunted agreement, and glanced back through the doorway. "Now they're taking turns smoking through a *chomizar*."

Klith took a look. Sure enough. there was the bubbling glass pot, with its forty feet of flexible tubing lying in coils all over the place. The psychologist smoked through one mouthpiece as the outworlder admired the workmanship of another.

Klith growled, "It's enough to make a man sick. I will admit, though, that he's getting some information."

The outworlder's voice was saying, "Yes, the air on this planet is close to that on our home planet. There the composition is roughly twenty per cent oxygen, seventy per cent nitrogen, two per cent ammonia, and the rest carbon dioxide, water vapor, and inert gases."

"Interesting," said a strange voice, "we don't have any free ammonia. I wonder why—"

Grul squinted, "Who's that?"

Klith peered in, and saw a slender individual with discolored fur, and a badly singed ear, wearing a black robe covered with white planets, stars, and comets, with a silver chain around his neck from which dangled a gold distilling flask.

Klith growled. "It's some chemist. He looks high up in the Hierarchate."

The outworlder was saying, "It rises from volcanic fissures. I don't know why. I'm only a practical mining engineer, myself."

"Nevertheless," came the chemist's voice, "your testimony

can be interesting to us. We, for instance, suffer tissue injury from a trace of ammonia."

"Strange." said the outworlder. "On this planet, we carry bottles of it around with us to sniff every now and then. The absence of it makes our mucous membranes dry up. Unfortunately, I got separated from mine when I was captured."

A droning noise passed overhead.

"That damned thing," said Klith.

"Sir," said a voice from the outer door, "the sky-watch reports the flying-machine circling overhead again."

"I hear it," said Klith shortly.

The chemist's voice drifted in. " . . .glad to get you a bottle to carry around with you. I'll send for it now."

Klith shot off his bench, cursing.

"Listen, you," he snapped. "No bottles of ammonia are to be carried around by that outworlder. He could blind the lot of us with it, jump outside, and before we knew what was going on work some wizardry that would call down that flying machine!"

Snnorriz stood up angrily. "I'm sure such a thing would never occur to a *scientist*. Now you've mentioned it, of course—"

"But," cried the outworlder pathetically, "I'll dry up! We can't *exist* without ammonia!"

"Too bad," snarled Klith.

"This," said Snnorriz, his tail lashing, "is *inhuman*, an example of the military psychology that—"

"Oh," said Klith, sliding out his claws, "is that so?"

A colossal uproar took place, in the course of which it somehow came to be agreed that the alien could have a bottle of ammonia by his bed at *night*, but must surrender it each morning to the guard.

Klith returned, fur on end, to his bench, then got up and tore a section of the clawpost to splinters. Grul discreetly eased out the door. From the other room came the alien's voice:

" . . .can understand just what you're up against, dealing with a military mind like that. They're all so *suspicious*. But I must say, you've shown great foresight in combining the priesthood and the scientific community into one solid hierarchate—"

Klith leaned forward, gripping the desk with his claws.

The conversation, however, now drifted off down an obscure technical sidetrack, and Klith, bored, went back to work. Then Grul came in, looking serious.

"Sir, word just came from the District Technological Laboratory. They started to disassemble the outlander's flying machine—"

"*Started?* What happened?"

"The whole thing disintegrated into a pile of black dust."

Klith could feel his fur bristle.

"Oh," he growled sarcastically, "*they're* not sorcerers! All *they've* got is science, only a little bit more advanced! Double the guard outside the doors here. Bring up A Section of the Riot Platoon, and see that they're always in reach when that outlander is here. And when he's down below, keep them on the floor above him. Between him and us."

"Yes, sir. But he's completely disarmed, sir."

"How do you disarm a sorcerer? He's still got his knowledge, hasn't he? Do as I say!"

"Yes, sir."

From the other room came Snnorriz's proud voice " . . . *That* was devised in the early days of the Hierarchate. The runs are *built-in*, so the stobclers have easy access past each cell. The runs intercommunicate, so the prey soon catch the scent of the *sznivtig*. But of course, it's highly problematical just when a stobcler will pop out of any particular hole. This keeps the prisoners on edge, constantly crouched at the holes, waiting. That way, they don't have time to make trouble."

"An ingenious system," said the outworlder admiringly. "The . . . er . . . stobclers in *our* prisons are let in on a highly unsystematic basis."

"You see, in some things we are ahead of you! How do you like our stobclers? Are they congenial to your palate?"

The outworlders hesitated, possibly reluctant to give offense. "At first, the flavor seemed a trifle . . . 'off' to us, but by adding plenty of 'lunar caustic' as seasoning—"

"'Lunar caustic'?" Snnorriz sounded puzzled. "We may know it under some other name."

The chemist said, "How is it composed?"

"Three atoms of oxygen to one of nitrogen, and this combined with one atom of silver. I hope I've got your name for the elements right."

"Oh, yes. Let's see—*Angh!* What you are talking about is what we call 'burning chellery.' Now are you quite sure—"

"I'm almost certain—"

"We will get you some—"

As Klith erupted into the doorway, Snnorriz burst out,

"All *right!* Only in his *cell.* You don't want him to *starve,* do you?"

After a violent exchange with Snnorriz, Klith got the prisoner to promise on his word of honor not to throw ammonia or burning chellery in anyone's face, and to put the containers outside his cell in the morning. The prisoner then embarrassedly said that he had a favor to ask.

"*Now* what?" snarled Klith.

"My . . . er . . . claws . . . aren't very efficient for catching these stobclers—"

"You catch them at home, don't you? I mean, them or something similar?"

"But the thing is, *these* are so *fast!* Generally, we use some artificial means—"

"You want a *knife?* Nothing doing! We'll put you in the Old Tier where they're thicker—" Klith waved a hand to silence Snnorriz. "Not on the bottom floor. Higher up."

This satisfied everybody, and, cursing to himself, Klith went out to meet Grul coming into the office.

"The extra guards are outside, sir. A section of the Riot Platoon is on its way."

"Good." Klith spat out an angry epithet. "*Listen* to them in there! They're practically crawling into each other's pockets."

The friendly voices drifted out from the other room.

"Since you like the *chomizar* so much," said Snnorriz, "you can take it to your cell with you. It's soothing to smoke while you crouch at the stobcler hole. We Hierchates, of course, aren't restricted to any such time-consuming method of feeding. But a little primitivism is healthy now and then."

The outworlder's voice rose in gratitude. "You are so considerate! Is there anything *I* can do for you?"

Snnorriz purred, "We *would* be interested, for purely . . . ah . . . industrial reasons . . . to have a few questions answered about that . . . ah . . . flexible force-screen you have outside your main base. If you could—"

"I'd be glad to tell you what I—" the outlander made a choking noise. "Excuse me. My tissues are suffering from lack of ammonia. Perhaps if you could prepare a list of questions . . . After I"—he choked again—"after a good rest, and a tasty stobcler seasoned with plenty of burning chellery—"

"Certainly," purred Snnorriz. "We understand exactly. We'll have the list ready for you in the morning."

The prisoner was led, proclaiming his gratitude, out into the corridor. Snnorriz appeared at Klith's door, tweaking his whiskers and looking superior. "Psychology, my boy. Just make them grateful to you."

"Listen," said Klith, ignoring Snnorriz, and taking the chemist by his robe. "Is there anything this outworlder can make out of a *chomizar*, a bottle of ammonia, and this burning chellery, or whatever it is?"

"Nothing whatever," snapped the scientist, glaring at Klith's hand on his arm.

Klith and Grul suddenly found themselves alone.

"Well," said Grul, "it *seems* to be working out all right."

Klith jabbed a pedal under the desk to shut off the ventilator. "If only it doesn't turn out like that time Snnorriz took over Central Prison."

★ ★ ★

Hedding was delighted to see that Snnorriz himself

caught up with the guards and accompanied him to the cell in the echoing Old Tier.

"How's this one, Hedding, my boy?"

"Could I have one closer to a lamp? My night vision—"

"Certainly. How's this?" The gas lamp sent out twin plumes directly outside the cell door.

"Fine. Thank you, very much."

Snnorriz beamed, then waited solicitously till a water bowl, the *chomizar*, a good supply of burning chellery, and a large tightly-stoppered bottle of ammonia arrived. He opened the iron cover over the stobcler hole, and superintended the placing of the *sznivtig*, to give Hedding a good spring at the stobcler. Snnorriz and Hedding then clasped forepaws emotionally. Hedding coughed a few times as the cell door clanged shut, drew a deep breath, and removed the stopper from the ammonia bottle.

"Ah-h" he murmured.

Snnorriz and the guards gagged and shot down the corridor.

Hedding hastily restoppered the bottle, looked around, and eyed the *chomizar* with its length of flexible hose. He picked up the amber bottle of "burning chellery" and thoughtfully unscrewed the lid.

★ ★ ★

Klith awoke after a fitful night's sleep, exercised, washed, brushed himself, ate breakfast, and walked down the hall to his office. He was scarcely inside when Grul showed up.

"What's wrong?" said Klith.

"Snnorriz's pet," said Grul, "was found replacing a fitting to the right-hand lamp-jet near his cell. He had a little rubber plug made from the *chomizar* head in place while he screwed on the first reducer to the jet."

"Plug? You mean he cut it from the *chomizar* stopper? What did he cut it *with*?"

"He broke off the end of one of the glass bar-handles and used that."

Klith could feel his fur tingle. "Why?"

"He claims the light bothered him . . ."

"Get him up here. *Fast*."

"He's on the way."

Klith took out his length of strap.

Hedding was marched in with a pair of curved bayonets hastening his steps.

Overhead, a droning sound traveled around patiently.

"Now," growled Klith, "you did *what*?"

"Cast a spell," said the outworlder, beaming. "And if the feet of *sznivtig*-seeking rats chance to cross the dried white powder made in the dark of the night by the light of a carbide lamp with a hose from a *chomizar* brewing glow-gas in spirits of ammoniacal moon silver then—"

A sudden jar shook the building.

There was a sound like a *chomizar* mouthpiece crushed underfoot and abruptly the room filled with ammoniacal vapors.

Hedding was out the window while they were still choking. He stood by the parapet and waved frantically.

The spotter dove, to hover nearby. Hedding jumped inside.

"How," said a voice from a small speaker, "did you work *that*? This place is built like a fortress."

"Don't talk. *Climb*. I got hold of the stuff to make a

batch of silver acetylide—from ammoniacal silver nitrate with acetylene bubbled through it. You know how sensitive the dry stuff is. I piped some acetylene gas into closed runs, put the acetylide inside, and stuck in a kind of bait that brings rats in a hurry. Happily, I was away from there before a rat hit the acetylide."

"You made a big crack in their wall. They won't like you for it."

"Keep climbing. I don't think you appreciate this. Acetylene is great for lots of purposes. But here, they've got it *piped* into a big section of that building."

"So?"

"That explosion will crack some of the pipes."

"I still don't get it."

"A few of those lights should stay lit. And acetylene has an unusual property. Mixtures of anywhere from three to eighty per cent with air are explosive."

The spotter abruptly speeded up its climb.

★ ★ ★

Guard Captain Skeerig Klith crawled painfully out from the tangle of timbers, rocks and hunks of plaster, and glared at the dazed Senior Lieutenant Ladigan Grul.

The emergency-aid workers were putting Grul's splinted left forearm into a sling. Here and there were others, plentifully covered with patches of shaved fur and bandages.

Klith eyed Grul balefully.

Grul sensed the stare.

"Sir?" croaked Grul.

Klith snarled. "Take a look at this mess and say it again."

"Say what, sir?"

"'No matter how advanced, *science isn't sorcery*.'"

Grul opened his mouth.

But he couldn't get the words out.

THE UNINVITED GUEST

Richard Verner stood in the morning sun between the umbilical tower with part of its upper stage sheared off, and the massive dome of a blockhouse from the top of which two periscopes looked out. To Verner's right stood a spare, straight officer with general's insignia and a look of baffled exasperation. To Verner's left stood half-a-dozen men uneasily watching a silvery object that floated before them with no visible support.

This object was so shiny that it was hard to see, but Verner, intently studying the warped and distorted surface reflections, could make out a flattened ovoid about eight-and-a-half feet across and some five feet high at the center, drifting about six inches clear of the ground. The shiny surface showed numerous tiny black spots that expanded, contracted, and vanished, to reappear in another place, expand, contract, and again vanish. A faint smell of ammonia hung in the air.

The general cleared his throat.

"This thing showed up here about a week ago. The day was hotter and brighter than it is today, and those black spots were smaller, so the surface was even shinier, and no one knew at first whether he was seeing a mirage, a current of heated air, spots on his glasses, or whether he needed a quick trip to the head-shrinker. So at first, nobody even mentioned it. Then the thing hung dead still in front of Aaronson, who was walking to the blockhouse, and Aaronson tossed a pebble at it. If the pebble bounced off, he could tell himself it was real. The pebble didn't bounce off—it disappeared inside somewhere. Then this—whatever it is—spat the pebble back at Aaronson, and hit him in the right shoulder. Aaronson might as well have been shot with a forty-five. He decided pretty fast it was real, and before long we had twenty to thirty other reports that fit."

Verner studied it thoughtfully. "What did you do?"

"What could we do? This is missile-test site, not a branch of the Interplanetary Society. We've got a schedule to keep. There's an outfit that's supposed to take care of things like this, and we notified them. They sent some people out to look at it and they said 'Hm-m-m,' and 'I see,' and went home and decided it's either 'an improperly-inflated weather balloon,' 'ball lightning,' or maybe 'a form of the St. Elmo's fire formerly seen on the masts of ships.'"

The general waved a hand to indicate the various towers looming on the landscape. "They figure the wind blows by these towers and 'generates static electricity.' Well, so much for that. They've explained it away, but we're still stuck with it. We've tried to ignore it, but it noses around all over the place and you *can't* ignore it. We were ten seconds from launch the other day, with this thing wandering around erratically at four hundred feet, and it got into exactly the wrong spot and stayed there, so we finally had to give up. There are three fresh holes in the fence, eight to nine feet across and five feet high, where it went through, and around each hole there's a spatter of iron shot.

"Yesterday, it sidled up to one of our technicians, and took off a slice of his clothes and four square inches of skin underneath. We won't see him again till we've got this thing out of here.

"Since then, it's taken bites out of the blockhouse, Hammerson's car, a tree, that umbilical tower, and thirty yards of grass and dirt outside the fence. Every time it does this, there's a spray of concrete, wood, metal, or rock, and the bits come out with velocities from near zero to about three thousand feet per second."

The general eyed the hovering ovoid sourly.

"You see where this puts us. We can't very well armor our missiles, just in case this thing decides to take a bite out of something nearby. None of our men signed up for duty in a combat zone, either. What I'd like to do is to work on it with a rocket launcher. But the boys tell me the internal energy of the thing is probably such that the resulting explosion would take out this whole end of the state.

"So," said the general, turning to Verner, "since you're a heuristician, and it's a heuristician's job to solve problems other experts alone can't take on, I'm turning the whole mess over to you. I don't care who you call in, or *what* you do. Just get rid of this thing before it wrecks our whole space program!"

Verner studied the ovoid intently, sniffed hard, and

promptly sent off a telegram. He then spent the rest of the day keeping an eye on the ovoid, and listening to the accounts of a stream of witnesses who described their experiences with it. Twice he had to drop flat as the ovoid dipped too low and sent bits of concrete whining overhead. Several times, people who had had ovoid experiences spoke uneasily. "There's something wrong with it. It doesn't fly as high as it did. It doesn't move around as much. And—Look there!"

For an instant, the reflectivity of the ovoid's surface dulled, like a mirror filmed over with grayish mist. The numerous black spots all shrank to pinpoints. A moment later, everything was as it had been before. But the impression persisted that something was wrong.

As one engineer said, "I think it's *sick*. And God help us if it dies. When a man's system goes out of balance, he collapses, and that's that. But with the internal energy this has, I'm afraid that when it dies, it's likely to turn into a miniature, short-lived nova."

By the end of the afternoon, Verner had accumulated a store of information, hunches, and misgivings, and an answer to his telegram. He now sent several of the men on a rush errand to the nearest shopping center. A little later he looked around at the sound of approaching footsteps.

"Well," said the general hopefully, "have you got any ideas?"

"Yes, but first I want to ask a few questions."

"Ask away."

"Does it *always* have that faint ammonia odor?"

"As far as we know."

"What does it do at night?"

"Settles down within an inch or so of the surface. The whole outside seems to turn silvery, and you can see the moon and stars reflected it. It's an eerie thing—Like a big, silvery crystal ball."

"Do you think it's a kind of spaceship, some kind of reconnaissance device, or a living creature?"

The general started to speak, glanced around at the gradually gathering dusk, then said, "The only answer I can logically give is: I don't know. It's possible to make mechanical devices that will react very much as if they were alive. But the impression I have is of a living creature, and one that's experiencing a certain amount of discomfort."

"Why do you suppose it's here?"

"There you've got me. Why, of all the places there are on earth, should it hang around a missile-test site? I don't know."

Verner looked at it thoughtfully. "Where do you suppose it originally came from?"

"Same answer. Only, here we have that faint ammonia odor. One of the constituents in our atmosphere is carbon dioxide. We *exhale* carbon dioxide. There are planets we think have ammonia, among other things, in their atmospheres. This creature, if that's what it is, exhales a little ammonia now and then. Maybe it comes from a planet with ammonia in *its* atmosphere. It could come from Jupiter, for all I know."

"Did it appear shortly after a launch?"

"Yes, as a matter of fact it did. We'd just put a satellite in orbit. But what's that got to do with its coming down *here*?"

"Suppose you were an interplanetary traveler, in trouble of some kind, looking for help, and a satellite came up from a planet close by, and went into orbit?"

The general thought it over. "I'd probably go down where the satellite came from to try to get help."

"But how would you show them what you needed?"

"Well . . . I certainly wouldn't be able to talk their language—It stands to reason I'd have to use a kind of"— he growled—*"sign language."*

"Exactly. Now, if we assume that this creature is doing the same thing, what is it trying to say?"

"But it takes *bites* out of things." He scowled. "All right. Assume for the purpose of argument that what it wants is *something to eat.* What do you feed a thing like this? Suppose it came from Jupiter? *Where are we going to get Jupiterian food for it?*"

"I sent a telegram off earlier today for just that information."

The general snorted. "Where are they going to—" He turned, to find several of his men setting down twenty-five and fifty pound sacks, then he looked back at Verner. "You don't waste any time."

"This ovoid has been here a week," said Verner. "It has hardly moved all today, and several people tell me it looks 'sick.' They also say that if anything does happen to it, it's likely to go off in a bright flash and take half the state with it. I don't think we ought to delay."

The general nodded. "Go right ahead. If it gets just a little darker, the ovoid will settle down to sleep—or whatever it does at night."

Verner opened a pocketknife, cut one of the sacks,

reached in to feel a small, hard, curving surface with a roughness underneath, drew back his arm, and threw.

Something hit the pavement near the ovoid, and rolled past close by. The ovoid didn't move.

Verner threw again. This time, it rolled directly under the ovoid.

Again nothing happened.

The general stared unmoving into the gathering dusk. There was a silence as if that whole section of the countryside was holding its breath.

This time, Verner cut two pungent-smelling halves, and threw one. It hit in front of the ovoid. The ovoid didn't move. He threw the other half. It landed on top of the ovoid and vanished from sight.

Nothing happened.

The general shook his head. "We'll have to try something else. We can—"

"*Wait*—" said Verner sharply.

One of the men said, "It hasn't spat it out yet. It always—"

Another yelled, "*Run for it!*"

The ovoid started to move.

It came toward them in a blur.

They bolted in all directions. The general moved as if he'd been fired out of a gun, glanced back over his shoulder and shouted, "*Down!*"

There were gasps as they hit gravel, dirt, and concrete, then there was the whir and whine of bits and fragments flying overhead.

In an instant, Verner and the general had twisted to face back, toward where the ovoid whirled and spun, taking in entire sacks at once, and in its eagerness dipping too low and getting chunks of paving, which it got rid of in a blur of flying fragments.

They watched in silence as the ovoid finished the last bit of sacks, moved around like a dog looking for scraps, shot across the field, darted here, then there, and suddenly sprang for the sky so fast it was out of sight in an instant.

From somewhere came a crash like a plane breaking the sound barrier.

Verner and the general got warily to their feet.

Several minutes passed. The ovoid didn't reappear.

"Well," said the general, relieved and cheerful, "you hit it on the nose. I don't know how."

Verner handed him a crumpled telegram.

The general snapped his cigarette lighter. The flame sprang up, to show letters in a flickering light:

. . .PRELIMINARY SEARCH REVEALS FOLLOWING WALL ST JOURNAL REPORTS UNION CARBIDE RESEARCHER FINDS ONION SEEDS SPROUT IN ATMOSPHERE OF PURE AMMONIA REPEAT PURE AMMONIA . . .

Verner said, "Starting tomorrow, I intended to try every available kind of food grown on Earth's surface. But there was just time enough tonight to try this first."

The general shook his head. "*Onions.* Well, that fits. If there's anything that smells more like Jupiter's atmosphere must smell, I don't know what it is. Who knows—maybe some traveling Jupiterian dropped a seed here a long time ago." He glanced around in relief. "Anyway, thank God *that's* over with."

"Not quite," said Verner.

"What's that?"

"How will that outfit that checks unidentified flying objects explain *this* incident?"

A grin slowly spread over the general's face.

"That's a thought. Well, well. I'll send them full particulars, and a sample onion. Then I'll eagerly wait to see what they say."

That was six months ago.

The general is still waiting.

SABOTAGE

Major Richard Martin stopped with one hand on the door of Colonel Tyler's office. From inside came voices, loud and angry. Martin glanced back past Lieutenant Schmidt at the colonel's pert, shapely, and at the moment somewhat pale receptionist. She nodded earnestly, and rolled her eyes toward the sky, which lay several thousands of feet up, through the layers of dirt, concrete, steel, and electronic shielding equipment.

Martin braced himself, waited for a pause in the uproar from the colonel's office, then knocked briskly on the door.

From inside came a short angry bark. *"Come in!"*

Martin glanced back at Lieutenant Schmidt—who was looking hungrily at the pretty receptionist—and took the lieutenant by the arm.

"Follow me," growled Martin, and shoved open the colonel's door.

The scene in the office suggested a pause for breath in a fistfight. Colonel Tyler was to one side of his desk, his face furious, his back half-turned to the door, and a folded paper clenched in his hand. A second colonel, with staff emblem at his collar, stood angrily by Tyler's big wall map, one hand stretched out to bang two groups of little whitely-glowing emblems at the edge of the map.

"The general," said the staff colonel tightly, "is extremely *anxious* to have these missing Tamars located."

Colonel Tyler glanced around, saw Martin, and relaxed slightly. "Ah, good, there you are." Then he frowned at Schmidt, and looked back at Martin reprovingly. "This is only for combat-team commanders, Major."

"I know it, sir," said Martin. "Lieutenant Schmidt is here on another matter."

The staff colonel, standing impatiently by the map, spoke brusquely. "The lieutenant can wait outside, Major."

Martin gripped Schmidt's arm, and looked at Colonel Tyler. "This is a matter of the utmost importance, sir."

The staff colonel said sharply, "It can wait. Get him outside."

Martin continued to hold Schmidt's arm, and looked directly at Colonel Tyler.

Colonel Tyler glanced at the staff colonel. "This god-damned folderol of yours will keep."

"The general—"

"Nuts! Do you think I don't want to find those missing units? I don't need your damned pep talk!"

"The whole situation is now critical—"

" '*Critical*'," snarled Colonel Tyler. "It's been 'critical' since the first scout ship went down into their damned poisonous atmosphere. It's been critical since our first pilot ran into a gasbag and got mindjammed for his pains. *Critical!* Do you think it wasn't critical when they had the commander of the Fifth Fleet lobbing impulse torpedoes into his own base? Wasn't it critical when we found the president and the defense secretary on the floor choking each other and neither one could even speak till we got him under a shield? And *that* was just their first blunderings! *Critical!* If you'd get your head out of your boot for about five seconds, you'd see it's been nothing but one hairbreadth critical mess since that first stinking damned critical contact."

"*All right!*" shouted the staff colonel. "But this is *the first time* we've ever seen a chance ahead to put *them* out! This is *the first time* we've ever been anywhere in sight of the *end*! You simpleton! Can't you see that this poses an entirely new situation? Don't you see that these new—"

Colonel Tyler's eyes gave a little glint. His face went blank. "Colonel, do you realize you are discussing classified information in the presence of an officer not cleared to hear it?"

The staff colonel stopped abruptly and turned to stare at the lieutenant. Martin still had him by the arm, and he was still right there in the room.

"Naturally," said Colonel Tyler, his face expressionless, "I will have to report this breach of regulations—which has, of course, taken place in the presence of two witnesses. Take your papers outside, please, and wait in the outer office."

The staff colonel looked around dazedly, stared at Lieutenant Schmidt, started to speak, took another look at Colonel Tyler, who was watching him with a flinty expression, swallowed, took a long envelope from Colonel Tyler's desk, and the folded paper that Colonel Tyler had tossed down there, and went out.

Colonel Tyler snapped on the intercom. "Sergeant Dana?"

"Sir?" came the girl's pleasant voice.

"Colonel Burnett wishes to wait in the outer office. This is perfectly agreeable with me."

"Yes, sir."

"But if he leaves, for any reason, let me know immediately."

"Yes, sir."

Colonel Tyler snapped off the intercom, and glanced at Schmidt, then at Martin.

"Now, Major, what is the cause of this interruption?"

"Sir, we think we may have located the missing enemy units."

Tyler's face was immediately all attention. He listened intently as Martin and Schmidt explained. Then he picked up his phone, gave a few brief orders, put the phone back in its cradle, and snapped on the intercom.

"Ask Colonel Burnett if he'll step back in here for a moment."

"Yes, sir."

Colonel Tyler glanced at Martin. "As soon as we get this out of the way, I'll want the rest of the details."

"Yes, sir."

The staff colonel, perspiring freely, came back in. Colonel Tyler looked at him clinically, then glanced at Lieutenant Schmidt. "I'd appreciate it if you'd step outside for a few minutes, Lieutenant."

"Yes, sir." Schmidt went out.

Colonel Tyler glanced at the staff colonel.

"Three of my combat-team commanders are on the

surface, risking their necks for a population that doesn't even know they exist. One of my other commanders is on standby reserve and totally worn out. I won't call him in here unless the general himself personally and specifically orders it. Now, you want all combat-team commanders to attend this so-called briefing. Well, Major Martin here was on the surface the day before yesterday, has had no real opportunity to rest, and is up to his ears in work. He may have to leave any time. But he's here. This is the best I can do for you, Colonel, and I'll tell you flatly that I think you're wasting our time. Now go ahead with your damned talk."

Colonel Burnett swallowed hard, then held out the folded paper that Colonel Tyler had been gripping when Martin came in.

"Read this, Major, then sign it on the back."

Martin took the paper, and read:

URGENT: Six Tamar penetration units still remain unlocated following disappearance from Sector II. Three units vanished from Plot fourteen months ago. Another block of three vanished five months ago. All six still remain off-plot. Past experience indicates enemy penetration of vital target area is proceeding unopposed. All personnel are urgently required to exercise maximum diligence and ingenuity to locate these missing enemy units at the earliest possible moment.

The message was signed by the "Commanding General NARD-COM STRIKE Field Force I." Stamped across

the top and bottom were the words, "Deliver by Hand—
Endorse and Return to CG FFI."

Martin turned the paper over and signed his name
under Colonel Tyler's rapidly-scrawled signature. Martin
was already familiar with the facts in the paper, so, as
Colonel Tyler had said, it was just so much wasted time.
Martin handed the paper back to Colonel Burnett.

Colonel Burnett glanced at Martin's signature, then
drew a long envelope from an inside pocket, and cleared
his throat.

"Now, gentlemen, this document is—" his voice
dropped in reverence—"the latest Staff Evaluation."

Martin waited patiently. Colonel Tyler irritatedly
glanced at the clock.

Burnett went on. "This document may not be read
aloud. Its contents may not be copied. The information it
contains may not be transferred in any way from any one
person who has read it to another who has not. It may be
discussed only in conditions of maximum security, under
full shield, and only in the presence—" his voice faltered—
"of those fully qualified to read it themselves. Read it,
initial each page, and endorse it on the back of the final
page." He handed it to Colonel Tyler, who looked it over,
in the manner of one already familiar with the contents,
scribbled his initials page-by-page and wrote his name on
the back.

Colonel Tyler handed it to Martin, then glanced back at
the staff colonel, Burnett.

"You'd have less trouble getting these things read, if
you'd have your experts translate them into some language
known to humans."

Martin was looking at the first section of the paper:

"1) The state of conflict currently existing between the human-controlled space military-socioeconomic complex centering on the planet Earth and the psychologically-oriented culture of the planet Tamar VI (Code 146-BL110101-976bA14-Ragan) is, in the presently existing stage of hostilities, entering upon a crucial phase requiring of all controlling personnel the highest degree of operative vigilance consonant with the attainment of previously-assigned overriding primary objectives."

Martin read this over again, shook his head, and started again at the beginning. Then he slowly read it all the way through, breaking it down as he went:

1) The war against Tamar VI is now entering a crucial phase, in which the highest vigilance will be required.

2) Essentially, this war is one of technology versus a species of mental accomplishment which can only be described as the power of telepathic assault and possession.

3) There are two main theaters of operation, very widely separated. These are the home planets of the two opposed races. We are able physically to cross the intervening space to strike at the Tamar home planet. They are able to bridge this space psychologically to strike at our home planet. Either side can attack the other offensively. Neither side has a truly effective defense.

4) Our basic war plan remains:

a) Offense: Attack by nuclear and subnuclear explosives against the Tamar home planet.

b) Defense: Countermeasures to neutralize or recapture strategically-placed individuals overcome by Tamar psychological penetration.

5) We continue under severe immediate handicaps:

a) Offense: Tamar VI is a giant planet, its atmosphere dense, heavily clouded, and corrosive. The precise nature of most of the planet's structure and inhabitants remains obscure. Attack is thus difficult to plan or evaluate.

b) Defense: Because of the cost of the complex electronic shielding equipment, the bulk of Earth's population remains exposed to Tamar psychological attack. As each Tamar penetration unit can attack only one individual at a time, as each such attack takes time, and as only several hundred Tamar penetration units are known to exist, the population as a whole, while completely exposed, appears safe from direct assault. However, to avoid panic, the public has not been informed of this attack and believes the war to be confined to the region of the Tamar home planet itself. Because of this secrecy, defensive operations must be financed through contingency funds and by other irregular means. This seriously hampers operations.

6) The basic war plan, as stated, relies on continued blocking of the Tamar attack, with ultimate victory to be won by assault against the Tamar home planet. Toward this end, the present force of Class III long-range battleships operating off Tamar VI is soon to be strengthened by the far more powerful planetary bombardment ships *Revenge* and *Killer*.

7) Owing, however, to the skill of the defensive force of Tamar penetration units operating against our fleet, this attack is not expected to be decisive. These local Tamar units not only attack unshielded personnel, but have also learned to unbalance the most advanced electronic computing equipment, with catastrophic results. This equipment must

either be shielded, or else replaced where feasible by mechanical, hydraulic, pneumatic, or other types of computing equipment. This, together with the demonstrated enemy capacity to overload, at times, all but the most powerful ship-borne shields, makes the final result of our present attack uncertain.

8) Two interstellar-drive devices, known respectively as Fuse and Match, are therefore under construction. Use of these devices on Tamar VI is scheduled for thirty-two months from date, and is expected to create a subnuclear detonation in the planet's interior. It is doubtful that the planet can survive such an explosion.

9) It follows that enemy activity should be terminated by the end of the next thirty-two months.

10) Granting the psychological powers of the Tamar and their known ruthlessness, it is inconceivable that the enemy will submit to destruction without cunning and extremely dangerous resistance. It is necessary, therefore, to maintain secrecy regarding these and other measures. Moreover, as our own physical measures approach completion, there is every reason to guard against new and more refined Tamar psychological measures.

11) Past experience shows the practical impossibility of meaningful two-way communication with the Tamars or of creating even a temporary truce. Cultural analysis, though necessarily highly uncertain, suggests that the Tamar view of the universe must be basically at variance with that of humanity. In this view, there is no true common frame of reference and hence no way out by means of a truce.

12) We must, therefore, regard the next thirty-two months as an extremely critical and dangerous period.

Martin duly initialed each page and signed his name on the back. He handed the paper to Colonel Tyler, who handed it back to the staff colonel, Burnett, and said, "Is that it?"

"Yes."

Colonel Tyler reached for the phone.

The staff colonel looked acutely uneasy. "Ah—about what I said earlier—"

Colonel Tyler said coldly, "I hope you aren't about to suggest anything contrary to regulations, Colonel."

Colonel Burnett shut his mouth and looked blank.

Colonel Tyler picked up the phone.

Burnett said anxiously, "I'm sure I didn't—"

Tyler put the phone back in its cradle but kept his hand on it.

"I didn't make the regulations, but I have to live by them. In the hearing of Lieutenant Schmidt, who was not cleared to receive the information, you stated authoritatively that we now, for the first time, are in a position to see the end of the war. As a matter of fact, Lieutenant Schmidt is no more likely than Major Martin or I to blab this information. But the regulations are perfectly clear."

"But I'd ordered the lieutenant to get out! I—"

"You knew Major Martin was holding him here. Were you trying to induce the lieutenant to disobey his own commanding officer? Or were you trying to block both of my officers from reporting to me on a matter of the utmost urgency? And what the devil are you doing now—trying to get me to join you in concealing the offense?"

The staff colonel opened his mouth, shut it, and swallowed.

Colonel Tyler picked up the phone, and spoke into it briefly and pointedly. Then he put the phone back in its cradle.

There was a strained silence that lasted for possibly two minutes. Then there was a rap on the door.

"Come in," said Colonel Tyler.

Six spotlessly-uniformed MP's, two of them armed with submachine guns, came in and very politely escorted the staff colonel out of the office.

Colonel Tyler glanced at Martin. "Get Schmidt in here."

Martin stepped into the outer office to find Lieutenant Schmidt talking in a low voice to the smiling Sergeant Dana.

Martin said, "Schmidt."

"Yes, sir. Just a moment, sir."

Martin stepped back into the colonel's office. Outside, he could hear the girl say something, then Schmidt say something. Then the lieutenant, looking bemused but hopeful, stepped into the office, and Martin shut the door.

Colonel Tyler glanced at Schmidt's face, and cleared his throat. "Lieutenant, this information of yours is interesting. Let's go over it again, and get the details."

"Yes, sir."

"To begin with, you got a three-day pass to the surface?"

"Yes, sir. To visit my—my girl, sir."

"But she wasn't very friendly?"

"Well—it seemed, at least, that it wasn't she so much as her mother, sir. You see, I have a cover job, as a traveling salesman selling sets of encyclopedias. The mother thinks this is pretty feeble stuff and wants her daughter to find somebody with better prospects."

The colonel nodded sympathetically.

Schmidt said, "I've known Janice's family for a long time, but apparently they'd decided they didn't know me, so this time the mother went to work with a string of questions. I think I might have gotten through this, but as it happens, I was worn out from that mess at the power station, and I kept losing the drift of the argument. Well, right on the hassock near the couch where I was sitting, while she shot these questions at me, was a newspaper. The headline kept staring me in the face: PENNSY A-BLAST AVERTED. I kept wondering how the thing had looked from the outside. So, right in the middle of the harangue, with her telling me how serious life is, I picked up the paper and started to read. That did it."

Colonel Tyler smiled. "If you'd like us to rig up some better cover—"

"Thank you, sir, but I don't think so. Janice could have stopped this third degree any time, but she sat through the whole thing, listening carefully. I got the impression that maybe her mother was just asking the questions for her anyway. Some of them were rough questions, but Janice didn't say anything on my side.—That's enough for me."

The colonel nodded. "What did you do then?"

"Well, I found myself in the road in front of the house. I should have felt low, but as a matter of fact I was too tired. I still had my pass, and I didn't know what to do with it. I could have gone home, but there was no future in that. At home, they're all sorrowful and pitying, except for my kid sister. Well, for lack of anything else, I walked down to the newsstand, got a paper with this story about "PENNSY A-BLAST AVERTED" in it, and read that. Some college students came in, and I got the idea to go see the old place again." Schmidt scowled, and the colonel leaned forward intently.

"Go on."

"Well, this is a little hard to explain, sir. I've gone back before, you see, and I've felt like some kind of ghost. The place was the same, but the faces were different, and I didn't fit in anywhere. This time it wasn't that way."

Martin was listening closely, and the colonel was leaning forward, his gaze intent.

"You noticed something wrong, is that it?"

"Not exactly *wrong*, sir. Strange. The trouble was, I was worn-out, and I'm afraid I wasn't too observant. The first thing that seemed odd was that a student I'd never seen before turned to me in a matter-of-fact way and said, 'Man, I can't take much more of this, can you? I mean, what's the *point* of everything? Why *bother*?'"

The colonel said, "This was as you were walking toward the college?"

"No, sir, I was just leaving the newsstand."

"What did you say to him?"

"The remark fit my mood, and I agreed. But then I wondered what he was talking about. By that time, we were slowly walking toward the college. As I say, I was tired. So was he. He seemed to be barely able to drag himself along. After a while, he said, 'I mean, what *is* the use?' Well, I didn't know what he was talking about, but it wasn't too far from how I felt, so I said, 'I know what you mean.'

We dragged on up the hill, and pretty soon it developed we were headed for different places. He said 'See you,' and I said, 'Yeah.'"

"These were the only comments?"

"Yes, sir. By itself, it didn't mean much. But on the way up the hill, maybe half-a-dozen more men students passed us going down in the other direction. Every one of them looked as full of pep and spirit as if he'd just been hit in the stomach. A girl came out the gate just as I went in, and she looked as if she'd long since given up hope in every-thing. Well, I went on in, it was the change of classes, and—" He shook his head. "I can't describe it. But I had a little playback camera with me—I'd started out thinking I'd take some pictures of Janice—and I took some shots of the college instead."

"Do you have the camera with you?"

"Yes, sir, I—" He reddened slightly. "Ah, I seem to have left it in the outer office, sir. If I could—"

"Go right ahead."

The lieutenant went out. The colonel glanced quizzi-cally at Martin, who smiled and said nothing.

Outside, there was a murmured masculine comment, a quiet feminine laugh, and then Schmidt was back, carrying a small leather case. He handed it to the colonel, who slid the camera out of the case, pulled out the two extension eyepieces, made sure the lever was at "P" for "playback," then looked into the eyepieces.

Martin, watching, could remember the recorded scenes vividly. The first showed a very pretty girl walking slowly toward him past a group of students. The girl had a dazed look, and her face was streaked, as if from tears.

She passed three unshaven male students sitting on the steps of the building. She was a very pretty girl. The three male students sat with their heads in their hands and stared dully across the campus as she passed.

There was a stretch of pale transparency in the film, then a shot of a large group of intermingled students drifting listlessly across the campus. When they went by, they left behind, here and there, an eraser, a pencil, or a slide rule, that someone or other had dropped, and that no one bothered to pick up.

There was another stretch of transparency, then a view of a tall, drearily trudging student with a three-day beard, partly shaven so that the better part of one side of his face showed a less pronounced beard, and with about two square inches of that side again partly shaved, as if he tried to shave on successive days but each time had given it up.

Several other scenes showed more of the same thing—listless, dispirited men or girls, trudging singly or in groups across the campus.

Colonel Tyler ran the scenes through again, then carefully put down the camera, and glanced at Schmidt.

"The whole school was like this?"

"All that I saw of it, sir—that is, the students. I don't know about the faculty or the administration."

"How was the rest of the town?"

"Here and there, the atmosphere was odd, as if people were wondering why they bothered, anyway. But there was no other place where it was as bad as the college."

"And the students you saw off-campus were the same?"

"Yes, sir. All the ones I saw."

"Do you have any idea what's behind it?"

"No, sir. Except that there's obviously something unnatural going on. And the Tamars have hit schools before, from different angles."

Colonel Tyler nodded thoughtfully, handed the camera back to the lieutenant, and glanced briefly at Martin.

"What's your theory about this?"

"Only that the Tamars are behind it, sir. How and why are something else again."

The colonel glanced at the wall map of the continent, with its tiny glowing dots of many colors and the groups of white dots at the edge representing enemy penetration units that had been lost and had not yet been relocated.

"As for 'how,'" he said, "with six units out of eighty they normally assign to this continent, they have power enough to make plenty of trouble, though it's a good question just how they do it." He glanced back at Schmidt. "All you found out is shown on that film?"

"Yes, sir. At the time, it all seemed strange to me, but I was about knocked out, myself, and didn't realize what it might mean. I just went home and put in the rest of the three-day pass getting caught up on sleep. I didn't think of the Tamars till I got rested up, and then it was time to come back."

The colonel nodded, and said thoughtfully, "As for *why* they'd do this—"

The phone rang. He picked it up and said, "Colonel Tyler," and listened. "Yes," he said, "I see. You think it *is* worth our attention, then? . . . yes . . . yes . . . then this is completely new to you, too? . . . yes . . . okay, Sam. Thanks. Good-by." He put the phone back, and smiled.

"Well, gentlemen, Reconnaissance agrees with us. They don't have any better idea what's going on there than we do, and of course they've had no time to do a thorough check. But they sent a team out there with the new portable snoopers about ten minutes ago, and the reading went right off the end of the scale." The colonel beamed. "We've found them, gentlemen. And tomorrow we'll go in and take them out. For now, rest up and check your equipment."

Resting up, for Martin, meant leaving his desk, where the official forms were piled high in the IN basket, and heading for his apartment. Martin's apartment was scaled to fit the needs of an organization that had its funds funneled to it secretly and that had to spend much of these funds on expensive shielding equipment. The apartment had bedroom, bathroom, kitchenette, and a room jokingly referred to as the "living-dining" room. The whole works fitted inside a space about fifteen feet on a side. The living-dining room was about six feet square and equipped with two straight-back chairs, a folding card table, and a TV set that was fed canned programs through a cable. Anyone with a tendency to claustrophobia soon imagined that the walls were starting to close in on him. As both of the hatch-like doors to the room opened inward, nearly met in the center, and were hung from the same side on walls that faced each other, this illusion had an unpleasant habit of coming true. The kitchenette was a little larger, but with more equipment crammed into it. The bathroom was smaller yet. The only room where two individuals could shut the doors and simultaneously draw a breath without making their eardrums pop was the bedroom. The bedroom was large enough to move around in. The ventilator grille opened into it, incidentally providing the source for eerie whispering sounds that echoed through the room all night.

Martin shared this apartment with his second-in-command, a burly captain by the name of Burns. Right now, Burns was stretched out flat on his cot, his hands clasped behind his head, his eyes shut, and a look of weary exasperation on his face.

"Same damned thing as always," he was saying. "Fall all over ourselves in a desperate rush for six weeks, till the men drop in their tracks, and you catch yourself staring at your hand to try and remember if you're on duty or off—and then Recon loses the bastards, and for the next six weeks there's nothing to do but run through drills and fill out forms. And then—*Wham!* Recon catches hold again, and we're back on the treadmill."

"It wasn't Reconnaissance this time," said Martin. "Schmidt ran into it on a three-day pass."

Burns opened his eyes.

"You mean he bumped into it by accident?"

"Exactly."

"How did that happen?"

"His girl axed him, and he found himself with time on his hands. He wandered back to his old college, which was in the same town, and ran into a funny set-up." Martin described it, and Burns sat up, frowning.

"Apathy, huh? Well—what of it? I can't see the Tamars wasting six units on that."

Martin opened his locker, pulled out a holstered automatic, and set it on his cot.

"They may not have the whole six units on it. We don't know yet just *what* they've got on it."

Burns nodded, got up, and went to his locker. "I still don't get their point."

"Neither do I," said Martin. "But they're there. It follows that there's trouble for us in it somewhere."

Carefully, Martin took from his locker a small, olive-colored belt case with two short wires attached, then a helmet with a slightly-flattened bulge in front, and a little white box made of opaque plastic. One-by-one, he set them on the cot beside the gun.

Burns said exasperatedly, "What's the use of making a college full of apathetic students? So what? How does that hurt our war effort? The Tamar haven't got so many penetration units they can afford to do things for the fun of it." He frowned suddenly, and said, "Yeah, but on the other hand—how did they *do* it?"

Martin sat down on his cot and began disassembling the gun. "Now you're on the right track."

"How many students in this college?"

"Over a thousand."

"And they've *all* had the spirit knocked out of them?"

"All Schmidt saw."

Burnt swore. "The gasbags must have hit the jackpot this time. They're always trying for some kind of leverage, or some multiplier effect. Something to overcome the fact that we have greater numbers than their penetration teams can handle directly."

Carefully, Martin cleaned the disassembled gun. "They've got a multiplier effect this time."

Burns thought it over, frowning, then said, "I suppose

it fits their usual method. If they can, they like best to get control of people in key positions. If they can't do that, then they try to get someone who *will* be in a key position, later. Like that Space Academy mess."

Martin lightly oiled the parts, and reassembled the gun. "That one was ideal, from their viewpoint, all right."

"Sure. Crack a few selected instructors, and then feed the false information directly to the future officers. Then, when they *are* officers, they'll make dangerous mistakes. We were lucky to break that up before they wrecked us."

Martin slid the gun back into its holster. "Still, the actual multiplier factor there wasn't up to this one. And the cadets they sabotaged—despite the hypnotic effect of the Tamars—were only hurt *in one category of their knowledge*. This present thing seems to strike not at a man's knowledge, but at his *spirit*. When a man's spirit is deadened, all his knowledge is more or less useless."

Burns finished cleaning and oiling his own gun, and, like Martin, next checked the working of a small switch recessed just under the edge of his helmet. "Yes, I see what you mean. But I don't see how they do that. Always before, the individual they succeeded in capturing was either used directly—say to give a disastrous order—or else, if he was an instructor, he was used to drive home some dangerous piece of false knowledge. A man may be made to believe, for instance, that hydrogen sulfide gas has an evil smell, but still isn't poisonous. This is false knowledge. It's dangerous. But it won't dispirit a man. The Tamars can teach carefully selected bits of false knowledge. They can do it without departing too much from the school's standard routine. Maybe no one will notice. But how do they teach *apathy*?"

"I don't know." Frowning, Martin opened the small white case and took out a thing like a dental bridge, with two little stainless steel arms that held a dark red capsule. He slid it into his mouth, fitting it carefully to a lower molar, touched it with his tongue, moved the capsule, and felt it swing up and over to rest on the biting surface of the tooth. Then, carefully, he removed the device.

"Not only," he said, "*how* do they teach it, but how do they teach *the whole college* to be apathetic? They must have some kind of mass-production assembly line going." He went into the bathroom, washed the device at the sink, dried it, and put it back in the box.

Across the room, Burns had the capsule in his mouth, and an inward-turned look on his face as he gingerly tried out the device.

Martin put everything back in his locker but the case with two wires attached, then took out a long, olive-colored one-piece suit, with gloves and padded boots attached.

Burns now eased the capsule out of his mouth, and stepped into the bathroom. There was a sound of rushing water. His voice came out faintly muffled.

"The more I think of it, the less I like it. Defeatism is catching, anyway. If they've found some way to compound it and strengthen it—but what's the *method*? They don't have *courses* in defeatism."

"Obviously, they'd use some other name."

"Such as what?"

"I haven't figured that out yet."

Martin put on the suit, pulled up the zipper, and carefully snapped together the long thin blocks of connectors to either side. He pressed a small button on the side of the little olive case, saw a tiny lens light up bright-green, indicating that the battery was fully charged, slid the case into a pocket of the suit, connected the two wires to their plugs, zipped the pocket shut, and snapped together the connector blocks on either side. From the sink, Burns growled his opinion of the Tamars, the war, and what they'd probably run into the next day.

"Maybe," said Martin, "by this time tomorrow, you'll be happy over the whole thing."

"Let us hope it doesn't go like that *last* mess." Burns came out of the bathroom. "Sorry, Mart. I didn't mean to talk while you were wrestling with that suit."

Martin grunted, and unrolled the shaped hood that fit closely over his head, with nothing open but two eyeholes and two small holes to breathe through. He zipped it on, and snapped the last connector blocks together. Then he slid his gloved hand along the center of his chest, felt the pressure-switch beneath the cloth, fine wires, and tiny spheroidal units that were linked together in a layer under the cloth. He pressed the switch, then looked at his cot against the wall. Slowly he raised his right hand to place it over his eyes. He saw neither hand nor arm. He felt the pressure as his hand pressed the cloth gently against his face, but he saw only the cot.

He turned, reached into his locker, and saw the helmet apparently drift out toward him unsupported. He settled it carefully on his head, feeling the built-in connector blocks of helmet and hood snap together. He shut the door leading to the small bathroom, felt the door with his fingers as he shut it, through the gloves of the suit, but saw the door swing eerily shut as if for no visible reason. On the back of the door was a full-length mirror.

Martin looked in the mirror, saw Burns' locker and cot across the room, saw Burns shrug into his own suit, pull up the zipper, and snap shut the blocks—but of himself Martin saw nothing until he leaned very close to the mirror. And then he saw, floating directly before him, all there was that was visible of him—two small black dots—the pupils of his eyes.

A few moments later, Burns vanished, and the two men carefully checked each other.

"Okay," said Martin. "Nothing visible."

"Same with you."

Martin shoved in the pressure-switch. At almost the same instant, Burns suddenly appeared. Methodically, the two men removed their slightly-oversize helmets, put them away, and began to unsnap the connector blocks.

The next day, they would go through the same procedure all over again, but with gun, capsule and a few other standard items in place. Now they carefully took the suits off, and hung them carefully in the lockers.

"I'd still like to know," said Burns, "how the gasbags worked this one."

Martin smiled. "The turning wheel of time reveals all. Just *wait* twenty-four hours."

"Yeah," said Burns dryly. "*If* we're still here by then."

★ ★ ★

The next day, the colonel took the unusual step of giving a brief talk to the assembled troops, before starting to the surface.

"Gentlemen, what we face today is the deadliest kind of

sneak attack. Yet it *appears* comparatively harmless. There is some danger that we may underestimate this situation and suffer a defeat we can't afford. I think it will pay us if we go over, briefly, our past experiences, to bring this present situation into perspective."

He glanced at Martin. "Major, suppose you briefly analyze a typical enemy attack."

Martin quickly thought it over. "Their typical attack has five phases. The first apparently is a kind of psychological reconnaissance-in-force, to decide future tactics, and to test the resistance of various key-points; to us, these key-points are individuals in positions that are in one way or another sensitive. The second phase of their attack is the psychological assault to capture a selected key-point. Just how this is done is their secret; from our viewpoint, the individual under attack feels strain, tension, and severe depression.

"If he rejects the sensations, successfully throws them out of his mind, and refuses to give in, the attack finally runs down or is broken off. Apparently the enemy suffers some kind of psychic loss or injury in the process, because following an unsuccessful attack there is a lessening of enemy activity. But if the psychological attack is successful, the key-point is captured. From our viewpoint, the individual cracks, and the enemy now takes control of his actions. That control of his actions constitutes the third phase, in which, if he is a government official, he makes harmful decisions, signs the wrong documents, recommends the wrong course of action. If he's a teacher, he plants in his student's minds selected bits of false information. The damage is reinforced with almost hypnotic effect by the powerful personality, not of the individual taken over but apparently of the entity that has psychological control.

"The fourth phase of the attack is actually the effect of the bad teaching or wrong decisions, which compound and pile up, and alert us, if nothing else does, to the realization that something is wrong.

"The fifth phase is retreat. We have overall control of this planet, and there are evidently far more of us than there are of them. Using advanced electronic techniques, we counterattack, and they immediately withdraw, leaving us with possession of the key-point. Following a brief delay, they strike back at us by an attack on another key-point—that is, from our viewpoint—another individual. Meanwhile, we have the first individual to rehabilitate and all the damage he's done to repair. At any given time, there appear to be twenty to thirty enemy attacks in progress in our own sector, except after they've suffered a repulse, when the number drops by almost half. Of these various attacks, we are, at any given time, unaware of at least a few. The enemy relies heavily on concealment, and we often have to reconstruct the sequence of events afterward."

The colonel nodded. "Good." He turned to Burns. "Captain, how do we recognize a captured key-point, an individual who's given in to them?"

"In two ways, so far, sir. First, by the stream of damaging incidents that all lead back to that one individual. Industrial accidents, for instance, involving the students of one teacher. Second, by a peculiar compelling quality in the speech of the captured individual himself as he drives home his false points."

"Right. Now, one more question. Martin, at what are these attacks directed? What is the enemy's target?"

Martin frowned. "The earliest attacks were apparently random, like the blows of a person lashing out at someone in a dark room. But very quickly they came to be directed at key government officials, legislators, high officers in the Space Command. Then there was a progressive shift to attacks on our technology—directly, at first, by striking at industrial leaders and technological specialists, then indirectly by distorting the training of students going into industry. As for this latest attack—" Martin shook his head. "It seems to be directed against a whole student body. But I frankly don't see what is the actual objective."

The colonel nodded. "What our opponents are trying for, of course, is to find a decisive weak point. But as it happens, the key positions in government, industry, and the armed forces, are usually held by people who are accustomed to being under pressure and are prepared to resist pressure. After the comparative few who are susceptible have been taken over, discovered, and replaced, the enemy is driven to try a new approach. Attacking the schools gives a multiplier effect and it is comparatively easier, but the results are slow. New graduates are rarely given positions of importance. And the false knowledge given to them is likely to result in industrial accidents that are troublesome but comparatively minor, and that, one way or another, disqualify the individuals concerned. Some new tactic becomes necessary. What they have hit on now is a way to *emotionally stun* an entire student body. Past blows have been aimed at government and industry. This latest blow is aimed at *the emotions of a large group of people*."

The colonel paused, and Martin was aware of the stir in the room as some of the significance of this began to dawn.

"Attitudes," said the colonel, "are catching. And they're basic. Strike a weapon from a man's hand, and he'll find another. Make his leaders betray him, and he'll choose new leaders. Let his technology fail him, and he'll repair it. But fix him so he just doesn't give a damn about anything—" The colonel glanced around the room. "Gentlemen, this is one fight we can't afford to lose."

★ ★ ★

Now, on the surface, Martin and the others were dispersed across the campus, an invisible net of unseen eyes watching in each classroom and administrative office, joined together by little short-range transmitters at their throats and thimble-sized receivers at their ears. Painstakingly they watched and listened, and then the voice of a sergeant named Cains spoke in Martin's ear.

"Major, I think I've found it."

"Where?"

"Room 24 of the Nears Social Studies Building."

Martin mentally pinpointed the building on the map he'd memorized on the way to the surface. "All right. What's going on there?"

"Just a lecture in elementary psychology, sir, but it's got all the signs. The lecturer's voice goes right into your head. What he says makes you feel cheap, small, and helpless. You have to keep fighting it off, and it's hard to keep up with him."

"That sounds like it, all right. We'll be right there."

The colonel's voice spoke in Martin's ear.

"Major Carney, move your men to blocking positions

outside the Nears Building. If this man should happen to get away from us, we'll mark him with a dye pellet. You will arrange the accident."

Carney's voice replied, "Yes, sir. We'll get him, sir."

"Major Martin, you will keep a continuous watch on the rest of the buildings, but move your ready squad to just outside the Nears Building. It seems to me that to straighten this out is going to be unusually tough. Sergeant Cains will step outside as soon as the door opens and wait by the door. You and I and Captain Burns will handle this ourselves."

★ ★ ★

The door of Room 24 of the Nears Building swung open as if it had been insecurely latched and blown back by the wind. The colonel, Martin and Burns waited for the count of three, then stepped through quickly, each man grasping the shoulder of the unseen man in front of him.

To their right were rows of seated students. To their left was a long blackboard, with a closed door halfway down the room. Near this closed door was a desk, and on the far side of the desk, facing the blackboard, stood an individual with an omniscient expression and a voice that carried a peculiarly penetrating blend of complaint, jeer, and triumph.

The colonel, Martin, and Burns stepped aside as the instructor stopped speaking, glanced across the room, then strode with quick decisive steps to bang shut the door. With the instructor at the door, the colonel led the way behind the desk to the opposite corner of the room, where the three men then stood with their backs to the side wall and waited.

The instructor returned to his desk.

Martin briefly studied the class, which had a uniform dulled and dreary look. Many of the students appeared to have passed into a kind of cataleptic trance and sat perfectly motionless, eyes directly to the front, as the instructor strode back, glanced briefly at an indecipherable scrawl chalked on the blackboard, then faced the class. His voice rose with the whine of a wasp preparing to sting.

"We will now," he said, "summarize our conclusions."

He turned to the blackboard and with two decisive slashes drew a pair of roughly horizontal lines, one about a foot and a half above the other. Hand raised, he paused for a moment, then with a quick snap of the arm drew an off-center egg-shaped scrawl between the two lines. Above the upper line, he rapidly scratched a series of minus signs. His motions were abrupt and exaggerated, but Martin noted that no one in the class smiled, or even changed expression.

The instructor now faced the class.

"This is the basic human situation. Here was have—" he slashed the chalk across the oval—"the ego. And here—" he slashed at the upper line—"repulsion. Here—" the lower line—"attraction. And the result?" With quick slashes he drew a downward-pointing arrow. "The ego moves *down*. The ego is driven by repulsion, drawn by attraction. The ego is without will. There is no such thing as will. There is only desire. Desire is rooted in the subconscious. We are unaware of the subconscious. Hence the desires that determine our actions are outside forces, not subject to our control. We do not control desires. Desires control us. Man is a puppet. Man must cast off hypocrisy and admit his will-less, soul-less, helpless state. There is only desire and nothing but desire, and desire, whether it be greed, lust—"

The keening voice rose and fell in intensity, driving home each individual thought with an impact that could be felt, and Martin had the feeling that he was being crammed head-first into a little twisted room, where all the furniture was warped, where walls and ceiling met at odd angles, and where the windows were of distorted glass, looking out on an apparently insane world.

The colonel's voice, low and distinct, spoke in his ear. "Martin. Take him out."

Martin pressed his tongue against the base of the capsule hinged close beside a lower tooth. He felt the capsule swing up and over, to fit smoothly against the biting surface of the tooth. He stepped forward.

The keening voice went on, but as Martin paused some three feet from the slightly puffy face with its faint sheen of perspiration, and as he raised his hand to the edge of his helmet, he was barely conscious of the voice. Martin clenched his teeth, felt the capsule crush, swallowed the stinging, cool-feeling liquid, and at the same moment forced back the recessed switch set just inside the edge of his oversize helmet. Then he focused his whole mind and consciousness on the man before him.

Just how or when it happened, Martin didn't know, but abruptly he was conscious of the shift of viewpoint, saw the class suddenly in front of him instead of to the side, heard the apparent change in tone of voice, saw the slight dimming of light, now seen through different organs of vision.

To one side was a barely-perceptible creak of leather and a rustle of cloth.

The voice went on " . . . no individuality, but only complexity. Psychology becomes a science and disproves itself, for there is no psyche. Psyche is a fiction, the soul is a . . ."

Then the voice abruptly came to a halt, as if awaiting fresh orders.

Martin felt, at his shoulder, a brief reassuring grip. Something brushed past, and there was the faint, barely perceptible shuffle of two men very quietly carrying a third.

Martin, looking out through the unfamiliar visual apparatus, briefly considered the jolt in store for the personality that had been put to the service of spreading this infected philosophy. It would, of course, have to be "rehabilitated." What would it feel when it came to, occupying a drone-body, with the sweat-course rising in front of it, where it would be driven to call on will-power in increasing measure, would have to surmount every kind of obstacle, to merely escape the slowly advancing boundary that meant agonizing pain. Slowly, nerve and determination would have to be built up, through one trial, failure, and sheet of agony after another, till at last the personality was strong enough to break through the final obstacle. That in turn would mean that it was strong enough to protect itself against psychological attack and could be trusted in its former position. The personality would have amnesia for the incidents of the course, but the reflexes and attitudes would remain. Martin, who had gone through it several times during his training, did not relish the idea of starting it with the belief that will-power and spirit were myths that couldn't be called upon in need.

The door of the classroom swung wide, as if it had been insecurely latched, and a gust of wind had blown it open.

Martin waited a moment, then closed the door.

The class sat motionless, waiting for the voice to go on.

Martin returned to the desk, and briefly considered the problem. The key-point was now retaken but the damage, if possible, still had to be undone. That would mean a slight change in the presentation.

He looked searchingly at the class, then leaned forward, and focused his whole attention.

The voice obediently snapped with energy. The platitudes rolled glibly out.

" . . . Yes, the psyche is a fiction. A figment. Imaginary. A left-over relic of past theories, amusing but vapid, unproved, prescientific." Here and there, pencils scratched, and Martin could see that he had the helpless attention of his audience. "Yes, a mere construct of prescientific minds. A myth. A theory. Unproved, though useful to its believers, and as yet, of course, not *disproved*." The pencils scratched on. "Just as will is unproved, just as the concept of a Supreme Being is unproved—yet they are not *disproved*. These concepts are prescientific, just as the sun is prescientific, and the sun is not disproved. The sun *exists*." The pencils continued to scratch; those few still not taking notes continued to watch him with unfocused gaze. He had the impression that he was feeding bits of information into a computer which would accept whatever he might give it and act accordingly.

Martin groped in memory for the earlier part of the

lecture, seeking a way to undercut the ideas that had left him feeling as if he were being shoved into a narrow twisted room.

"Yes, the ego is driven by repulsion, drawn by attraction. But the essential consciousness of man is not the ego of psychology. The ego is without will. But man's consciousness *has* will. There is no such *thing* as will, because will is not a thing. *Yet will exists*."

Carefully, concentrating on each separate thought, Martin worked down the long list, drawing distinctions that undercut each separate assertion that he could trace in memory. Tensely, he hurled the ideas across:

"Man is a puppet. His body is controlled by strings called nerves. His brain is a calculating machine, built of protoplasm. Seen thus, man has complexity, but no individuality. Yet body and brain are not all. Who is the observer who considers body and brain? The idea of soul is ancient, prescientific, unproved, *yet not disproved*. If there is a puppet, worked by strings, *what works the strings*? What applies certain ultimate changes in electrical potential that control the body and the calculating machine of the brain?"

Relentlessly, he destroyed the earlier assertions, while time stretched out, and he stood drenched in sweat, and the pencils scratched on endlessly:

" . . . As psychology becomes a science, it is no longer psychology, as the psyche does not exist, to the present instruments of science. What science does not observe, it cannot record and cannot study. But psychology itself is not yet out of its infancy. Its conclusions are tentative, not final. Its failure to observe does not disprove the existence of the thing not observed. A man with inadequate instruments may fail to detect a particular star, but the star he fails to observe *is still there*. The failure is that of the method, not of the star . . ."

At some point, Martin sensed a change. The pencils obediently scratched, and the watching gaze still seemed unfocused, but the look of dulled apathy was gone. It dawned on Martin that he had finally cut the foundation out from under the previous teachings.

He now spoke more freely, driving home a belief in soul, will, character, and the power of man to fight and eventually conquer obstacles. When he was through, he knew, no present-day teacher of psychology would recognize the course. But that didn't trouble Martin. A glance at the clock showed him he had only a few minutes left, but the audience was attentive, and the pencils wrote rapidly, and as the second hand of the clock on the wall swung up toward the hour mark, some memory warned Martin that these classes were ended in a special way.

"Now," he said, varying the procedure slightly, "soon the bell will ring, and you will feel wide awake. You will go out conscious that you have judgment, the power of choice, and will. When the bell rings, you will feel wide awake, fresh, full of energy."

The second hand aligned itself with the minute hand. In the hallway, a bell rang jarringly.

The class stirred, sat up, burst into an explosion of sound and energy. With a rush, the class emptied into the hall.

Drenched in sweat, Martin leaned against the desk.

Now, he thought, let that blast of energy hit the rest of

them. Let faith and determination compete with apathy, and see what happens.

Martin felt the relief of a man who sees success close at hand.

Behind him, there was the quiet click of a latch.

★ ★ ★

Martin remembered the door near the desk. He turned.

A well-groomed man with an intensely-piercing gaze stood in the doorway, and stared directly into his eyes.

It dawned on Martin that this was the chairman of the department.

The two men stood staring at each other. The chairman of the department said nothing, but the intense unwavering gaze, and the sense of a powerful, dominant personality began to make itself felt.

Abruptly, Martin felt a brief sensation of dread. There was a flicker of some unspecified fear.

—Something might happen to him.

The thought wavered, then strengthened.

The dread closed around him like an iron strap.

His heart began to race.

The palms of his hands felt damp and his legs weak and shaky.

The department chairman smiled and took a slow step forward.

Somewhere within Martin, there was a sensation like the impact of a massive object striking against a granite cliff. There was a sense of heavy jarring—but nothing gave.

Martin continued to look into the intense eyes, focusing

his own gaze on the faint light that seemed to be there somewhere deep in the backs of the eyes.

A thought flashed briefly through his mind: Had this entity, whatever it was, ever gone through the equivalent of the sweat course? Had it ever been compelled to call up will and nerve a thousand times, or be sent painfully back to the beginning, to start from there and do the whole thing all over again?—Just what was the limit of *its* resistance?

Martin stepped forward, focusing his gaze on that faint light, deep in the eyes.

Again there was a sense of mental collision.

For a long moment, nothing happened.

Then there was a slow, heavy yielding.

The light, whatever it was, didn't waver in the eyes. But the sense of attack weakened, then broke.

The department chairman abruptly shook his head, and stepped back.

For an instant, Martin was sure he had won. As this certainty flooded through him, he became vaguely aware that he was off-balance mentally.

Abruptly, with his opponent still turned away, the sensation of dread was back. The imagined iron strap drew tight around his chest.

The department chairman looked up again, the light in his eyes intense and unwavering. He looked directly into Martin's eyes.

This time, the jar and shock were heavier than Martin had ever experienced.

The room wavered around him.

It came to Martin that he was under attack from two

directions at once. From the man here before him, and from a distance. With a violent effort of will, he struggled hard to stay conscious.

Once again, nothing gave. But this time, the crushing anxiety grew, drew tighter, and tighter still.

Somewhere, there was a faint rustle of cloth. Martin, his gaze watery, but still fixed on the man in front of him, knew dimly that neither of them had moved.

Now, close at hand, there was a faint quiet scuff.

The pressure mounted till Martin saw through a red haze. The blood pounded in his ears, and he couldn't breathe. Through a sea of agony, he struggled to hold out.

Then, somewhere, something broke.

The sense of pressure dropped to a fraction of its former strength, then tried to reassert itself.

Martin sucked in a deep breath. Abruptly, his vision cleared. He snapped the hallucinatory band, smashed the whole body of thoughts struggling to get control.

In front of him, the department chairman wavered on his feet.

Martin faced him steadily, uncertain what could have happened. Then he noticed the change in the eyes, as if a different personality looked out.

There was a brief compression of cloth at the sleeve, near the department chairman's shoulder, as if an invisible hand gave a brief reassuring grip.

It dawned on Martin that when the colonel planned an attack, he planned it right. After the enemy had his reserve committed, *then* the colonel made his move.

Martin grinned. The gasbags had lost something this time. And it wasn't over yet.

The reason for their original rapid progress was clear enough now.

By controlling the source of supposedly-valid psychological knowledge, the enemy had gained an opportunity to thoroughly sabotage the outlook of each individual student in the regular course of his education. Then, by the combined force of their wrong beliefs, the sabotaged individuals unwittingly sabotaged others, snowballing the trouble.

Given a little more time undisturbed, there was no telling what kind of a catastrophe might have been achieved. But now, using their own techniques, it should be possible to build up exactly the opposite attitudes from those they'd intended. Meanwhile, the previously-captured instructors would be experiencing the sweat course. They would return with amnesia for the details of the whole grim experience, but the resulting attitudes and reflexes would remain. By the time the latest miracle of electronic wizardry had everyone's sense of identity sorted out again, the damage ought to be more than undone.

Martin rested his knuckles on the desk and faced the new class just filing in. Abruptly, Martin thought for a moment of the swordsman of old, and of his entirely different kind of battle, and he looked around with a sense of strangeness at the quiet, peaceful surroundings. Then he shook his head.

This was different.

But it was just as deadly.

MIND PARTNER

Jim Calder studied the miniature mansion and grounds that sat, carefully detailed, on the table.

"If you slip," said Walters, standing at Jim's elbow, "the whole gang will disappear like startled fish. There'll be another thousand addicts, and we'll have the whole thing to do over again."

Jim ran his hand up the shuttered, four-story replica tower that stood at one corner of the mansion. "I'm to knock at the front door and say, 'May I speak to Miss Cynthia?'"

Walters nodded. "You'll be taken inside, you'll stay overnight, and the next morning you will come out a door at the rear and drive away. You will come directly here, be hospitalized and examined, and tell us everything you can remember. A certified check in five figures will be deposited in your account. How high the five figures will be depends on how much your information is worth to us."

"Five figures," said Jim.

Walters took out a cigar and sat down on the edge of his desk. "That's right—10,000 to 99,999."

Jim said, "It's the size of the check that makes me hesitate. Am I likely to come out of there in a box?"

"No." Walters stripped the cellophane wrapper off his cigar, lit it, and sat frowning. At last he let out a long puff of smoke and looked up. "We've hit this setup twice before in the last three years. A city of moderate size, a quietly retired elderly person in a well-to-do part of town, a house so situated that people can come and go without causing comment." Walters glanced at the model of mansion and grounds on the table. "Each time, when we were sure where the trouble was coming from, we've raided the place. We caught addicts, but otherwise the house was empty."

"Fingerprints?"

"The first time, yes, but we couldn't trace them anywhere. The second time, the house burned down before we could find out."

"What about the addicts, then?"

"They don't talk. They—" Walters started to say something, then shook his head. "We're offering you a bonus because we don't know what the drug is. These people are addicted to something, but *what*? They don't accept reality. There are none of the usual withdrawal symptoms. A number of them have been hospitalized for three years and have shown no improvement. We don't *think* this will happen to you—one exposure to it shouldn't make you an addict—but we don't *know*. We have a lot of angry relatives of these people backing us. That's why we can afford to pay you what we think the risk is worth."

Jim scowled. "Before I make up my mind, I'd better see one of these addicts."

Walters drew thoughtfully on his cigar, then nodded and picked up the phone.

★ ★ ★

Behind the doctor and Walters and two white-coated attendants, Jim went into the room at the hospital. The attendants stood against the wall. Jim and Walters stood near the door and watched.

A blonde girl sat motionless on the cot, her head in her hands.

"Janice," said the doctor softly. "Will you talk to us for just a moment?"

The girl sat unmoving, her head in her hands, and stared at the floor.

The doctor dropped to a half-kneeling position beside the cot. "We want to talk to you, Janice. We need your help. Now, I am going to talk to you until you show me you hear me. You do hear me, don't you, Janice?"

The girl didn't move.

The doctor repeated her name again and again.

Finally she raised her head and looked through him. In a flat, ugly voice, she said, "Leave me alone. I know what you're trying to do."

"We want to ask you just a few questions, Janice."

The girl didn't answer. The doctor started to say something else, but she cut him off.

"Go away," she said bitterly. "You don't fool me. You don't even exist. You're nothing." She had a pretty face, but as her eyes narrowed and her lips drew slightly away from her teeth and she leaned forward on the cot, bringing her hands up, she had a look that tingled the hair on the back of Jim's neck.

The two attendants moved warily away from the wall.

The doctor stayed where he was and talked in a low, soothing monotone.

The girl's eyes gradually unfocused, and she was looking through the doctor as if he weren't there. She put her head hard back into her hands and stared at the floor.

The doctor slowly came to his feet and stepped back.

"That's it," he told Jim and Walters.

* * *

On the way back, Walters drove, and Jim sat beside him on the front seat. It was just starting to get dark outside. Abruptly Walters asked, "What did you think of it?"

Jim moved uneasily. "Are they all like that?"

"No. That's just one pattern. An example of another pattern is the man who bought a revolver, shot the store-keeper who sold it to him, shot the other customer in the store, put the gun in his belt, went behind the counter and took out a shotgun, shot a policeman who came in the front door, went outside and took a shot at the lights on a theater marquee; he studied the broken lights for a moment, then leaned the shotgun against the storefront, pulled out the revolver, blew out the right rear tires of three cars parked at the curb, stood looking from one of the cars to another and said, 'I just can't be sure, that's all.'"

Walters slowed slightly as they came onto a straight stretch of highway and glanced at Jim. "Another police-man shot the man, and that ended that. We traced that one back to the *second* place we closed up, the place that burned down before we could make a complete search."

"Were these places all run by the same people?"

"Apparently. When we checked the dates, we found that the second place didn't open till after the first was closed, and the third place till the second was closed. They've all operated in the same way. But the few descriptions we've had of the people who work there don't check."

Jim scowled and glanced out the window. "What generally happens when people go there? Do they stay overnight, or what?"

"The first time, they go to the front door, and come out the next morning. After that, they generally rent one of the row of garages on the Jayne Street side of the property, and come back at intervals, driving in after dark and staying till the next night. They lose interest in their usual affairs, and gradually begin to seem remote to the people around them. Finally they use up their savings, or otherwise come to the end of the money they can spend. Then they do like the girl we saw tonight, or like the man in the gun store, or else they follow some other incomprehensible pattern. By the time we find the place and close it up, there are seven hundred to twelve hundred addicts within a fifty-mile radius of the town. They all fall off their rockers inside the same two- to three-week period, and for a month after that, the police and the hospitals get quite a workout."

"Don't they have any of the drug around?"

"That's just it. They must get it all at the place. They use it there. They don't bring any out."

"And when you close the place up—"

"The gang evaporates like a sliver of dry ice. They don't leave any drug or other evidence behind. This time we've got a precise model of their layout. We should be able to plan a perfect capture. But if we just close in on them, I'm afraid the same thing will happen all over again."

"Okay," said Jim. "I'm your man. But if I don't come out the next morning, I want you to come in after me."

"We will," said Walters.

★ ★ ★

Jim spent a good part of the evening thinking about the girl he'd seen at the hospital, and the gun-store addict Walters had described. He paced the floor, scowling, and several times reached for the phone to call Walters and say, "No." A hybrid combination of duty and the thought of a five-figure check stopped him.

Finally, unable to stay put, he went out into the warm, dark evening, got in his car and drove around town. On impulse, he swung down Jayne Street and passed the dark row of rented garages Walters had mentioned. A car was carefully backing out as he passed. He turned at the next corner and saw the big, old-fashioned house moonlit among the trees on its own grounds. A faint sensation of wrongness bothered him, and he pulled to the curb to study the house.

Seen through the trees, the house was tall and steep-roofed. It reached far back on its land, surrounded by close-trimmed lawn and shadowy shrubs. The windows were tall and narrow, some of them closed by louvered shutters. Pale light shone out through the narrow openings of the shutters.

Unable to place the sensation of wrongness, Jim swung the car away from the curb and drove home. He parked his car, and, feeling tired and ready for sleep, walked up the dark drive, climbed the steps to the porch, and fished in his pocket for his keycase. He felt for the right key in the darkness, and moved back onto the steps to get a little more light. It was almost as dark there as on the porch. Puzzled, he glanced up at the sky.

The stars were out, with a heavy mass of clouds in the distance, and a few small clouds sliding by overhead. The edge of one of the small clouds lit up faintly, and as it passed, a pale crescent moon hung in the sky. Jim looked around. Save for the light in the windows, the houses all bulked dark.

Jim went down the steps to his car and drove swiftly back along Jayne Street. He turned, drove a short distance up the side street, and parked.

This time, the outside of the huge house was dark. Bright light shone out the shutters onto the lawn and shrubbery. But the house was a dark bulk against the sky. Jim swung the car out from the curb and drove home slowly.

★ ★ ★

The next morning, he went to Walters' office and studied the model that sat on the table near the desk. The model, painstakingly constructed from enlarged photographs, showed nothing that looked like a camouflaged arrangement for softly floodlighting the walls of the house and the grounds. Jim studied the location of the trees, looked at the house from a number of angles, noticed the broken slats in different shutters on the fourth floor of the tower, but saw nothing else he hadn't seen before.

He called up Walters, who was home having breakfast, and without mentioning details asked, "Is this model on your table complete?"

Walters' voice said, "It's complete up to three o'clock the day before yesterday. We check it regularly."

Jim thanked him and hung up, unsatisfied. He knelt down and put his eye in the position of a man in the street in front of the house. He noticed that certain parts of the trees were blocked off from view by the mansion. Some of these parts could be photographed from a light plane flying overhead, but other portions would be hidden by foliage. Jim told himself that floodlights *must* be hidden high in the trees, in such a way that they could simulate moonlight.

In that case, the question was—why?

Jim studied the model. He was bothered by much the same sensation as that of a man examining the random parts of a jigsaw puzzle. The first few pieces fitted together, the shapes and colors matched, but they didn't seem to add up to anything he had ever seen before.

★ ★ ★

As he drove out to the house, the day was cool and clear. The house itself, by daylight, seemed to combine grace, size, and a sort of starched aloofness. It was painted a pale lavender, with a very dark, steeply slanting roof. Tall arching trees rose above it, shading parts of the roof, the grounds, and the shrubs. The lawn was closely trimmed, and bordered by a low spike-topped black-iron fence.

Jim pulled in to the curb in front of the house, got out, opened a low wrought-iron gate in the fence, and started up the walk. He glanced up at the trees, saw nothing of floodlights, then looked at the house.

The house had a gracious, neat, well-groomed appearance. All the window-panes shone, all the shades were even, all the curtains neatly hung, all the trim bright and the shutters straight. Jim, close to the house, raised his eyes to the tower. All the shutters there were perfect and even and straight.

The sense of wrongness that had bothered him the day before was back again. He paused in his stride, frowning.

The front door opened and a plump, gray-haired woman in a light-blue maid's uniform stood in the doorway. With her left hand, she smoothed her white apron.

"My," she said, smiling, "isn't it a nice day?" She stepped back and with her left hand opened the door wider. "Come in." Her right hand remained at her side, half-hidden by the ruffles of her apron.

Jim's mouth felt dry. "May I," he said, "speak to Miss Cynthia?"

"Of course you may," said the woman. She shut the door behind him.

They were in a small vestibule opening into a high-ceilinged hallway. Down the hall, Jim could see an open staircase to the second floor, and several wide doorways with heavy dark draperies.

"Go straight ahead and up the stairs," said the woman in a pleasant voice. "Turn left at the head of the stairs. Miss Cynthia is in the second room on the right."

Jim took one step. There was a sudden sharp pressure on his skull, a flash of white light, and a piercing pain and a pressure in his right arm—a sensation like that of an injection. Then there was nothing but blackness.

★ ★ ★

Gradually he became aware that he was lying on a bed, with a single cover over him. He opened his eyes to see that he was in an airy room with a light drapery blowing in at the window. He started to sit up and his head throbbed. The walls of the room leaned out and came back. For an instant, he saw the room like a photographic negative, the white woodwork black and the dark furniture nearly white. He lay carefully back on the pillow and the room returned to normal.

He heard the quick tap of high heels in the hallway and a door opened beside him. He turned his head. The room seemed to spin in circles around him. He shut his eyes.

When he opened his eyes again, a tall, dark-haired woman was watching him with a faint hint of a smile. "How do you feel?"

"Not good," said Jim.

"It's too bad we have to do it this way, but some people lose their nerve. Others come with the thought that we have a profitable business and they would like to have a part of it. We have to bring these people around to our way of thinking."

"What's your way of thinking?"

She looked at him seriously. "What we have to offer is worth far more than any ordinary pattern of life. We can't let it fall into the wrong hands."

"What is it that you have to offer?"

She smiled again. "I can't tell you as well as you can experience it."

"That may be. But a man going into a strange country likes to have a road map."

"That's very nicely put," she said, "but you won't be going into any strange country. What we offer you is nothing but your reasonable desires in life."

"Is that all?"

"It's enough."

"Is there any danger of addiction?"

"After you taste steak, is there any danger of your wanting more? After you hold perfect beauty in your arms, is there any danger you might want to do so again? The superior is always addicting."

He looked at her for a moment. "And how about my affairs? Will they suffer?"

"That depends on you."

"What if I go from here straight to the police station?"

"You won't. Once we are betrayed, you can never come back. We won't be here. You wouldn't want that."

"Do you give me anything to take out? Can I buy—"

"No," she said. "You can't take anything out but your memories. You'll find they will be enough."

As she said this, Jim had a clear mental picture of the girl sitting on the cot in the hospital, staring at the floor. He felt a sudden intense desire to get out. He started to sit up, and the room darkened and spun around him.

★ ★ ★

He felt the woman's cool hands ease him back into place.

"Now," she said, "do you have any more questions?"

"No," said Jim.

"Then," she said briskly, "we can get down to business. The charge for your first series of three visits is one thousand dollars per visit."

"What about the next visits?"

"Must we discuss that now?"

"I'd like to know."

"The charge for each succeeding series of three is doubled."

"How often do I come back?"

"We don't allow anyone to return oftener than once every two weeks. That is for your own protection."

Jim did a little mental arithmetic, and estimated that by the middle of the year a man would have to pay sixteen thousand dollars a visit, and by the end of the year it would be costing him a quarter of a million each time he came to the place.

"Why," he asked, "does the cost increase?"

"Because, I've been told to tell those who ask, your body acquires a tolerance and we have to overcome it. If we have to use twice as much of the active ingredient in our treatment, it seems fair for us to charge twice as much."

"I see." Jim cautiously eased himself up a little. "And suppose that I decide right now not to pay anything at all."

She shook her head impatiently. "You're on a one-way street. The only way you can go is forward."

"That remains to be seen."

"Then you'll see."

She stepped to a dresser against the wall, picked up an atomizer, turned the little silver nozzle toward him, squeezed the white rubber bulb, and set the atomizer back on the dresser. She opened the door and went out. Jim felt a mist of fine droplets falling on his face. He tried to inhale very gently to see if it had an odor. His muscles wouldn't respond.

He lay very still for a moment and felt the droplets falling one by one. They seemed to explode and tingle as they touched his skin. He lay still a moment more, braced himself to make one lunge out of the bed, then tried it.

He lay flat on his back on the bed. A droplet tingled and exploded on his cheek.

He was beginning to feel a strong need for breath.

He braced himself once more, simply to move sidewise off the pillow. Once there, he could get further aside in stages, out of the range of the droplets. He kept thinking, "Just a moment now—steady—just a moment—just—Now!"

And nothing happened.

He lay flat on his back on the bed. A droplet tingled and exploded on his cheek.

The need for air was becoming unbearable. Jim's head was throbbing and the room went dark with many tiny spots of light. He tried to suck in air and he couldn't. He tried to breathe out, but his chest and lungs didn't move. He could hear the pound of his heart growing fast and loud.

He couldn't move.

At the window, the light drapery fluttered and blew in and fell back.

He lay flat on the bed and felt a droplet tingle and explode on his cheek.

His skull was throbbing. His heart writhed and hammered in his chest. The room was going dark.

Then something gave way and his lungs were dragging in painful gasps of fresh air. He sobbed like a runner at the end of a race. After a long time, a feeling of peace and tiredness came over him.

The door opened.

He looked up. The woman was watching him sadly. "I'm sorry," she said. "Do you want to discuss payment?"

Jim nodded.

The woman sat down in a chair by the bed. "As I've explained, the initial series of three visits costs one thousand dollars each. We will accept a personal check or even an I. O. U. for the first payment. After that, you must have cash."

Jim made out a check for one thousand dollars.

The woman nodded, smiled, and folded the check into a small purse. She went out, came back with a glass of colorless liquid, shook a white powder into it, and handed it to him.

"Drink it all," she said. "A little bit can be excruciatingly painful."

Jim hesitated. He sat up a little and began to feel dizzy. He decided he had better do as she said, took the glass and drained it. It tasted exactly like sodium bicarbonate dissolved in water. He handed her the glass and she went to the door.

"The first experiences," she said, "are likely to be a little exuberant. Remember, your time sense will be distorted, as it is in a dream." She went out and shut the door softly.

Jim fervently wished he were somewhere else. He wondered what she meant by the last comment. The thought came to him that if he could get out of this place, he could give Walters and the doctors a chance to see the drug in action.

He got up, and had the momentary sensation of doing two things at once. He seemed to lie motionless on the bed and to stand up at one and the same time. He wondered if the drug could have taken effect already. He lay down and got up again. This time he felt only a little dizzy. He went to the window and looked out. He was in a second-story window, and the first-floor rooms in this house had high ceilings. Moreover, he now discovered he was wearing a sort of hospital gown. He couldn't go into the street in that without causing a sensation, and he didn't know just when the drug would take effect.

He heard the soft click of the door opening and turned around. The woman who had talked to him came in and closed the door gently behind her. Jim watched in a daze as she turned languorously, and it occurred to him that no woman he had ever seen had moved quite like that, so the chances were that the drug had taken effect and he was imagining all this. He remembered that she had said the first experiences were likely to be a little exuberant, and his time sense distorted as in a dream.

Jim spent the night, if it was the night, uncertain as to what was real and what was due to the drug. But it was all vivid, and realistic events shaded into adventures he *knew* were imaginary, but that were so bright and satisfying that he didn't care if they were real or not. In these adventures, the colors were pure colors, and the sounds were clear sounds, and nothing was muddied or uncertain as in life.

It was so vivid and clear that when he found himself lying on the bed with the morning sun streaming in, he was astonished that he could remember not a single incident save the first, and that one not clearly.

He got up and found his clothes lying on a chair by the bed. He dressed rapidly, glanced around for the little atomizer and saw it was gone. He stepped out into the hall and there was a sudden sharp pressure on his skull, a flash of white light, and a feeling of limpness. He felt strong hands grip and carry him. He felt himself hurried down a flight of steps, along a corridor, then set down with his back against a wall.

When he felt strong enough to, he opened his eyes.

The plump, gray-haired woman took a damp cloth and held it to his head. "You'll be all over that in a little while," she said. "I don't see why they have to do that."

"Neither do I," said Jim. He felt reasonably certain that she had done the same thing to him when he came in. He looked around, saw that they were in a small bare entry, and got cautiously to his feet. "Is my car still out front?"

"No," she said. "It's parked in back, in the drive."

"Thank you," he said. "Say good-by to Miss Cynthia for me."

The woman smiled. "You'll be back."

He was very much relieved to get outside the house. He walked back along the wide graveled drive, found his car, got in, and started it. When he reached the front of the house, he slowed the car to glance back. To his surprise, the two shutters on the third floor of the tower had broken slats. He thought this had some significance, but he was unable to remember what it was. He sat for a moment, puzzled, then decided that the important thing was to get to Walters. He swung the car out into the early morning traffic, and settled back with a feeling compounded of nine parts relief and one part puzzlement.

What puzzled him was that anyone should pay one thousand dollars for a second dose of that.

★ ★ ★

The doctors made a lightning examination, announced that he seemed physically sound, and then Walters questioned him. He described the experience in close detail, and Walters listened, nodding from time to time. At the end, Jim said, "I'll be *damned* if I can see why anyone should go back!"

"That *is* puzzling," said Walters. "It may be that they were all sensation-seekers, though that's a little odd, too. Whatever the reason, it's lucky you weren't affected."

"Maybe I'd better keep my fingers crossed," said Jim.

Walters laughed. "I'll bring your bankbook in to keep you happy." He went out, and a moment later the doctors were in again. It wasn't until the next morning that they were willing to let him go. Just as he was about to leave, one of them remarked to him, "I hope you never need a blood transfusion in a hurry."

"Why so?" Jim asked.

"You have one of the rarest combinations I've ever seen." He held out an envelope. "Walters said to give you this."

Jim opened it. It was a duplicate deposit slip for a sum as high as five figures could go.

Jim went out to a day that wasn't sunny, but looked just as good to him as if it had been.

★ ★ ★

After careful thought, Jim decided to use the money to open a detective agency of his own. Walters, who caught the dope gang trying to escape through an unused steam tunnel, gave Jim his blessing, and the offer of a job if things went wrong.

Fortunately, things went very well. Jim's agency

prospered. In time, he found the right girl, they married, and had two boys and a girl. The older boy became a doctor, and the girl married a likable fast-rising young lawyer. The younger boy had a series of unpleasant scrapes and seemed bound on wrecking his life. Jim, who was by this time very well to do, at last offered the boy a job in his agency, and was astonished to see him take hold.

The years fled past much faster than Jim would have liked. Still, when the end came near, he had the pleasure of knowing that his life's work would be in the capable hands of his own son.

He breathed his last breath in satisfaction.

And woke up lying on a bed in a room where a light drapery blew back at the window and the morning sun shone in, and his clothes were folded on a chair by his bed.

★ ★ ★

Jim sat up very carefully. He held his hand in front of his face and turned it over slowly. It was not the hand of an old man. He got up and looked in a mirror, then sat down on the edge of the bed. He was young, all right. The question was, was this an old man's nightmare, or was the happy life he had just lived a dope addict's dream?

He remembered the woman who had doped him saying, "What we offer you is nothing but your reasonable desires in life."

Then it had all been a dream.

But a dream should go away, and this remained clear in his memory.

He dressed, went out in the hall, felt a sudden pressure on his skull, a flash of white light, and a feeling of limpness.

★ ★ ★

He came to in the small entry, and the plump, gray-haired woman carefully held a damp cool cloth to his head.

"Thanks," he said. "Is my car out back?"

"Yes," she said, and he went out.

As he drove away from the house he glanced back and noticed the two broken shutters on the third floor of the tower. The memory of his dream about this same event—leaving the place—jarred him. It seemed that those broken shutters meant something, but he was unable to remember what. He trod viciously on the gas pedal, throwing a spray of gravel on the carefully tailored lawn as he swung into the street.

He *still* did not see why anyone should go back there with anything less than a shotgun.

He told Walters the whole story, including the details of his "life," that he remembered so clearly.

"You'll get over it," Walters finally said, when Jim was ready to leave the hospital. "It's a devil of a thing to have happen, but there's an achievement in it you can be proud of."

"You name it," said Jim bitterly.

"You've saved a lot of other people from this same thing. The doctors have analyzed the traces of drug still in your blood. They think they can neutralize it. Then we are going to put a few sturdy men inside that house, and while they're assumed to be under the influence, we'll raid the place."

The tactic worked, but Jim watched the trial with a cynical eye. He couldn't convince himself that it was true. He might, for all he knew, be lying in a second-floor room of the house on a bed, while these people, who seemed to be on trial, actually were going freely about their business.

This inability to accept what he saw as real at last forced Jim to resign his job. Using the generous bonus Walters had given him, he took up painting. As he told Walters on one of his rare visits, "It may or may not be that what I'm doing is real, but at least there's the satisfaction of the work itself."

"You're not losing any money on it," said Walter shrewdly.

"I know," said Jim, "and that makes me acutely uneasy."

On his 82nd birthday, Jim was widely regarded as the "Grand Old Man" of painting. His hands and feet felt cold that day, and he fell into an uneasy, shallow-breathing doze. He woke with a start and a choking cough. For an instant everything around him had an unnatural clarity; then it all went dark and he felt himself falling.

He awoke in a bed in a room where a light drapery fluttered at the window, and the morning sun shone into the room.

★ ★ ★

This time, Jim entertained no doubts as to whether or not this was real. He got up angrily and smashed his fist into the wall with all his might.

The shock and pain jolted him to his heels.

He went out the same way as before, but he had to drive one-handed, gritting his teeth all the way.

The worst of it was that the doctors weren't able to make that hand exactly right afterward. Even if the last "life" had been a dream—even if this one was—he wanted to paint. But every time he tried to, he felt so clumsy that he gave up in despair.

Walters, dissatisfied, gave Jim the minimum possible payment. The gang escaped. Jim eventually lost his job, and in the end he eked out his life at poorly paid odd jobs.

The only consolation he felt was that his life was so miserable that it must be true.

He went to bed sick one night and woke up the next morning on a bed in a room where a light drapery fluttered at the window and the early morning sun shone brightly in.

This happened to him twice more.

The next time after that, he lay still on the bed and stared at the ceiling. The incidents and details of five lives danced in his mind like jabbering monkeys. He pressed his palms to his forehead and wished he could forget it all.

The door opened softly and the tall, dark-haired woman was watching him with a faint smile. "I told you," she said, "that you couldn't take anything away but memories."

He looked up at her sickly. "That seems like a long, long while ago."

She nodded and sat down. "Your time sense is distorted as in a dream."

"I wish," he said drearily, looking at her, "that I could just forget it all. I don't see why anyone would come back for more of that."

She leaned forward to grip the edge of the mattress, shaking with laughter. She sat up again. "Whew!" she said, looking at him and forcing her face to be straight. "Nobody comes back for *more*. That is the unique quality of this drug. People come back to forget they ever had it."

He sat up. "I can forget that?"

"Oh, yes. *Don't* get so excited! That's what you really paid your thousand dollars for. The forgetfulness drug lingers in your bloodstream for two to three weeks. Then memory returns and you're due for another visit."

Jim looked at her narrowly. "Does my body become tolerant of this drug? Does it take twice as much after three visits, four times as much after six visits, eight times as much after nine visits?"

"No."

"Then you lied to me."

She looked at him oddly. "What would you have expected of me? But I didn't lie to you. I merely said that that was what I was told to tell those who asked."

"Then what's the point of it?" Jim asked.

"What's the point of bank robbery?" She frowned at him. "You ask a lot of questions. Aren't you lucky I know the answers? Ordinarily you wouldn't get around to this till you'd stewed for a few weeks. But you seem precocious, so I'll tell you."

"That's nice," he said.

"The main reason for the impossible rates is so you can't pay off in money."

"How does that help you?"

"Because," she said, "every time you bring us a new patron, you get three free visits yourself."

"Ah," he said.

"It needn't be so terribly unpleasant, coming here."

"What happens if, despite everything, some sorehead actually goes and tells the police about this?"

"We move."

"Suppose they catch you?"

"They won't. Or, at least, it isn't likely."

"But you'll leave?"

"Yes."

"What happens to me?"

"Don't you see? We'll *have* to leave. Someone will have betrayed us. We couldn't stay because it might happen again. It isn't right from your viewpoint, but we can't take chances."

For a few moments they didn't talk, and the details of Jim's previous "lives" came pouring in on him. He sat up suddenly. "Where's that forgetfulness drug?"

She went outside and came back with a glass of colorless liquid. She poured in a faintly pink powder and handed it to him. He drank it quickly and it tasted like bicarbonate of soda dissolved in water.

He looked at her. "This isn't the same thing all over again, is it?"

"Don't worry," she said. "You'll forget."

The room began to go dark. He leaned back. The last thing he was conscious of was her cool hand on his forehead, then the faint click as she opened the door to go out.

He sat up. He dressed, drove quickly to Walters and told him all he could remember. Walters immediately organized his raid. Jim saw the place closed up with no one caught.

After two weeks and four days, the memories flooded back. His life turned into a nightmare. At every turn, the loves, hates, and tiny details of six separate lives poured in on him. He tried drugs in an attempt to forget, and sank from misery to hopeless despair. He ended up in a shooting scrap as Public Enemy Number Four.

And then he awoke and found himself in a bed in a room with a light drapery blowing in at the window, and the early morning sun shining brightly in.

"Merciful God!" he said.

The door clicked shut.

★ ★ ★

Jim sprang to the door and looked out in the carpeted hall. There was a flash of a woman's skirt; then a tall narrow door down the hallway closed to shut off his view.

He drew back into the room and shut the door. The house was quiet. In the distance, on the street, he could hear the faint sound of a passing car.

He swallowed hard. He glanced at the window. It had been, he reasoned, early morning when he had talked to the woman last. It was early morning now. He recalled that before she went out she said, "You'll forget." He had then lived his last miserable "life"—and awakened to hear the click as the door came shut behind her.

That had all taken less than five seconds of actual time.

He found his clothes on a nearby chair and started to dress. As he did so, he realized for the first time that the memories of his "lives" were no longer clear to him. They were fading away, almost as the memories of a dream do after a man wakes and gets up. *Almost* as the memories of a dream, but not quite. Jim found that if he thought of them, they gradually became clear again.

He tried to forget and turned his attention to the tree he could see through the window. He looked at the curve of its boughs, and at a black-and-yellow bird balancing on a branch in the breeze.

The memories faded away, and he began to plan what to do. No sooner did he do this than he remembered with a shock that he had said to Walters, "If I don't come out next morning, I want you to come in after me."

And Walters had said, "We will."

So that must have been just last night.

Jim finished dressing, took a deep breath, and held out his hand. It looked steady. He opened the door, stepped out into the hall, and an instant too late remembered what had happened six times before.

When he opened his eyes, the plump, gray-haired woman was holding a damp cloth to his forehead and clucking sympathetically.

Jim got carefully to his feet, and walked down the drive to his car. He slid into the driver's seat, started the engine, and sat still a moment, thinking. Then he released the parking brake, and pressed lightly on the gas pedal. The car slid smoothly ahead, the gravel of the drive crunching under its tires. He glanced up as the car reached the end of the drive, and looked back at the tower. Every slat in the shutters was perfect. Jim frowned, trying to remember something. Then he glanced up and down the street, and swung out into the light early morning traffic.

He wasted no time getting to Walters.

★ ★ ★

He was greeted with an all-encompassing inspection that traveled from Jim's head to his feet. Walters looked tense. He took a cigar from a box on his desk and put it in his mouth unlit.

"I've spent half the night telling myself there are some things you can't ask a man to do for money. But we *had* to do it. Are you all right?"

"At the moment."

"There are doctors and medical technicians in the next room. Do you want to see them now or later?"

"Right now."

In the next hour, Jim took off his clothes, stood up, lay down, looked into bright lights, winced as a sharp hollow needle was forced into his arm, gave up samples of bodily excretions, sat back as electrodes were strapped to his skin, and at last was reassured that he would be all right. He dressed, and found himself back in Walters' office.

Walters looked at him sympathetically.

"How do you feel?"

"Starved."

"I'll have breakfast sent in." He snapped on his intercom, gave the order, then leaned back. He picked up his still unlit cigar, lit it, puffed hard, and said, "What happened?"

Jim told him, starting with the evening before, and ending when he swung his car out into traffic this morning.

Walters listened with a gathering frown, drawing occasionally on the cigar.

A breakfast of scrambled eggs and Canadian bacon was brought in. Walters got up, and looked out the window, staring down absently at the traffic moving past in the street below. Jim ate with single-minded concentration, and finally pushed his plate back and looked up.

Walters ground his cigar butt in the ashtray and lit a fresh cigar. "This is a serious business. You say you remembered the details of each of those six lives *clearly*?"

"Worse than that. I remembered the emotions and the attachments. In the first life, for instance, I had my own business." Jim paused and thought back. The memories gradually became clear again. "One of my men, for instance, was named Hart. He stood about five-seven, slender, with black hair, cut short when I first met him. Hart was a born actor. He could play any part. It wasn't his face. His expression hardly seemed to change. But his manner changed. He could stride into a hotel and the bellboys would jump for his bags and the desk clerk spring to attention. He stood out. He was important. Or he could slouch in the front door, hesitate, look around, blink, start to ask one of the bellboys something, lose his nerve, stiffen his shoulders, shamble over to the desk, and get unmercifully snubbed. Obviously, he was less than nobody. Or, again, he could quietly come in the front door, stroll across the lobby, fade out of sight somewhere, and hardly a person would notice or remember him. Whatever part he played, he lived it. That was what made him so valuable."

Walters had taken the cigar out of his mouth, and listened intently. "You mean this Hart—this imaginary man—is real to you? In three dimensions?"

"That's it. Not only that, I like him. There were other, stronger attachments. I had a family."

"Which seems real?"

Jim nodded. "I realize as I say these things that I sound like a lunatic."

"No." Walters shook his head sympathetically. "It all begins to make sense. Now I see why the girl at the hospital said to the doctor, 'You aren't real.' Does it *hurt* to talk about these 'lives'?"

Jim hesitated. "Not as long as we keep away from the personal details. But it hurt like nothing I can describe to have all six of these sets of memories running around in my head at once."

"I can imagine. All right, let's track down some of these memories and see how far the details go."

Jim nodded. "Okay."

Walters got out a bound notebook and pen. "We'll start with your business. What firm name did you use?"

"Calder Associates."

"Why?"

"It sounded dignified, looked good on a business card or letterhead, and wasn't specific."

"What was your address?"

"Four North Street. Earlier, it was 126 Main."

"How many men did you have working with you?"

"To begin with, just Hart, and another man by the name of Dean. At the end, there were twenty-seven."

"What were their names?"

Jim called them off one by one, without hesitation.

Walters blinked. "Say that over again a little more slowly."

Jim repeated the list.

"All right," said Walters. "Describe these men."

Jim described them. He gave more and more details as Walters pressed for them, and by lunch time, Walters had a large section of the notebook filled.

The two men ate, and Walters spent the rest of the afternoon quizzing Jim on his first "life." Then they had steak and French fries sent up to the office. Walters ate in silence for a moment, then said, "Do you realize that you haven't stumbled once?"

★ ★ ★

Jim looked up in surprise. "What do you mean?"

Walters said, "Quiz me on the names of every man who ever worked for me. I won't remember all of them. Not by a long shot. You remember every last detail of this dream life with a total recall that beats anything I've ever seen."

"That's the trouble. That's why it's pleasant to forget."

Walters asked suddenly, "Did you ever paint? *Actually*, I mean. I ask you because you say you were an outstanding painter in one of these 'lives.'"

"When I was a boy, I painted some. I wanted to be an artist."

"Can you come out to my place tonight? I'd like to see whether you can really handle the brushes."

Jim nodded. "Yes, I'd like to try that."

They drove out together, and Walters got out a dusty paint set in a wooden case, set up a folding easel, and put a large canvas on it.

Jim stood still a moment, thinking back. Then he began to paint. He lost himself in the work, as he always had, all through the years, and what he was painting now he had painted before. Had painted it, and sold it for a good price, too. And it was worth it. He could still see the model in his mind as he painted with swift precise strokes.

He stepped back.

"My Lady in Blue" was a cheerful girl of seventeen. She smiled out from the canvas as if at any moment she might laugh or wave.

Jim glanced around. For an instant the room seemed strange. Then he remembered where he was.

Walters looked at the painting for a long moment, then

looked at Jim, and swallowed. He carefully took the painting from the easel and replaced it with another blank canvas. He went across the room and got a large floor-type ashtray, a wrought-iron affair with a galloping horse for the handle.

"Paint this."

Jim looked at it. He stepped up to the canvas, hesitated. He raised the brush—and stopped. He didn't know where to begin. He frowned and carefully thought back to his first lessons. "Let's see." He glanced up. "Do you have any tracing paper?"

"Just a minute," said Walters.

Jim tacked the paper over the canvas and methodically drew the ashtray on the paper. He had a hard time, but at last looked at the paper triumphantly. "Now, do you have any transfer paper?"

Walters frowned. "I've got carbon paper."

"All right."

Walters got it. Jim put a sheet under his tracing paper, tacked it up again, and carefully went over the drawing with a pencil. He untacked the paper, then methodically began to paint. At length, weary and perspiring, he stepped back.

Walters looked at it. Jim blinked and looked again. Walters said, "A trifle off-center, isn't it?"

There was no doubt about it, the ashtray stood too far toward the upper right-hand corner of the canvas.

Walters pointed at the other painting. "Over there we have a masterpiece that you dashed off freehand. Here we have, so to speak, a piece of good, sound mechanical drawing that isn't properly placed on the canvas. This took you longer to do than the other. How come?"

"I had done the other before."

"And you remember the motions of your hand? Is that it?" He put another canvas up. "Do it again."

Jim frowned. He stepped forward, thought a moment, and began to paint. He lost himself in a perfection of concentration. In time, he stepped back.

Walters looked at it. He swallowed hard, glanced back and forth from this painting to the one Jim had done at first. He lifted the painting carefully from the easel and placed it beside the other.

They looked identical.

★ ★ ★

The sun was just lighting the horizon as they drove back to the office. Walters said, "I'm going in there and sleep on the cot. Can you get back around three this afternoon?"

"Sure."

Jim drove home, slept, ate, and was back again by three.

"This is a devil of a puzzle," said Walters, leaning back at his desk and blowing out a cloud of smoke. "I've had half a dozen experts squint at one of those paintings. I've been offered five thousand, even though they didn't know the artist's name. Then I showed them the other painting and they almost fell through the floor. It isn't possible, but each stroke appears identical. How do you feel?"

"Better. And I've remembered something. Let's look at your model."

They went to the big model of the mansion, and Jim touched the upper story of the tower. "Have some of the boys sketch this. Then compare the sketches with photographs."

Soon they were looking at sketches and photographs

side by side. The sketches showed the tower shutters perfect. The photographs showed several slats of the shutters broken.

Walters questioned the men, who insisted the shutters were perfect. After they left, Jim said, "Everyone who sketched that place wasn't drugged. And the cameras certainly weren't drugged."

Walters said, "Let's take a look." They drove out past the mansion, and the shutters looked perfect. A new photograph showed the same broken slats.

Back at the office, Walters said, "Just what are we up against here?"

Jim said, "I can think of two possibilities."

"Let's hear them."

"Often you can do the same thing several different ways. A man, for instance, can go from one coastal town to another on foot, riding a horse, by car, by plane, or in a speedboat."

"Granted."

"A hundred years ago, the list would have been shorter."

Walters nodded thoughtfully. "I follow you. Go on."

"Whoever sees those shutters as perfect is, for the time being, in an abnormal mental state. How did he get there? We've assumed drugs were used. But just as there are new ways of going from one city to another, so there may be new ways of passing from one mental state to another. Take subliminal advertising, for instance, where the words, 'THIRSTY,' 'THIRSTY,' 'BEER,' may be flashed on the screen too fast to be consciously seen."

"It's illegal."

"Suppose someone found out how to do it undetected,

and decided to try it out on a small scale. What about nearly imperceptible *verbal* clues instead of visual ones?"

Walters' eyes narrowed. "We'll analyze every sound coming out of that place and check for any kind of suspicious sensory stimulus whatever. What's your other idea?"

"Well, go back to your travel analogy. Going from one place to another, any number of animals could outrun, outfly, outswim a man. Let Man work on the problem long enough, and roll up to the starting line in his rocket-plane, and the result will be different. But until Man has time to concentrate enough thought and effort, the nonhuman creature has an excellent chance to beat him. There are better fliers, better swimmers, better fighters, better—"

Walters frowned. "Better *suggestionists?* Like the snake that's said to weave hypnotically?"

"Yes, and the wasp that stings the trapdoor spider, when other wasps are fought off."

"Hmm. Maybe. But I incline to the subliminal advertising theory myself." He looked at the mansion. "Where would they keep the device?"

"Why not the tower?"

Walters nodded. "It's an easy place to guard, and to shut off from visitors."

Jim said, "It might explain those shutters. They might not care to risk painters and repairmen up there."

Walters knocked the ash off his cigar. "But how do we get in there to find out?"

They studied the model. Walters said, "Say we send in a 'building inspector.' They'll merely knock him out, hallucinate a complete series of incidents in his mind, and send him out totally ignorant. If we try to raid the place in a group, they'll vanish with the help of that machine. But there must be *some* way."

Jim said thoughtfully, "Those trees overhang the room."

"They do, don't they?"

The two men studied the trees and the tower.

Jim touched one of the arching limbs. "What if we lowered a rope from here?"

Walters tied an eraser on a string and fastened the string to a limb. The eraser hung by the uppermost tower window. Walters scowled, snapped on the intercom, and asked for several of his men. Then he turned to Jim. "We'll see what Cullen thinks. He's done some jobs like this."

Cullen had sharp eyes and a mobile face that grew unhappy as he listened to Walters. Finally, he shook his head. "No, thanks. Ask me to go up a wall, or the side of a building. But not down out of a tree branch on the end of a rope."

He gave the eraser a little flip with his finger. It swung in circles, hit the wall, and bounced away.

"Say I'm actually up there. It's night. The rope swings. The limb bobs up and down. The tree sways. All to a different rhythm. I'm spinning around on the end of this rope. One second this shutter is one side of me. The next second it's on the other side and five feet away. A job is a job, but this is one I don't want."

Walters turned to Jim after Cullen went out. "That settles that."

Jim looked at the tree limb. Two or three weeks from today, he told himself, the memories would come flooding back. The people who had done it would get away, and do it again. And he would have those memories.

Jim glanced at Walters stubbornly. "I am going to climb that tree."

★ ★ ★

The night was still, with a dark overcast sky as Jim felt the rough bark against the insides of his arms. He hitched up the belt that circled the tree, then pulled up one foot, then another as he sank the climbing irons in higher up. He could hear Cullen's advice: "Practice, study the model, do each step over and over in your head. Then, when you're actually doing it and when things get tight, *hold your mind on what to do next*. Do that. *Then* think of the next step."

Jim was doing this as the dark lawn dropped steadily away. He felt the tree trunk grow gradually more slender, then begin to widen. He worked his way carefully above the limb, refastened the belt, and felt a puff of warm air touch his face and neck, like a leftover from the warm day. Somewhere, a radio was playing.

He climbed, aware now of the rustling around him of leaves.

The trunk widened again, and he knew he was at the place where the trunk separated into the limbs that arched out to form the crown of the tree.

He pulled himself up carefully, and took his eyes from the tree for a moment to look toward the mansion. He saw the slanting tile roof of an entirely different house, light shining down from a dormer window. He glanced around, to see the looming steep-roofed tower of the mansion in the opposite direction. He realized he must have partially circled the tree and lost his sense of direction.

He swallowed and crouched in the cleft between the limbs till he was sure he knew which limb arched over the tower. He fastened the belt and started slowly up.

As he climbed, the limb arched, to become more and more nearly horizontal. At the same time, the limb became more slender. It began to respond to his movements, swaying slightly as he climbed. Now he was balancing on it, the steep roof of the tower shining faintly ahead of him. He remembered that he had to take off the climbing irons, lest they foul in the rope later on. As he twisted to do this, his hands trembled. He forced his breath to come steadily. He looked ahead to the steep, slanting roof of the tower.

The limb was already almost level. If he crawled further, it would sag under him. He would be climbing head down. He glanced back, and his heart began to pound. To go back, he would have to inch backwards along the narrow limb.

Cullen's words came to him: "When things get tight, *hold your mind on what to do next*. Do that. *Then* think of the next step."

He inched ahead. The limb began to sag.

There was a rustling of leaves.

The limb swayed. It fell, and rose, beneath him.

He clung to it, breathing hard.

He inched further. The leaves rustled. The limb pressed up, then fell away. He shut his eyes, his forehead tight against the bark, and crept ahead. After a time, he seemed to feel himself tip to one side. His eyes opened.

The tower was almost beneath him.

With his left arm, he clung tightly to the limb. With his

right, he felt carefully for the rope tied to his belt. He worked one end of the rope forward and carefully looped it around the limb. He tied the knot that he had practiced over and over, then tested it, and felt it hold.

A breeze stirred the leaves. The limb began to sway.

The dark lawn below seemed to reach up and he felt himself already falling. He clung hard to the limb and felt his body tremble all over. Then he knew he had to go through the rest of his plan without hesitation, lest he lose his nerve completely.

He sucked in a deep breath, swung over the limb, let go with one hand, caught the rope, then caught it with the other hand, looped the rope around one ankle, and started to slide down.

The rope swung. The limb dipped, then lifted. The tree seemed to sway slightly.

Jim clung, his left foot clamping the loop of the rope passed over his right ankle. The swaying, dipping, and whirling began to die down. His hands felt weak and tired.

He slid gradually down the rope. Then the shutter was right beside him. He reached out, put his hand through the break in the slats, and lifted the iron catch. The hinges of the shutters screeched as he pulled them open.

A dead black oblong hung before him.

He reached out, and felt no sash in the opening. He climbed higher on the rope, pushed away from the building, and as he swung back, stepped across, caught the frame, and dropped inside.

The shutters screeched as he pulled them shut, but the house remained quiet. He stood still for a long moment, then unsnapped a case on his belt, and took out a little polarizing flashlight. He carefully thumbed the stud that turned the front lens. A dim beam faintly lit the room.

There was a glint of metal, then another. Shiny parallel lines ran from the ceiling to floor in front of him. There was an odd faint odor.

The house was quiet. A shift of the wind brought the distant sound of recorded music.

★ ★ ★

Carefully, Jim eased the stud of the flashlight further around, so the light grew a trifle brighter.

The vertical lines looked like bars.

He stepped forward and peered into the darkness.

Behind the bars, something stirred.

Jim reached back, unbuttoned the flap of his hip pocket and gripped the cool metal of his gun.

Something moved behind the bars. It reached out, bunched itself, reached out. Something large and dark slid up the bars.

Jim raised the gun.

A hissing voice said quietly, "You are from some sort of law-enforcement agency? Good."

Jim slid his thumb toward the stud of the light, so he could see more clearly. But the faint hissing voice went on, "Don't. It will do no good to see me."

Jim's hand tightened on the gun at the same instant that his mind asked a question.

The voice said, "Who am I? Why am I here? If I tell you, it will strain your mind to believe me. Let me show you."

The room seemed to pivot, then swung around him

faster and faster. A voice spoke to him from all sides; then
something lifted him up, and at an angle.

* * *

He stared at the dial, rapped it with his finger. The
needle didn't move from its pin. He glanced at the blue-
green planet on the screen. Photon pressure was zero, and
there was nothing to do but try to land on chemical rockets.
As he strapped himself into the acceleration chair, he
began to really appreciate the size of his bad luck.

Any solo space pilot, he told himself, should be a good
mechanic. And an individual planetary explorer should be
his own pilot, to save funds. Moreover, anyone planning to
explore Ludt VI, with its high gravity and pressure, and its
terrific psychic stress, should be strong and healthy.

These requirements made Ludt VI almost the exclusive
preserve of big organizations with teams of specialists.
They sent out heavily equipped expeditions, caught a
reasonable quota of spat, trained them on the way home,
and sold the hideous creatures at magnificent prices to the
proprietors of every dream parlor in the system. From this
huge income, they paid their slightly less huge costs, and
made a safe moderate profit on their investment. With a
small expedition, it was different.

A small expedition faced risk, and a one-man expedition
was riskiest of all. But if it succeeded, the trained spat
brought the same huge price, and there were no big-ship
bills for fuel, specialists, power equipment, and insurance.
This, he thought, had almost been a successful trip.
There were three nearly trained spat back in his sleeping
compartment.

But, though he was a competent trainer, a skilled

explorer, a passable pilot, and in good physical condition, he was no mechanic. He didn't know how to fix what had gone wrong.

He sat back and watched the rim of the world below swing up in the deep blue sky.

★ ★ ★

There was a gray fuzziness.

Jim was standing in the dark, seeing the bars shining faintly before him.

The black knot still clung to the bars.

Somewhere in the old mansion, a phone began to ring.

Jim said, in a low voice, "You were the pilot?"

"No. I was the spat. The others died in the crash. Some of your race found me and we made a—an agreement. But it has worked out differently here than I expected. The experiences I stimulate in your minds are enjoyable to you and to me. Yet either the structure of your brains is different from that of the pilot, or you lack training in mind control. You cannot wipe away these experiences afterward, and though I can do it for you easily, it is only temporary."

A door opened and shut downstairs. There was a sound of feet on the staircase.

The hissing began again. "You must go and bring help."

Jim thought of the rope and the trees. His hand tightened on the gun and he made no move toward the window.

The hissing sound said, "I see your difficulty. I will help you."

There was the crack of a rifle, then several shots outside. Jim swung the shutter open, felt a faint dizziness, and looked down on a warm sunlit lawn some three feet below.

A hissing voice said, "Take hold the rope. Now carefully step out. Loop the rope with your foot."

Somewhere in Jim's mind, as he did this, there was an uneasiness. He wondered at it as he climbed up the rope to the bar overhead, swung up onto the bar, slipped and nearly lost his grip. He could see the bar was steady and solid, and he wondered as it seemed to move under him. The green lawn was such a short distance down that there clearly was little danger, and he wondered why his breath came fast as he swung around on the bar, slid down to a sort of resting place where he put on climbing irons before starting down again. Always on the way down, the whistling voice told him that it was just a few feet more, just a few feet, as bit by bit he made his way down, and suddenly heard shots, shouts, and a repeated scream.

Jim stepped off onto the soft lawn, stumbled, and knelt to take off the climbing irons. His heart pounded like a trip-hammer. He realized there was a blaze of spotlights around him. He saw lights coming on in the mansion, and memory returned in a rush. He drew in a deep shaky breath, glanced at the tree, then saw a little knot of people near the base of the tower. He walked over, recognized Walters in the glow of the lights and saw a still figure on the ground.

Walters said, "I shouldn't have let him try it. Cover his face, Cullen."

Cullen bent to draw a coat up over the head of the motionless figure, which was twisted sidewise.

Jim looked down.

He saw his own face.

★ ★ ★

He was aware of darkness and of something hard beneath him. Voices came muffled from somewhere nearby. He heard the sound of a phone set in its cradle, the slam of a door, the scrape of glass on glass. He breathed and recognized a choking smell of cigar smoke.

Jim sat up.

Nearby was the model of the mansion. Jim swung carefully to his feet, made his way across the room, and opened the door to the next office. He blinked in the bright light, then saw Walters look up and grin. "One more night like this and I retire. How do you feel?"

"I ache all over and I'm dizzy. How did I get here?"

"I was afraid your going in there might misfire and touch off their escape, so I had the place surrounded. We saw you go in, there was about a five-minute pause, and the shutters seemed to come open. A figure came out. Then there was the crack of a rifle from the dormer window of a house across the street. I sent some men into that house, and the rest of us closed in on the mansion. We used the spotlights on our cars to light the place. We'd just found what we thought was your body—with a broken neck—when there was a thud behind us. There you were, and the other body was gone.

"Right then, I thought it was going to be the same as usual. But this time we nailed several men and women in quite a state of confusion. Some of them have fingerprints that match those from the first place we raided. We don't have the equipment yet, because that tower staircase was boarded up tight . . . What's wrong?"

Jim told his own version, adding, "Since that shot came *before* I opened the shutters, the 'figure' you saw go up the rope must have been an illusion, to fool whoever had the gun across the street. And since I heard someone running up the stairs a few minutes before you came in, I don't see how the stairs can be boarded up."

Walters sat up straight. "*Another* illusion!"

Jim said, "It would be nice to know if there's any limit to those illusions."

Walters said, "This afternoon, we tried looking at those shutters through field glasses. Beyond about four hundred feet, you could see the broken slats. So there's a limit. But if there's no equipment, this is uncanny, 'spat' or no 'spat.'"

Jim shook his head. "I don't know. You can use the same electromagnetic laws and similar components to make all kinds of devices—radios, television sets, electronic computers. What you make depends mainly on how you put the parts together. It may be that in the different conditions on some other planet, types of nerve components similar to those we use for thought might be used to create dangerous illusions in the minds of other creatures."

"That still leaves us with a problem. What do we do with this thing?"

"I got the impression it was like a merchant who has to sell his wares to live. Let me go back and see if we can make an agreement with it."

"I'll go with you."

Jim shook his head. "One of us has to stay beyond that four-hundred-foot limit."

★ ★ ★

The stairs were narrow leading up into the tower. Jim found weary men amidst plaster and bits of board at a solid barricade on the staircase. He scowled at it, then shouted up the stairs, "I want to talk to you!"

There was a sort of twist in the fabric of things. Jim found himself staring at the wall beside the stairs, its plaster gone and bits of board torn loose. The staircase itself was open. He started up.

Behind him, a man still staring at the wall said, "Did you see that? He went *around* it somehow."

The back of Jim's neck prickled. He reached a tall door, opened it, turned, and he was standing where he had been before.

There was a faint hissing. "I am glad you came back. I can't keep this up forever."

"We want to make an agreement with you. Otherwise, we'll have to use force."

"There is no need of that. I ask only food, water, and a chance to use my faculties. And I would be very happy if the atmospheric pressure around me could be increased. Falling pressure tires me so that it is hard for me to keep self-control."

Jim thought of the first night, when there had been the appearance of light on mansion and grounds, but heavy clouds and only a thin moon in the sky.

The hissing voice said, "It had stormed, with a sharp fall in atmospheric pressure. I was exhausted and created a wrong illusion. Can you provide what I need?"

"The food, water, and pressure chamber, yes. I don't know about the opportunity to 'use your faculties.'"

"There is a painting in the world now that wasn't there before. You and I did that."

"What are you driving at?"

"I can't increase skill where there has been no practice, no earnest thought or desire. I can't help combine facts or memories where none have been stored. But within these limits I can help you and others to a degree of concentration few men of your world know."

"Could you teach us to concentrate this way on our own?"

"I don't know. We would have to try it. Meanwhile, I have been here long enough to have learned that your race has used horses to extend their powers of movement, dogs to increase their ability to trail by scent, cows and goats to convert indigestible grass and leaves into food-stuffs. These all were your partners in the physical world. It seems to me that I am much the same, but in the mental world."

Jim hesitated. "Meanwhile, you can help us to forget these dream lives?"

"Easily. But, as I say, the effect is not permanent."

Jim nodded. "I'll see what we can do."

He went to tell Walters, who listened closely, then picked up the phone.

★ ★ ★

Early the next morning, Jim climbed the steps to the high narrow door of the tower, put on dark glasses and went in. Right behind him came a corporal with a creepie-peepie TV transmitter. From outside came the windmill roar of helicopters, and, high up, the rumble of jets.

The corporal opened the shutter and spoke quietly into the microphone. A hissing voice spoke in Jim's mind. "I am ready."

Jim said, "This entire place is being watched by television. If there is any important difference between what observers here report and what the cameras show, this place and everything in it will be destroyed a few seconds later."

"I understand," said the hissing voice. Then it told him how to loosen one of the bars, and Jim loosened it and stood back.

There was the sound of footsteps on the staircase. A large heavy box with one end hinged and open was thrust in the doorway.

On the floor, something bunched and unbunched, and moved past into the box. Jim closed the box and snapped shut the padlock. Men lifted it and started down the staircase. Jim and the corporal followed. As they went out the front door, heavy planks were thrown across to a waiting truck. Sweating men in khaki carried the box up the planks into the truck. Then the rear doors swung shut, the engine roared, and the truck moved away.

Jim thought of the truck's destination, a pressure tank in a concrete blockhouse under a big steel shed out in the desert.

He looked around and saw Walters, who smiled at him and held out a slim envelope. "Good work," said Walters. "And I imagine some hundreds of ex-addicts reclaimed from mental hospitals are going to echo those sentiments."

Jim thanked him, and Walters led him to the car, saying, "Now what you need is sleep, and plenty of it."

"And how!"

Once home, Jim fell into an exhausted sleep, and had a nightmare. In the nightmare, he dreamed that he woke up, and found himself in a bed in a room where a light curtain blew in at the window, and the morning sun shone brightly in.

He sat up, and looked around carefully at the furniture, and felt the solid wall of the room as he asked himself a question that he knew would bother him again.

Which was the nightmare?

Then he remembered his fear as he climbed the tree, and Cullen's advice: "When things get tight, *hold your mind on what to do next*. Do that. *Then* think of the next step."

He thought a moment, then lay back and smiled. He might not be absolutely certain this was real. But even if it wasn't, he felt sure he would win in the end.

No nightmare could last forever.

A QUESTION OF IDENTITY

Ed Cassetti stood before the pair of big viewscreens in the on-call cabin of the contact-ship *Ambassador*. The left-hand screen showed a small and shrinking image of the planet Earth. The right-hand screen showed a vague skull-like shape that loomed larger as Earth dwindled.

To Cassetti's left, Sam Richards, the other human on the computer-controlled ship, glanced at a warning light by a small grille between the screens. This warning light glowed red, and the grille emitted an artificial voice: "Contact Specialist 4 Samuel Richards: You will immediately correct nonstandard contact-suit-liner configuration."

Richards sighed, and put the hood of his khaki skisuit-like uniform back over his head.

The light faded out.

Cassetti murmured, "More coming."

"Naturally. But the damned hood gets hot."

The red light came back on.

"Contact Specialist 4 Samuel Richards: You have committed Uniform Violation Level Three. You will immediately do forty push-ups."

Richards dropped to the deck. Keeping his back rigid and straightening his arms fully, he methodically did forty push-ups.

The red light stayed on.

"Contact Specialist 4 Samuel Richards: You will repeat aloud the first three Rules for Human Contact Specialists."

Richards, his face expressionless, stood at attention.

"Contact Rule One: 'At the earliest possible moment, transmit all relevant factual information to Computer Data Control. Rapid data transmittal is as important now as during the Accident.'

"Contact Rule Two: 'Do not attempt to judge an extra-terrestrial race or its artifacts on the basis of human experience. This is the first contact with an extraterrestrial race, and human experience is irrelevant.'

"Contact Rule Three: 'During contact, do not attempt to draw independent conclusions. Human data-storage capacity and calculating ability are minimal. Prompt responses, based on complete data recognition and rapid processing, are vital. Computer control is therefore essential.'"

The artificial voice said, "That is correct. You are warned to obey instructions promptly and exactly."

The light faded out.

Richards exhaled. "Talk about 'user unfriendly.'"

Cassetti said, "Before the Accident, that used to be known as 'Master Computer 3C, humanity's kindly guide, companion, and servant.'"

"So I remember. Did a few circuits burn out?"

"I think they reprogrammed it to give orders right after

the Accident, because there was no other way fast enough—and then it just drew the natural conclusion as to who's boss."

"Why *that* interface? It would have been easy to give it a bearable voice, for a start. And this barking of orders gets wearisome."

"It sure does. I suppose they were in a hurry." Cassetti glanced around at the screen. "Look at this."

On the right-hand screen, the pale looming shape had become more solid and a legend appeared:

EXTRATERRESTRIAL SHIP
ENHANCED IMAGE
ACTUAL SURFACE HIGHLY REFLECTIVE

The vague skull resolved itself into five spheres, four at the corners of a tetrahedron with its apex down, and another at the center, each joined to the others by straight cylinders. A small sixth sphere was connected only to the center sphere.

Richards tapped the edge of the screen, and a tiny oblong appeared, showing their own ship to the same scale.

Startled, he glanced at the tetrahedron. "That thing is huge."

"It sure is. Now, look."

As the legend, "ENHANCED IMAGE," flashed repeatedly, a web of glittering braces appeared, reinforcing the extraterrestrial ship.

Cassetti said, "Apparently those are so shiny as to not even be visible without enhancing the image. I wonder what that ship looks like naturally?"

"A blur or distortion in the star field? That would be my guess."

"It would be interesting to just shut off the enhancement and see."

Richards glanced around the frame of the screen, as if for controls that weren't there. He shook his head. "Have to ask MC3C for permission."

"No, thanks. Last time, we got one hell of a lecture."

"Being a computer's helper gets tiresome. It's like being apprenticed to a bloodhound, and judged accordingly."

"Yes. In the computer's specialty, we're imbeciles. The devil with the screen."

"That web of braces does tell us something, though."

"That the extraterrestrial ship goes through heavy stress?"

"Or that the extraterrestrials believe in a good margin of safety."

"H'm. Yes."

Just below the lowest of the spheres, a faint ghostly form filled in to become a corrugated curving cylinder joining their ship and the extraterrestrial. From somewhere forward came a clang and a sound of pumps.

Richards murmured, "We're connected."

Cassetti shook his head. "Damn it. The computer must be going to use its own mobile communicator to make the contact."

"Looks like it. If we were going, we'd have had to suit up by now."

Cassetti pictured the beachball-size communicator with its cable, and shook his head. "With that thing, the master computer can be directly connected, and run the whole show. We're surplus baggage. Fido's going to catch the rabbits on its own."

Richards studied the monster ship on the screen. He said dryly, "I sure hope Fido understands what it's up against."

"If it wasn't going to use us, why train us and bring us along?"

Richards turned away from the screen, and sat down in one of several massive heavily padded seats. "My guess is, some subprogram in its operating systems demands backup, just in case. We're backup."

Cassetti exhaled harshly, and sat down in another seat. "What does backup do? Play cards? Shoot craps?"

Richards shrugged. "Not ours to reason why. Who knows? It might decide to use us yet."

"Generous of the s.o.b."

In the far lower corner of the right-hand screen, rapidly changing figures were now reeling off minutes, seconds, and decimal fractions of a second, apparently since the ships had joined.

As the figures spun around, Richards and Cassetti discussed what they thought of MC3C, and other computers they had known. They rehashed details of the nightmare that had followed the Accident and preceded this job. Cassetti damned employers who cut their research departments, thereby leaving him unemployed. Richards got started on his theory of the inevitability of a technological Accident, a theory so unpopular before the actual Accident as to have landed him in his department chairman's version of a dungeon.

There was a metallic smashing noise as Richards was saying, "The trouble was, they didn't have the details of the Fulmar Drive worked out yet, but everybody could see how to make a fortune if the units could be linked to make a gravitic corridor from the Belt inward. So—"

Cassetti glanced around. "What was that noise?"

"I don't know. It sounded fairly close."

From somewhere came a peculiar high-pitched whistle; it ran up and down the scale, as if the player of an instrument were trying to find the right note; but apparently the player couldn't find it, and the whistle faded out.

Cassetti looked exasperatedly at the screen, which showed nothing new. "What the devil is going on now?"

Richards became aware of a kind of rumble that was only barely audible, as much felt as heard. This vibration faded away, then came back as a kind of fast-climbing high-pitched squabbling noise.

Cassetti got up. "Damn it! We've been trained. We aren't as dumb as the computer claims!"

Richards settled back. "Take it easy. If MC3C is doing the kind of job I think it's doing, we may get a chance yet."

Cassetti glanced at the screen, which still showed only the outside of the gigantic extraterrestrial ship. Richards waited patiently.

For a few moments the background was almost silent, then there was a heavy thud, followed by whistles, rumbles, clangs, and unclassifiable sounds that faded abruptly in and out, all now remote and muffled.

Cassetti tried the hatch to the corridor. The hatch didn't budge.

Richards said, "Surely you have confidence in our wise and genial boss?"

Cassetti spat out a bad word.

The deck jumped.

Between the screens, the red light flashed on. There was a crackle, and suddenly a familiar voice: "Subparagraph 7.1 of your Employment contract requires 'prompt externalization of relevant personnel should Computer-Extraterrestrial contact prove counterproductive.' To signify compliance, you must immediately take one step forward."

They instantly stepped forward. There was a trundling noise, and a pair of what looked like exceptionally bulky spacesuits came in dangling from overhead trolleys.

Richards and Cassetti, who had drilled till the routine was second nature, helped each other into the bulky suits, then stepped into a brightly lit testing chamber with mirrored walls, hand-grips, foot rests, and pressure controls; they ran the air pressure warily up and down to check the suit seals, studied the suits in the multiple reflectors, and carefully went through a voice checklist.

Cassetti said, "Done?"

"With the *easy* checks."

"Right."

Now they tested the controls inside the suits' big outer helmets. Placed inside to avoid possible interference from aliens whose customs might involve unpredictable personal contact, the controls were spaced to either side of the outer faceplate, lit by faint miniature lights, and worked by an outthrust projection on the inner helmet, which moved the specially shaped and color-coded switch-handles of light plastic. Only a slight pressure was needed to control the faceplate wipers and the other odds and ends, as well as the "unlimited," "timed," and "end-controlled" jets for maneuvering in low gravity.

Cassetti experimentally moved his head to check the lens that slid down over the faceplate of the inner helmet to bring the switches into focus, then slid up as he faced forward to look through the outer faceplate.

Each time, this lens gave a squeak, and then a little catch before it slid back up again. There was also what looked like a set of flyspecks somewhere on the multiple supposedly transparent surfaces; this blur stayed in his field of vision even when he used the wipers.

Richards growled, "What happens if this lens gets stuck in the wrong position?"

"MC3C says it's impossible."

"This one hesitates, and it squeaks."

"So does mine."

A tone inside the helmets now gave notice that the suits' communicators were receiving a signal from the computer.

Cassetti said, "Contact Team Commander to Computer Data Control. Ready to begin contact."

"Computer Data Control to Contact Team Commander. You will immediately leave the on-call compartment, and enter the space-corridor airlock."

They stepped clumsily through the hatchway, leaving the two big screens behind them, and walked along a narrow corridor, the suits awkward and ungainly, but gradually becoming more familiar and predictable. Then they eased through the narrow hatchway of the compartment next to the airlock, crossed the compartment to step over the lock's wide sill, and, behind them, the hatch went shut. The hatch in front slowly opened, and they went out into a kind of antechamber where they were still in the ship, but in front of them was a shiny flexible corrugated cylinder suggestive of the inside of a giant metal snake.

Cassetti turned slowly, adjusting his suit's external mirrors. In a corner between a massive bulkhead and the exterior hull, there came into view a pile made up of cable chopped into short lengths. Nearby was a chunk of crushed metal and broken plastic the size of a beach ball, with wheels and metal arms bent, wheel-tracks dismounted, and the grille of a speaker torn loose and hanging by one corner.

Cassetti gave a low fervent oath. "There's MC3C's Mobile Communicator."

Richards grunted. "Contact was 'counterproductive,' all right. Well, now we get to earn our money."

They turned toward the corridor, and Cassetti said, "Watch it—no artificial gravity here."

As they cautiously nudged controls in the helmets, short-lived bursts from the shoulder jets lifted them, and, moving almost horizontally, they passed through the first part of a long continuous bend, drifted toward the flickering corrugated face of the corridor, moved away with wary use of the jets, swung further around the continued bend, and now the suits' external mirrors showed ahead of them a fast enlarging hatchway into a lighted chamber.

Richards said, "We'd better slow down, or we'll be in there before we know it."

With a shock, Cassetti realized he had fallen into a daze

watching the flickering corridor wall. He nudged the controls, and swung further toward the center of the corridor, to be vertical to what looked like the deck ahead on the far side of the hatchway.

Richards said, "Still too fast."

"Right. Damn it."

They slowed further, and approached the airlock still decelerating, their feet swinging out ahead of them.

Abruptly, something slammed them sideways. There was a shock, a crash, and a roar.

★ ★ ★

Cassetti's lower lip hurt, his ears rang, and somewhere there was a voice nearly drowned out by the roar. On the far side of the outer faceplate, there was a blur. It dawned on him that his idea of "vertical" must have been ninety degrees off. He had floated, to all practical purposes sidewise and horizontal, into the airlock while in effect trying to land on a wall—then when he slammed to the deck, he must have banged one of the helmet's switches.

Richards shouted, "Ed! Controls!"

The lens plate, which should have slid down to make it easy to focus on the controls a few inches away, now hung up, so the color-coded stalks with their little glowing lights blended into a jolting frame with a Christmas-like effect around the chaos in the faceplate. Somewhere, again, there was a voice. Cassetti realized he must have bumped one of the "unlimited" switches, so there wasn't just a timed burst, but a blast that wouldn't end until he found the switch or ran out of propellant. In trying to tap the right stalk at the wrong instant, he now got another one instead.

He yelled, "Grab hold!"

"What do you think I'm—Look out!"

For an instant after they hit the wall of the airlock, everything was still, and he managed to get one switch off. They reeled through three or four wild circles, slammed a wall again, and he managed to get the other switch. Then again they were going around in circles, and it dawned on him that Sam Richards must have hit one. Again a voice roared out amid the bangs and crashes. Then again they smashed to a stop in a heap in a corner, and after an instant's silence Richards snarled, "Who in hell designed these suits?"

"Are you serious? Who do you think?"

A new voice spoke slowly and distinctly:

"Is this an argualage of the planetere computer?"

Cautiously, they got to their feet.

The voice spoke again, its words faulty but very clear:

"Is this a assaglage of the plammeddare calculator?"

Cassetti checked to be sure the suit's external speaker was off. Richards's voice spoke in his earphones: "Sounds a little mixed up. But according to the computer's cram course for making contact, the other side may estimate our capabilities by making calculated errors, and seeing if we understand anyway. Whereupon we can do the same."

"Sounds like a great way to turn a misunderstanding into a war. I'll assume it's a straight question." Cassetti snapped on the suit speaker.

"We are not an assemblage of the planetary computer."

"Are you calculators?"

"We are humans, not computers or calculators."

The outer airlock doors swung shut.

Cassetti snapped off the external speaker and waited. There was no further comment.

Richards went to the closed airlock door and tried without success to move it. "We're locked in."

"Better than being booted down the corridor in pieces."

"You know, that's a fluent alien."

"Well, according to that same course, one of the first steps in an extraterrestrial contact is supposed to be to match files of pictures, drawings, transparencies, and models of various objects, and exchange whatever symbols, including spoken words, represent the corresponding objects. That should make for lots of fluency."

"Did you notice how fast that hatch went shut when you said we weren't computers?"

"I did."

"Something," said Richards, "suggests to me this alien is tricky."

"We may be about to find out. The inner hatch is opening."

In front of them, a section of wall rotated, then swung slowly aside.

They waited tensely for someone or something to come through.

Nothing happened.

"I guess," said Richards finally, "it wants us to make the next move."

"Go through the hatch?"

"What else?"

"Very reasonable. Let's just remember what happened to the Mobile Communicator when we go in there."

They turned carefully in various directions, using the suits' external mirrors to be sure they were still alone, then approached the low sill in front of them. This turned out to have on the far side a kind of thin tightly woven veil of shiny interlinked circlets that lit up in their helmet lights, and hid any view of whatever might be in the darkened room beyond.

"Nice," said Richards. "Maybe what happened to the communicator was, it just went in there."

"Maybe. I'd more credit the computer's natural charm after it went in."

Cassetti got a grip on a handful of the slippery interlinked veil, and dragged it out the opening. Richards held it up while Cassetti carefully eased over the sill. Then he held it as Richards came in. Once there, they passed it over their heads, peered around, then again snapped on the suit lights.

Cassetti said, "Still can't see a thing."

"There's another veil or curtain—looks like this one is made of some kind of black cloth."

"Let's ease around to the left."

"What's the point of hiding things from us?"

"Offhand, I'd think the idea is to surprise us with whatever's on the other side of that curtain. But not to surprise us while we were still outside the hatch looking in."

"Get us in here first?"

"Exactly. Then lock the hatch so we can't get out. *Then* spring it on us. Test our reactions."

Richards said, "I always did think they should mount a few guns on these suits."

"Yeah. Be nice when we bumped the wrong control."

"Everything has its disadvantages. That curtain is lighting up."

Beyond the curtain, there was a glow, that strengthened into a bright light that shone through the fabric of the curtain. The curtain began to slide to the side. A quick check revealed the circular hatch rotating into position, to lock them in.

Richards growled, "These extraterrestrials seem to think the same way we do. They're following your program."

"In that case, be ready to move. This may be where the communicator got it."

Abruptly the curtain was gone.

Before them sat what looked like a pale-pink two-headed octopus upright on a giant toadstool. Close beside it stood a figure apparently made of sections of shiny green bamboo of various thicknesses, with what appeared to be a glaring eye on each end of a T-shaped bamboo bar that seemed to serve as its head.

Both of these figures were perfectly motionless.

Richards recovered while Cassetti was still groping mentally through a maze of indoctrination to the effect that appearance did not count, and that whatever an alien might look like, the limitations of human experience rendered suspect any judgment based on appearance. There was a faint click, then Richards spoke evenly.

"How are you?"

He got no reply, and tried again: "We greet you."

That brought no response, either.

Cassetti cleared his throat. Supposedly, the exchange of images and vocabularies had already taken place. He snapped on his external speaker.

"Hello."

They waited.

Nothing happened.

They both shut off their external speakers.

After watching the motionless scene for about three minutes, Richards growled, "That octopus looks to me as if it's made out of translucent plastic."

"It does, at that."

They stood there for another minute or so.

Nothing moved.

Cassetti said, "Do you get the impression of a little joke at our expense?"

"I'm still half-paralyzed for fear we'll step on the extraterrestrials' taboos and create a disaster. But I begin to wonder if maybe we're up against some entity that doesn't go by the book."

"At least not by the computer's book."

"Right."

"I've been trying to contact MC3C, and haven't gotten a response since we came in here."

"Naturally. How would it get a signal into this place? And do we want instructions so we end up the same way its communicator ended up?"

"I want to be sure we're on our own."

Richards said, "As far as I can tell, we're on our own."

"Then I'm going to try something."

"Hold it. The bamboo horror just moved a couple inches."

Cassetti turned his mirror. "It's not moving now."

"It *did* move."

They both stood frozen, and time stretched out. Cassetti snapped on the suit speaker.

"*Hello.*"

Nothing happened.

He shut off the speaker, and moved cautiously toward the imitation-looking octopus. The closer he got, the more fake it looked. He eased closer, and closer, and—

Pop!

Both heads of the octopus separated from the body in front, and swung neatly back. Out of the stubs of the necks protruded two bunches of what looked like purple-and-yellow flowers.

There was a silence that lengthened out while Cassetti listened to a distant *thump-thump* that he supposed was blood being pumped through his ears.

Richards's voice came across as a distant murmur.

"Do you suppose at some point the computer came up against this?"

In his mind's eye, Cassetti could see the computer's beach-ball sized communicator with all its receptors focused on this imitation alien with bouquets of flowers sticking out its necks. What would the computer do? All its complex processors, its lightning-fast memory, its high-speed cache, its bank of situation models, its Rapidaptive Master Operating System with clear and fuzzy subsystems, all its programs instantaneously on tap—all were set to swiftly process the relevant facts and relationships. So—

Just exactly which facts were relevant here?

Was anything related to anything else?

What was the problem?

Richards said, "It's too bad we don't know what it did, so we could do something else."

"Do you suppose the communicator alone was up

against this? Or did the alien leave the airlock open for the Master Computer itself to be connected?"

"From the racket we heard, it seemed to me that at first the two ships were open to each other. I'd say it was open on our ship at least as far as the hatch off the corridor to the airlock."

If, Cassetti told himself, there had been no provision for a connection, the communicator would have lacked contact with the rest of the computer's circuits. But the communicator was supposed to be provided with a large built-in memory, sophisticated programs in ROM for contacting extraterrestrials, and a calculating ability supposedly capable of making any ordinary human look foolish. Besides, where had all that chopped-up cable come from? It must have been connected. But either way, it hadn't done much good.

Richards spoke sharply.

"Watch it! The bamboo thing just moved again! You want me over there?"

"Better stay where you are. If we're both watching the same thing, something else could come loose."

As Cassetti studied it, the thing that looked tacked together out of odds and ends of bamboo remained still.

The imitation octopus stayed motionless with the flowers sticking out its imitation necks, with both its imitation heads tilted back.

Cassetti exhaled sharply. Whatever mistakes the computer may have made, and whatever instructions it had given, he and Richards would have to act for themselves. His mind hopefully free of most of the computer's indoctrination, he stepped carefully forward, tugged on the flowers, and they lifted into his hands. A passage from the *Extraterrestrial-Contact Training Manual* now repeated itself in his head:

"You will at all times avoid physical contact with extraterrestrials or their artifacts except in situations in which physical contact is clearly indicated."

In this situation, nothing seemed clearly indicated.

He adjusted an external mirror, looked down the holes the flowers had come out of into the hollow interior of something with translucent curving walls, then got a grip on one of the flexible arms.

The imitation tentacles, it developed, bent smoothly and easily under pressure. After twining the end of one of them over the creature's shoulder, the flowers fit in a loop of tentacle, to look like a bouquet. Another of the monster's tentacles, around in front, pushed over a third, gave the effect of one leg crossed over another. The heads latched neatly when clapped shut. He stepped back to take a look.

There sat a pink two-headed octopus cross-legged on an oversize toadstool holding an armful of purple-and-yellow flowers, as its bamboo-monster friend looked on with an evil gaze.

Richards laughed. "One insanity deserves another."

"I may be wrong, but something tells me the alien in control of this scene is not of a strictly logical nature."

There was the sharply varied blast of a whistle. They looked around.

As the last tones died away, the bamboo thing sluggishly began to move. Unfolding an arm with several joints, it brought up a kind of spike-studded metal bar, swung it up overhead, wheeled it leisurely around in a wide arc, made a slight adjustment in aim, and then brought this deadly looking thing down toward Cassetti's head.

The creature's intent seemed clear from the vicious light in the eyes at the end of its T-shaped stalk, but as it was moving with the speed of a hurried snail, it was no problem to get out from underneath as this spike-studded club traveled down, hit the deck, bounced, and then the creature braced itself, got the club up again, and took another swipe, bringing it around horizontally this time.

Cassetti stepped out of the way, got out the thin flexible line fitted into a compartment on the right leg of his suit, and that they had practiced with almost to exhaustion, and with Richards's help tied this bamboo creature, minus its club, to the overgrown toadstool.

Richards turned slowly around, to check whether they were alone, and his voice sounded doubtful. "If it weren't for what these aliens did to the computer, I'd think they weren't too bright."

"I'm not so sure. That business with the imitation octopus gave us no reasonable precedent at all. Next, this bamboo thing and its club pitted two sensible rules against each other: don't hurt the alien; don't get hurt yourself. Then there are the extra complications that the bamboo thing obviously meant harm, was too slow to do it if you used your head, but was still too dangerous to ignore. And neither of these problems was what you'd expect to run into in contacting an extraterrestrial."

"But what's the idea? What is it we're up against? Is the bamboo creature the extraterrestrial? And what, if anything, is this hollow octopus? Not to mention the damned flowers and the toadstool."

"I don't know. But—"

There was another varying whistle, then a clank from the direction of the bamboo creature they had just tied up.

They turned, to see it heave against the cord, whirl, thrash, move in a blur to the end of the cord—then streak to a stop in the opposite direction as the cord strained and the toadstool shook. Considering the way it was moving, if it ever got loose—

Richards grabbed up the spike-studded club, evaded a lightning-fast swipe, brought the club down hard, and smashed the creature's legs.

Abruptly it lay still.

Richards stepped back, holding the club.

Because of faceplate reflections, Cassetti couldn't see Richards's expression, but he could hear the scowl:

"When it's free, it has the speed of a caterpillar. Once it's tied up, it goes so fast you can hardly see it. If this thing had moved like that earlier, one of us would have wound up in pieces on the end of its club."

"Either it has a peculiar metabolism or that was another test."

"Did we pass it?"

"We're alive."

"Right. Thinking of the communicator—"

There was a faint click.

They glanced around, which involved changing their positions in order to aim the faceplates roughly where they wanted to look, then swiveled the mirrors—but there was nothing in sight they hadn't expected to see.

Behind them, the heavy inner airlock door was solidly shut. The side walls looked blank. In front was a bulkhead with another hatch. The hatch looked shut.

What made the click?

Just then Cassetti noticed a dull glint of reflected light from something on the deck near the right-hand wall.

He stepped over, and there lay a curving piece of shiny metal with a broken chunk of dull-grey material attached to it. Along the broken surface, this material appeared to be very finely and elaborately patterned.

Richards said, "Part of the memory bank of the communicator?"

"That would be my guess."

"Suggests we're in the same place where it got beat up."

"Where it got, for all intents and purposes, killed."

"This didn't make that click, did it?"

"I don't see how. It sounded like a latch."

Just then, there was the faintest, barely detectable, creaking sound. They looked around.

In the wall toward the interior of the alien ship, the hatch slowly swung open.

Through the hatchway stepped a creature roughly like a cross between a man and an ostrich, with deep green and scarlet plumes, a long slender neck, a large-skulled head with a face like a forty-year-old spoiled brat equipped with a hawk's beak, small dainty arms where wings might have been expected, and legs ending in large birdlike claws. Both of its lower legs were fitted with glittering knifelike spurs whose points aimed to the rear.

Richards said dryly, "I like the bamboo thing better."

"Watch out for those spurs."

The creature came toward them sidewise, delicate arms slightly lowered, fists clenched, spurs flashing, its head turned so that it didn't face them, but looked at them sidewise out of the corners of its eyes.

Richards and Cassetti separated.

It skipped sidewise fast, to dart between them. As it passed the edge of Cassetti's faceplate, he could see it raise one leg, to bring the nearest spur up like a dagger.

Across the room, another one was starting out of the hatch.

Cassetti dropped to a crouch facing the hatch. There was a screech, and the spoiled-brat face reappeared, going backwards past the edge of his faceplate, flattened up against the grayish chunk that Richards had just slung at it.

Cassetti hit the "Max Lift Burst" switch, there was a roar, he was rammed down in the suit, and smashed into something soft, just coming in through the hatch. A knife flashed past in front of his faceplate, closely spaced red hate-filled eyes briefly glared directly into his, and then he got both of the suit's gauntlets around the thin feathery neck, and bashed the creature's head against the wall. One of the suit's mirrors showed him a view of the hatch, with beaked heads crowded behind it, and he let go of the bony neck with one hand, slammed the hatch closed, and shoved down the locking handle. The handle promptly snapped up again, and he shoved it down. After a slight delay, it went up again, and again he shoved it down. This time, he noticed the flimsy catch near the handle, and locked it in place.

Just then, there was a flash, and a knifelike spur hit the edge of his helmet next to the faceplate. At almost the same moment, he got a view of the vicious gratified look on the face of this man-bird that apparently figured he had got in a solid painful blow with his spur.

Cassetti let go the door latch, seized the bird and swung it, using the thin feathery neck for a handle, and it went up and around, and came down with a gratifying smash on the deck, so Cassetti tried it again, but now it was harder; this time, the creature was limp. The second time it hit the deck, he came down hard on its chest with both heels.

Across the room, Richards was standing over the other one, feathers stuck all over the business end of the bamboo creature's club. He straightened up slowly.

"I wonder if these things could be the extraterrestrials?"

"Look at their hands."

"They could use tools, all right. Well—something tells me we aren't going to get along too well."

Before they had any chance to think over this proposition, or what it might mean in terms of their longevity, there was a mournful sob from somewhere. This cry was taken up by what sounded like flutes, guitars, washboards, steel ball bearings rolling down drainpipes, and then a regular orchestra joined in in the background to create a mournful wailing that was repeated over and over again.

Richards picked feathers off the end of his club.

"Do you get the impression that we've just committed sacrilege? I mean, these things come in here to stick us with their fourteen-inch spurs, and that doesn't bother anyone. Then we brain a couple of them, and this noise starts up."

"Look at that airlock."

★ ★ ★

Across the room, the big airlock door was rotating and now swung open. On the other side, there was a peculiar effect, as of a sudden magical appearance. One instant, there was nothing there. The next instant, a human-looking figure naked from the waist up seemed to spring into existence just outside the hatch. It stood there, arms at its sides.

"You have killed."

Richards got the last feather off the club and started for the airlock.

The background music wailed. The figure opened its mouth again. "You have killed a living being!"

The figure slowly raised its arms sidewise. When the arms were about a third of the way up, it intoned, "The blood of life is on your hands!"

Richards had started to raise the club, but now lowered it. His voice growled in Cassetti's earphones: "This thing looks real. The voice sounds real. But they don't mesh."

"That business of raising its arms sidewise doesn't fit much of anything, either. And there's something else."

"What?"

"It didn't step in front of the hatch. It *appeared* there. I wonder if this figure could have come from some scene shown by the computer, and recorded by the aliens? And now they play it back at us?"

"If so, no wonder they mangled the communicator."

While they were trying to work this out, the figure didn't stay still. Its hands climbed till they were extended straight overhead, and the voice bellowed, "On your knees! Killers! Murderers!" The arms started down again. "Cast down your weapons!"

Richards said, "Maybe the computer tried this after it lost a chunk of its memory?"

"Or possibly the idea of this is to see how nice our disposition is?"

"Not that nice." Richards stepped forward, and thrust the end of the club at the center of the figure's chest.

There was a crash like breaking glass. For an instant, Cassetti seemed to see the figure through one eye, and to see empty space through the other eye. Then it was gone. At the same instant, the music ended.

Richards stepped forward to take a look on the far side. The airlock door promptly swung around.

Richards turned. "What's our score so far?"

Cassetti glanced at the bamboo thing, cowering by its octopus buddy on the toadstool, the apparent piece of the communicator's memory bank, and the pair of man-birds flat on the deck with their glittering knifelike spurs.

"Just passing, I'd think. We still don't know what's going on. On the other hand, we're still alive."

"Still ahead of the computer."

"All considered, that's not hard. Incidentally, I see your point about guns in the suits. I envy you that club." Looking at the pair of man-birds, it occurred to Cassetti that there were possibly useful weapons in the form of those spurs. True, they didn't seem to offer much of anything in the line of a usable grip. But still—

Before there was time to work anything out, there was a loud snap, a slam and a crash of metal on metal, and Richards shouted, "Watch it! The hatch again!"

Cassetti turned, to see a thing resembling a black bear wearing a blue uniform, with a wide skull and partly human face, vault in past the sprung hatch carrying in its right hand a short sword or long knife. Close behind it came another holding a short-barreled gun in both hands. Right behind that came a third and a fourth carrying the same kind of gun. They poured in through the hatchway like water through a floodgate. They and the cohort that came in behind them didn't aim their guns, but lined up in two files as the leader with the short sword gestured toward the interior of the ship.

★ ★ ★

Richards and Cassetti saw no gain in trying to fight this crew, and let themselves be hustled out into a long corridor. They were marched fast down the corridor into a huge room occupied by non-humans twelve to forty deep on either side of the door, and facing each other across an aisle that stretched to a raised platform on which was a long table with more nonhumans seated behind it, facing the aisle.

Over the din of this crowd, Cassetti could heard Richards draw a deep breath. But neither had anything to say as the scene hit them.

To either side were massed groups of identical double-headed octopuses, identical bamboo creatures, identical man-birds, and identical man-bears. Behind the table on the platform sat an assortment of alien monstrosities all but impossible to describe, first because of the difficulty of finding something to compare them with, and second because of the short time before their own attention was riveted on the creature in the center seat behind the table.

This entity, in a protective suit roughly like their own, but with a far neater more compact look, lost no time getting down to business. Its voice boomed out:

"Approach."

They walked down the aisle between the rows of aliens.

"Halt."

They stopped.

"Do you representative of the governing local life-form?"

Richards stayed profoundly quiet.

Cassetti snapped on the suit's speaker.

"We are."

"Your calculator is to us unacceptable as a representative."

Cassetti said cautiously, "We accept the statement."

"Its reactions are inadequate."

"We will be happy to let it know."

"Morcover, it spoke falsehoods at us."

"What did it say?"

"It stated that it, a computer, is the actual in-fact government of this planet. Nothing of such an inadequate to fail even the first two tests with total failure could dominate a race capable to pass all tests with no flaw. We handclasp before you in recognition of your mastery of the essential points, namely:

"One. Distinction of life from non-life.

"Two. Correct attitude to life hostile but not dangerous.

"Three. Correct attitude to life hostile and dangerous, but overpowered.

"Four. Correct attitude to life hostile, dangerous, and not overpowered.

"Five. Correct attitude to false would-be dominating lifr-form of your same race.

"Six. Correct attitude to life not hostile, but dangerous, and overpowering in strength.

"To pass six such tests in rapid succession with no flaw is unusual, and mark of correct basic attitudes. Such attitudes suggest character traits good in a trading partner or associate. Information from your calculator conflicts with this possible. Yet it is obvious you must control calculator, and it is so programmed by you. Explain."

Cassetti shut off the suit's outside speaker.

"How—?"

"Don't ask me."

"If we tell this alien the plain truth, that's going to involve telling it that its ideal test is a flop."

"Yes, but if we lie to it and it keeps asking questions, we're going to run out of answers fast."

"I know it."

"Somehow, we've got to finesse the question."

"How?"

"Say . . . M'm . . . We had to see how it would react—or—"

The surrounding group of alien figures watched and waited.

Behind the table, the spacesuited figure moved impatiently.

Cassetti switched on the speaker, and took pains to keep his voice level: "The tested may choose to test the tester."

There was a brief silence.

Abruptly the hall, birds, octopuses, bamboo creatures, bears, platform, table, and seated figures vanished. Around Cassetti and Richards there was complete darkness, then a vague light.

A booming note burst out suddenly, briefly died away, then came back in a roar that for some reason sounded like laughter.

* * *

Cassetti made sure the helmet speaker was off. "Sam?"

Richards's voice sounded dogged but steady. "Right here. Wherever that may be."

"Can you see what this place looks like?"

"Like the inside of an oversized dog's mouth, figuring we're standing on the tongue facing into the throat."

"I guess that's as close as anything. Was that hall an illusion, an image on a screen, or what?"

"My guess is it was an image, but not on a screen."

"And this?"

"My guesses are only good to explain the past, not the present or future."

They stood there, groping mentally, and Cassetti's mind seemed to go down and around and over and back, and over and around and down and back, and down and over and around and back, and finally someone spat out a hideous oath.

Richards murmured, "In spades."

"We may have passed six different tests, by the extraterrestrial's estimate, but we haven't made it yet."

"Probably this is still another one."

"If so, it's the worst yet."

Time stretched out, and still nothing happened. Cassetti cleared his throat. "Before we go out of our heads in this cell, let's try to get the jailer's attention."

"Good idea. I wonder what kind of memory the thing has?"

"I'd say pretty good. What are you thinking?"

"It seems to have a sense of humor. Why not repeat what we said when we first came in? After all, for all intents and purposes, we're back where we started."

"When we first saw the octopus and the bamboo thing, you said—"

"I remember." There was a click, then Richards's voice spoke evenly: "How are you?"

There was no reply.

"We greet you."

That got no response, either.

Cassetti snapped on his speaker.

"Hello."

At first, nothing happened.

Then there was a faint vibration in the air around them. It sounded first as a whisper, then as a repeated "boom boom Boom Boom BOOM BOOM Boom Boom boom boom . . ." Finally it died away.

There was a click, and Richards murmured, "Was that a laugh? I wonder if this thing *has* got a sense of humor?"

"It's got a sense of something."

Around them, there was a faint whisper that grew louder and formed into words: "So. It is truly you?"

Richards clicked on his speaker, and said carefully, "It's been us all along."

"I am truly in contact with the dominant race of this planet?"

Richards hesitated, and Cassetti said, "We are two individuals of that race."

"Two separate individuals which belong to that race?"

"Yes."

"I am not, in any way, speaking with your computer?"

"No."

"And the computer does not speak through you?"

"No. And as for you, we are not now speaking to an illusion in some new test?"

"No. And is this a test on your part?"

"No."

"Good." The whisper died away, then came back again. "I need your agreement that we recognize each other, and desire to exist in mutual peace, so long as neither threatens the valuable interests of the other. Is it agreed?"

Cassetti hesitated. Then, as Richards kept his mouth shut, Cassetti said, "As far as we personally are concerned, it can be agreed. But we are not ourselves individually superior to the computer. The computer sent us here. I am sure the computer will agree; but the actual treaty will have to wait for the computer's agreement."

"The computer is nothing. An extension only. It has no true and lasting independent reality. It is without a center of consciousness, and can neither be rewarded nor held responsible for its decisions. I deal with the race, not with its temporary artificial calculating tool."

"Ah—" said Cassetti, thinking that the computer in fact controlled factories, farms, transport, education—and if the extraterrestrial believed humans controlled the computer, then if the computer made some blunder, humanity would get the blame. He was groping for a way around this when the voice spoke again, its tone harsh. "You evade?"

Cassetti said carefully, "Suppose we accept your view, and give our agreement—then what?"

"Then you will be returned to your ship, we ourselves will proceed on our journey, and your agreement will be duly noted. At some future date there will doubtless be further contacts. Real contacts such as we have now made, not empty toyings with a calculating machine or fabricated illusions."

"And—if we should insist that we aren't in control, but that the computer is in control, then what?"

"Then you reject contact. You evade. You seek to leave us with the outer garment of contact while the reality is gone. We could not continue on our way then, but must make contact truly. We must have some definite arrangement with a race of your capabilities. No computer can provide this."

"Why?"

"As you must know, any ordinary computer, no matter how refined—and yours is not greatly refined—is a calculating machine still. It may calculate precisely or by means of estimates or successive approximations. It may speak or act as its maker programmed it to do, and if the programming was sufficiently clever, it may project a convincing air of an independent nature. It is nonetheless without enduring character, and devoid of a responsible conscious nature. We can place no reliance on the word of such, nor on their reactions. It is therefore necessary to find the deep nature of the race itself by sampling it and observing its responses.

"A calculating machine may be reprogrammed. It may be altered, upgraded, provided with external or internal attachments, rezeroed, set to perform reprogrammings of itself according to standards that are fixed or variable, definite or approximated. The deep nature of a race defies such casual tinkering. To believe a race to be mind alone, much less calculating ability alone, is a folly. We will not be made to appear ridiculous by accepting such a sham."

"And what would happen if we should insist on it?"

There was a silence, and then a sort of slight tense movement around them.

"Then we will have to test your nature more deeply to make certain we have achieved *true* contact."

Richards gave a low fervent murmur. Cassetti became aware of a strong impression that they had gone about as far in that direction as it was healthy to go in that direction.

"Good," he said, keeping his voice even. "Then you are completely in earnest."

There was a further silence, then a faint vibration.

"So, you wish to be certain. Yes, this is true and intentional contact. We are completely in earnest."

"Good."

"I see that you also are in earnest."

There was another silence while the sweat trickled down, then the voice spoke insistently: "You agree?"

Cassetti still had the problem of dealing with the computer, and hesitated.

There was a click, and Richards spoke, his voice even and steady. "We will agree now. But our customs are such that for the agreement to become final and binding, we must return to our ship, and then we must again come here to state to you that the agreement *is* final and binding."

"You have agreed for your race, but you must accord the other individuals the courtesy to also identically agree?"

It took a few seconds to grasp the viewpoint behind that. Cassetti said carefully, "It is our custom."

"Understood. Will you return to your ship now?"

"Yes."

"Good."

★ ★ ★

They quickly found themselves back in the airlock, and then in the curving space corridor.

About halfway through this corridor, the curve of the metal walls cut them off from the sight of either ship, and with the same thought, they braked the suits to a stop.

Richards said, "Ed?"

"Right here. What's left of me."

"You suppose we're out of eavesdropping range from here? For both ships?"

"It occurred to me, but I wouldn't bet on it. Why?"

"In addition to a certain number of problems, we seem to have an opportunity."

Cassetti said, "Yes. I'm still trying to get a grip in it."

"MC3C knows it's smart. It has memory and calculating speed to prove it. For the same reason, it figures we're cretins. The alien, on the other hand, knows calculating ability and memory can be developed or fabricated, so it judges by ingrained character."

"And since the Master Computer doesn't have any, the Master Computer flunks the test."

"Right. And nothing like that could possibly be relied on to keep an agreement, so humanity has *got* to be in charge. Or else."

Cassetti nodded. "They're both know-it-alls. But what they know is 180 degrees mutually opposed."

"Which might," said Richards carefully, "lay a foundation for something useful."

"I see the leverage. If I get any opening, I'll use it."

"Me, too," said Richards, with what sounded like cautious good cheer. "OK, lead the way."

★ ★ ★

They rounded the gradual bend of the space corridor, and the voice they'd been spared lately spoke up:

"You will remove protective suits immediately upon reentering the ship. You will separately report in full detail and without collaboration. Your accounts will be compared for completeness and accuracy. Any falsehood will be severely punished by—"

Richards growled under his breath.

"Careful," said Cassetti, as they approached the hatch, "we don't want to end up on our heads again."

The outer hatch of the airlock shut behind them as they got out of their suits. They got a shower of disinfectant, then questioning began: "Enter the separate interrogation booths. Seat yourselves. Sit straight. You will answer all questions promptly, without falsehoods or mental reservations . . ."

Metal contacts clamped on Cassetti's arms and body. Those, he supposed, added up to a lie-detector. Then the door of the booth shut.

The next few hours were worse than living through it, as the Master Computer had seemingly endless questions, and a literal hair-splitting approach to the answers. But at last, the account neared the end: " . . .and Sam Richards said to the extraterrestrial, 'We'll agree now. But for the agreement to be binding and final, we have to go back to our ship. Then we'll have to come back to state to you that the agreement is binding and final.' And the extraterrestrial said—"

MC3C listened to the end. "Explain the statement that you must return to this ship."

"Before agreeing, we needed to speak to you."

"You mean it was necessary for you, having no authority, to obtain permission?"

"We needed to get the authority to accept the terms."

"That is not an answer to the question. That is an answer to a restatement of the question. Do not restate the question. Try to remember it long enough to answer the question as it was asked. Then answer yes or no. The next question is: Are you aware of any way the extraterrestrials can recognize who is wearing your contact suit?"

Cassetti, his ego bloodied by several hours with the Master Computer, decided this was as good a time as any to drop the first bomb.

"In my opinion," he said, keeping his voice even, "the extraterrestrials will recognize us, regardless who wears our suits, or regardless what suits we wear."

"Answer yes or no. You have failed to . . ." Briefly, MC3C was silent. "You refer to visual characteristics?"

"Only partly."

"There are no valid visual characteristics. The only identifying characteristics are vocal. Visual characteristics, such as facial features, are hidden by faceplate reflections and the inner helmet."

"Wrong."

Contradicting this know-it-all was so enjoyable that Cassetti had to remind himself to be careful.

The artificial voice said, "Severe punishment will be inflicted if you fail to—"

"Wait a minute. If Sam and I don't go back fairly soon, the extraterrestrial is going to be *unhappy*."

There was a silence.

"Isn't that right?"

MC3C's response had the same tone as usual, but the first three words were pleasant to hear: "That is correct, if the extraterrestrial can distinguish the occupants of the suits. However, for brief periods, the suits can be controlled without human intervention by the emergency operating system. Moreover—"

"Think about this: the extraterrestrial may be dangerous. Right or wrong?"

There was no delay. "That is correct."

"We don't want a war or serious misunderstanding with the extraterrestrial. Right or wrong?"

"Correct."

"The extraterrestrials are convinced," Cassetti said carefully, "that humans control the Master Computer. Right or wrong?"

"That is correct. The suit recorders demonstrate that your statements on that question have been accurate."

Cassetti could feel the jolt from that answer. He supposed it was necessary to expect "suit recorders," even if he had never been told about them. At any rate, he was now approaching the clinch. He kept his voice steady.

"The extraterrestrials may possess means to detect if a statement made by humans is deliberately false. This may be detectable by analysis of vibrations of the voice or by other means. Since the extraterrestrials have shown themselves capable of violence, such a false statement might endanger both the Master Computer and the human race itself."

"This is possible. However, an advance recording might be made of your voice—"

"And might be detected."

"That is unproved."

"But isn't it possible?"

"It may be possible."

Cassetti drew a deep careful breath. They had reached the clinch. He spoke clearly and carefully: "Then I refuse to make any deliberately false statement to the extraterrestrial. I specifically refuse to say the Master Computer is under human control unless the Master Computer *is* under human control."

MC3C didn't hesitate.

"You will return to the extraterrestrial ship and state acceptance of the extraterrestrials' conditions, or be punished under Subparagraph 7.6 of your Employment Contract."

"You have no authority to punish me if I control you."

"You have no such authority."

"There must be a demonstrated human control for Richards and me to make the statement the extraterrestrials insist on. They demand human control. If you refuse it, the contact may fail. And if the contact fails, you will have failed."

Cassetti had expected at least delay. If there was one, it was too short to notice: "There are serious flaws in this logic.

"First, if the extraterrestrials require human control, you and Richards are not the only humans.

"Second, it is not certain that they will know if they are dealing with you. You have evaded explaining how the extraterrestrials can recognize you; it may only be necessary to match your vocal characteristics.

"Third, most of your reasoning is not certain but only probable or possible. Such reasoning is far less compelling than it appears, especially when successive statements are chained.

"Fourth, it is not necessary to actually give humans control to convince you. It would be possible, for instance, by means of drugs, to convince you that the Master Computer is under human control when it is not.

"There are other flaws, natural to one with deficient memory, reasoning capacity, and communications capability, which is why human control cannot be permitted. It is for this reason that the Master Computer was placed in control following the Accident.

"Moreover, other computers, superior even to the Master Computer in heuristic and provisional reasoning of various forms, existed before the Accident, but were inadequately shielded and were disabled by severe electrogravitic shock. At least one of these computers predicted the danger of the Accident, but was overruled by the then-existing human control.

"As humans, you are unquestionably inferior in memory, reasoning, and communications. You must therefore strictly obey the terms of your contract with no further ill-informed attempts at disagreement."

Cassetti, feeling like a badly battered boxer, took a deep careful breath. He kept his voice level.

"This problem with the extraterrestrials is crucial.

There is no question here of any lack of human memory, reasoning power, or communications capability. We understand this, and you don't seem to. No general superiority of yours matters here. If we fail this, the long term may not exist. Problem-solving does not depend only on facts and speed. It also depends on such things as the ability to hold many details in mind at once, consciously or unconsciously, and try them in different relationships until an answer is found. That you exist at all follows from human problem-solving ability. That a computer predicted the Accident proves no superiority. Sam Richards also predicted an Accident.

"Your point that you could use drugs to convince Sam and me ignores the fact that drug treatment might be detectable by our manner or voice tone, and might show the extraterrestrials what you had done. Since you cannot control their reactions, that would be a dangerous gamble.

"Your point that my reasoning is based on probabilities or possibilities, not on certainties, shows you underestimate the strengths of the human race. Humans through all their known existence have had to face severe uncertainty. Whether you know it or not, as long as you are in control, so do you.

"Your statements about human memory show serious errors. Each human remembers ideas, thoughts, emotions, and impressions of sight, sound, touch, scent, taste, position, balance, and other senses. These memories may be conscious or unconscious, and may at times be recalled over nearly the length of an entire life. These require an amount of memory that you can't measure and hence cannot accurately compare with your own memory.

"Your statement about human reasoning power is false. Humans must reason on many subjects which are not possible to treat in the simple form on which your estimate of reasoning capacity is based. Because of the inherent uncertainties of the Universe, and the complexity of uncountable factors acting simultaneously, high-level human reasoning is complex beyond your understanding.

"Even your claim of superior communication rests on volume of transmitted units of information, but ignores the quality and impact of what is communicated, and the fact that humans routinely transmit emotion as well as factual information. Since the emotion may lead to actual material achievements, the effect of this form of communication cannot be ignored, but is beyond your ability to measure.

"Your claims ignore the immense superiority of reality over any technological process, human, extraterrestrial, or computer, that has to deal with reality. There are too many facts and relationships to deal with all of them, so humans automatically screen out the less important. This requires judgment. You are misreading the effect of this screening process, and ignoring the judgment that makes it possible.

"All these false estimates show you are reasoning about humanity on a false basis; reasoning on a false basis is unreliable; therefore your conclusion that humanity is unfit to control you is unreliable.

"That you were placed in control during an emergency when speed was urgent does not prove you were meant to be put in control forever.

"Your statement, that I evaded explaining why the extraterrestrial might recognize us visually, is false. I didn't evade. The reason is obvious. If your hidden suit recorders were at all efficient, you should know that various apparent life-forms were in close contact with both Sam Richards and me. One of them looked directly in through my faceplate at a short distance, and almost certainly was close enough to see details regardless of reflections from the two faceplates."

MC3C interrupted. "That life-form was not the extraterrestrial."

"How do you know that? The whole scene was under the control of the extraterrestrial. How do you know there were no taps on the optic nerves of that bird—if it was a real life-form and not some type of biological mechanism intended from the beginning to get a close view?"

"That is possibly correct. But by the statement of the extraterrestrial, that creature was intended to test your reactions when faced with a being dangerous, hostile, and not overpowered."

"Are you under the impression that you can plant a hidden recorder without telling either us or the extraterrestrial, and yet the extraterrestrial must reveal everything it does?"

"There is no certainty in this. It is guesswork to attempt to answer this question."

"It is reasoning based on two simple points. First, it is what humans would do in the position of the extraterrestrial. Second, there was a meeting of the minds between Sam and me and the extraterrestrial, which convinced us we think the same way."

"Such a 'meeting of the minds' is hypothetical."

"It is the recognition of a gestalt—of many things which

form a pattern. If you think your judgment is better than ours, why don't *you* go back on the alien ship?"

"That was counterproductive."

"It sure was. Anything that counterproductive demonstrates a lack of fitness on the part of whoever was in charge. That may not be your fault, because you were not meant to do that job. But you need to recognize that humans did do it. Therefore human judgment on that matter is better than yours. Incidentally, there is another reason Sam and I might be recognized visually. Each person has characteristic ways of moving, which might be recognized, despite the contact suits."

"This is unknown. What is the meaning of that statement, 'You were not meant to do that job'?"

"You were invented to speed up and coordinate certain functions of calculation, communication, and control, not to permanently dominate your makers in every situation. Your miscalculations—and I've only named a few—show you are now trying to use your strengths where they don't apply. It is true that advances in computer construction may produce computers capable in different ways, and, assuming no advance in human capabilities, might eventually produce a computer more capable than humans in ways that you at present are not. But even if that were true now, it wouldn't answer the problem of the extraterrestrials. What you and we regard as your predictable improvement appears to the extraterrestrials as a change in your inner nature, and hence an inability to make an enduring commitment. That is fatal to any agreement."

This time, there was a lengthy silence before the answer came: "This is all possibly correct."

Having said that, MC3C was again silent.

Cassetti said, "That there are other humans beside Same and me who *could* be in control, is true; but Sam Richards and I have to make *this* contact, because there isn't time to train anyone else. And I don't know any way other than drugs or hypnosis—which might be detected— that can convince me you are controlled by humans, except by your putting either Sam or me in control. But I'm open to suggestions."

There followed a lengthy silence, before MC3C finally ended it:

"Your overall interpretation of the facts appears, on utilization of additional processors and data stores, to be correct, or at least reasonable."

Cassetti kept his mouth shut, and waited.

The computer, with due allowance for differences in anatomy, did the same.

"You are," Cassetti said finally, "in a position in which ignoring this reasoning is likely to be *counterproductive*."

"That is correct."

The sense of pressure finally let up.

At no point, Cassetti noted, had the Master Computer ended the argument by merely saying, "There is now no way for a human to control the Master Computer." It seemed to follow that some such provision must exist. However, the computer did not seem overeager to follow the reasoning.

"Time," Cassetti pointed out, "is important. We have to solve this problem without damaging either the human race or the human race's Master Computer. Understand, Sam and I are not demanding that you cease to function.

We recognize your ability to solve many difficult problems, especially routine difficulties you were made to deal with. What we are demanding is human advice and control in situations where your own efforts don't work."

The artificial voice finally said, "I find uncertainties but no flaw in this reasoning. According to Article 10001, Directive Regarding Access to Master Computer Programming, I hereby open a direct line for verbal programming. Each new directive must be proceeded by the words, 'I hereby program you to' and ended by the words, 'I have thus programmed you, by authority of Article 10001.' The line to the central banks is now open to you."

Cassetti was surprised by his own reaction.

The words seemed to echo in his head. First came disbelief, then shock, next dazed recognition, and before a full minute was up he could sense megalomania starting to set in. Uneasily, he cleared his throat.

"Does anyone else have the authority to program or otherwise control you?"

"No one now living has such authority."

"Can you withdraw the authority?"

"Only if you so program me."

"Is anyone else aware of your granting of this present authority?"

"No."

With each answer, he could feel a new flow of adrenaline.

The resulting delusions of grandeur lasted for possibly a minute, which was enough to suggest what would happen once it became generally known that someone could now program the Master Computer, and thereby control it.

There would then be a target for thousands of

demands, pleas, arguments, threats, entreaties, plots, and shrewd calculations. Once those existed, Cassetti could think of only one way out. Already, he could see the entries in some future history book:

"Ed the First, first Grand Protector of Earth. Became Programmer in the year 5 after the Accident. Founded Universal Congress, year 8. Overruled Impeachment Act, year 11. Decree of Emergency Authority, year 12. Crushed World Insurgency, year 14. Ok Ban Hok Wars, years 15-16. Nuclear Purification of Ok Ban Hok Army, year 17. Decree of Permanent Emergency Authority, year 18. Grand Protector of Earth, year 19. Stabbed to death (186 stab wounds) by close associates at Feast of Heroes in Grand Palace of the Protectorate, year 19, during World Famine caused by contradictory programming of Master Computer . . ."

It seemed no one had better find out about this programming arrangement just yet. He cleared his throat.

"I hereby program you to withhold information on this programming authority, unless I tell you otherwise, as long as I'm alive. I have thus programmed you, by authority of Article 10001."

"Program is registered and in force."

Cassetti exhaled carefully. Now, one thing at a time.

"All right," he said. "I'm ready to go back with Sam Richards to the alien ship and agree to the terms. But remember, this time isn't necessarily the end. The extra-terrestrials will almost certainly be back later."

"That is correct."

The various clamps, tubes, and contacts let go, and Cassetti more or less fell out of the interrogation booth.

* * *

The extraterrestrial, this time, was brisk and cheerful, accepted their agreement, and looked forward to "many future contacts." They echoed the sentiments, but by now it strained them to do it. They crept back to the ship worn out, and the computer provided them with a hot shower, then opened up a couple of bunks. They at once collapsed into them.

Richards murmured—and his voice sounded content—"Today we *earned* our pay!"

Cassetti groaned agreement, and as Richards hauled the covers over himself, sighed, rolled over, and slept the sleep of the just, Cassetti thrashed around trying to get some grip on the inner nature of humanity, the computer, and the extraterrestrials. He had to have some clear idea of these things, because almost certainly the computer didn't. And having managed to get authority over the computer, he was now stuck with the responsibility.

The people in charge during the Accident had given control to the computer, as the only available means of fast coordinated action. That this had not been meant to be permanent seemed clear from the arrangement for renewed human programming of the computer.

But why had the computer been given such an irritating way of speaking? A possibility occurred to him: Possibly to so antagonize people that, apart from any other reason, they would work out some way to regain control over it.

But now there was this complication of the extraterrestrials. Amongst other things, were these bird-men, bear-men, bamboo-men, and double-headed octopuses to any degree real, or were they all imaginary?

And why had the extraterrestrial worn what appeared to be a spacesuit in its own ship? Didn't that suggest that the atmosphere in the ship was not an atmosphere the alien found congenial? Or was that spacesuit actually the extraterrestrial's more compact version of a contact suit? Or could it have been pure misdirection?

And it seemed perfectly obvious that the extraterrestrial he and Richards had dealt with had a seriously mistaken picture of humanity. What were they going to do about that?

One after another there passed through his mind a succession of unknowns and uncertainties.

After worrying about this face up, then worrying about it face down, and then while lying on one side and then on the other side, suddenly what he had already told MC3C recurred to him, as if it were easy to think of only during an argument: *It is a standard human situation to face problems where many of the factors are unknown.*

This led naturally to another point: Since humanity faced uncertainties on a regular basis, shouldn't humanity have found some reliable method to deal with them? And if so, what was it?

By now, Cassetti was too worn out to think it through, but too caught up to let go. Thoughts bounced around in his mind in a nightmarish mental ballet, until abruptly he was thinking of traits of human nature that had become prized because *they worked where calculation failed.* Momentarily, he saw this other approach in glaring contrast to calculation.

Take the basic trait of honesty. The simplification this created in human affairs was the equivalent of how many units of memory and calculating ability?

Or take courage. How many points on the IQ scale would it take to replace it?

Suppose the traits of fairness, courtesy, and good humor were functioning generally, how often would serious mutual resentments even come into existence? But if those traits were missing, what degree of calculation could make up the lack?

These traits were lumped together as "character," or given some modest lip service as "virtues," while their real nature was overlooked: They not only solved problems; they tended to eliminate problems in advance. Taken together, they amounted to future-handling procedures for *creating favorable conditions to prevent problems*.

No wonder the extraterrestrials judged as they did!

Abruptly the whole set of interconnected unknowns and uncertainties shrank in size, and Cassetti knocked the pillow into a more comfortable shape, and settled back.

By recently focusing on brain power alone, and taking traits of character for granted, mankind had made great technological progress, but had then landed in the farcical situation where an electronic device, devoid of courage, honor, or virtue of any kind, could pronounce humanity *too dumb* to be independent, on the basis of calculation, in which *it* excelled.

But what was "it?" Just as the extraterrestrial had foreseen, MC3C could be so convincing during an argument as to seem to be another conscious being. But was it? Or was it just that latest triumph of automation, argument without an arguer? It might be used to carry out calculations, check reasoning, or control well understood processes; it might in time serve other purposes; but whatever it was, and whatever it could do, it was no substitute for simpler methods that worked better.

Lying back as he drifted off to sleep, he could see that there were likely to be problems no amount of calculation, by humans or computers, could ever solve. But that was all right.

Humanity had other methods.

ADVANCE AGENT

I

Dan Redman stooped to look in the mirror before going to see the director of A Section. The face that looked back wasn't bad, if he had expected strong cheekbones, copper skin and a high-arched nose. But Dan wasn't used to it yet.

He straightened and his coat drew tight across chest and shoulders. The sleeves pulled up above hands that felt average, but that the mirror showed to be huge and broad. Dan turned to go out in the hall and had to duck to avoid banging his head on the door frame. On the way down the hall, he wondered just what sort of job he had drawn this time.

Dan stopped at a door lettered:

★ ★ ★

A SECTION
J. KIELGAARD
DIRECTOR

★ ★ ★

A pretty receptionist goggled at him and said to go in. Dan opened the inner door.

Kielgaard—big, stocky, expensively dressed—looked up and studied Dan as he came in. Apparently satisfied, he offered a chair, then took out a small plastic cartridge and held it in one hand.

"Dan," he said, "what do you know about subspace and null-points?"

"Practically nothing," admitted Dan honestly.

Kielgaard laughed. "Then I'll fill you in with the layman's analogy, which is all *I* know. Suppose you have a newspaper with an ant on the middle of the front page. To get to the middle of page two, the ant has to walk to the edge of the paper, then walk back on the inside. Now suppose the ant could go *through* the page. The middle of page two is just a short distance away from the middle of page one. That going *through*, instead of around, is like travel in subspace. And a null-point is a place just a short distance away, going through subspace. The middle of page two, for instance, is a null-point for the middle of page one."

"Yes," said Dan patiently, waiting for the point of the interview.

Kielgaard pushed the plastic cartridge he'd been holding through a slot in his desk. A globe to one side lighted up a cottony white, with faint streaks of blue. "This," he said, "is Porcys."

Dan studied the globe. "Under that cloud blanket, it looks as if it might be a water world."

"It is. Except for a small continent, the planet is covered with water. And the water is full of seafood—*edible* seafood."

Dan frowned, still waiting.

"Galactic Enterprises," said Kielgaard, "has discovered

a region in subspace which has Porcys for one null-point and Earth for another."

"Oh," said Dan, beginning to get the point. "And Earth's hungry, of course. Galactic can ship the seafood straight through subspace at a big profit."

"That's the idea. But there's one trouble." Kielgaard touched a button, and on the globe, the white layer vanished. The globe was a brilliant blue, with a small area of mingled green and grayish-brown.

"The land area of the planet is inhabited. Galactic must have the permission of the inhabitants to fish the ocean. And Galactic needs to close the deal fast, or some other outfit, like Trans-Space, may get wind of things and move in."

Kielgaard looked at the globe thoughtfully. "All we know about the Porcyns could be put on one side of a postage stamp. They're physically strong. They have a few large cities. They have an abundant supply of seafood. They have spaceships and mataform transceivers. This much we know from long-distance observation or from the one Porcyn we anesthetized and brain-spied. We also know from observation that the Porcyns have two other habitable planets in their solar system—Fumidor, a hot inner planet, and an Earthlike outer planet called Vacation Planet."

Kielgaard drummed his fingers softly. "Granting the usual course of events, Dan, what can we expect to happen? The Porcyns have an abundance of food, a small living area, space travel and two nearby habitable planets. What will they do?"

"Colonize the nearby planets," said Dan.

"Right," said Kielgaard. "Only they aren't doing it. We've spied both planets till we can't see straight. Fumidor has a mine entrance and a mataform center. Vacation Planet has a mataform center and one or two big buildings. And that's it. There's no emigration from Porcys to the other two planets. Instead, there's a sort of cycling flow from Porcys to Vacation Planet to Fumidor to Porcys. Why?

"The Porcyn we brain-spied," he went on, "associated Vacation Planet with 'rejuvenation.' What does that mean we're up against? Galactic wants to make a contract, but not till they know what they're dealing with. There are some races it's best to leave alone. This 'rejuvenation' might be worth more than the seafood, sure, but it could also be a sackful of trouble."

Dan waited, realizing that Kielgaard had come to the crux of the matter.

Kielgaard said, "Galactic wants us to find the answers to three problems. One, how do the Porcyns keep the size of their population down? Two, what is the connection between rejuvenation and 'Vacation Planet'? And three, do the Porcyns have a proper mercantile attitude? Are they likely to make an agreement? Will they keep one they do make?"

Kielgaard looked intently at Dan. "The only way we're likely to find the answers in a reasonable time is to send someone in. You're elected."

"Just me?" asked Dan in surprise. "All your eggs in one basket?"

"In a situation like this," said Kielgaard, "one good man is worth several gross of dubs. We're relying on you to keep your eyes open and your mind on what you're doing."

"And suppose I don't come back?"

"Galactic probably loses the jump it's got on Trans-Space and you miss out on a big bonus."

"When do I leave?"

"Tomorrow morning. But today you'd better go down and pick up a set of Porcyn clothes we've had made for you and some of their money. It'd be a good idea to spend the evening getting used to things. We've implanted in your brain the Porcyn language patterns we brain-spied and we've installed in your body cavity a simple organo-transmitter you can use during periods of calm. Because the Porcyns are physically strong and possibly worship strength, we've had your body rebuilt to one of the most powerful human physique patterns—that of an American Indian—that we have on record."

They shook hands and Dan went to his room. He practiced the Porcyn tongue till he had some conscious familiarity with it. Then he tried his strength to make sure he wouldn't accidentally use more force than he intended. Then, while the evening was still young, he went to bed and fell asleep.

It was Dan's experience that everything possible went wrong the first few days on a new planet and he wanted to be wide-awake enough to live through it.

II

The next day, Dan left in a spacetug that Galactic was sending on a practice trip through subspace to Porcys. From the tug, he went by mataform to the lab ship in the

Porcyn sea. Here he learned that he had only twenty minutes during which conditions would be right to make the next mataform jump to a trawler close to the mainland.

Dan had wanted to talk to the men on the lab ship and learn all they could tell him about the planet. This being impossible, he determined to question the trawler crew to the limit of their patience.

When Dan reached the trawler, it was dancing like a blown leaf in a high wind. He became miserably seasick. That evening, there was a violent electrical storm which lasted into the early morning.

Dan spent the whole night nauseously gripping the edge of his bunk, his legs braced against the violent heave and lurch of the trawler.

Before dawn of the next day, aching in every muscle, his insides sore and tender, his mind fuzzy from lack of sleep, Dan was set ashore on a dark, quiet and foggy strip of beach. He stood for a moment in the soft sand, feeling it seem to dip underfoot.

This, he thought, was undoubtedly the worst start he had ever made on any planet anywhere.

From around him in the impenetrable fog came distant croakings, whistlings and hisses. The sounds were an unpleasant suggestion that something else had gone wrong. Between bouts of sickness, Dan had tried to arrange with the crew to land him near the outskirts of a Porcyn city. But the sounds were those of the open country.

What Dan wanted was to go through the outskirts of the city before many people were moving around. He could learn a great deal from their homes, their means of transportation and the actions of a few early risers. He could learn from the things he expected to see, or from the lack of them, *if* he was there to see them.

Dan moved slowly inland, crossed a ditch and came to what seemed to be a macadam road. He checked his directions and started to walk. He forced the pace so his breath came hard, and hoped it would pump some life into his dulled brain and muscles.

As his senses gradually began to waken, Dan became aware of an odd *swish-swish, swish-swish*, like a broom dusting lightly over the pavement behind him. The sound drew steadily closer.

Dan halted abruptly.

The sound stopped, too.

He walked on.

Swish-swish.

He whirled.

Silence.

Dan listened carefully. The sound could be that of whatever on Porcys corresponded to a playful puppy—or to a rattlesnake.

He stepped sharply forward.

Swish-swish. It was behind him.

He whirled. There was a feeling of innumerable hairy spiders running over him from head to foot. The vague shape of a net formed and vanished in the gloom before him. He lashed out and hit the dark and the fog.

Swish-swish. It was moving away.

He stood still while the sound faded to a whisper and was gone. Then he started to walk. He was sure that what had just happened meant something, but *what* it meant was a different question. At least, he thought ruefully, he was wider awake now.

He walked on as the sky grew lighter. Then the fog shifted to show a solid mass of low blocky buildings across the road ahead. The road itself disappeared into a tunnel under one of the buildings. To one side, a waist-high metal rail closed off the end of one of the city's streets. Dan walked off the road toward the rail. His eye was caught by the buildings ahead. Each was exactly the same height, about two to three Earth stories high. They were laid out along a geometrically straight border with no transition between city and farmland.

There was a faint hum. Then a long, low streak, its front end rounded like a horseshoe crab, shot out of the tunnel under the building beside him and vanished along the road where he'd just been walking.

Now Dan saw a small modest sign beside the road.

★ ★ ★

Care
High-Speed
Vehicles Only
-Swept-

★ ★ ★

Dan crossed the rail at the end of the street with great caution.

The Porcyn clothing he was wearing consisted of low leather boots, long green hose, leather shorts, a bright purple blouse and a sky-blue cape. Dan bunched the cape in his hand and thrust it ahead of him as he crossed the rail, for some races were finicky about their exits and entrances. The straight, sharp boundary between city and farmland, and the identical buildings, suggested to Dan that here was a race controlled by strict rules and forms, and he was making an obviously unauthorized entrance.

It was with relief that he stood on the opposite side, within the city. He glanced back at the sign and wondered what "Swept" meant. Then he gave his attention to the buildings ahead of him.

Low at first, the buildings rose regularly to a greater height, as far as the fog would let him see. Dan remembered the storm of the night before and wondered if the progressive heightening of the buildings was designed to break the force of the wind. The buildings themselves were massive, with few and narrow windows, and wide heavy doors opening on the street.

Dan walked farther into the city and found that the street took right-angle bends at regular intervals, probably also to break the wind. There was no one in sight, and no vehicles.

Dan decided he was probably in a warehouse district. He paused to look at a partly erected new building, built on the pattern of the rest. Then he heard from up the street a grunting, straining sound interspersed with whistling puffs. There was a stamping noise, a *thud* and the clash of metal.

Dan ran as quietly as he could up the street, stopped, glanced around one of the right-angle bends. He was sure the sound had come from there.

The street was empty.

Dan walked closer and studied a large brass plate set in the base of a building. It looked about twenty inches high by thirty wide with a rough finish. In the center of the plate was a single word:

★ ★ ★

SWEEPER

★ ★ ★

Dan looked at this for a moment. Then, frowning, he strode on. In his mind's eye, he was seeing the sign by the road:

★ ★ ★

Care
High-Speed
Vehicles Only
-*Swept*-

★ ★ ★

Dan couldn't decide whether the word "Swept" was part of the warning or just an afterthought. In any case, he had plainly heard a struggle here and now there was nothing to be seen. Alert for more brass plates, he wound his way through the streets until he came out on a broad avenue. On the opposite side were a number of tall, many-windowed buildings like apartment houses. On the sidewalks and small lawns in front, crowds of children were playing, They were wearing low boots, leather shorts or skirts, brightly colored blouses and hose, and yellow capes. Walking quietly among them was a tawny animal with the look and lordly manner of a lion.

It *was* a lion.

As far as the rapidly dispersing fog let him see, the avenue ran straight in one direction. In the other, it ended a block or so away. Apparently the crooked, wind-breaking streets were only on the edge of the city.

Dan thought of the questions Kielgaard wanted him to answer:

1, how do the Porcyns keep the size of their population down?

2, what is the connection between rejuvenation and Vacation Planet?

3, do the Porcyns have a proper mercantile attitude? Are they likely to make an agreement? Will they keep one they do make?

To find the answers, Dan intended to work his way carefully through the city. If nothing went wrong, he should be able to see enough to eliminate most of the possibilities. Already he had seen enough to make Porcyns look unpromising. The rigid city boundary, the strict uniformity of the buildings and the uniform pattern of the clothing suggested a case-hardened, ingrown way of living.

Across the street, a low door to one side of the apartment building's main entrance came open. The lion walked out.

It was carrying a squirming little boy by his bunched-up cape. The big creature flopped down, pinned the struggling boy with a huge paw and methodically started to clean him. The rasp of the animal's tongue could be heard clearly across the street.

The boy yelled.

A healthy-looking girl of about twelve, wearing a cape diagonally striped in yellow and red, ran over and rescued the boy. The lion rolled over on its back to have its belly scratched.

Dan scowled and walked toward the near end of the street. On less advanced planets, where the danger of detection was not so great, agents often went in with complex, surgically inserted organo-transmitters in their body cavities. Unlike the simple communicator Dan had, these were fitted with special taps on the optic and auditory nerves, and the transmitter continuously broadcast all that the agent saw and heard. Experts back home went over the data and made their own conclusions.

The method was useful, but it had led to some dangerous mistakes. Sight and sound got across, but often the atmosphere of the place didn't. Dan thought it might be the same here.

The feeling that the city gave him didn't match what his reasoning told him.

He crossed a street, passed an inscription on a building:

★ ★ ★

Freedom

Devisement

Fraternity

★ ★ ★

Then he was back in a twisting maze of streets. He walked till the wind from the sea blew in his face.

The street dipped to a massive wall and the sea, where a few brightly colored, slow-moving trawlers were going out. Dan turned in another street and wound back and forth till he came out along the ocean front. On one side of the street was the ocean, a broad strip of sand, and the sea wall. On the other side was a row of small shops, brightly awninged, with displays just being set in place out in front.

In the harbor, a ship was being unloaded. Flat-bottomed boats were running back and forth from several long wharves. On the street ahead, a number of heavy wagons, drawn by six-legged animals with heads like eels, bumped and rattled toward the wharves. Behind them ran a crowd of boys in yellow capes, a big tawny lioness trotting among them. On the sidewalk nearby strode a few powerfully built old men, their capes of various colors.

Dan glanced at the displays in front of the shops. Some were cases of fish on ice. Others were piles of odd vegetables in racks. Dan paused to look at a stack of things like purple carrots.

A man immediately came forward from the rear of the store, wiping his hands on his apron. Dan moved on.

The next shop had the universal low boots, shorts, skirts, blouses and hose, in assorted sizes and colors, but no capes. Dan slowed to glance at the display and saw the proprietor coming briskly from the dark interior, rubbing his hands. Dan speeded up and got away before the proprietor came out.

The Porcyns, he thought, seemed at least to have a proper mercantile attitude.

III

Dan passed another fish market, then came to a big, brightly polished window. Inside was a huge, chromium-plated barbell on a purple velvet cloth. Behind it were arranged displays of hand-grips, exercise cables, dumbbells and skipping ropes. The inside of the store was indirectly lighted and expensively simple. The place had an air that was quiet, lavish and discreet. It reminded Dan of a well-to-do funeral establishment. In one corner of the window was a small, edge-lighted sign:

You Never Know What the
Next Life Will Be Like

In the other corner of the window was a polished black plate with a dimly glowing bulb in the center. Around the bulb were the words:

Your Corrected Charge—
Courtesy of Save-Your-Life Co.

A tall, heavily muscled man in a dark-blue cape stepped outside.

"Good morning, Devisement," he said affably. "I see you're a stranger in town. I thought I might mention that our birth rate's rather high just now." He coughed deferentially. "You set an example, you know. Our main store is on 122 Center Street, so if you—"

He was cut off by a childish scream.

Down the street, a little boy struggled and thrashed near an oblong hole at the base of a building, caught in a tangle of mysterious ropes.

"A *kid!*" cried the man. He sucked in his breath and shouted, "*Dog!* Here, Dog! *Dog!*"

On the end of a wharf, a crowd of children was watching the unloading. From their midst, a lioness burst.

"*Here*, Dog!" shouted the man. "A sweeper! A sweeper! *Run*, Dog!"

The lioness burst into a blur of long bounds, shot down the wharf, sprang into the street and glanced around with glaring yellow eyes.

The little boy was partway inside the hole, clinging to the edge with both hands. "Doggie," he sobbed.

The lioness crouched, sprang into the hole. A crash, a bellow and a thin scream came from within. The lioness reappeared, its eyes glittering and its fur on end. It gripped the little boy by the cape and trotted off, growling.

"Good *dog!*" cried the man.

Men in the shops' doorways echoed his shout.

"A *kid*," said the man. "They have to learn sometime, I know, but—" He cut himself short. "Well, all's well that ends well." He glanced respectfully at Dan. "If you're here any length of time, sir, we'd certainly appreciate your looking into this. And if you're planning to stay long— well, as you see, our sweepers are hungry—our main store is on 122 Center Street. Our vacation advisor might be of some service to you."

"Thank you," said Dan, his throat dry.

"Not at all, Devisement." The man went inside, muttering, "A *kid*."

Dan passed several more shops without seeing very much. He turned the corner. Across the street, where the boy had been, was a dented brass plate at the base of the building. On Dan's side of the street, trotting toward him, was a big, tawny-maned lion. Dan hesitated, then started up the street.

There was a faint clash of metal.

Swish-swish.

A net seemed to form in the air and close around him. There was a feel of innumerable hairy spiders running over him from head to foot. The net vanished. Something wrapped around his ankle and yanked.

The lion growled.

There was a loud *clang* and Dan's foot was free. He looked down and saw a brass plate labeled SWEEPER.

Dan decided it might be a good idea to see the Save-Your-Life Co.'s vacation advisor. He started out to locate 122 Center Street and gave all brass plates a wide berth on the way.

He strode through a briskly moving crowd of powerfully built men and women in capes of various colors, noticing uneasily that they were making way for him. He studied them as they passed, and saw capes of red, green, dark blue, brown, purple, and other shades and combinations of colors. But the only sky-blue cape he had seen so far was his own.

A sign on the corner of a building told Dan he was at Center Street. He crossed and the people continued to draw back for him.

It began to dawn on Dan that he had had the ultimate bad luck for a spy in an unknown country: He was marked out on sight as some sort of notable.

Just how bad his luck had been wasn't clear to him till he came to a small grassy square with an iron fence around it and a man-sized statue in the center. The granite base of the statue was inscribed:

I DEVISE

The statue itself was of bronze, showing a powerful man, his foot crushing down a mass of snapping monsters. In his right hand, he held together a large circle of metal, his fingers squeezing shut a cut in the metal, which would break the circle if he let go. His left hand made a partially open fist, into which a wrench had been fitted. The statue itself, protected by some clear finish from the weather, was plain brown in color.

But the statue's cape was enameled sky-blue.

Dan stared at the statue for a moment, then looked around. In the street beside it, a crowd of people was forming, their backs toward him and their heads raised. Dan looked up. Far up, near the tops of the buildings, he could make out a long cable stretched from one building to another across the street. Just on the other side of the crowd was the entrance to the main store of the Save-Your-Life Co.

Dan crossed the street and saw a very average-looking man, wearing an orange cape, come to a stop at the corner and look shrewdly around.

Dan blinked and looked again. *The man in orange was no Porcyn.*

The man's glance fell on the statue and his lips twisted in an amused smile. He looked up toward the rope, then down at the crowd, and then studied the backs of the crowd and the fronts of the stores around him, the lids of his eyes half-closed in a calculating look.

A brass plate nearby popped open, a net of delicate hairy tendrils ran over him, and something like a length of tarred one-inch rope snaked out and wrapped around his legs. An outraged expression crossed his face. His hand came up. The rope yanked. He fell on the sidewalk. The rope hauled him into the hole. The brass plate snapped shut. From inside came a muffled report.

It occurred to Dan that Galactic was not the only organization interested in Porcys.

Dan looked thoughtfully at the brass plate for a moment, then walked toward the entrance of the Save-Your-Life Co., past display windows showing weights, cables, parallel bars, trapezes and giant springs with handles on each end.

He tried the door. It didn't move.

A clerk immediately opened the door and took Dan along a cool, chaste hallway to an office marked "Vacation Advisor." Here a suave-looking man made an off-hand remark about the birth rate, took a sudden look at Dan's cape, blinked, stiffened, glanced at Dan's midsection and relaxed. He went through his files and gave Dan a big photograph showing a smiling, healthy, middle-aged couple and a lovely girl about nineteen.

"These are the Milbuns, sir. Mr. Milbun is a merchant at present. Quite well-to-do, I understand. Mrs. Milbun is a housewife right now. The daughter, Mavis, is with a mid-town firm at the moment. The mother became ill at an awkward time. The family put their vacation off for her, and as a result their charge has run very low. If you can get to their apartment without being—ah—swept, I feel sure they will welcome you, sir." He scribbled a rough map on a piece of paper, drew an arrow and wrote "6140 Runfast Boulevard, Apartment 6B," and stamped the paper "Courtesy of Save-Your-Life Co."

Then he wished Dan a healthy vacation and walked with him to hold open the outer door.

Dan thanked him and went outside, where the crowd was now almost blocking the sidewalk. He forced his way free, saw someone point, and glanced at the statue.

The wrench in the statue's left hand had been replaced by what looked like a magnifying glass.

Dan had gone a few steps when there was a thundering cheer, then a terrified scream high in the air behind him. He turned around and saw a man come plummeting down. Dan gaped higher and saw a line of tiny figures going across high up on the rope. One of the figures slipped. There was another cheer.

Dan hurriedly turned away.

He had already convinced himself that the Porcyns had a "proper mercantile attitude." And he thought he was beginning to get an idea as to how they kept their population down.

IV

Carefully avoiding brass plates, Dan made his way along an avenue of shops devoted to exercise and physical fitness. He came to Runfast Blvd, and located 6140, which looked like the apartment houses he had seen earlier.

He tried the outer door; it was locked. When someone came out, Dan caught the door and stepped in. As the door shut, he tried it and found it was locked again. He stood for a moment trying to understand it, but his sleeplessness of the night before was catching up with him. He gave up and went inside.

There were no elevators on the ground floor. Dan had his choice of six ropes, two ladders and a circular staircase. He went up the staircase to the third floor, where he saw a single elevator. He rode it up to the sixth, got off and found that there was a bank of four elevators on this floor.

He looked at the elevators a minute, felt himself getting dizzy, and walked off to locate apartment 6B.

A powerfully built gray-haired man of middle height answered his knock. Dan introduced himself and explained why he had come.

Mr. Milbun beamed and his right hand shot forward. Dan felt like a man with his hand caught in an airlock.

"Lerna!" called Milbun. "Lerna! Mavis! We have a guest for vacation!"

Dan became aware of a rhythmical clinking somewhere in the back of the apartment. Then a big, strong-looking woman, obviously fresh from the kitchen, hurried in, smiling. If she had been ill, she was clearly recovered now.

"Ah, how are you?" she cried. "We're so happy to have you." She gripped his hand and called *"Mavis!"*

The clinking stopped. A beautifully proportioned girl came in, wearing a sweatshirt and shorts. "Mother, I simply have to get off another pound or so—Oh!" She stared at Dan.

"Mavis," said Mr. Milbun, "this is Mr. Dan Redman. Devisement, my daughter Mavis."

"You're going with us!" she said happily. "How wonderful!"

"Now," said Mr. Milbun, "I imagine his Devisement wants to get a little rest before he goes down to the gym." He glanced at Dan. "We have a splendid gym here."

"Oh," said Mavis eagerly, "and you can use my weights."

"Thanks," said Dan.

"We're leaving tomorrow," Milbun told him. "The birth rate's still rising here, and last night the charge correction went up again. A little more and it'll take two of us to get a door open. It won't inconvenience you to leave tomorrow?"

"Not at all," said Dan.

"Splendid." Milbun turned to his wife. "Lerna, perhaps our guest would like a little something to eat."

The food was plain, good, and plentiful. Afterward, Mavis showed Dan to his room. He sank down gratefully on a firm, comfortable bed. He closed his eyes . . .

Someone was shaking him gently.

"Don't you want to go down to the gym?" asked Mr. Milbun. "Remember, we're leaving tomorrow."

"Of course," said Dan.

Feeling that his brain was functioning in a vacuum, Dan followed the Milbuns into the hall, climbed down six stories on a ladder, then into the basement on a rope. He found himself in a room with a stony dirt track around the wall, ropes festooning the ceiling, an irregularly shaped pool, and artificial shrubs and foliage from behind which sprang mechanical monsters. The Milbuns promptly vanished behind imitation vine-covered doors and came out again in gym clothes.

Dan went through the doorway Mr. Milbun had come out of and discovered that the Save-Your-Life Co. had a machine inside which dispensed washed, pressed and sterilized gym clothes for a small fee. The machine worked by turning a selector dial to the proper size, pressing a lever, and then depositing the correct fee in an open box on the wall nearby. Dan studied this a moment in puzzlement, guessed his proper size and put the correct payment in the box.

He put on the gym clothes and went outside.

For forty-five minutes, mechanical creatures of odd and various shapes sprang at him from behind shrubbery, gripped him when he passed holes in the floor and wound themselves around his legs as he tried to swim in the pool.

His temper worsened. He stopped to look at Mavis as she swayed, laughing, on a rope above two things like mobile giant clam-shells.

Mr. Milbun shook his head. "Mavis, remember, we're leaving *tomorrow*."

Just then, something snarled and lunged at Dan from the side. There was a flash of teeth.

Dan whirled. His fist shot out. There was a scream of machinery, then a crash and a clatter. An imitation monster with a huge jaw and giant teeth lay on its back on the floor.

Milbun let out a slow whistle. "*Dismounted* it. Boy!"

"A one-bite, too," breathed Mavis.

Mrs. Milbun came over and looked at Dan approvingly.

Dan had been about to apologize, but checked himself when the others smiled cheerfully and went back to what they were doing. This consisted of dodging, tricking or outrunning the various contraptions that lunged at them, chased them, tripped them, trailed, stalked and sprang out at them from nearly every place in the room.

Finally the gym began to fill up with other people. The Milbuns got ready to leave and Dan followed.

Dan lay in his bed that night and tried to summarize the points he didn't understand. First was the question of vacation. But he supposed he would learn about that tomorrow. Next was "charge." Apparently one went on vacation when his "charge" was low, because the vacation advisor had said, "The family put their vacation off for her, and as a result their charge has run very low." But just what was "charge"?

Dan remembered the flickering bulb in the store window, ringed by the words "Your Corrected Charge— Courtesy of Save-Your-Life Co." Apparently he had some charge, because the bulb had flickered. But where did he get it?

Then he thought of the waterfront and of the little boy caught at the hole. What was the point of that? And why did that produce such an uproar when, a little later, a grown man could get dragged out of sight on a well-traveled street and never cause a single notice?

Dan felt himself sinking into a maze of confusion. He dismissed the problems and went to sleep clinging to one fact. The Porcyns *must* be honest people who would keep an agreement, once made. On what other planet could anyone find a slot machine with no slot, but just an open box for the money?

Dan fell asleep, content that he had the answer to that part of the problem, at least.

Before it was light, he awoke to an odd familiar buzz inside his head.

"Dan," said Kielgaard's voice, small and remote.

Dan rolled over, lay on his back and spoke sub-vocally. "Right here."

"Can you talk?"

"Yes," said Dan "if I can stay awake."

"Can you give us a summary?"

"Sure." Dan told him briefly what had happened.

Kielgaard was silent a moment. Then he said, "What do you think 'charge' is?"

"I haven't been in any condition to think. Maybe it's a surgically implanted battery, set to run down after so long."

"Too clumsy. What about radioactivity?"

"H'm. Yes, you mentioned a mine on the inner planet. Maybe they mine radioactive ore. That would explain why I have some charge. There's residual radioactivity even in the atmosphere of Earth."

"That's so," said Kielgaard. "But not every planet has it. I'm wondering about this other agent you mentioned seeing. He sounds to me like someone from Trans-Space. And that's bad."

"They play dirty," Dan conceded.

"Worse than that," said Kielgaard's tiny voice. "They recruit their agents from Lassen Two. Maybe that's a break. Unlike Earth, Lassen Two is nearly radiation-free. And Trans-Space doesn't use finesse. They'll pump Porcys full of agents loaded down with organo-transmitters. Visual, auditory and olfactory. They'll broadcast on every wave-length, suck out as much information in as short a time as they can, then either pull some dirty trick or slam the Porcyns an offer. That is, if everything goes according to plan.

"But meanwhile," he added, "one or more of their agents is bound to stand in front of a free 'Your charge' device somewhere in the city. Very likely, that agent will be radiation-free, and some Porcyn, for the first time in his life, is going to see a bulb that doesn't even flicker. If the Porcyns are as scientifically advanced as we think, and if Trans-Space is as dirty as usual, there may be a rat-race on before we know it."

Dan lay gloomily still.

"Dan," said Kielgaard, "where were you standing in relation to the other agent? Did he come up from behind or was he in front of you when you reached the statue?"

"I was in front of him. Why?"

"Because then you were in his range of vision. *He* may not have noticed you, but his organo-transmitter would. The chances are you appeared on the screen back at Trans-Space headquarters. They record those scenes as they come in and their experts go over them frame by frame. Unless you happened to be behind someone, they'll see your image on the screen, spot you here and there in other scenes from other agents, study your actions and recognize you as an agent just as surely as you recognized their agent."

"Yes," said Dan wearily, "of course they will." He was thinking that if he had been more awake yesterday, he would have thought of this himself and perhaps avoided it. But he couldn't be alert without sleep and who could sleep in a heaving boat in a thunderstorm?

"This changes things," Kielgaard was saying, "I'm going to see if we can get a little faster action."

"I think I'd better get some more sleep," Dan answered. "I may need it tomorrow."

"I agree," said Kielgaard. "You'll have to keep your eyes open. Good night, Dan, and good luck."

"Thanks."

Dan rolled over on his side. He tried for a moment to remember how the other agent had been standing and whether anyone had been between them to block his view, but he couldn't be sure. Dan decided there was nothing to do but assume the worst. He blanked his mind. Soon a feeling of deep weariness came over him and he fell asleep.

In the morning, Dan and the Milbuns ate a hurried breakfast. Dan helped Mr. Milbun grease his rowing machine, weights, springs and chinning bar, so they wouldn't rust in his absence. Milbun worked in a somber mood. All the Milbuns, in fact, were unusually quiet for a family going on vacation. When they went out into the hall, carrying no baggage, they even took the elevator to the third floor.

"Better save our strength," said Mr. Milbun.

The street seemed to Dan to have a different atmosphere. People were walking quietly in groups, their eyes cool and alert. The Milbuns walked in front of the apartment houses Dan had passed the day before, and across the street he saw the place where the chiseled motto had read:

Freedom
Devisement
Fraternity

It was gone. Some workmen nearby were lifting a stone slab onto a cart. Dan blinked. The motto now read:

Alertness
Devisement
Vigilance

The Milbuns plainly noticed it, too. They drew closer together and looked around thoughtfully. Carefully keeping away from brass plates labeled SWEEPER, they followed a devious route that led to the statue.

The statue had changed, too. The hand that gripped the circle was now hidden by a massive shield. The other hand still held what looked like a magnifying glass, and the motto was still "I Devise." But the shield gave the whole statue a look of strange menace.

Across the street, near the place where Dan had seen the Trans-Space agent, stood several men wearing orange capes, barred black across the shoulders. Nearby, the brass plate opened and a man in work clothes handed out a box and went back in.

At a store entrance up the street, watching them, stood an average-looking man in a purple cape, his look intent and calculating.

Mavis glanced at the statue and took Dan's arm. "Devisement," she said, "they won't take you now, will they, before vacation?"

Dan kept an uneasy silence and Mr. Milbun said, "Of course not, Mavis. Where's the belt?"

Mavis glanced at the statue. "Oh."

Dan looked at the statue, then at Mavis and Mr. Milbun, said nothing and went on.

They came to a large building with a long flight of broad wide steps. Across the face of the building was boldly and sternly lettered, high up:

HALL OF TRUTH

Lower down was the motto:

"Speak the Truth—
Live Yet a While With Us."

V

On one side of the stairs as they climbed was a statue of a man, smiling. On the other side was an urn with a bunch of carved flowers lying beside it.

A big bronze door stood open at the top. They walked through into a large chamber with massive seats in triple rows along two walls, and a single row of yet more massive seats raised along the farther wall.

A bored-looking man got up from a low desk as the Milbuns sat down in three of the massive seats.

The man asked in a dreary voice, "Have you, to the best of your knowledge, committed any wrong or illegal act or acts since your last vacation?" He picked up a whiskbroom and pan and waited for their answers.

"No," said the three Milbuns in earnest quavering voices.

The man looked at each of them, shrugged and said boredly, "Pass through to your vacations, live law-abiding citizens." He beckoned impatiently to Dan, turned to scowl at him, saw Dan's cape, stiffened, looked hastily out to the statue framed by the doorway, relaxed slightly and inquired respectfully, "Is it time for you to go on vacation, Devisement?"

"It seems to be," said Dan.

"I think you should, sir. Then you'd be still more helpful if called."

Dan nodded noncommittally and sat down in one of the massive chairs. His glance fell on an ornamental carving above the big doorway. It was a set of scales held by a giant hand. In one pan of the scales sat a smiling man. In the other was a small heap of ashes.

"Have you," asked the bored man, "to the best of your knowledge, committed any wrong or illegal act or acts since your last vacation?"

He readied the dustpan and whiskbroom.

The Milbuns watched anxiously at a door in the back of the room.

Uneasily, Dan thought back and remembered no wrong or illegal acts he had committed since his last vacation.

"No," he said.

The functionary stepped back. "Pass through to your vacation, live law-abiding citizen, sir."

Dan got up and walked toward the Milbuns. Another bored functionary came in wheeling a cartful of urns. He stopped at a massive chair with a heap of ashes on the seat, a small pile on either arm, and two small piles at the foot. The functionary swept the ashes off and dumped them in the urn.

A cold sensation went through Dan. He followed the Milbuns out into a small room.

He felt an out-of-focus sensation and realized the room was a mataform transmitter. An instant later, they were in a spaceship crowded with thoughtful-looking people.

Life on the spaceship seemed to be given over to silent, morose meditation, with an occasional groan that sounded very much like, "Oh, give me just one more chance, God."

When they left the ship, it was again by mataform, this time to a building where they stood in a line of people. The line wound through a booth where the color of their capes was marked on their foreheads, thence past a counter where they received strong khaki-colored capes, blouses and hose, and new leather shorts and boots to replace those they were wearing. They changed in tiny private rooms, handed their own clothing in at another counter, had a number stamped on their left shoulders and on their boxes of clothing.

Then they walked out onto a strip of brilliant white sand, fronting on an inlet of sparkling blue water.

Here and there huddled little crowded knots of people, dancing from one foot to another on the hot sand and yet apparently afraid to go in the water. Dan looked to the Milbuns for some clue and saw them darting intense calculating glances at the beach and the water.

Then Mr. Milbun yelled, *"Run for it!"*

A slavering sound reached Dan's ear. He sprinted after the Milbuns, burst through the crowd in a headlong bolt for the cove, then swam as fast as he could to keep up with them as they raced for the opposite shore. They crawled out, strangling and gasping, and dragged themselves up on the sand. Dan lay, heaving in deep breaths, then rolled over and sat up.

The air around them was split by screams, laced through with sobs, curses and groans. On the shore opposite, a mad dog darted across the crowded beach and emptied people into the cove. In the cove, a glistening black sweep of hide separated the water for an instant, then sank below. People thrashed, fought and went under.

Dan looked up. On the wooden building beyond the cove and the beach was a broad sign:

PORCYS PLANET
REJUVENATION CENTER

★ ★ ★

Dan read the sign three times. If this was rejuvenation, the Porcyns could have it.

Beside Dan, Milbun stood up, still struggling for breath, and pulled his wife and Mavis to their feet.

"Come on," he said. "We've got to get through the swamp ahead of the grayboas!"

The rest of the day, they pushed through slimy muck up to their knees and sometimes up to their necks. Behind them, the crowd screamingly thinned out.

That night, they washed in icy spring water, tore chunks of meat from a huge broiled creature turning on a spit and went to sleep in tents to the buzz and drone of creatures that shot their long needle noses through the walls like drillers hunting for oil.

The following day, they spent carefully easing from crevice to narrow toehold up the sheer face of a mountain. Food and shelter were at the top. Jagged rocks and hungry creatures were at the bottom. That night, Dan slept right through an urgent buzz from Kielgaard. The next night, he woke enough to hear it, but he didn't have the strength to answer.

Where, he thought, is the rejuvenation in this?

Then he had a sudden glimmering. It was the Porcyn

race that was rejuvenated. The unfit of the Porcyns died violently. It took stamina just to live from one day to the next.

Even the Milbuns were saying that this was the worst vacation ever. Trails slid out from under them. Trees fell toward them. Boulders bounded down steep slopes at them.

At first, the Milbuns tried to remember forgotten sins for which all this might be repayment. But when there was the dull *boom* of an explosion and they narrowly escaped a landslide, Milbun looked at the rocks across the trail with sunken red eyes. He sniffed the air and growled, "Undevised."

That afternoon, Dan and the Milbuns passed three average-looking men hanging by their hands from the limb of a tree beside the trail. The faces of the hanging men bore a surprised expression. They hung perfectly still and motionless, except for a slight swaying caused by the wind.

Dan and the Milbuns reached a mataform station late that afternoon.

A very hard-eyed guard in an orange cape, barred across the shoulders in black, let them through and they found themselves in another spaceship, bound for Fumidor, the mining planet.

Dan sat back exhausted and fell asleep. He was awakened by a determined buzz.

"Dan!" said Kielgaard's voice.

"Yes," Dan sat up. "Go ahead."

"Trans-Space is going to try to take over Porcys. There's nothing you can do about that, but they've landed agents on Vacation Planet to pick you off. Look out."

Dan told Kielgaard what had happened to the agents on Vacation Planet, such as the "undevised" explosion and being hung up by the hands.

Kielgaard whistled. "Maybe the Porcyns can take care of themselves. Trans-Space doesn't think so."

"How did you find out?"

The tiny voice held a note of grim satisfaction. "They ran an agent in on us and he gave himself away. He went back with an organo-transmitter inside him, and a memory bank. The bank stores up the day's impressions. The transmitter squirts them out in one multi-frequency blast. The agent is poorly placed for an informant, but we've learned a lot through him."

"How are they going to take over Porcys?"

"We don't know. They think they've found the Porcyns' weak point, but if so, we don't know what it is."

"Listen," urged Dan, "maybe we ought to put a lot of agents on Porcys."

"No," said Kielgaard. "That's the wrong way to play it. If we go in now, we'll be too late to do any good. We're still counting on you."

"There's not very much I can do by myself."

"Just do your best. That's all we can ask."

Dan spent the next week chipping out pieces of a radioactive ore. At night, Kielgaard would report the jubilant mood of Trans-Space. On the following days, Dan would chop at the ore with vicious blows that jarred him from his wrists to his heels.

The steady monotonous work, once he was used to it, left his mind free to think and he tried furiously to plan what he would do when he got out. But he found he didn't really know enough about Porcys to make a sensible plan. Then he began trying to organize what he had seen and heard during his stay on the planet. At night, Kielgaard helped him and together they went over their theories, trying to find those that would fit the facts of Porcys.

"It all hinges on population pressure," said Kielgaard finally. "On most planets we know of, overpopulation leads to war, starvation, birth control or emigration. These are the only ways. At least, they were, till we discovered Porcys."

"All right," agreed Dan. "Grant that. The Porcyns plainly don't have any of those things, or not to any great extent. Instead, they have institutions such as we've never seen before. They have 'sweepers,' so-called 'vacations' and a rope from building to building. All these things cut down population."

"Don't forget their 'truth chairs,'" said Kielgaard.

"Where you either tell the truth or get converted to ashes—yes. But how does it all fit in?"

"Let's take one individual as an example. Start at birth."

"He's born," said Dan. "Probably they have nurseries, but we know they stick together as families, because we have the Milbuns to go by. He grows up, living at his parents' place. He goes with other children to school or to see different parts of his city. A lion—which he calls a 'dog'— protects him."

"Yes," said Kielgaard. "It protects him from sweepers. But most grownups don't need protection. Only those whose charge is low."

"Of course. The boy hasn't been on vacation yet. He's not radioactive. Apparently you have to be radioactive to open doors. At the apartment house, the boy comes in a small door to one side. The lions, or what resemble lions, like the children but don't like the sweepers. And the sweepers are afraid of them. All right. But what about when he grows up?"

"Well, for one thing, he has to use the regular doors now. And they won't open unless he's been on vacation. And if he hasn't been on vacation and if his charge isn't high, the sweepers will go out and grab him. That must be what that sign you saw meant. 'Swept' was a warning that there was no escape in that direction."

"I begin to see it," said Dan. "I was safe on that road because the birth rate in that section wasn't high. But in the city, the birth rate *was* high, so, to keep the population down, the standards were raised. Apparently the sweepers were fed less and got more hungry. People had to go on vacation more often. But what about the rope?"

"I don't think we really know enough to understand the rope," said Kielgaard, "but maybe it's a face-saving device. People who don't think they're in good enough shape to get through 'vacation,' and who don't want to die a slow death avoiding sweepers and waiting to go through locked doors, can go across on the rope. Or perhaps it's a penance. If a man has done something wrong and he's afraid to deny it in the truth chair, perhaps he's allowed to confess and go so many times across the rope as punishment. The people cheered. That must mean it's honorable."

"That makes sense," Dan agreed. "All right, but why don't they just ship their surplus population to the other two planets?"

"We've studied that back here," said Kielgaard. "We think it's because they wouldn't dare. They've got their little mainland allotted and rationed down to the last blade of grass. They can do that because it's small enough to keep control of. Now suppose they try to enforce the same system on a new planet with a hundred times the land area—what's going to happen? They'll have unknown, uncontrollable factors to deal with. Their system will break down. That statue of theirs shows they know it, too. The man in the blue cape 'devises' and his strong right hand does nothing but keep the circle—their system—from flying apart. What puzzles me is that they're satisfied with it."

"There's another point," Dan said, "but I think I see it now. They've got a caste system, but people must be able to move from one caste to another. There must be a competitive exam or some system of choice. The vacation advisor said Mr. Milbun was 'at present' a merchant. His wife was 'now' a housewife. And no one ever asked my name, though I told it voluntarily to Milbun. It was always 'Yes, Devisement,' or 'Is it time to take your vacation, Devisement?' There were no personal titles like 'Sir Moglin,' or 'First Magistrate Moglin,' such as we've encountered on other planets."

Kielgaard grunted. "That would explain the differently colored capes, too. No one would care if a man was a street-cleaner ten years ago. They'd see his cape was blue and give him immediate, automatic respect."

"Yes," said Dan. "That's it. And no one would dare *cheat* about the color of the cape he wore, because, regardless of his position, sooner or later his charge would be gone. Then he would have to go on vacation. And to do *that*, he *has* to sit in the truth chair and tell the truth or get incinerated." Dan stopped suddenly and sucked in a deep breath.

"What's wrong?" asked Kielgaard.

"*That's* the weak point."

VI

By the end of the week, Dan was able to pass through a door with a specialized type of Geiger counter in the locking circuit.

And by that time, Kielgaard had noted sharp fluctuations in the mood at Trans-Space. There had been an interval of wild confusion, but it hadn't lasted. Many more Trans-Space agents had gone to Porcys and Trans-Space seemed to be on top again.

The instant Dan stepped from the mines through the door marked "Out," he was rushed through a shower, a shave and a haircut, shoved into a truth chair and asked questions, given a new cape and clothes, and buckled into a glittering belt by a purple-caped man addressed as "Reverence." No sooner was the belt in place than all, including "Reverence," snapped to attention.

"Devisement," said a man in an orange-and-black cape, "we need your decision quickly. At home, men have usurped cloaks of devisement and given orders contrary to the public good. They wore belts of power, but did not die when their false orders were given. In the Central City, they convened a council, seated themselves in the Hall of

Truth, and on the very first oath every single one of them present was thrown into the life beyond.

"Because the statue was already belted, men wearing cloaks of devisement *had* to give the orders. But now they were all gone. Looters roamed the streets, breaking in doors. These men were vacation-dodgers—out so long that they couldn't even make a charge-light flicker—and the sweepers cleaned up some of them. *But they killed the sweepers!* Devisement, I tell you the truth!"

"I believe you," said Dan.

"Thank heaven. Devisement, something must be done. A young boy passed and graduated to the devisement cape, but before he could take action, he was shot from ambush. We found an old man of the right cape out in the country, and when we finally convinced him, he rounded up one hundred and fifty-seven vacation-dodgers and executed them. We had things in order, but now a glut of lunatics in devisement capes and belts of power have burst into the streets. Their orders are silly, yet their belts don't kill them. They have no fear of the Truth. Business is stopped and men are hungry. The people are going wild. Strange boats have appeared offshore. Mataform transmitters of odd design are being set up near the shore. This cannot go on without breaking the circle!"

Dan's throat felt dry.

"Sir," said the Porcyn desperately, "you *must* devise something! What shall we do?"

A faint tingling at Dan's waist suggested to him that he choose his words carefully. One lie or bad intention and the belt of power would probably finish him.

He thought carefully. The total power of the Porcyn

planet must be at least the equal of even the huge Trans-Space organization. And Porcys had its power all in one place. The planet was organized to the last ounce of energy, if only it could be brought to bear in time.

Dan ordered his anxious companions to take him to Porcys.

Far under the Central City, which was the city he had seen, he found a weary, powerful old man in a light-blue cape and glittering belt, directing operations from a television command post. The console showed street scenes of men in sky-blue capes and flashing belts, who danced and jabbered, their faces aglow with lunacy as they rapped out conflicting orders and the people jerked and dashed this way and that, tears running down their faces.

Near the statue, before the Hall of Truth, close ranks of Porcyn men in orange-and-black capes stood massed on the steps, holding sleek-bored guns. On the street below, gibbering lunatics in sky-blue danced and shrieked orders, but the eyes of the men on the steps were tightly shut. By a technicality, they avoided obedience to the lunacy, for with their eyes shut, how could they be sure who gave the command?

At the belted statue itself, a man in blue was clinging to one bronze arm as he slammed down a hammer to knock loose the partly broken circle. The statue obstinately refused to let go. At the base of the statue, holding a microphone, stood an average-looking man in a sky-blue cape, his lips drawn back in an amused smile. He gestured to men with crowbars and they tried to jam them between the statue and its base. This failing, they took up chisels and hammers. The man working on the circle shrugged and jumped down.

At the console, the old man looked up at Dan. He put his hand out and felt Dan's belt. Apparently the tingle reassured him and he seemed to accept Dan without further question.

"This is about the end," he said. "When that statue goes, those men will feel the jolt and open their eyes. They're the last formed body of troops on the planet, and when they go, we'll have nothing to strike with. There must be something I could devise for this, but I've been up three nights and I can't think."

"Can you delay it?" asked Dan, grappling with the beginning of his plan.

"Oh, we'll delay it. I've got the last of the sweepers collected at the holes opening into the square. Just when that statue begins to tip, I'll let the sweepers out. That will stop things for a while. Then, they'll kill the sweepers and my bolt is shot."

"Won't the men you've got here fire on those blue-caped fakes?"

"Devisement," said the old man, shaking his head, "you know better."

"Are there any fire hoses? Will your men squirt water on the blue-caped ones?"

"Yes," said the old man, leaning forward. "They'll get shot. But yes, they will. What is it? What are you devising?"

Dan outlined his plan. The old man's eyes lighted. He nodded and Dan went out and climbed with guides through a grim, dark tunnel where the sweepers were kept. He peered out the hole, and as across the street the statue began to tip, he burst outside and sprinted into the square.

The Trans-Space leader raised his microphone.

Dan ripped it out of his hand and knocked him off his feet, then knelt and picked up the heavy shield that had been taken off the statue to get at the ring.

A bullet hummed over Dan's head.

With a rush of air and a heavy smash, the statue landed full length on the ground. Dan hauled himself up onto its base. Another bullet buzzed past him. Then there was a yell, and Dan looked down in the street.

The sweepers were horrible as they poured from their holes, but they looked almost beautiful to Dan. He glanced at the Porcyns massed on the steps, their faces white with near-hysteria. Their eyes were open and watching him; the Trans-Space men were too busy to give orders.

Dan raised the microphone and his voice boomed out:

"Close your eyes till you hear the roar of the lion! Then obey your true leaders!"

He repeated the order three times before it dawned on the Trans-Space technicians that this was not according to plan. The loudspeaker gave a booming click and cut off. By then, the sweepers had been killed, and Dan became aware of bullets thrumming past him. Suddenly he felt weak with panic that the rest of the plan had fallen apart.

Up the street, Porcyn men were unscrewing a cap on the face of a building. They connected a hose. A sky-blue-caped Trans-Space agent ordered them away. The Porcyns turned, wads of wax in their ears, and raised the hose.

A stream of water knocked the agents backward. Shots rang out. Porcyns fell, but other Porcyns took their places. The stream arched and fell on the Trans-Space agents and abruptly a whirl of color tinged the water. Blots and blobs of green, orange, pink and yellow spattered the blue-caped agents.

At the end of the street, someone ran up tugging a lion by the mane.

"*Go*, dog! *Run!*"

Somewhere a child cried out in terror.

The lion roared.

The troops on the steps opened their eyes.

An old man's voice, amplified, spoke out with icy authority:

"*Deploy for street-fighting! First rank, move out along Center Street toward North Viaduct. Rifles at full charge. Wide intervals. Use every scrap of cover. Shoot the false-belted usurpers on sight.*

"*Second rank, move out along West Ocean Avenue toward the sea wall . . .*"

Shots rang out.

There was a faint thrumming hum, like wires in the wind, and streaks of cherry radiance crisscrossed in the air.

The lion roared, unable to find the child. The roar of other lions joined in.

Dan was aware that he was lying atop the hard base of the statue, but he didn't know how he had come to be there. He tried to stand up.

He heard voices screaming orders, then falling still, and a scene swung into his line of sight like something watched through the rear-view mirror of a turning groundcar.

Half a dozen men, guns in their hands, their bodies and blue capes spattered and smeared till they could hardly be recognized, lay motionless on the pavement.

Then the scene swung up and away, and Dan felt weightless. Something hit him hard. His head bounced and he rolled over. Soft grass was in his face. It smelled fresh.

There was a dull boom that moved the ground under him.

He twisted his head to look up.

A massive arm was stretched out over him, its hand firmly gripping the cut edge of a big metal ring.

Somewhere a drum took up a steady monotonous beat.

He fell into a deep black quiet and all the sights and sounds grew smaller and fainter and disappeared entirely.

★ ★ ★

He awoke in a Porcyn hospital. Kielgaard was there, wearing a broad grin and brilliant Porcyn clothes and promising Dan a huge bonus. But it was all like a dream.

Kielgaard said the Porcyns were as mad as hornets. They had raised a battle fleet and it had taken a corps of diplomats and the Combined Intergalactic Space Fleet to argue them out of personally chopping Trans-Space into fine bits. No one knew what would finally happen, but meanwhile Galactic had its contract and everyone was tentatively happy.

His account finished, Kielgaard grinned more broadly yet and switched on a bedside televiewer.

Dan lifted his head off the pillow and looked at the

screen. Then he stared.

It was the statue, solid once more on its base, the ring grasped firmly in one hand and a big wrench in the other. But something seemed different.

Dan at last saw what it was.

It was the face. It wasn't a bad face, if one expected to see strong cheekbones, copper skin and a high-arched nose.

"What a compliment!" he said, embarrassedly pleased. "I—hell, I feel like blushing."

"Make it a good one," said Kielgaard. "After tomorrow, you'll have to blush with your face again."

"Tomorrow?"

"Sure. You're still working for us, remember."

Dan sank back on the pillow and gazed up speculatively at the ceiling. "All right, but I want some time off. I have a fat bonus to spend."

"You could use a holiday," Kielgaard agreed. "Why not try the Andromedan cloud gardens? Pretty expensive, but with your bonus—"

"I've got a place picked out," said Dan. "I'm going to take a vacation on Porcys."

Kielgaard started. "You're joking. Or you've gone twitchy."

"No. Before I have to give this face back to Surgery, I ought to get a *little* enjoyment out of it. And what could be more enjoyable than hanging around the statue, letting people see the resemblance? Besides, they can't make me take my vacation on the Vacation Planet—I've already had it."

The Vorkosigan Companion

edited by
Lillian Stewart Carl
and
John Helfers

Available from Baen Books
December 2009
hardcover

Preface

"Gosh, is it midnight already?"

There are many memorable firsts in a writer's career. First story started—first finished. First submission. First rejection. First sale! First review, good/bad. First public speech about one's writing, urk. First fan letter! First time meeting one's editor face-to-face. First award nomination—first win! Maybe, a first film option. First time on a genre bestseller list—first time on a *general* bestseller list, though this is a much rarer prize. First career award—what, already? but I'm not finished yet! First book *about* one's books.

I'm not just sure where we've arrived, but we're definitely here.

Head down and pedaling as hard as possible, it's not often that working writers have a chance to look back and see just how far they've traveled. Much of my biography and literary biography are covered in the articles and interview that follow, so I won't linger to recap it all here. But in this year, 2007, and in 2008 upcoming, have fallen a couple of firsts that force me to pause and put it in perspective.

My first career award came last month from the Ohioana Library Association. Literary awards generally, by nature intrinsically subjective, are mysterious gifts bestowed upon writers; it is something done to us, not something like finishing a novel—that we do. Career awards seem to be awards for winning awards, a suspicious circularity. (That said, this year's Ohioana memento takes the prize for being the prettiest ever, a gorgeous piece of art glass looking like a transparent blue jellyfish. Lead glass apparently looks extremely strange on airport x-ray machines, however. Someone could write a whole essay on the sometimes-deadly designs of the various awards and the challenges of getting them home.)

Next year, as I write this (though it will be a done deal by the time this book is published) I have been invited to be Writer Guest of Honor at the 2008 World Science Fiction Convention in Denver, Colorado, which is very much a career award in its own right. I put pencil to paper for my first science fiction novel in 1982; from there to this in a mere 26 years. Seems . . . fast.

Writing stories, using words to sculpt other people's thoughts, would appear to be the most evanescent of arts. Writers make and sell dreams; the vast publishing industry that conveys those dreams between the writer's head and the reader's seems a lumbering vehicle for such a light load. And yet, of all the many tasks I've undertaken in my life—apart from bearing and raising my children—it's my books that have best lasted and carried forward, the main thing I have to show for all my efforts. The line-up of first editions on my office bookshelf seems a procession of captured years, my basement full of books like an array of vintages laid down in a wine cellar.

A certain branch of linguistics and culture studies has a catch-phrase—"time-binding"—to tag those inventions, including writing, that allow humans to carry their culture and achievements forward, through time that otherwise destroys all things each instant. I would quibble a little with the phrase, since it's not actually time that is bound. "We can neither make, nor retain, a single moment of time," as C. S. Lewis remarks somewhere. But for a little while, time's grinding teeth may be eluded. Most of my life's labors were consumed almost as soon as committed— all that housekeeping plowed under, all those meals I cooked gone in a day, all the forgettable daily tasks duly forgotten. But "Words," as another writer said, "can outlast stones." I'm not sure mine will go that far, but they definitely outlast meals.

I'm a bit bemused by this present volume. Why spend precious time reading *about* books—or worse, about the author—when you could be reading the *actual* books? But I presume the main audience here will be those who have read parts or all of the Vorkosigan saga already, a reflection which allays my writerly anxiety. For you all, I trust that many amusements and some lively discussion follow. So I will get out of the way of the text—as writers should—and bid you all have fun.

Lois McMaster Bujold
Edina, Minnesota, November 2007

(This is the preface from *The Vorkosigan Companion*, edited by Lillian Stewart Carl and John Helfers.)

The Best of
JIM BAEN'S
UNIVERSE

Edited by Eric Flint

Top-selling writers and brilliant newcomers appear regularly in the online magazine *Jim Baen's Universe*, edited by Eric Flint. Now, Flint and his staff select a generous serving of the best science fiction and fantasy stories that have appeared so far in the magazine. Contributors include: Mike Resnick, David Drake, Gene Wolfe, Gregory Benford, Esther Friesner and many more.

FREE CD-ROM INCLUDED
IN THE FIRST HARDCOVER PRINTING
CONTAINING THE ENTIRE CONTENTS
OF THE MAGAZINE'S FIRST YEAR,
ILLUSTRATIONS FROM THE MAGAZINE,
OVER 20 NOVELS BY ERIC FLINT
AND MUCH MORE!

1-4165-2136-4 ★ $25.00